DEATH OF A DUCHESS

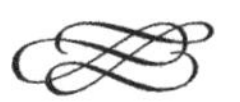

ALSO BY NELLIE H. STEELE

Cate Kensie Mysteries:

The Secret of Dunhaven Castle

Murder at Dunhaven Castle

Holiday Heist at Dunhaven Castle

Shadow Slayer Stories:

Shadows of the Past

Stolen Portrait Stolen Soul

Gone

Maggie Edwards Adventures:

Cleopatra's Tomb

DEATH OF A DUCHESS

A DUCHESS OF BLACKMOORE MYSTERY

NELLIE H. STEELE

A Novel Idea Publishing

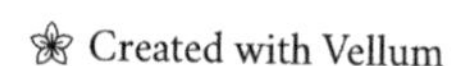
Created with Vellum

For my Aunt Michelle

ACKNOWLEDGMENTS

A HUGE thank you to everyone who helped get this book published! Special shout outs to: Stephanie Sovak, Paul Sovak, Michelle Cheplic, Cathi Colas, Mark D'Angelo and Lori D'Angelo.

Finally, a HUGE thank you to you, the reader!

CHAPTER 1

The imposing silhouette of Blackmoore Castle rose from the mist, standing in stark contrast against the ominous gray sky. Its grand towers and turrets with banners waving rose high above the landscape. The castle, perched on the cliffs, beckoned me home as my carriage trundled up the path toward it.

It still had the power to take my breath away as it did when I first laid eyes upon it, drenched in moonlight, some three months ago when I arrived. I recalled the journey into the Scottish Highlands as though it were yesterday. Filled with a mix of excitement and trepidation of what would become of me, I rode in silence with my traveling companion, Henry Langford, a middle-aged estate agent with a kind face in the service of Duke Blackmoore, the castle's proprietor.

The foreboding façade of the castle may have sent shivers up the spine of most women my age. However, the turmoil of my short life of eighteen years and two months created within me a façade almost as formidable as the castle's, if not more so. Instead, the brooding castle with its gothic design and blackened stones generated a stirring of home inside me. And despite my questioning mind regarding what would become of me, I feared not what secrets the ominous castle held within its walls.

As the carriage bounced over the rocky pathway to the castle, I closed my eyes, recalling the night I had first arrived. My day had started like any other, with no indication of difference from the days before it. At the orphanage, my home for ten years, six months and three weeks, days were rarely unique. Mundaneness and routine thrived at the orphanage above all things. I passed most of my time reading and learning. I had, in fact, been returning from the orphanage's paltry library on that morning when I overheard the tail end of the conversation between Duke Blackmoore's man and the headmistress. I shall make clear one thing: I was not eavesdropping. However, upon passing through the foyer to the staircase leading to bedrooms, I overheard my name. Naturally intrigued, I stopped to listen.

Headmistress Williamson protested, "There are far better girls beyond Miss Hastings in this orphanage for this sort of thing."

"Far better for what?" my mind questioned. Though her comment did not surprise me. Her dislike for me was well known. She despised my quick wit among other aspects of my personality. As much as she hoped to rid herself of me, she sabotaged every possibility of my departure. I had long since resigned myself to becoming a teacher at the orphanage.

I did not recognize the voice that answered her. "Miss Williamson, I am not here to ask your opinion, merely to pay for any expenses Miss Hastings accumulated during her time at your facility and to retrieve her," he argued.

My brow furrowed at the mention of retrieving me. Who was this mystery man, I wondered, and what right of claim did he have to me? He wasn't my father, of this much I was sure. An uncle, perhaps. My mind wandered from possibility to possibility as the doors to Headmistress Williamson's office flung open.

Headmistress Williamson spotted me in an instant, her eyes wide as she noted my proximity to her office doors. Her mouth set itself into its usual scowl as her eyes settled on me. Her mousy brown hair, pulled back into its low bun at the nape of her neck, added to the dour expression on her face.

"Miss Hastings," she growled, glowering at me with those fiery emerald eyes, "how fortuitous to find you here. Mr. Langford," she said, motioning to the man who stepped behind her to fill the doorway, "is here to collect you."

I glanced to the man, exploring his features as I searched them for an answer. None came. Instead of explanations, what came was a quick swat on my upper arm. "Do not stand there dumbfounded, girl!" Headmistress Williamson exclaimed. "Mr. Langford does not have all day. He'd like to get as early a start as possible!"

The headmistress offering a contrite glance to Mr. Langford before spinning me on my feet and shoving me up the stairs. She huffed as we hurried down the hall toward the bedroom I occupied with seven other girls. "Quickly, now, Lenora, pack your things. You won't be needing this." She ripped the book still clutched in my hands away, discarding it on a nearby dresser.

I had come to the orphanage with a small, well-worn suitcase which I kept shoved under my sagging mattress. Retrieving it from its hiding spot, I placed it on the bed and set about gathering the few possessions I had accumulated over the years. My meager belongings, consisting of a second dress, a tarnished gold hair comb missing the jewels that once adorned it and a well-worn copy of *Frankenstein* gifted to me by a former teacher, were packed within minutes. I pulled on a tattered pair of gloves and secured a frayed cape at my neck.

"Well, I suppose this is goodbye... for now," the headmistress replied as I stood in my cape, suitcase in my hand.

"For now?" I questioned.

"I wouldn't be surprised if you are not returned within a month's time," she commented, a skeptical expression clouding her features as she considered my journey.

I heaved a sigh and stepped past her, making my way to the doorway. There I turned, giving one last glance at my home for just over a decade. I held no melancholy in my heart despite the extended time I had spent here. Without a word, I continued through the doorway, descending the stairs to the waiting man below. Headmistress Williamson followed on my heels. "I do apologize for the wait, Mr. Langford. And please, if Miss Hastings does not work out for any reason, do not hesitate to contact me. I am certain we can suggest a more appropriate placement for you and Duke Blackmoore."

The vote of confidence in my ability was staggering, and I fought to restrain my tongue. "I am certain there will be no need for that," Mr. Langford replied with a curt smile. He shifted his gaze to me. "Come, Miss Hastings. We've a long journey ahead of us. Good day, Headmistress Williamson." He placed his hat on his head, tipping it to her and extending his arm to usher me from the building. I nodded to him, eager to leave the place behind.

Outside, a carriage awaited, drawn by four large horses. As we exited into the street, Mr. Langford lifted the suitcase from my hands. I opened my mouth to protest, but he insisted, passing my case off to the coachman. The man held it as he opened the carriage door, offering his hand to assist me into the contraption. I climbed inside followed by Mr. Langford and the door was closed behind us. The coachman set about securing my case to the rear of the carriage with what I assumed to be Mr. Langford's luggage.

I glanced to Mr. Langford, who fiddled with the latch on an attaché case. After clearing my throat, I inquired, "May I ask where we are going?"

"Blackmoore Castle. Highlands of Scotland. Settle in, Miss Hastings, we've a long journey ahead of us," he replied, removing a stack of papers and fixing a pair of spectacles to his nose.

Though I had more questions, I quieted my tongue. Mr. Langford's focus on the papers in front of him made it clear my queries were unwelcome at present.

The buggy shimmied as the coachmen climbed into his seat, taking hold of the reins. The carriage lurched forward and the characteristic sound of horseshoes on cobblestones filled my ears. I leaned forward, peering from the window at the orphanage as it slid away from my view.

I folded by hands, placing them in my lap as I continued to watch the city fade away. After several hours, rolling green hills dotted with autumn foliage filled the view in all directions. The scene, though charming, became monotonous after a time and I nodded off, soothed by the swaying motion of the carriage ride.

When I woke, the moon, already high in the darkened sky, glowed brightly. Mountainous terrain now surrounded us, and I assumed we had entered the Scottish Highlands, though having never traveled there, I could not be sure.

I straightened in my seat, drawing my threadbare cape closer around me. The air, markedly cooler and damper here, penetrated my bones. Heavy mists clung to the moors, obscuring some of them completely. The large white moon glowed over the land, casting an eerie image across the landscape.

The carriage slowed, and I was pitched backward as we

began to climb. "We're nearly there, Lenora," Mr. Langford said with a smile. It was the first time he'd used my first name. I noted he was devoid of his paperwork, likely unable to view it as the light waned to darkness. "All that remains is the climb to the castle."

I gazed out the window as the carriage lurched around a bend, noticing the large structure perched on the top of the moor. Lit by moonlight, I distinguished multiple features of the castle looming above us. Turrets and towers jutted from various areas of the sprawling framework. The moonlit castle struck an imposing silhouette against the night sky.

I returned my gaze to Mr. Langford. "Am I to be a governess?" I inquired.

An amused smile crossed the man's face. "No, you are not to be a governess."

"A companion, then? A ladies' maid?" I continued, not understanding what my new role was to be when we arrived.

"No, Lenora," he answered, "Duke Blackmoore has far better uses for your special skills in mind. He has far bigger plans for you." I furrowed my brow in confusion at his answer as he continued. "You, my dear Lenora, are to be a duchess!"

* * *

My mind snapped back to the present as the carriage slowed to a halt outside the castle. I waited inside as the coachman dismounted from his driving perch and opened the door, unfurling the steps and offering his hand for me to disembark. How quickly one becomes used to the genteel things, my mind contemplated during my short wait. Accepting his hand, I stepped out onto the gravel drive below, pulling my fur-trimmed velvet cape closer around me to keep out the winter chill.

For a moment, I glanced up at the castle's exterior, recalling my thoughts just three months prior when I arrived. The odd blackening on some parts of the stones, always a source of local gossip, cast a sinister countenance on what would otherwise pass for a fairytale castle. Some of the more levelheaded townsfolk attributed the blackening to some internal quality of the stones used or the growth of local flora. Still others insisted it represented the veins of the castle. As though, somehow, the castle had become alive and its very soul was blackening as a result of the strange goings-on here. Or perhaps because it defiled some ancient sacred ground.

I paid little attention to the histrionics of most of the locals, many of whom warned me to flee before I should meet a gruesome end. I had grown accustomed to people like this in my life and had learned to ignore them at a very young age. They based most of their opinion on lack of knowledge, understanding, superstition and a general sense of foolishness.

When I arrived three months ago, the castle, lit by moonlight, its network of blackened veins crawling through the stones, conjured no apprehensive reactions but only contentment. The serenity and peace I felt that night had never waned, it had only grown. Each time I returned here, I experienced the same emotion, as though I had found my place in the world.

Three months later, the only change in my emotion was the lack of curiosity in my heart over my new life. I now possessed a firm understanding of what my life would become and what my role was here.

The gravel crunched under my feet as I stepped toward my home, ready to continue my odyssey within the castle walls.

At this moment, it occurs to me that I haven't properly

introduced myself to you, dear reader. Now seems an opportune moment to make a proper introduction before we continue together.

My name is Lenora Fletcher. I am the Duchess of Blackmoore. And I can communicate with the dead. Within these pages, dear reader, I have recorded one of my stories.

CHAPTER 2

"Welcome home, Your Grace," Mr. Buchanan, our butler, greeted me as I entered the castle's foyer. I handed my cape to him and began removing my gloves. "Was your trip successful, Your Grace?"

"It was," I informed him. "The dress is as lovely as promised and with a few minor adjustments should be perfect."

"Wonderful, Your Grace."

"Have I much time before the dressing gong for dinner?" I inquired. Despite the general lack of guests and other family, my husband maintained the custom of dressing for dinner.

"Two hours, Your Grace."

I finished removing my gloves and nodded. "I shall be in my tower room reading if I am needed."

"Very good, Your Grace. May I fetch you anything?"

"No, thank you, Buchanan."

I spun on my heel, ascending the massive stone staircase flanking the right wall. I navigated to my bedroom, setting my gloves on my dressing table before climbing the steep stairs to the tower room where I spent a good deal of my time.

When I first arrived at the castle, I found the room while exploring. Its high turret overlooked the countryside with enormous windows giving a panoramic view. Glancing to the ground may provide one with a disorienting effect as the tower resides on the side of the castle where the cliffs drop sharply away. The height of the tower coupled with the sheer drop below gives one the impression of flying, soaring above the earth like large birds of prey.

I stepped inside the room and the familiar sense of peace washed over me as I entered. The room's furnishings had been sparse when I found it, but the views so inviting and incredible, I immediately took to the space. I'd taken it upon myself to add furnishings and other details, to add comfort to the space. After our marriage, my husband offered me the freedom to do with the castle as I saw fit. I'd taken the most license in this room, choosing to leave the other rooms untouched and in the tradition in which they were furnished upon my arrival.

This particular turret, devoid of any human touch, had been the one exception. I'd added cushions and pillows to the window seats, a writing desk, a chaise and side table and a small bookcase. The library in the castle was well-fitted with book storage and books to fill it, however, I wanted a small space for those books I chose to keep close as I did a large amount of reading in this room, often late into the night.

I nestled under a fur blanket near one of the windows. The winter chill frosted the glass outside, creating icy patterns that crept from the corners inward. My beloved book, *Frankenstein*, lay across my lap, though it could not capture my interest today.

Instead, I gazed out the window, lost in my own thoughts. My mind wandered to the events of the day. The dress for which I had my fitting earlier would be delivered tomorrow morning, and I would wear it tomorrow evening to a New Year's Eve ball. The occasion, a popular holiday in Scotland, was being marked by Lord and Lady Cunningham in an ostentatious event. My husband and I accepted the invitation, much to Lady Cunningham's delight.

I reflected on my turn of fortune as the year approached its close. At the start of the year, I was an orphan, a creature spurned by her own parents and left alone in the world. I would finish the year a duchess. Despite ours being a marriage of convenience, I experienced more acceptance and tenderness from my new husband than I'd experienced from most others for the entirety of my life.

My thoughts turned to my marriage, specifically, to the manner in which it was announced. Mr. Langford's revelation of my impending nuptials as we climbed the moors to the castle astounded me. I had assumed I had been engaged for a governess position. My training at the orphanage had prepared me well for such a venture. I had excelled in my classes there. Miss Pepperidge, one of my favorite teachers, who had taken a shine to me despite my curious traits, had called me the cleverest student she had ever taught. Indeed, I clung to my studies as a child clings to a cherished toy. Despite my quick mind and academic talent, I had never been engaged as a governess by anyone who sought such a girl at the orphanage. Though qualified, Headmistress Williamson had a knack for guiding the employing family away from me and on to "more suitable" girls. She told me once, in a private meeting in her office, that she preferred I not be selected in case there were any "incidents" caused by my wicked vice, as though I had some control over my ability to see the dead.

Still, it seemed the most likely conclusion when Mr. Langford loaded me into a carriage and transported me to the Scottish countryside. I recalled my reaction to his announcement that I was to become the Duchess of Blackmoore.

"Married? A duchess?" I cried. "Sir, do you jest?"

He chuckled before answering. "No, Lenora, I do not. However, I shall allow Duke Blackmoore to explain further."

I sat back in my seat, considering the information. I had not anticipated such a turn of events. In truth, given the revelation, I wondered if the events of the morning were as fortuitous as I originally assumed. Still, I assured myself in the quiet moments as the castle drew ever nearer to us, that whatever may come, I should survive it.

"Fear not, Lenora," Mr. Langford commented, breaking the silence between us. "There is nothing nefarious in the offer."

The carriage slowed to a stop in front of the castle and we disembarked. Mr. Langford led me into the castle where Mr. Buchanan met us. "Good evening, Mr. Langford. His Grace is awaiting your arrival in the drawing room."

"Thank you, Buchanan. Before we seek an audience, allow me to introduce Miss Lenora Hastings, Duke Blackmoore's fiancée."

I managed a tight-lipped smile and a soft hello, still finding the words of my engagement strange sounding to my ears.

Buchanan bowed his head to me. "A pleasure, Miss Hastings. I shall anticipate working for you as mistress of Blackmoore with much eagerness."

My mind, still reeling, struggled to comprehend his words. Overseeing a castle as mistress was never a position I imagined I'd find myself in. "As shall I," I managed with another curt smile.

"To begin, may I take your cape, miss?"

"Oh!" I answered, feeling foolish and raising my eyebrows as I undid the tie. "Certainly and thank you."

"I shall place it with the others. Should you need it merely ask myself or one of the servants."

"Oh," Mr. Langford interjected, waving a hand in the air. "I do not mean to overstep, Lenora, but the cape may be given away. Duke Blackmoore has already arranged several articles of clothing for you. And the dressmaker shall arrive tomorrow. Should you find the cape already ordered unacceptable, she can see to a new one for you."

I handed the cape to Buchanan as I stared in disbelief at Mr. Langford. So, my things were to be discarded? "Mr. Langford…" I began to protest.

He held up a hand to hush my tongue. "Do not dispose of it yet, Buchanan, however, I am quite sure Lenora will find no more use for it after this evening."

I blinked my eyes several times, stunned by the situation, yet allowed it to unfold around me.

"Very good, Mr. Langford," Buchanan's deep voice boomed as he bowed his head and trundled across the room and down the hall. I followed his large form as it disappeared down the hallway, my cape with him.

"Come, Lenora," Mr. Langford encouraged me. "It is time to meet Duke Blackmoore." I didn't move for a moment, my hesitation clear as the situation spiraled beyond my grasp. I possessed no details and only a vague understanding of the expectations of me. My discomfort with the lack of information must have been apparent to Mr. Langford, because he continued speaking when I did not budge from my spot. "There is nothing to fear, Lenora. I expect after discussing the details with Duke Blackmoore, you shall find yourself most comfortable with the arrangement."

I drew in a deep breath and nodded my head. I had come this far. There was no harm in hearing the man out. Mr.

Langford ushered me into a room off the large foyer. A fire roared in the massive fireplace across the room. The rest of the colossal room remained dimly lit. A man's figure, visible only from the side, stared at the dancing flames.

"Duke Blackmoore," Mr. Langford addressed him.

The man spun in his seat to face us. "Henry," he answered without standing. "And Lenora, I presume?" His gaze rested on me.

"Yes, Duke Blackmoore," Mr. Langford confirmed, "allow me to present Miss Lenora Hastings."

"Come closer, my dear," Duke Blackmoore instructed.

With my hands folded in front of me, I approached the man in his chair. He struggled to standing with the assistance of a cane. As I approached, I noticed his thick, dark, unruly hair was streaked with gray and hard lines cut into his face. He could easily pass for my father. His light gray eyes studied me. Though his face, hair and reliance on a walking aid suggested old age, his eyes disagreed. I detected something unusual in them, as though he was seeing for the first time. "Good evening, Duke Blackmoore," I greeted him with a curtsy as I had been instructed in the orphanage.

"Do not curtsy, my dear," he chided. "You shall soon be a duchess. We shall share the same rank. Hmm, you are more beautiful than I expected."

I swallowed hard, finding my voice. "Your Grace..." I began but was stopped by Duke Blackmoore's waving hand as he teetered on his cane.

"Please dispense with the formality, Lenora. My name is Robert, you shall address me as such."

I swallowed again. "Robert," I began, my voice faltering as I struggled to speak his name outright, "I hope you will not find my comments out of turn, but I am quite in the dark regarding my role at the castle. Mr. Langford has explained what I am NOT to be, yet my mind struggles to comprehend the implication of the role I shall fulfill."

Robert smiled at me, the expression softening his face immeasurably. He motioned to the chair across from him. "Please, sit down, Lenora. I shall explain." He collapsed in a heap into the chair behind him, still clutching his cane. I crossed to the open chair, perching on it as I set my gaze on him.

Mr. Langford poured himself a brandy from the bar, bringing a glass to Robert. He offered me a brandy, though I refused. After a sip of the amber liquid, Robert began his explanation. "Allow me to apologize first for the lack of detail provided to you. I instructed Mr. Langford to leave the details to me. It is, after all, my request. I should have preferred to retrieve you myself from the orphanage, however," he disclosed, waving his cane in the air, "I am still recovering from a recent spill while riding my horse. Rather careless of me. Though I should be up and about soon.

"As Mr. Langford may have alluded to, you are not here to take up a position on the staff, you are here to become mistress of this house." He said the words so matter-of-factly, I wondered if he may be mad, suffering from some head injury after falling from his steed.

"Sir, forgive me, but are you quite certain you understand what you are saying?"

My query elicited a hearty laugh from the man. I glanced to Mr. Langford, who also enjoyed a chuckle over my question. "I assure you, Lenora, Duke Blackmoore is quite sane."

"Yes, yes, my dear," Robert assured me. "I am in full command of all my faculties. Are you quite sure YOU understand what you are saying?" he posed.

"Sir?" I asked, not understanding the question.

"I'm not certain I have come across a girl less eager to become a duchess, Lenora."

"May I speak in earnest?" I inquired.

"By all means," Robert granted.

"It has little to do with assuming the position you offer and more to do with a lack of understanding as to why the offer is being made. What is expected of me? Why have you sought me out? Surely there are many women who long for such a position, who may be better suited for the position, having been bred for it. Yet you seem to have sought me, an orphan, out very specifically."

He offered a sly half-grin. "And you are not one of these women? A woman who longs for a position?"

"I have come to expect nothing in particular from life, sir. And you have not answered my questions."

"You are quick-witted, Lenora. A trait I admire. Yet you, also, avoid my question. Have you some aversion to assuming such a social position?"

I considered the question a moment, then responded, "No. I have no aversion, yet, I still fail to understand why I have been sought for it. It is an odd turn of events for an orphan. What is it you expect me to provide in return?"

Robert smiled at me again, leaning forward in his chair, steadying himself on the cane. "Again, I admire your tenacity. You wish to learn the terms. I shall lay them out for you. This shall be a marriage of convenience. I shall provide you with a prestigious position, a lavish home, any goods your heart may desire, a comfortable life from here forward. You shall provide me with something very special in return. You are correct, I have sought you out for a specific reason. You have a unique ability, do you not, Lenora?"

I swallowed hard as I contemplated my response. Without doubt, he referred to my consciousness of the dead that walked among us. But how much did he know of my situation, I wondered? And how had he learned it? "I suffer from a peculiar view of the world," I hedged.

"By this you mean you can see those who have died. As plainly as you can see me in front of you?"

I nodded. "Yes."

Robert shared a glance with Henry before continuing. "This is why I sought you out."

"You wish to use my ability for yourself?" I questioned.

He nodded. "Yes. You see." He paused, his face darkening. "My first wife passed away three years ago. Took her own life. I haven't a clue as to why and I must learn the reason."

"She left no missive? No explanation?"

He shook his head, remaining silent for a breath. "I have no other options. Lenora, you are my only hope to determine why my beloved Annie chose such a tragic end."

My brow furrowed as I considered the exchange. "What if you are displeased with the answers I find?"

He shook his head. "I must learn the truth, no matter what it is. There is no expectation on your behalf to provide me with an answer I approve of."

"The offer seems to favor me," I noted aloud as I grappled with the revelation.

"Then you agree?" Robert pressed, leaning further forward, his eagerness obvious. I glanced at him as I weighed the options. "Please, Lenora, you are my only hope."

"I do not suppose I have much choice to refuse. It appears the decision has been made."

"You have every right to refuse," Robert informed me. "And I shall return you to your life, posthaste. You have no obligation. You are not a prisoner. Though I pray you choose to stay."

I studied the man's face. The firelight cast shadows across it, though the darker shadows were not caused by the fire's light, but rather by the sorrow he experienced. It was etched in every line of his face, in the way he clutched at the cane, in his posture, hidden behind his stormy gray eyes.

The man has experienced true grief and had not yet recovered. My heart experienced a great deal of pity for him. In his desperation, he offered anything he could to win me to his cause.

Despite his sorrow, though, I caught a glimpse of something else in his eyes: hope. I could not extinguish that small glimmer that kept him clinging to life. I nodded slowly. "Yes. I agree."

He breathed a visible sigh of relief as he leaned back in the chair, sharing a relieved glance at Mr. Langford. He nodded toward Henry who said, "I will see that all the appropriate changes are made to the estate documents first thing in the morning. And make the necessary final arrangements." Henry swallowed the last of his brandy, setting the glass down. "I shall have documents to you by afternoon for signatures. I shall take my leave now. Lenora, I hope you enjoy a restful first night in your new home. Good night, Your Grace," he said, bowing toward Duke Blackmoore. He strode from the room.

"Thank you, Lenora," Robert said, once we were alone. "We shall wed at mid-week. A simple ceremony. My apologies that you won't receive a lavish wedding. The dressmaker has been engaged to come tomorrow. She should have a dress prepared by the wedding, along with whatever else you desire. I've had several dresses ordered along with other things you may need. Feel free to order whatever may appeal to you."

The statements confounded me. I still wrestled to comprehend the sudden turn of events. My husband-to-be set a generous bounty at my feet. And he continued as my mind struggled to catch up. "If there is anything you prefer to change within the household, you have free rein. Make the castle what you want, Lenora. It hasn't known a female touch in three years."

I mustered a tight-lipped smile. "Thank you, your offer continues to prove most generous."

"Do not thank me, Lenora. I offer no more than any man should offer his wife. What you provide in return goes beyond anything material."

"Concerning your request," I began. "I do not control my ability. That is, I cannot initiate it at the snap of a finger. This may take time..."

Robert interrupted me. "I understand, my dear. I ask only that you keep me apprised of anything you learn as you learn it."

"I shall," I agreed.

"Do you require any ...details?" The man's face contorted with grief as he asked the question.

I shook my head. "No, Robert. I shall not press you for details. I am capable of retrieving them on my own and should prefer to. I shall not ask you to relive the painful memory."

He offered a weak smile. "I am most grateful." We sat for a moment near the fireside, allowing the conversation to settle around us. "Your journey must have been tiring. I am sure you would like to retire."

"Yes," I agreed. I stood from my chair as he rose, steadying himself with the cane. "Please do not trouble yourself. If you provide direction, I am certain I am capable of finding my place."

"You must learn to be less accommodating, Lenora," Robert answered with a chuckle. "You are soon to be a duchess."

"Duchess or not, I shall remain the same independent woman I was when I arrived on the property," I assured him, earning a half-smile from him. "And I do not wish to trouble you with your injury."

"If you are determined to be so understanding of me, I

shall ring for Buchanan, who will show you to your room and ensure you have everything you need."

I returned his slight smile. "I am determined and am capable of ringing," I informed him, pulling the cord on the wall.

Within seconds, Buchanan appeared, obviously awaiting word on whether or not I would join the household. "Buchanan," Robert said as Buchanan entered the room, "please show Miss Hastings to her room and ensure she has everything she needs for her first night in the castle."

"Very good, Your Grace," Buchanan said with a head bow. He turned to me. "If you'll follow me, Miss Hastings, I shall show you to your room and arrange for anything that may be lacking." He motioned for me to precede him through the doors leading to the foyer.

I stepped toward the door, turning back before leaving. "Good night," I said.

Robert craned his neck around the chair. "Good night, Lenora. Sleep well."

I stepped into the foyer and waited for Buchanan to lead the way to the bedroom. We ascended the curving stairway to the balcony overlooking the foyer. He led me through several hallways, arriving outside of large peaked double doors. He pushed both doors open into the room, standing aside to allow me to enter first.

I stepped through the doorway, my eyes drawn upward within the impressive room. A fire roared in the enormous stone fireplace near to which stood a four-poster bed with heavy navy wool draperies. A white dressing gown and heavy red velvet robe were laid out on the bed, their colors contrasting with the navy bed covering. A chaise lounge was positioned near another fireplace in the room, along with a small table and two wing-backed armchairs. A large wardrobe adorned the space as well. Overall, the room was elaborately decorated. I noticed my well-worn copy of *Frankenstein* laid out on the night table next to the bed.

The entire room had been prepared for my arrival. The room and its preparations left me speechless for a moment. As I gaped around, Buchanan cleared his throat. The small sound reminded me of his presence. I had forgotten, so caught up in the beauty of the room. "I have taken the liberty of having your case unpacked. Everything you need should be available. I shall send a maid to assist you with undressing. If there is anything I have not attended to, please inform her and I shall see to it at once."

"Thank you, Buchanan. It appears you have taken care of everything. I do not require a maid this evening. What time should I present myself for breakfast?"

"Duke Blackmoore takes his breakfast in the dining room at six-thirty. Ring for the maid when you would like to dress," he replied, motioning to the pull cord on the wall. "Or I can inform her to arrive at the time of your choosing." He paused, awaiting my answer.

At the orphanage, I dressed myself, never requiring assistance, though I had no ladies' maid at my disposal even if I needed it. I evaded the question. "I shall ring if I require assistance," I informed him.

"Very good, miss." He nodded his head to me, taking a step toward the door. He hesitated a moment as though considering something, then said, "And welcome to Blackmoore Castle. I do hope you will find yourself at home here." He offered a kind smile.

"Thank you," I responded, matching his expression. "The castle and my room are quite beautiful. I am sure I will find myself content here."

He nodded again and departed, pulling the doors shut behind him. Alone, I continued gawking at the room. The bedroom I shared with seven other girls at the orphanage was smaller. I wondered if the room may compete in size with the entirety of the upper floor at the orphanage. A silly thought, of course, but it adequately conveys the overwhelming size of the room in comparison to what I was accustomed.

Despite the journey being tiring, I sank onto the chaise lounge before undressing. I took several deep breaths as I surveyed my surroundings again, each time noticing something new. Shock began to set in as silence settled around me. What had I agreed to, I pondered? I was engaged to be married in three days' time to a man I'd only met one hour ago. A man who had me driven sight unseen from an orphanage to a castle in the Scottish Highlands.

I shook my head. I'd given my response, and I intended to keep to my word. Dwelling on my choice would only prove to drive me mad. It appeared my life had taken a turn for the better, regardless of the strange circumstances that brought this to fruition.

Before my mind chose to wander any further, I rose from my seat and dressed for bed. Carefully, I folded my dress and opened the wardrobe to place it inside. I found three other dresses inside, none of which were mine. Fine materials made up each elaborate dress. Two appeared to be for day and one for evening.

I placed my dress in an empty spot and closed the wardrobe, crossed the room and climbed into bed. As I slid beneath the bed linens, my feet touched warmth. A bed warmer had been placed at the bottom of the bed. I'd never experienced the luxury of warm sheets on a chilly night in the past. The sensation was pleasant. I laid in bed staring at the canopy over me, my thoughts crowding my mind, each vying for my attention.

I recalled those thoughts as I gazed out of the window from my tower room. Thoughts which seemed foreign to me now. In three months, I had grown into my role. Tomorrow night, we would attend our first event as a married couple, my first event in high society. I would ring in the New Year as a duchess among the lords and ladies of the land.

The dinner gong sounded, breaking into my thoughts. I pulled myself from my ruminating, setting my book down on the nearby table. I traversed the many halls to my room, pulling the cord on the wall as I entered to summon the maid.

She arrived within moments, undoubtedly anticipating the call. "Good evening, Your Grace," the girl greeted me.

"Good evening, Elsie."

The girl, a housemaid, doubled as a ladies' maid, helping me to fasten my dresses and finish my hair. I used her as little as possible since it pulled her from her other duties. It was a rather unfair situation to have thrusted upon the poor girl and one that I planned to remedy soon. I thanked her for her assistance as I pulled on my gloves. She excused herself from the room with a curtsy and I found my way to the drawing room where Robert and Henry Langford awaited me.

"Good evening, Your Grace," Henry addressed me.

"Good evening, Mr. Langford. I am so pleased you could join us for dinner."

"Good evening, Lenora," Robert said. "And how was the dress fitting? Ready for tomorrow?"

"Yes," I replied.

"Are you looking forward to the party?" Mr. Langford inquired as we made our way into the dining room.

"I'm afraid Lenora may be rather dreading it," Robert admitted as he took his chair at the head of the table.

"I am not," I countered. "Though I cannot imagine you are looking forward to explaining my humble beginnings on our first outing."

"You care too much of others' opinions, Lenora," Robert

warned. "I shall explain nothing to anyone beyond what I want them to know."

We continued the meal, discussing the advent of the new year and Robert's upcoming trip to Glasgow in early January. I excused myself after dinner, allowing the men to speak about their business, and retired to my bedroom.

CHAPTER 3

I presented myself early the following morning, awaiting Robert's arrival at the breakfast table. "Good morning, Lenora," he greeted me. "You are up early." He seated himself at the head of the table, retrieving his newspaper.

"Good morning, Robert. Indeed, I am. I confess to having an ulterior motive."

"Oh?" he inquired, setting his paper aside.

Our breakfast was served, and I proceeded with my request prior to my meal. "I should like to take on a ladies' maid. I hoped to travel with you to Glasgow to engage one. Are you agreeable?"

"To Glasgow? Have you someone specific in mind?"

"Yes," I confirmed. "I won't be any trouble. I shall not interfere with your business dealings, I promise."

Robert chuckled and set his gaze on me. "Dear Lenora, you could never be trouble."

"So, you agree?"

"Yes, I agree. It is a splendid idea." I offered a slight smile, beginning my breakfast. "I'm quite pleased, Lenora. You are finally settling in to your new role."

"I am quite settled," I assured him. "The castle is most comfortable. I have no complaints."

"No, I do not imagine you would, dear, even if something was not to your liking. Yet you've held yourself just beyond accepting your role fully. I worried you may never accept it."

My brows pinched together as he spoke. I fulfilled all duties required of a mistress of a dwelling such as this. I consulted with the staff regarding meals, ran the household and performed other tasks a lady such as myself was responsible for. I attempted to create an atmosphere in which my husband was at ease. It was, after all, his castle. Though we were a married couple, our marriage was in name only.

I set my spoon on the underplate, prepared to discuss the issue. "Have I been remiss in some duty?" I inquired.

"No, Lenora. You fulfill every duty expected of you, with expert precision, from what Buchanan has told me. The staff quite enjoys working for you."

"While I am pleased to hear this, I am troubled over your statements. If there is something lacking in my duties, I should prefer to be informed."

"There is nothing lacking on your part, Lenora. I merely refer to your tendency to disallow yourself to truly become part of the household. Your delay in seeking a ladies' maid, or making any household changes, for example. I suppose the fault is mine. With our rather rushed marriage, you've been brought into the house more like a staff member than family."

"There is no fault on your part. Your offer was and continues to be generous. I shall work harder to..."

Robert waved his hand to interrupt me. "I understand some of your reluctance may stem from the less-than-courteous treatment you've received throughout your life. You should not work harder, though, dear, you should not work at it at all."

I pondered his statements. Had I a reluctance to allow myself to be folded into a family? Family was not a foreign concept, but I had not experienced the comforts of a family for most of my adolescent life. Did I hold myself at a distance? In a marriage of convenience, this seemed expected. Yet…

Robert interrupted my thoughts. "Eat your breakfast, Lenora. Do not dwell on it. There are no shortcomings on your behalf."

I nodded, retrieving my spoon to eat my porridge. "I shall not dwell on it," I promised, though I was certain my mind would return to it.

Robert eyed me sideways for a moment but did not return to the conversation. Instead, he moved on to a new topic. "The party this evening will provide a good opportunity to introduce you to many of the country's society members."

I nodded with a curt smile. "Indeed."

Robert offered a small smile and returned to his newspaper. We finished our breakfast, and I excused myself to prepare for my final dress fitting, pleased that my plan had been approved.

Buchanan showed my dressmaker to my room by midmorning. She carried the garment for the event this evening with her. The maid followed her, prepared to assist me in dressing. I gazed at the dress as the dressmaker fussed at its form, which she draped over the chaise. She faced me, a pleased expression on her face.

"It is lovely," I commented. "The detailing is exquisite. Shall I try it?"

"Yes," Madame Worth encouraged. "It should be perfect.

But let us be sure. We must ensure your first outing is *magnifique*!"

I nodded as the maid collected the dress and we disappeared behind the dressing screen. As Elsie began securing the dress, I gazed down at the gathered beige-gold fabric, at the bow and rose detail intricately stitched at the shoulder and around the bottom of the top skirt. The train of the dress was bustled thrice, roses adorning each gather. I fretted for a moment, worried I had allowed myself to be led into an overly extravagant choice.

Elsie continued pulling at the bodice to tighten it around my waist. After a few moments, she finished the task. "Finished, Your Grace," she said, stepping back. I emerged from the dressing screen and approached the full-length mirror.

Madame Worth clasped her hands together in front of her face, thrilled with the result. "OH! Your Grace! You shall be the belle of the ball!"

I gazed into the mirror, admiring the dress. The fabric, the cut and the detailing were impeccable. Madame Worth's talent was obvious. "Is there anything amiss, Your Grace?" the woman asked when I did not respond.

"No!" I assured her, rousing myself from my own thoughts. "I was lost in admiration of your work."

The woman placed a hand over her heart. "Your Grace, you are too kind."

"I am not," I countered. "Your talent is obvious." I glanced into the mirror again. "Are you sure it isn't too ostentatious?"

"Not at all, madam," Madame Worth assured me, approaching me. "You must remember, you will be the highest-ranking lady at the party. I was sure to check the guest list before designing for you."

I nodded at her, catching her eye in the reflection. "I am very pleased. I shall feel as though I am the loveliest woman at the party, I am certain."

"As you should, Your Grace."

With Elsie's assistance, I changed into my day dress and dismissed her to her other duties. Madame Worth and I chatted over tea. After she departed and I finished my lunch, I climbed to my tower room, settling into the window seat for a few hours of reading before dressing for the ball.

After glancing over the winter landscape, I focused on the book I'd selected from the library. When I arrived, the library and its selections had thrilled me. I'd never beheld such an abundance of books in one place. The library at the orphanage had been small, tiny in comparison. I struggled to find suitable books to read that were new to me. Here, I should be kept satisfied for a long while.

My most recent read, *The Scarlet Letter,* came from this library and was new to me. Published only thirteen years earlier, the orphanage's library would never have included something so new.

As I settled into the engaging story, a noise sounded from across the room. A low rattling growl called my attention to the doorway. I glanced up from my book, finding what I expected standing in the doorway. A dark-haired woman stood there, her disheveled hair escaping in every direction from her swept-up style. Dirt smudged her red dress. Her dark eyes bored into me, a sneer on her lips.

"Hello, Annie," I greeted her. "Are you planning to stay this time?"

The preceding Duchess of Blackmoore narrowed her eyes at me. Her gray, sunken cheeks puffed at me as she elicited a hiss in my direction. I set my book aside and swung my legs over the side of the window seat. The movement spooked my specter, and she hastened away from my view. I sighed, regaining my perch next to the window. I would not give chase, I had tried that on a prior occasion and it had ended in disaster.

On my second encounter with Annie, almost two months after my arrival, Annie had appeared to me in the hallway leading to my bedroom. She pawed at my bedroom door as I approached it when returning from dinner. When my proximity to her became too close for her comfort, she dashed down the hall. I followed. She led me in a winding chase through the castle, ending up in another turret, the very tower from which she had thrown herself. As I entered the room, my eyes fixed on her figure, I realized the error I'd made. What I beheld in front of me was no more than a mirror image. Annie stood behind me, slamming the door shut with a growl and locking me in the tower.

I raced toward the door as it swung shut. Annie's eyes glowed red as she sneered at me from beyond the threshold. I pushed against the door with all my strength, but it did not budge. I pounded against the door, calling for help from Annie first, then anyone who may hear me. No one came.

I spent a cold night on the stone floor before a maid found me early the following morning after a search had commenced when I failed to turn up for breakfast. Despite insisting my well-being had not been compromised by the incident, I was put to bed with a hot toddy. An unfamiliar sensation for me since, even when ill, one was not permitted to remain in one's bed at the orphanage.

Mid-morning, Robert visited me, concerned over the episode. "Foolish of me," I fibbed. "The door swung shut behind me and I had failed to check the lock." I did not see a reason to provide the whole story. The living did not often understand the machinations of the dead. They sometimes operated in a curious way. In many cases, they were the antithesis of themselves when alive. The entire escapade was only a bit of mischief, an attempt to frighten me or exert some dominance. Robert studied me a moment as he weighed my words. "I am really quite fine." I pushed myself up to sit straighter.

"What were you doing in that tower at night?" he questioned.

I pondered my response before giving it. "Following a lead on my special project," I replied.

He cocked his head, staring at me with his stormy gray eyes. "You have encountered Annie again," he surmised.

I nodded, confirming my second experience with the ghost of Annie Fletcher. "Yes, she awaited me at my door after dinner last night."

"Did she speak to you?" he inquired.

"No," I responded. "She is not up to communicating yet."

He nodded, his disappointment clear. "She will come around," I promised. "It takes them time. They go unnoticed in most instances. It is often shocking to them when they do not. And they do not always communicate as we do."

His gaze fell to the bedcovers, and he failed to respond. "She will come around," I reiterated, understanding the emotional toll the process took on him.

"My apologies, Lenora. It pains me to learn of Annie's apprehension."

"I understand. I shall be gentler with her in future encounters."

He waved his hand at me, dismissing the comment. He stood, stalking across the room. "It also troubles me that you endure this treatment."

"I have endured nothing," I responded.

"A night locked in a cold tower is not to be dismissed," he countered.

"That was my own foolishness."

"Lenora," Robert chided, "the door does not lock itself." He gleaned my explanation a deception. The jig was up.

"There is no cause for worry," I assured him. He glanced toward me. "I have sustained no injury."

"She was not like this in life," he stated, returning his gaze out the window.

"I am sure she was not," I assured him. "The dead behave differently than they did in life. They can be confused and disturbed. They need time and understanding."

"I have endangered you by bringing you here. Lenora," he paused, turning toward me, "I am sorry. I did not expect this when I sought answers."

"You owe me no apology," I asserted. "I was aware of what I was taking on when I accepted. Besides, there is no harm done."

He offered a half-smile. "You take the situation very much in stride, Lenora."

"I am well-acquainted with it. It has been my entire life." I pushed the bedcovers back, intent on rising and going about my day. At the orphanage, a day spent in bed was not permitted unless one could not remain on one's feet.

Robert approached the bed. "Is there something you require?"

"No," I responded, standing. "I do not need to remain abed."

He raised his eyebrows. "Yet you shall."

"It is unnecessary," I contended.

"Necessary or not, I insist upon it." He paused. "As your husband," he added, a coy expression on his face.

"As my husband?" I queried with a chuckle. He raised his eyebrows again, cocking his head at me. I raised an eyebrow but climbed back into my bed. "Very well. I shall agree only by virtue of protecting the investment you made in me and to remain a dutiful wife. I have yet to provide you any answers. I do not wish to become ill and fail to hold up my end of our bargain."

"I do not wish you to become ill for any reason, bargain or otherwise."

I pulled the bedsheets around me. "Here I shall stay then."

* * *

My mind snapped back to the present. I'd made little headway since then. In three months, I'd had three encounters with the former mistress of Blackmoore. She was testing the boundaries with me, determining what she could and could not do. With any luck, as our comfort with each other grew, I would glean some evidence about her demise.

Until then, I had other business to attend to. The dressing gong rang early. Given our travel plans, dressing would take place earlier than normal. I set my book aside and made my way to my bedroom.

Elsie met me there to begin the process. Elsie's hair styling ability had improved considerably in the few months she attended me. Using a recently learned technique, she swept my hair up in a smart style. I commended her on the style as I pulled my gloves on. She spritzed perfume on my hair. Though unaccustomed to wearing such frivolities, I was adapting to the habits of ladies in my station.

After a glance in the mirror, I smoothed my skirts and navigated to the foyer. Buchanan awaited me, though Robert did not. I glanced at the grandfather clock that ticked away the time. Was I early?

"Your Grace," Buchanan greeted me. "Duke Blackmoore has requested you meet him in the drawing room."

"Thank you, Buchanan," I responded and made my way to the drawing room doors. I entered the room, lit mostly by the roaring fire. Robert sat in his usual chair, fireside. "Robert?" I questioned, drawing his attention. I wondered for a moment if he had changed his mind about attending.

"Lenora," he said, standing and facing me. "Oh!"

I swallowed as his gaze fell on me, his eyebrows raising. "Is anything wrong? Is the dress inappropriate? I considered it perhaps too much, though Madame Worth assured me..."

"Yes, I would say something is wrong," he interrupted. "I am quite sure every woman at the party will be eaten away with jealousy when they view you in this dress."

I let out a relieved sigh. "Oh, is that all?" I quipped. "Buchanan informed me you wished me to meet you here."

"Yes," Robert answered, retrieving a box from the nearby table. "I have a gift for you. To mark the occasion."

"A gift?" I inquired. "Thank you, though it was unnecessary." He motioned for me to join him, and I approached him as he opened the box. My eyes widened at the contents. My jaw dropped open, and I clutched my stomach. "Robert!" Inside the box lay a jeweled necklace with a large yellow, teardrop-shaped stone in the middle surrounded by deep blue gems. Sparkling diamonds jutted from each side, forming the chain.

"Do you fancy it?" he inquired.

"Fancy it? It is absolutely stunning!" I glanced up to him, shaking my head. "It is too much. I cannot accept this."

"Nonsense," he quibbled, removing the necklace from the box. "Of course you can, and you will. You cannot deny your husband the opportunity to bestow such a gift. Turn around while I fasten it."

Shock still coursed through me, but I complied with his request. He placed the necklace around my neck, its heavy coolness caressing my skin. "The large stone is a yellow sapphire, which I'm told is rare, but I was assured by Madame Worth that it would complement your dress. The smaller stones are traditional sapphires. Often, they are set to contrast their yellow cousins. The color reminds me of your eyes. And, of course, the diamonds, no woman should be without them." He clasped the necklace. I grasped it between my thumb and forefinger, glancing down at it.

"You spoil me," I murmured, turning back toward him.

"You are a duchess, you deserve to be spoiled. Now that your outfit is complete, shall we depart?" He held out his arm to escort me to don my cape and climb into the carriage.

During our journey, my hand found its way under my cape several times, my fingers grazing the necklace. I had never seen anything so ostentatious in my life, and certainly never expected to wear anything so extravagant.

We arrived at Lord Cunningham's estate and were announced. The broadcasting of our names into the room reminded me how truly odd the situation remained in my mind. Lord and Lady Cunningham greeted us, making polite conversation before moving to another guest. We mingled with several guests and I was introduced to a plethora of people. I possess a good memory, which, at that moment, came in handy for the multitude of names, positions and peerage imparted to me in a short time.

As the dancing began, a wiry gentleman approached us. He appeared to be near to my husband's age. Sir Richard Prescott shook Robert's hand and Robert introduced him to me. "So," he inquired, sipping his brandy, "you are the orphan with the special talent?"

My reputation preceded me, though I hadn't expected it not to. However, the other guests had possessed enough good manners not to mention it, particularly in my husband's presence. I opened my mouth to answer, but Robert responded first. "She is my wife, Sir Richard, beyond that is not your concern. Come, dear," he retorted, guiding me away by the elbow.

I glanced behind me as Robert escorted me away. Sir Richard stared after us, his eyes narrowed as he followed our retreat across the room. We chatted with several others before two gentlemen stole Robert away to discuss some form of business. I remained in the company of several ladies.

As our group broke up, I made my way to the fringes of the room to await Robert's return. As I watched the dancers twirl across the ballroom, Sir Richard cornered me. "Well, if it isn't the orphan duchess," he remarked. As he closed in nearer to me, the thick scent of alcohol became apparent. "What a beautiful necklace. Is this the going rate for your special skills?"

I did not dignify his remark with a response, instead I turned to escape his drunken ramblings. He grasped my arm, pulling me toward him and into the hallway outside the ballroom. "Tell me, orphan duchess, do your special skills extend to the bedroom? Is this how you've earned your position?"

I tugged at my arm but failed to loosen his grasp. His hand's crushing grasp twisted to pull me closer, and he forced his lips upon mine. I pushed against him with all my strength but was no match for his overpowering brawn. As I struggled, he began to fall backward, and I wondered if he might be having some sort of attack.

As I followed his falling form, I caught sight of Robert, pulling the man by the collar. He struck him square on the jaw, knocking his sinewy form to the floor. "I informed you once, my wife is no concern of yours. Do not lay a hand on her again."

Sir Richard wiped a trace of blood from the corner of his mouth where Robert's fist landed moments earlier. He pulled himself up to standing. "The whore cannot possibly be worth this much to you, Robert," he hissed.

Robert's eyes burned with fury. "Robert," I whispered, "leave it. It is no bother."

"Listen to her, she understands her worth," Prescott breathed. With that comment, Robert cocked his fist, striking him again, sending him sprawling. I exclaimed aloud, covering my mouth with my hand as he landed.

Several gentlemen rushed into the hall. "Is something amiss?" one questioned.

"Sir Richard seems to have had too much to drink. He is having trouble keeping to his feet. Call for his carriage, he should be on his way," Robert answered, then guided me across the ballroom and outside to the balcony.

He squared my shoulders, forcing me to face him. "Are you all right, Lenora? Did he harm you?"

I shook my head, still catching my breath. "No," I answered after a few breaths. "I am not hurt." He relaxed, and I continued, "Robert, I am sorry."

"Sorry?" he exclaimed. "Dear Lenora, you have nothing to be sorry about!"

"You shouldn't have struck him on my account."

"I damn well should have done more than that," Robert responded, leaning against the balustrade. "Oh, please excuse my language."

"There was no need to cause a scuffle over me."

"The man is an insufferable jackass. He's made enough money in the rail system to buy his way into society. Unfortunately, he did not buy any manners. Are you certain you are unharmed, Lenora?"

I nodded. "Yes, I am certain."

Robert shook his head. "It seems what you maintain as a generous offer on my behalf has caused you more trouble than any woman should encounter."

"That isn't true," I insisted. "Your offer remains generous. It is my reputation that causes the trouble."

"Lenora," Robert said, taking my hands in his, "do not take this upon yourself. You share no blame in this."

"Nor do you," I asserted.

Robert stared off in the distance for a moment. "Would

you prefer to depart?" he inquired after a breath, focusing his gaze on me.

"There is no need to depart on my account," I assured him.

"Then perhaps you'd care to dance with your husband?"

"But your leg…" I began.

"It is quite fine, my dear," Robert promised. "I use the cane only because I prefer the rakish appeal it lends me." He grinned, and I matched his expression. He offered his arm, and I accepted, being led to the dance floor to join the others.

I had never danced with a man before, nor at a ball, though I had learned the steps for most popular dances at the orphanage. We were expected to learn them in the event we were engaged by a wealthy family and needed the skill. In a cloud of giggles, the girls would practice with each other and dream of being swept off their feet. I silently thanked my instructors for providing the lessons as Robert whisked me across the dance floor. My dream had come true. I had the world at my feet.

A smile crept across my face as we continued to swirl around the floor. When the music ended and we applauded the orchestra and dancers, my smile had not diminished. Robert glanced to me, leaning closer to say, "I've never seen you smile so much, Lenora. It is quite beautiful. You should do it more often."

We spent the rest of the party enjoying the company and entertainment, remaining unbothered by any additional rude guests. We returned home in the wee hours of the morning. Poor Elsie was roused from her bed to help me undress.

I climbed into my bed, exhausted but exhilarated. As I relaxed into the pillows, I considered my task over the next several days. I'd prepare for our trip to Glasgow to engage my ladies' maid. I considered the packing to be done before the trip, planning what I might need.

My musings were interrupted by a loud banging at the door. I shot up to sitting, listening as the pounding continued. The sound, enough to rattle my bed, could not emanate from an earthly source.

I swung my legs over the side of the bed, sliding onto the floor. My bare feet touched the cold floor as I crossed the room to the door, pulling on my dressing gown. Dust shook from the ceiling as the battering of my bedroom door continued.

I pulled the door open, staring out at an empty hallway. Moonlight cast shadows down the corridor from the large window at the hall's end. I peered up and down the hall, searching for the cause of the disturbance. I found nothing.

Sighing, I latched the door behind me, shuffling back to my bed. I climbed in and settled back into my pillows. The moment I relaxed into the bed, the pounding began anew. I did not rise this time, hoping the noise would stop on its own. I waited for several moments until I could stand it no longer. The noise grew so loud I shook within the bed each time it sounded.

I rose again, plodding to the door and opening it. Silence and emptiness stared back at me. This time I ventured into the hall, striding up and down but finding nothing. I returned to my quarters and closed the door behind me. I ambled back to bed, pulling the covers high around me as I settled for a third time into the pillows.

Several minutes passed in silence. Perhaps the game was over. I closed my eyes, prepared to sleep. I took a deep, steadying breath and as I felt my body relax, a new sound reached my ears. A creak sounded, and I snapped my eyes open. My bedroom door swung open on its hinges.

I sat up, staring at it as it made its slow journey into the room. "Annie?" I called, wondering if she'd halted her antics and was prepared to be reasonable. I received no answer. I waited a few more moments, staying still so as not to spook her. No one appeared.

I slid from the bed for a third time, crossing the room and closing the door. This round, I locked it behind me. I strode across the room and crawled into bed for what I hoped was the final time. With the sheets gathered around me, I closed my eyes again.

As I lay on my back, a small breeze caressed my cheek. I ignored it until it tickled my cheek again. With a groan, I opened my eyes. I sat up, glancing around. Nothing appeared amiss in the room.

I was almost ready to lay down when the room erupted into pandemonium. Both bedroom doors swung open, along with all the windows. Wind whipped through the room, blowing the bed curtains in a frenzied display. The linens were lifted off the bed and flung across the room. The doors and windows banged open and shut. The bed began to shake, bouncing off the floor. I tumbled out, falling on my rear. I climbed to my feet and fled the room.

I glanced back toward the room as I stood in the hallway, barefoot and in only my nightclothes. The commotion had settled. I took a step toward the door, but it slammed shut. I jiggled the handle, finding it locked. I pounded against the door with my hand. "Annie? Annie! Open this door!" I pushed on the door, twisting the handle, but to no avail. "Annie!" I shouted again. "Your mischief has gone far enough. Open the door!" I tried again but found the door stuck fast.

With a sigh, I considered my options. I would not upend the household at this hour to retrieve a key for my room. I settled on climbing the winding stairs to my tower room. There a fur blanket awaited me, and I could curl up on the chaise and perhaps sleep would come.

I weaved my way through the halls, my arms wrapped tightly around me. I cursed the loss of my dressing gown behind the locked bedroom door. I had spent many a cold evening at the orphanage though, so I would survive.

I climbed the frigid stone steps to the tower and retrieved my fur blanket from the window seat. I curled in a ball on the chaise, draping the fur blanket over me. I rubbed my arms and legs until I felt warmth returning to my body. I nestled further under the blanket, tucking it around me.

The next sensation I experienced was a gentle shaking. Startled, I snapped my eyes open, flailing at my attacker. "Lenora," Robert soothed, "it's me. It's Robert." I breathed a sigh of relief, relaxing. "You're freezing. Where is your dressing gown? What happened?" Robert removed his suit coat, placing it around my shoulders.

"Thank you," I replied, shrugging it tighter around my shoulders. "There was a disturbance in my room last night."

"To say the least," Robert replied. "When you didn't appear at breakfast this morning, I came to check on you. We found your door locked and when Buchanan opened it, the room was in shambles."

"Yes," I explained, sitting up straighter, "after the uproar I retreated to the hallway and found myself locked from my room. I'm sorry for the trouble, I did not intend to sleep this late."

"You need not apologize. You must be quite tired. What happened, Lenora?"

"After I climbed into bed, there was a pounding at my door. When I investigated, I found nothing. It happened once more. Then my door opened. I locked it and returned to bed. That is when the melee ensued. The windows and doors rattled open and shut. Winds whirled through the room and the bed shuddered until I was thrown from it."

"Was it…" Robert began, his voice trailing off.

I nodded. "Yes, I believe so. I did not see her, but I'm convinced it was her."

"I do not understand this. Why does she behave so?" Robert questioned with a shake of his head. He stood and stalked a few steps away.

"This is not abnormal. She met with a violent end. She is confused, agitated. Her mind is troubled. But last night's occurrences indicate a step in the positive direction."

"Positive?" Robert twisted to stare at me, an incredulous expression on his face. "Lenora! Only you can discern being thrown from your bed, chased from your room and risking illness in freezing temperatures as positive!"

"This is her first attempt at communicating," I explained. "In the past, she's only appeared to me. Last night went well beyond that. This is her reaching out."

Robert pondered my comments for a moment. He gave a slight nod. "I'm glad you are traveling with me to Glasgow tomorrow. I should be uncomfortable leaving you in the castle alone. And if this should happen again, you shall wake the household no matter what time of night it is. I will not risk you catching a chill."

I nodded in agreement. In the three months of our marriage, I had already learned not to argue with my husband. I climbed from under my blanket to return to my room to dress. "I hope to have a better encounter with Annie in the future."

"If it is not, you shall awaken me, and I shall rouse Buchanan."

Elsie appeared in the doorway, carrying my dressing robe and slippers. "Your Graces," she greeted us. "I have your dressing gown and slippers."

"Thank you, Elsie," I replied as she slipped the robe around my shoulders after I returned Robert's jacket. She placed the slippers on my feet.

"Would you like to dress for the day now, Your Grace?" she inquired.

"Yes..." I began when I was interrupted by Robert.

"No, she would not. She is to go straight to bed and spend the day there. Has the room been restored yet?"

"Yes, Your Grace," Elsie responded. "Everything is restored. I shall take Her Grace there and see that she is brought hot tea."

"Thank you, Elsie. Do not object, Lenora. It will do you no good. You shall spend the day resting. You must recover your energy before we travel tomorrow."

"I must oversee preparations for the trip," I protested.

"And you may oversee them from your bed," Robert countered. Exasperated as I was, arguing was futile. Robert doted on me for reasons unknown to me. As foreign as it was to me, I was learning to accept it.

I nodded, collecting my book from the side table. "I shall rest," I agreed.

Elsie saw me to my bedroom which had been restored already. A few small items were still being handled. "Your Grace," Buchanan greeted me with a bow of his head. "I shall have a tray of breakfast brought to you at once."

"Thank you, Buchanan. I shall also require assistance to prepare for our journey to Glasgow tomorrow. I have been confined to my bed by Duke Blackmoore."

"I shall arrange the maids to assist at once, Your Grace."

"Thank you, Buchanan."

CHAPTER 4

Despite my stay in bed, I managed to be ready for travel the next day. After assuring Robert of my ability to travel after my experience, we climbed into the carriage with Mr. Langford for the long trip to Glasgow.

The countryside passed us by as we traveled away from the castle. While I possessed a purpose on my trip, I found myself already missing Blackmoore Castle. The castle which had been my home for only three months, provided me more stability and comfort than I'd ever experienced in my eighteen years. Homesickness swept over me as we traveled away from the castle.

I pushed it aside. We would return in four days. Though I would anticipate it with much eagerness, I had business to attend to. My mind turned to my goal: engaging a ladies' maid. I had a specific girl in mind. My mind dwelled on the girl of late, and I hoped my good fortune could become a turn of fortune for her in kind. The idea had occurred to me when, as I was reading in my tower room, a former classmate of mine, had pervaded my thoughts.

Tilly, a friend close in age to me, had resided at the

orphanage when I did. She left the orphanage several months before my surprise engagement. A romantic dreamer, Tilly insisted she'd be better off outside of the orphanage walls. According to Tilly, the orphanage quashed any chance she had at romantic happiness. She insisted if she could only live outside the restrictive walls, she would, without doubt, find a nice gentleman and settle into a good marriage rather than a life of servitude. The appeal of married life was more attractive than even a governess position, no matter how prestigious the household.

Tilly ran away days after her seventeenth birthday. As the clock struck midnight, she and I stood in the foyer. I pleaded with her to remain at the orphanage, maintaining her scheme would turn disastrous. My pleas fell on deaf ears and, with a wink and a grin, fair-haired Tilly snuck from the front door and disappeared into the moonlight. I recall her flaxen hair flowing behind her, her cheeks pink with anticipation and excitement for her new adventure.

I fretted for days, worrying over her plight. But over the course of a week, my worry subsided when she did not return. My mind assured me that, had the situation been intolerable, Tilly would simply have returned to the orphanage. Though her punishment would have been swift and serious, she would be safe and cared for. Perhaps my tainted view of the world prevented me from being open to more possibilities as Tilly was.

Three months passed before I heard from Tilly again. In a letter, she detailed her luck after escaping the orphanage. She'd had wonderful luck in meeting several gentlemen who took a shine to her. She hadn't settled on any as yet, but she hoped she would soon. The description of her situation gave me hope for her.

I smiled as I read the letter, tucking it away in a secret spot where Headmistress Williamson would not find it, but not before I memorized the return address. At the orphanage, older girls were often required to run errands to assist with the running of the facility. It was during one of my errand outings, I planned a daring mission. I would visit Tilly and speak with her.

I completed my tasks as quickly as possible, dashing, in some cases, from place to place. Once completed, I checked the time. I would not be expected back this soon, so my plan would work.

I navigated to the address given on the envelope I'd tucked in my purse. Despite having the address memorized, I worried my memory may fail me. I checked it twice as I closed in on the location, concerned I had traveled to the incorrect area.

While I did not anticipate the area to be opulent, I expected it to exhibit some charm. However, as I approached closer and closer to the address, the buildings became more and more dilapidated. Rough characters lurked in dark corners. I began to fear I had made a grave error in judgement.

However, I steeled my nerves and approached the address. I knocked at the door and was met by a scantily dressed woman. Surely I must have the wrong address, I reflected, though I asked for Tilly, anyway. Shock coursed through me as the woman invited me in and disappeared up the stairs to fetch Tilly.

As I waited in the building's foyer, I glanced into the rooms visible from the entryway. Couches and chaise lounges in loud colors and the like were scattered around the rooms. Gauzy draperies hung at various angles. A piano sat in the middle of the largest room.

My mind tried to process what I was witnessing, but before it could, Tilly rushed down the stairs. "Lenora!?" she exclaimed.

"Tilly!" I greeted her, surprised I had the address correct.

"Lenora," she said, hurrying down the rest of the steps. "What are you doing here?"

"I came to visit. The orphanage does not expect me back for a bit. I wanted to see how you were getting on." I gazed at her, noting several changes. Her long flaxen hair, always a source of pride and which she kept carefully groomed while at the orphanage, hung in tangles. Her plump cheeks with their rosy countenance were sunken and colorless. Her sparkling blue eyes had lost their sparkle. Her dress, tattered now, hung loosely on her frame.

Tilly glanced around before suggesting we step outside to speak. She ushered me out the door and down the street a few steps. "Tilly," I queried as she tugged me further from the building, "whatever are you doing?"

"You shouldn't have come, Lenora," Tilly stated as we came to a stop near the corner.

"Why, Tilly?" Tilly glanced around, avoiding my eyes. "Tilly?"

She met my gaze. "Oh, Lenora, I cannot explain. I am quite embarrassed. It is why I was not truthful in my letter to you, though that must be obvious to you now."

"Tilly, are you in some sort of trouble?"

Tilly let out a long sigh, her shoulders sinking and a tear falling to her cheek. She wiped it away. "Tilly? What is it?"

"Oh, Lenora," she cried.

I put my arms around her. "Tilly, you need not share any details with me. Come home where you are safe and cared for."

"I cannot." Tilly sobbed in my arms. She righted herself, pulling away and drying her eyes. "That place is not a home, Lenora."

"It is," I insisted. "It is OUR home."

Tilly shook her head. "No, it is no home. And they wouldn't take me back. Not now."

"I am sure they would. Please, Tilly, you are miserable."

Tilly sniffled, swallowing hard. "I am not miserable. Forgive my outburst. It is not as bad as it may have seemed moments ago."

"What is 'it,' Tilly?" I inquired.

"Oh, Lenora," Tilly replied, with a roll of her eyes, "you must have deduced already."

My mind whirled at her words. I considered the information in front of me. My brow furrowed as I pieced the puzzle together. "Tilly!" I exclaimed in disbelief. "No!"

"Yes," Tilly admitted with a sheepish grin. "Yes, Lenora, I am a prostitute."

I shook my head, more in disbelief than in judgement. "Oh, Tilly…" I began.

Tilly held up her hand. "So, you see, I would no longer be welcome at Saint Mary's."

"No one must know, Tilly. I would never tell! Please, come home, this is no life!"

"You were always a good friend, Lenora," Tilly responded. "But I cannot."

"Why? What holds you here?"

Tilly offered a slight smile. "Love."

"Love?" I cried. "Tilly, I believe you may be mistaking lust for love."

Tilly shook her head. "No, Lenora, no. Not everything in my letter to you was a lie. I have met someone. He is keen on me and I am keen on him."

"Has he made a promise?"

Tilly gazed to the sky as she shrugged. "Not in so many words," she began. I opened my mouth to reply, raising my eyebrows, but she interrupted. "Oh, he will, Lenora, he will!

You do not know him as I do." I imagined not. "He is not like the others. He is kind, caring, sweet and tender."

My heart broke for Tilly in that moment. She desperately clung to the hope that her supposed sweetheart would rescue her from her current situation. I imagined the likelihood of this to be slim. Though Tilly, always the dreamer, did not agree. I wouldn't ruin the illusion for her. Perhaps she required the fantasy, desired to clutch at this fairytale to endure her new life.

I nodded, pasting on a smile and hoping she could not glean it was disingenuous. "I am glad you have found him, Tilly. And I hope he offers soon. Will you keep in touch? Make me aware of where I can find you should you move?"

Tilly smiled at me. "Of course, Lenora!" She flung her arms around my neck. "Oh, I hope it is soon! I cannot imagine it will be long with the words he speaks to me."

I grasped her hands as she released me. "I hope it to be true. Please take care, Tilly."

"I will," she answered. "And you, Lenora. I wish you the best. I hope you will find happiness as I have."

With a smile and a nod, I stepped away, leaving Tilly on that street corner. I held back a tear as I continued down the street. My beautiful and vivacious friend reduced to this. My mind refused to fill in the word describing her new profession. I refused to glance back as I continued to put one foot in front of the other. I prayed as I journeyed back to the orphanage that Tilly's narrative was not fiction but truth and that she soon would be removed from the situation she found herself in.

CHAPTER 5

Another mile passed by the carriage window as I contemplated what I may find when I sought Tilly. I had heard from her only once more before my fantastic adventure began. She had received no offer yet, but still maintained a proposal was forthcoming. I would be shocked if, when I sought her at the same brothel, I found her to be gone. Though my heart hoped this would be the case. Despite my hope to engage Tilly as my ladies' maid, I wished her to be unavailable for the position.

After a day's journey, we arrived in Glasgow. Henry had made arrangements at a local hotel where we also dined that evening. "Has the journey tired you very much, dear?" Robert asked me as we ate.

"No," I responded, "I do not mind travel. Though I do admit I shall be pleased to journey in the opposite direction."

"You do not like the city?" Henry inquired.

"I prefer my home," I responded, garnering a smile from Robert.

"Will you call at the orphanage to engage your ladies' maid?" Robert questioned.

"No." I hesitated. "The girl I had in mind no longer resides there."

Robert furrowed his brow. "She is engaged in another position and you hope to lure her away, is it, Lenora?"

"Yes," I confirmed, speaking no further.

"I wish you luck, my dear. Should you call upon the girl alone? Perhaps Henry should accompany you, or perhaps you should wait until I've concluded my business." While he did not press the issue, Robert obviously suspected there was more to the story than my simple explanation suggested.

I offered a brief smile as I wiped the corners of my mouth. "I shall be fine. I require no assistance."

Robert chuckled. "No, I do not imagine you require assistance to do much of anything, Lenora. But as your husband, I must ensure you are not placed in any harm."

"I will not be in any danger. I have visited Tilly before and survived it."

"A fact for which I am most grateful," Robert replied.

We finished our dinner and retired for the evening. My mind could not settle as I crawled into bed that evening. Anticipation of my upcoming conversation with Tilly raced through my thoughts, as did a general sense of unease. As I tossed in my bed, I attempted to allay my anxiety by suggesting to myself it was merely the change of scenery causing it. I longed to return to Blackmoore Castle. Soon, I reminded myself, soon.

* * *

Morning came at long last and I rose from my bed, dressing for the day. I'd received little sleep, hoping a resolution to my ladies' maid position would set my mind at ease. Robert kissed my forehead, an affectionate habit he had developed of late, as he left on his business, reminding me to be safe today and wishing me luck. I thanked him as I pulled on my gloves and retrieved my purse.

I stepped onto the pavement, purpose filling my stride. I wound through the streets, reminded again of my first journey to visit Tilly. I quickened my pace, wanting the conversation to be resolved.

I approached the questionable section of town. The last time I'd traveled here, I likely looked out of place. This time, there was no doubt I appeared out of place. I wondered if Robert's concern was less unfounded than I'd originally believed. My clothing on this trip made it clear I did not belong.

Still, I pressed on, intent on speaking with Tilly. I approached the ramshackle building and knocked. A woman, or rather a girl, answered, and I asked for Tilly. The girl shouted up the stairs for her, assuring me she'd be down in a minute. She inspected me up and down, but Tilly appeared before any conversation could be struck.

My jaw dropped open as Tilly waddled down the stairs. I covered my surprise, at least I hoped, by plastering a smile on my face. "Tilly!" I greeted her as she crossed the foyer.

Tilly offered a brief smile. "Lenora," she said with some effort.

"May we speak outside?" I requested.

Tilly nodded, and we proceeded several steps away from the building. I eyed Tilly sideways as we walked, realizing I could no longer ask her to become my ladies' maid. "How are you, dear Tilly?" I inquired as we halted on the sidewalk.

She offered a weak smile. "I am well. You look… quite well!" she responded, eyeing my clothing. Though I worked hard to remain kempt during my orphanage days, the clothing I wore now was obviously a better grade.

"I am," I answered. "I have had… an interesting development in my life."

"Oh?" Tilly prodded.

I licked my lips, contemplating how to explain. "Yes." I hesitated. "I am married."

Tilly's eyebrows shot up in surprise. "Married?"

I nodded. "Yes, I am three months wed. I reside in the highlands now. My husband is in town on business. I traveled with him to engage a ladies' maid."

"Ladies' maid? Lenora! To whom are you married? The Prince of Wales?"

I chuckled. "No," I assured her. "Robert is the Duke of Blackmoore."

Tilly's eyes were wide with shock. "You... you... you are a duchess?"

"I am," I responded, feeling rather foolish for not having broken it more gently. I followed up quickly with, "But I am here to visit you, Tilly. I hope you are well."

"Well enough," Tilly answered, both of us avoiding the obvious.

I offered a polite smile, deciding to inquire after a moment. "I had hoped to speak with you about the position of ladies' maid, but..." Again, I hesitated. "You are... with child?"

Tilly glanced to her swollen belly. "Yes," she admitted. "How sweet of you to consider me, Lenora. But as you can see, I am in no position to accept."

I offered a tight-lipped smile, worried about my friend. The offer for the position could no longer be made given her condition. I was uncertain of how my husband would react and, while he had proven to be understanding beyond measure, this scandal may prove too much. I was unwilling to risk displeasing Robert. "Tilly..." I began hesitantly, unsure what to say next.

Tilly smiled at me, grasping my hand and squeezing. "Even if I weren't in this position, I couldn't accept, Lenora."

"Oh?" I questioned.

She nodded, a grin on her face. "I'll soon be in your position… married."

"Oh!" I exclaimed, squeezing her hand. "How wonderful. Have you set a date for when you shall wed? What sort of gentleman is he? Where will you reside?"

Tilly's smile faltered. After a moment, she forced the smile back on her face. "We… we have not set any date yet." She paused before continuing. "He… he does not know yet… about the baby. Oh, but as soon as he's aware, he will offer," Tilly assured me.

My brow furrowed at her statements. By her size, I judged her to be at least seven months along. "Doesn't know?" I queried, unable to formulate a full thought.

Tilly shrugged. "I… I was not aware when I saw him last. I suspected but did not want to mislead him. Oh, but once the precious babe is with us, he will be overcome with joy as I am, and we shall form our own little family."

I smiled, though my heart broke for her. Tilly, always the optimist, assumed the birth of her child would spur a proposal. Perhaps my realism colored my expectations too darkly, but I doubted the events would pan out as Tilly hoped.

"I wish you the best of luck, Tilly. I am certain the birth of your child will bring you much joy."

"Oh, I'm so sorry you wasted your trip," Tilly replied, embracing me.

"It was not a waste, Tilly! I have been able to visit with you, which is never a waste. I hope to visit again. If I do not return before your child is born and you are settled, will you leave a forwarding address?"

"Of course, Lenora. How exciting, I expect the next we see each other, we shall both be settled into married life!"

I offered another weak smile. And Tilly continued, "Now,

walk me back and tell me all about your new life!"

Before we began our return journey to Tilly's home, Sir Richard Prescott approached us.

"Duchess Blackmoore?" he inquired, squinting his eyes as though they deceived him.

"Sir Richard, hello," I answered.

"Whatever are you doing in THIS part of town? And alone no less." His eyes traveled up and down my form, sending a shiver up my spine.

"She is not alone," Tilly chimed in. She linked her arm in mine and pulled me closer to her.

"I stand corrected," Sir Richard said. "Though I do not imagine you plan to accompany Duchess Blackmoore to wherever she is staying, do you?"

Tilly remained silent and Sir Richard continued. "Perhaps, duchess, I could escort you to your next destination."

"Thank you for the kind offer, Sir Richard," I began.

"But her business is not yet finished," Tilly finished for me.

"I could wait," Sir Richard offered.

"It is not necessary, Sir Richard. I am certain you have pressing matters to attend to, and I have no set time to return. Again, thank you for your kind offer."

Sir Richard nodded. "Please pass along my regards to your husband."

"I shall. Good day, Sir Richard."

Sir Richard tipped his hat to us. "Good day, Duchess Blackmoore." He glanced to Tilly, repeating his gesture. "Miss."

He disappeared down the street. Tilly turned me to face her, staring in my eyes, a serious expression on her face. "Lenora," she said in a low tone, "do not trust that man."

While I agreed with her sentiment, I was surprised at her comments. "I do not."

"Good," she answered. "He is a cruel, heartless man. A terrible man." I raised my eyebrows at her statement. It confirmed the experience I had with him was not a singular event. She read my expression and continued her explanation. "He is a frequent visitor to our establishment. On occasion, he is rough with the girls. He bruised Minnie terribly and gave her a nasty cut on her head."

"I have not had a pleasant experience with Sir Richard either," I admitted, though I did not explain the details. "I would prefer not to be alone with the man."

Tilly nodded at me. "Now, about that wonderful new life of yours."

I imparted a few details as we strode down the street, arm-in-arm. Tilly acted genuinely enthusiastic for my change in circumstances. Each statement I imparted stabbed at my heart. I felt as though I bragged even as Tilly suffered. I attempted to keep my statements brief and factual, though when Tilly asked if Duke Blackmoore's estate was grand, the admittance that my new home was a castle felt awkward.

On that note, we arrived at the brothel's doorstep. Embracing, we wished each other well, and I watched her climb the steps into the building. She waved and smiled as she entered the building. I did the same as she disappeared through the door. A thought wandered across my mind, depressing and disheartening. I wondered if, or rather worried that, this would be the last time we spoke. I dismissed it, pushing the desolate notion from my mind, and forced myself to walk away.

I glanced back at the building, resisting the urge to return and drag Tilly from inside. Though, despite my intentions being admirable, I overstepped my rights by assuming I knew what was best for Tilly. Instead, I pushed myself to continue across the street, convincing myself with every step that my decision to leave was correct.

CHAPTER 6

I pushed the peas around on my plate as we dined that evening. "You've been quiet, Lenora," Robert mentioned. "Did your plan not come to fruition?"

"It did not," I admitted with a sigh. "The girl I considered suitable… was not able to accept."

"I'm sorry, though the position should not be difficult to fill," he answered.

"Not at all," Henry agreed. "I could assist you."

I smiled at him. "Thank you, though I have another avenue to pursue first."

"Oh?" Robert inquired.

"Yes," I informed my companions. "I shall try at the orphanage, my former home. I am well acquainted with many of the girls there. It is a good position. I hope to find someone suitable there to accept."

"Indeed," Robert agreed.

"If you find no success there," Henry said, "I shall be happy to assist in the matter."

"Thank you, Mr. Langford," I responded with a nod.

After dinner, I undressed, considering both the events of

my day and the task ahead. Nervousness filled me, though I did not understand if the cause was my reunion with Tilly or my upcoming encounter with Headmistress Williamson. Returning to the orphanage after three short months as a duchess overwhelmed me. I could only imagine the reaction such news would garner from the headmistress.

As I eased back into the pillows, I attempted to push both events from my mind. Tilly's life was her own, not mine to interfere in. She made her choices. I fell asleep repeating this to myself as disturbing thoughts crept through my mind.

* * *

I stood outside the run-down form of St. Mary's Orphanage for Girls, staring up at the building. I had spent over one decade here, yet it now seemed so foreign to me. Invisible hands held me back from crossing the street and entering the place I'd once considered my home.

Nervousness was a sentiment I rarely suffered from. Given my experience with the dead, I seldom found many circumstances with the living that flustered me. Still, my experience here, while not horrid, could not be categorized as pleasant. My life had taken a tremendous turn for the better, and I had no desire to return to my previous world.

Nevertheless, I had a task to complete. I drew in a deep breath, steadied myself, and took my first step toward the building. I drew confidence with every step I took. And by the time I climbed to the top step, I knocked on the door without hesitation.

One of the younger girls, with whom I was not well acquainted, opened the door. "May I help you?" she asked in a crisp voice, as we were instructed.

"Yes, Mrs. Lenora Fletcher to see Headmistress

Williamson," I announced. The girl stood aside, motioning for me to enter the foyer.

"Wait here, please, madam, I shall announce you," she responded.

"Thank you," I said, clutching my purse in both hands as I stood awaiting an audience with the headmistress. Normally being in this position was not something to be enthusiastic about, however, this time was different. Still, my stomach disagreed with my breakfast as old sentiments swept over me.

The girl disappeared into the headmistress' office, then returned a moment later. "You may enter," she stated, motioning to the door.

I nodded at her, entering the room and closing the door behind me. Headmistress Williamson tended a plant near her window. She glanced to me as I entered, nodding her head as she returned her gaze to the plant.

"Headmistress Williamson," I began, though the waving of the headmistress' hand interrupted me.

She finished watering her plant before speaking. I expected an offer to be seated, however none came. "Well, Lenora," she stated as she set the watering can aside, "I cannot say I am surprised to see you. I suspected it was you when Molly announced the name, though I was not sure. I believe she misspoke your name, assuming you a married woman. I shall speak to the child about the danger of assumptions."

"But…" I began, attempting to set the record straight.

Another dismissive wave as Headmistress Williamson spoke over me. "Lenora, please. You have not been given permission to speak! Now," she continued as she paced behind her desk, "you may NOT have your old room back. I am afraid you shall be given the only available bed remaining in the facility in the attic. You are quite lucky there is any space at all, girl!"

I sighed and the headmistress finally set her gaze upon me. I prepared myself for the inevitable chiding about my sighing, but she stopped short. I glanced up at her, noting her furrowed brow and slack jaw. For the first time in my visit, she had looked at me and actually seen me. My appearance should have made it obvious I did not plan a return to the orphanage for boarding.

I took advantage of her lost voice to fill in the details before any embarrassment occurred on either of our parts. "Headmistress Williamson, please allow me to make clear my purpose here. I have not returned to reclaim a space at the orphanage, quite the opposite."

"Oh?" Headmistress Williamson queried in a hoarse voice.

"Yes," I continued. "I am here seeking a girl to fulfill the position of ladies' maid."

Her brow remained furrowed as she processed the information. "You... wish... You wish to fulfill a ladies' maid position for your mistress?"

"No," I corrected. "I wish to fulfill a ladies' maid position for myself."

"Yourself? Lenora, stop talking nonsense and explain yourself. How many times have I told you to be clear when you speak? Now, what is it you wish to achieve?"

My shoulders sagged for a moment as I bit my tongue. After a clarifying breath, I explained, "Headmistress Williamson, I apologize if I've been unclear. I wish to fulfill a ladies' maid position within MY household. I am married and mistress of the Blackmoore estate."

Shock was apparent on the woman's face. She blinked at me as though understanding would not come to her. "You..."

she gasped, hesitating and struggling to find words. "You are… the Duchess of Blackmoore?"

"Yes, I am," I confirmed.

The woman collapsed to her chair. After a moment, she motioned for me to sit across from her. Perplexed, she gazed at me. I perched on the edge of my chair, wondering if I should fetch a glass of water for the poor woman. "I see," she murmured. She raised her eyebrows, swallowed hard, and sat straighter in her seat. "Well," she began, pushing her shoulders back and raising her chin, "unfortunately, I am unable to assist you."

This time, my brow crinkled. Surely, I reflected, there were girls seeking positions at the orphanage. Within three months' time, all eligible girls could not have found positions. I opened my mouth to question her meaning, but she continued speaking. "There are simply no suitable girls at this time. None that would be able to fill such a role within your particular household."

"Oh," I muttered, formulating my response. "I assumed there may be girls seeking a position. Since I have not been gone long and there were several when I departed. How fortunate they have all been placed."

"Well," Headmistress Williamson explained, "they have not ALL been placed, but again, there are none suitable to join your staff."

"Has Margaret found placement?" I inquired.

"No," the headmistress answered, drawing the word out. "But I could not let her go at this time, though your husband may prefer I did, pretty girl that she is." She narrowed her eyes at me, letting out a harsh cackle.

"Well," I retorted as I rose to stand, "it appears our business is concluded." Headmistress Williamson also stood. "I shall see myself out."

I approached the door when the headmistress ceased my departure, calling, "Oh, Lenora..."

"Yes?" I questioned, turning to face her from the doorway.

"If you are in any position to make a request of your husband, it would prove most helpful for Duke Blackmoore to make a donation to the orphanage."

Try as I might, I could not force my lips into a smile, fake or otherwise. Instead, I struggled to stop them from forming into a grimace. "I shall speak with him regarding your request with the utmost haste." With those words, I stormed across the foyer and departed through the front door. Only once outside did I take a moment to allow the emotions boiling under the surface to bubble up.

I breathed a shaky breath, my hand still gripping the door handle leading to my former home. My change of position failed to affect Headmistress Williamson's attitude toward me. Had I expected it to? I was not certain, though in my deepest heart, I had hoped for a different result.

I set my jaw, pulling myself straighter. I released the door handle and smoothed my skirts, drawing in a deep breath. I should not let it affect me, I decided. As I descended the steps, I caught sight of Robert crossing the street.

"Robert!" I exclaimed. "Whatever are you doing here?"

"Collecting you," he responded. "My business concluded early. I hoped to locate you and lunch at my favorite restaurant. I warn you, it is a pub. Are you game?"

"I am," I answered, accepting his arm to walk. We wound through the streets, ending our journey outside a pub.

Robert stared up at the building, then eyed me. "I hope you don't find the establishment too coarse. The food is quite good."

I smiled at him. "I do not object."

"You are quite a good sport, Lenora," Robert mentioned, holding the door open for me.

We sat in a booth near the fireplace. Warmth flowed from its crackling fire. "How was your visit to the orphanage?" Robert asked after our order was placed.

"Brief," I stated, not meeting Robert's eye. "Headmistress Williamson is very busy."

"Was she able to help you settle the position?"

"No," I admitted, "she had no suitable girls available."

"Really?" Robert questioned. "I am quite surprised."

"As was I," I conceded. "I have not been gone long. I assumed several of the girls there when I departed remained. Had I realized she had no suitable girls, I would not have wasted her time and mine."

"The headmistress must be well-connected to have gained placements for all of them," Robert commented.

"I did not gather the impression they were all placed, merely that none of them were suitable to join our household."

"That seems an odd statement," Robert commented.

"Odd or not, it was the entirety of her response. I am not surprised. She and I were not cordial. Though I admit not to have expected the cool reception I received. Despite her lack of help, she did solicit a donation request on your behalf."

Robert lifted his eyebrows but allowed the subject to drop. "Unfortunate she was unable to settle the position. Though, allow Henry to handle it. He will make short work of the matter, I imagine."

"I will," I agreed.

Our food was served, and I realized as a whiff passed under my nostrils, how hungry I was. "Are you anxious to return to the castle?" Robert inquired as we began eating.

"Yes," I confirmed, "I am most anxious to return home."

Robert offered a half-smile. "It warms me to hear you call it your home."

"I am glad it pleases you," I answered.

"And I am glad it pleases YOU," Robert replied with a chuckle.

"It does," I disclosed. "I have a tremendous sense of contentment there."

"Despite your midnight hauntings?"

"I am accustomed to these phenomena."

"I must admit, it is odd to me how you take these events in stride." I nodded, familiar with the sentiment. Most others with whom I was acquainted found me odd. "Do not misunderstand me, Lenora. I do not find YOU odd. Merely the ease with which you accept the events surrounding you."

A half-smile crossed my face as, for the first time in my life, I experienced acceptance from another living person. "I am glad," I murmured, unsure how to respond, having no experience with this feeling.

We spent the remainder of the meal discussing household details. During the afternoon, we took in the scenery in a park despite the chill in the air before returning to our hotel. As we approached the building, Robert confessed he had a surprise for me.

"A surprise?" I questioned, shocked but curious.

"Yes," he mentioned as we entered our suite of rooms. A crate sat on the table inside the entryway. "I hope you shall be pleased." Robert removed the lid, allowing me to view the contents.

Books filled the crate to the brim. "For your library," Robert added, with a grin.

I smiled at him, a genuine, open smile. "Robert!" I exclaimed.

"Are you pleased?"

"Pleased is an understatement," I assured him, returning my gaze to the books. I reached out to touch them, feeling their covers beneath my fingertips. Excitement coursed through me at the thrill of discovery and promise of new adventure the books brought. I imagined the words on each page, inhaled the scent of the paper and bindings.

"Your books seem to bring you much joy. Again, I confess to have seldom used the library at Blackmoore Castle, though, your zeal for reading is obvious. I hope these additions will bring you delight."

"I have no doubt they will," I voiced, eyeing the books with eagerness. I turned to Robert and, with a wide grin, exclaimed, "Thank you!"

He matched my expression. "You are most welcome, Lenora." He kissed my forehead before suggesting we change for dinner.

The following morning brought a dreary January day. Eager to return home, I awoke early and prepared for the journey. Dressed in my peach traveling dress, I awaited the carriage to be loaded for the return trip. My crate of books was placed with the luggage, bringing a smile to my face.

We departed following breakfast, and I settled in for the long journey to the highlands. "Oh, I hope you do not mind, Lenora," Robert stated as we climbed into the carriage, "I have one stop to make. I trust it shall be brief."

"Not at all," I replied. With a crack of the whip, the carriage lurched forward, and we set off. The buildings passed by the window as the carriage wound through the streets.

After a few moments, the buildings passing us became shabbier. I did not recall traveling into town past these squalid buildings. Within another moment, I recognized my surroundings. Our carriage approached the orphanage.

Surprise surged through me as the carriage pulled to a stop outside St. Mary's. Perhaps Robert planned to acquiesce to Mistress Williamson's request for a donation. The door to the carriage popped open and Robert exited, reaching inside for my hand. "Come, Lenora, this shan't take long."

I accepted his hand as I climbed out of the carriage, still unclear on the nature of our business. We climbed the steps and Robert introduced us to the child who answered the door. We were shown inside and asked to wait while we were announced.

The child ushered us into the headmistress' office moments later. The headmistress sat overlooking papers on her desk. Without glancing up, Headmistress Williamson began speaking. "Lenora, I informed you yesterday that..."

"Excuse me, madam," Robert interrupted. Headmistress Williamson's head shot up from her desk and her mouth gaped open.

"Duke Blackmoore!" she exclaimed, leaping from her chair.

"Yes, and my wife. You should take greater care, madam, to address her in the proper fashion."

"Oh," she hesitated, "yes. My apologies, Duchess Blackmoore. Won't you both be seated?" Headmistress Williamson motioned to chairs across from her. I had never witnessed the headmistress flustered before, though it was obvious she was at this moment. "May I offer you tea?"

"No, we shan't be long," Robert responded. Turning to me, he said, "Please sit, dear."

I took a seat across from the headmistress, still unclear on the purpose of our visit. Robert remained standing. "What may I help you with, Duke Blackmoore?" she inquired.

"Yesterday, my wife called upon you to discuss the placement of a girl from your school as a ladies' maid. You were unable to accommodate the request. I find it surprising you were unable to assist her, though I suspect that had little to do with the lack of availability of a suitable girl."

"Well..." Headmistress Williamson began, her eyes darting around the room as though searching for an answer. "I... I..." The headmistress swallowed hard. "I am not sure what Len… Duchess Blackmoore imparted about our discussion, but the fact is, Duke Blackmoore, there were simply no girls I felt acceptable for the position."

"No girls acceptable for the position or my wife not acceptable for your girls?" Robert pushed. I realized in that instant the true nature of the visit. My husband had no intention on offering a donation. He meant to scold the headmistress for her treatment of me. Guilt washed over me. I should not have mentioned my disappointment over the incident yesterday.

"Robert," I whispered, reaching for his hand behind his back.

Headmistress Williamson's mouth quavered as she considered her answer. "I... That is…"

"That is what, headmistress?" Robert pressed on.

"This isn't necessary," I breathed as I stood.

"An apology from Headmistress Williamson is completely necessary," Robert assured me. "Please sit, dear." I regained my seat at my husband's behest.

"Apology?" Headmistress Williamson queried as she seated herself. "Yes, I do apologize for our inability to fill your staff position, however…" Her voice faltered as she glanced to Robert. Robert raised his eyebrows at the word, waiting for her to continue. "However, given Duchess Blackmoore's… unique view of the world…" she paused. "I am not sure if you are aware of it, but I felt it most inappropriate to …"

Robert held up his hand. "I shall stop you there, madam." Robert clasped his hands behind his back again, pacing in front of the desk. "Your apology should be directed toward my wife for your less than courteous treatment of her. I am very much aware of her 'unique view of the world,' as you put it. And it has carved her into a beautiful, caring, compassionate individual. Qualities that should be prized but instead are scorned. Qualities you obviously lack, headmistress."

"I am sorry if you deigned my behavior less than suitable, Duchess Blackmoore," Headmistress Williamson responded. "It was not my intention. I merely considered the situation less than ideal. Though I..."

Robert held up his hand again, stopping her. He raised his voice, heat entering it. "That's quite enough. You misunderstand my meaning, headmistress. I do not wish you to apologize for my wife's perception of your attitude. I wish you to apologize for your attitude, intended or otherwise."

Headmistress Williamson stared at Robert, swallowing hard again. She offered a brief smile at him, turning her gaze to me and repeating the gesture. "I am sorry, Duchess Blackmoore," she responded just above a whisper.

For a decade, I had endured poor treatment at this woman's hands. She spurned me for my ability, though, as with most, she failed to understand it. Instead, she viewed it as abnormal, evil, a thing to be reviled. Her attitudes regarding my capabilities with the dead led her to treat me as subhuman in many instances.

Still, in this moment, as uneasiness bordering on fear flashed through her eyes, I experienced only empathy for the woman. "Thank you, Headmistress Williamson," I replied. "Please let us consider the matter concluded."

Headmistress Williamson glanced to Robert, her eyes questioning his evaluation of her performance. "My wife is most gracious," he noted.

"Indeed," Headmistress Williamson breathed. "Again, I meant no disrespect."

"Understood, though in the future," Robert responded, "you may consider exercising greater judgement in your behavior. You oversee the development of several young women who should be taught better judgement than you displayed."

"Indeed," the headmistress repeated.

Robert nodded his head at her. "We shall take up no more of your time, Headmistress Williamson. Come, Lenora."

Headmistress Williamson stood as I did. "Perhaps an arrangement can still be made..." Headmistress Williamson began.

Robert turned back toward her. "That will not be necessary," Robert replied. "We have made other arrangements. I am afraid you may be correct in your assessment that girls from your school would not fit within our household."

"I see," the headmistress responded. "Then perhaps you would consider a..."

Robert interrupted her for the third time. "A donation?" he inquired.

Headmistress Williamson paused a moment. "It would further the girls' educations so that perhaps we would provide a more appropriate match for households such as yours in the future."

Robert considered her request for a moment. "I leave the decision of your request to my wife," Robert answered, setting his gaze on me.

I glanced between the two of them before responding. "I am sure the girls here would benefit from a donation," I responded.

Robert nodded. "I shall see that my man provides you a generous donation within the week, headmistress. Good day." Robert drew me through the door, guiding me across the foyer.

"Thank you!" Headmistress Williamson called from behind her desk. "We are most grateful!" Her voice echoed in the entryway as we departed the building. We descended the stairs, climbing into the carriage, and set off.

As the carriage pulled away, I glanced to Robert. "You are more generous than I am, Lenora," he admitted.

"That was unnecessary," I replied. "I do not mean to be ungrateful nor lecture you, though I did not require an apology for her poor behavior."

"Require or not, you deserved one. I cannot imagine how you tolerated that woman for over ten years."

"I had little choice," I conceded. "One becomes accustomed to their surroundings and learns to accept them."

"One should never accept such poor treatment."

"Which is why I chose generosity. Those girls do not have a choice to accept their lives or not."

Robert gazed at me a moment. "The wisdom you display at your young age is a constant surprise to me."

"I have a significant advantage," I quipped, referencing my ability.

Robert smiled at my attempt at humor. "Well, at the very least, she should not trouble you any further if you have any future dealings with her. Though I would not recommend it."

I smiled and nodded at him, settling back into my seat for the journey.

CHAPTER 7

As the carriage rumbled along beneath me, a smile crossed my face as the notion of us inching closer to Blackmoore Castle, my home, swirled in my mind. My thoughts turned from my impending arrival at home to the life I'd left behind. The confrontation with Headmistress Williamson frothed in my mind. Competing memories fought for my attention. I replayed the conversation between my husband and the headmistress over. Despite the harrowing years spent at the orphanage, I'd experienced compassion for her in that moment. With the reputation of the orphanage on the line, she had been backed into a corner and forced to apologize. I doubted the sincerity of the apology, but she had still made it, if only to save her own job.

My mind regressed further, pouring over that decade spent at St. Mary's. Following the unceremonious drop off by my previous guardians, who imparted the details of my mysterious affliction to the headmistress, I had endured less than pleasant treatment. Headmistress Williamson viewed my special talent as a curse. I spent my first night in the orphanage in the attic. No bed existed at that time in the attic of St. Mary's. Instead, I spent a chilly night on the floor, a tattered blanket the only item offered to me. I curled under it as tears spilled down my cheeks. A second time abandoned in less than two years, I, a child of seven, struggled to accept my fate.

As I sobbed, a woman, appearing aged and frail, approached. She pulled me into her arms, drying my tears with the papery skin on her fingers. She possessed surprising strength for a woman of her age. I buried my face in her bosom, weeping as she pulled me close. She offered no warmth, but the comfort of her presence soothed me enough to sleep.

The next morning when I awoke, prodded by a stick I would later be struck with for oversleeping, I confessed my midnight visitor. I inquired about her, hoping she would be a teacher there, some kind soul I could draw strength from. After providing a careful description of the woman several times, I managed to raise Headmistress Williamson's ire. She slapped me, calling me a wicked child and scolded me about the evils of lying.

"I'm not lying!" I cried, my face smarting from the crisp smack.

"You are you wicked child!" she screamed at me, her face red and twisted with fury.

"I am not!" I insisted, a tear escaping my eye and sliding down my cheek.

Another slap landed across the other cheek as I sniveled. "You are lying, admit it. Admit it, Lenora! Say you are lying, and you will spare yourself some of the further punishment you will receive for your wicked ways."

I remained silent, sniffling and choking back sobs. "Stop your sniveling, you wicked brat. If anyone should shed tears, it is I. I, out of the kindness that resides deep in my heart, took you in, against my better judgement. Your former guardians at the convent informed me of your… vice. What have you to say for yourself?"

Again, I remained quiet. She spun to face me. "Answer, girl!" she shrieked. "Speak when you are spoken to!"

I sucked in air, my breath unsteady. "I cannot control it," I wept, tears falling to my cheeks. "They are real to me."

Her slap knocked me from my chair. I fell to the floor on my knees, gasping as I clutched my cheek. "Stand up," Headmistress Williamson insisted. I did not move. "STAND UP!" she yelled, yanking me to my feet. "Now, admit your lie."

I stared at the floor, tensing my muscles, my jaw tightening. I swallowed hard, firming not only my posture but my heart as well. I would know no peace here, no acceptance. To survive, I would need to adapt. I licked my lips, my gaze flickering up to the headmistress' face. My bottom lip quavered as I spoke. "I lied."

"About?" she queried.

"I did not see the woman," I responded.

The woman's lips curled into a cruel smile. She paced the floor behind her desk. "You shall be punished for your lies. You shall go without dinner and you shall spend your night scrubbing the entry floor on your hands and knees. While you do so, you shall consider the sin you are committing with your lies. It is a habit you should break, Lenora. My punishments will seem kind compared to the wrath of God you shall incur. Tomorrow you will write one hundred times the words 'I shall not lie' in good penmanship. If your penmanship is lacking in any way, you shall write it again. Do you understand?"

"Yes, headmistress," I responded, my head bowed.

It was not the last night I would spend paying for my purported vice. Though I tried to hide my gift, it was, at times, impossible. On several occasions, unable to hide the truth, I had paid a terrible price.

As the years passed, I learned to control my reactions and ability, earning me less hostility from Headmistress Williamson and the other girls. At the age of thirteen, nearly an entire year had passed without incident when I was awakened from my winter slumber at quarter after midnight.

An older woman, her hair white as snow, wrinkles set deeply into her face, stood at the bedside. I ignored her, rolling onto my side with my back toward her. Her brown eyes bore into my back. I closed my eyes, attempting to shut out her presence.

An icy hand pressed against my shoulder. I shrugged away from it, pulling the bed covers higher. A moment later, the covers slid off me. I clutched at them, attempting to stop the woman from stripping them from my bed. "No!" I whispered, glaring at her.

Her eyes, fixed on me, made a silent plea. "Please, go!" I begged. "I cannot help you." As forlorn as her gaze, my plea matched hers in desperation. While the dead had visited me over the course of the past year, I had experienced no additional instances with the headmistress. I did not wish to incur her wrath again.

I pulled the covers from her cold, gnarled hands, twisting to face away from her. But that would not be the end of the experience. Cold hands grasped my shoulders, shaking me with enough force to drive me from my bed. "All right," I acquiesced in a whisper. I held my finger to my lips, not wanting to wake the other girls. I motioned for her to follow me as I tiptoed into the hall.

She followed, though her footsteps made no sound. Glassy eyes stared at me as I eased the door shut. "What is it you want?" I questioned, wrapping my arms around me as I shivered from the cold.

Her arm raised and a frail finger pointed down the hall.

Her eyes met mine as she continued to point. I shook my head. "No!" I insisted.

I spun to reenter the bedroom when her icy hand grasped my wrist. "No!" I maintained, yanking on my arm. The woman did not relent. "Please," I begged. "You do not understand."

She cupped my face in her hand, pulling me closer to her. Cool air caressed my skin as she whispered in my ear. My jaw fell open at her words. I met her gaze, swallowing hard. I nodded. "All right," I acceded.

Together, we proceeded down the hall in the direction she signaled moments earlier. With much trepidation, I turned the door handle, easing the door open. The moonlight cast long shadows in the room. I had never seen the interior of the room before. It was decorated with rich woods and thick velvet draperies.

A large bed stood against the far wall. Headmistress Williamson lay sleeping under a thick coverlet. With a quick glance at the woman, I crept into the room, approaching the bed. My trembling hand reached toward Headmistress Williamson. I touched her shoulder, and I gently rocked her.

It took several attempts, but eventually I roused her from her slumber. She startled awake, staring at me with bleary eyes. "Lenora?" she barked, recognizing me. "What are you doing here? How dare you enter my bedroom!"

"I apologize," I replied, shrinking back from her bed. I glanced toward the specter behind me. "It is urgent."

"Has something happened to one of the girls?" Headmistress Williamson questioned, rising from her bed and donning her robe.

I shook my head. "No," I choked out.

"Well, what is it then, girl? Do you find this an amusing game?"

"No, headmistress. My apologies, however..." I paused.

"Spit it out, girl!" Headmistress Williamson responded, approaching me.

"It is your mother," I explained.

Her face changed, anger at being awoken replaced by confusion. Her brows knit together, and her jaw slackened. She stared at me, silent for a moment.

The ghost clutched my shoulder, whispering in my ear. "She has several things she would like to say," I began.

Headmistress Williamson found her voice, cutting me off. "This stunt is not entertaining, Lenora. And you shall be punished for it in the morning. I am too tired to deal with your games now."

"You do not understand..." I protested.

"I understand perfectly well, it is YOU, Lenora, who does not understand. You consider yourself clever, playing this ruse of my mother visiting you. However, my mother is alive."

I pressed my lips together as sorrow filled my heart. "She passed earlier this evening, headmistress. I am so very sorry."

Headmistress Williamson stared at me, frozen in her place for a moment. "What a horrible girl you are, Lenora. Your antics disgust me."

"I am sorry, but it is the truth. She has suffered from pneumonia these past months and succumbed to it earlier this evening."

She grimaced at me, but I continued. "I can prove it," I claimed.

"Prove it?" she scoffed.

"Yes," I insisted. Cool air brushed past my ear as the specter whispered into it. I spoke, recounting what she told me. "When you were young, about six, you found a kitten, gray striped, tiny and with a malformed back foot. You took it in, caring for it. You hid it from your mother, assuming she would not allow you to keep it. Despite the care you gave it, it died. And you wept for three nights over it. Your mother knew, and she wasn't cross with you. In fact, she admired you for it. And she wanted to tell you its death was not your fault. The kitten could not have been saved, but your care of it made its only days on earth tolerable. It knew love, and she was very proud of you for what you did."

Tears filled Headmistress Williamson's eyes and her breath caught in her throat. "How..." she choked out.

I continued, information still flowing into my ear from the specter of Headmistress Williamson's mother. "She wants to tell you she is very proud of you. Your position here is an achievement. She forgives you for not coming when she wrote to say she fell ill. You could do nothing to change the outcome."

A tear fell from Headmistress Williamson's eye and she clutched her stomach. With a gasp, she collapsed onto the bed. I approached her, putting my hand on her shoulder. "Your father's departure was not your fault." Headmistress Williamson's head bobbed up. Her eyes stared into mine. Her lips trembled as she held back sobs. "He and your mother had a terrible falling out. He rushed out of the house. Your mother let him go. He did not return. She heard a rumor later that he had been drinking. He was always an angry drunk. An altercation occurred, and he died. She did not have the courage to determine if the story was truth or rumor, so she continued to deny it. It led you to believe your father may return, that he had left because of something you did. But that isn't true. She wanted you to know. She did not want you living the rest of your life believing you drove your father away." I paused. "She loved you, Miriam." I offered a slight smile as she gazed at me.

She wept, bending at the waist and resting her head on her knees. I eased onto the bed next to her, allowing her time to grieve. I placed my hand on her back as I fixed my gaze on her mother. The specter stared at the huddled form next to me. She shifted her gaze to me, a tiny smile crossing her lips. She nodded to me. I returned the gesture, and she stalked across the room without a sound. She glanced back before passing through the door.

After several moments, Headmistress Williamson regained her posture. She wiped at her face. I offered her a handkerchief from her night table. She dried her eyes. We sat for several more breaths in silence before Headmistress Williamson stood. I rose as she did.

She breathed a deep breath, squaring her shoulders and raising her chin. She set her jaw and made eye contact. "Go to bed, Lenora. Speak of this to no one," she instructed.

I nodded and crossed the room without comment. As I stepped through the doorway, I reached behind me to shut the door. "Oh, Lenora," Headmistress Williamson added, "do not expect this incident to change my opinion regarding you and your ... ability. I still find it abnormal, amoral and foul."

I nodded to her again and pulled the door shut, retiring to my bed. After that night, while there was still no love lost between us, Headmistress Williamson and I avoided each other as much as we could. My treatment, though still callous, lacked the usual cruelty I endured as a younger child.

The carriage rocked after hitting a bump in the road and my mind snapped back to the present. My situation no longer depended on the whims of a harsh and spiteful woman. I drew in a deep breath, gazing at the scenery as it passed. Each passing moment brought me one step closer to my home. The thought brought a small smile to my face, and I rested my head against the side wall as I continued to gaze out the window.

CHAPTER 8

Blackmoore Castle rose from the mists high atop the moor. The sight delighted me, setting my heart aglow with excitement. This had been my first extended trip away from my new home since I'd arrived three months prior. Even in that short time, the attachment I'd formed to the property ran deep.

The connection surprised me. After bouncing between three locations in eighteen years, I grew unsure that I could ever truly feel at home. I assumed, unless I obtained a suitable placement in another's household, I would stay at the orphanage. A home, it was not. The concept that I had my own home still astounded me.

I leaned forward, focusing on the growing outline of the castle. "Anxious to return home, Lenora?" Robert inquired.

"Very," I replied with a grin.

Robert matched my expression. "You must be eager to rest after the long journey."

"I am eager to be in my home," I responded.

The carriage slanted as we began the climb to the castle. "Soon, my dear, soon."

We drew up alongside the castle's main entrance, greeted by the staff. I entered the foyer, allowing the sense of comfort to wash over me. Buchanan collected our outerwear. Movement drew my eyes upward as I removed my gloves. I glanced to the balcony above. Annie stood overlooking the floor below. Her tattered and dirty red dress hung around her frame. Her dark hair remained as mussed as the first day I witnessed her specter. Perhaps she had missed me in my absence, I pondered.

I stared at her, making eye contact. Robert, noting my fixed stare, followed my gaze. Before he could inquire about my behavior, the doors to the drawing room burst open. A young, dark-haired man emerged from the room beyond. Even from a distance, he smelled of liquor.

He stumbled from the doorway into the foyer toward us. He eyed Robert, then me. His lips curled into a scornful sneer as he returned his glare to Robert. "I see you've brought the harlot back after I warned you…" he slurred.

"You're drunk," Robert hollered at him. "Get out of this house before I throw you out."

"No, Robert," he argued, "we're not finished with our discussion."

"We are quite finished, Edwin, now get out."

Edwin struggled to focus his gaze on Robert. "But we're not. Not until that strumpet is out of this house!" He lunged toward me. Robert placed himself between us and Edwin fell against him.

Robert shoved him back. "Get out, you drunken dolt. You are not welcome here until you understand how to behave. In particular, how to show the proper respect to my wife."

Edwin teetered on his feet but managed to remain upright. He scoffed at Robert's last statement. A grimace settled on his face. "I shall have what is rightfully mine,

Robert. Not you, nor her," he shouted, pointing his finger at both of us, "will stop me."

Robert lunged toward him, but Edwin leaned away, escaping his grasp. He held his hands up in defeat. "Fine. I shall leave." He spun on his heel, coming close to losing his balance and sprawling across the floor. Righting himself, he stalked from the castle.

Robert faced me, searching my face in an attempt to discover my reaction. "I am sorry, Lenora. My brother is…"

"Angry and upset," I finished for him. "And drunk. He is lashing out, nothing more."

"He does not deserve your generosity. You are gracious to a fault. Still, I shall make every attempt to ensure you do not endure any more of his poisonous hostility."

"You defend my honor quite well," I assured him.

"I am certain you would like to rest after our journey," Robert responded. "If you prefer to take dinner in your suite, I do not object."

"If you prefer it, I shall. Though I am capable of attending dinner despite the travel."

Robert smiled at me. "Then I shall see you for dinner, my dear," he replied with a kiss to my forehead.

Before ascending the stairs, I glanced to the balcony above. Annie no longer stood overhead. The outburst between Robert and his brother, Edwin, must have frightened her off. Perhaps I'd find her waiting for me upstairs. I navigated to my bedroom, finding it empty, even of ghosts.

I left the room behind after discarding my purse in favor of climbing to my tower room. As I entered, warmth washed over me. A fire blazed in the room's fireplace. Buchanan, anticipating my affinity to be in the room after my journey, must have ordered the fire be lit upon my return. The thoughtfulness brought a smile to my face.

I retrieved my book and fur blanket, curling on my

window seat. The book lay in my lap as my gaze fell to the landscape outside. I had missed the moors even with their colorless winter landscape. My mind processed the encounter with Edwin earlier. It was the second of such encounters. Neither was pleasant.

My mind flitted to the first clash with Robert's brother. Days after our wedding, Edwin appeared at the castle, riding furiously to our door on his jet-black steed. His dark, curly hair, a match to Robert's minus the graying bits, was unruly on his head after the hard ride. I witnessed his frenzied ride from this very room.

He dismounted and raced to the main doors, throwing them open. Curious, I descended from my hideaway, overhearing the argument occurring in the drawing room.

"... demand to know if this is true!" a voice unknown to me shouted.

"I owe you no explanations, brother," Robert's voice responded.

Brother, I pondered, as the argument continued. "You owe me a hell of a lot more than that, Robert," the voice countered, heat entering it.

"I owe you nothing! And with your crass behavior, you shall have no more from this estate."

"You are cheating me out of my inheritance."

"I am doing nothing of the sort. How dare you accuse me of this? You received what was due you from this estate. You are owed nothing more."

"Do not expect you can swindle from me from what is rightfully mine. I shall challenge any will that contains her name!"

"Lenora is my wife. No court will agree with you."

"Wife or not, she is a woman. So, I stand to inherit the bulk of this estate upon your death..."

"That is where you are wrong, Edwin," Robert retaliated. "My chosen heir will inherit the bulk of my estate, not you."

"Your heir? Oh!" Edwin exclaimed, letting out a callous laugh. "The reason for the rushed marriage is revealed! Are you sure the little slut is carrying YOUR child, Robert?"

A loud crash emanated from the room. I jumped at the sound as I stood at the bottom of the staircase. Another harsh laugh. "My, we are sensitive about this. I suspect you do question if she has made you or some other man a father."

"I question nothing about my wife," Robert roared. "And I will not stand here and allow you to impugn her virtue. Get out of this house, Edwin, before I throw you from it."

"Oh, Robert," Edwin replied, "I will go further than impugning. I will destroy her if I must. I will NOT be robbed by that little whore."

A scuffle sounded behind the doors. I recoiled as the doors flung open. A dark-haired man slid sprawling on the floor in front of me. He appeared at least a decade younger than Robert. His lip was bloodied, his eye purple-red and already swelling. He rubbed his jaw as he pulled himself to sitting.

"Lenora!" Robert exclaimed at the sight of me as he entered the foyer.

Edwin glanced up to me. "I… I heard a commotion," I stuttered.

Edwin climbed to his feet, his eyes surveying me from head to toe. "Ah, here is the little tart now. I suppose…"

His statement hung unfinished as Robert flung his cane aside and grasped him by the collar. "I have warned you once about your foul mouth and using it in regard to my wife. Do not EVER speak about her in this manner again. Now get out!" Robert dragged him to the door, tossing him through it into the autumn air.

Robert shoved the doors shut, bolting them as Edwin

threatened to return. He crossed the foyer, straightening his jacket. My eyes remained downcast, studying the marble floor below my feet. Our rushed nuptials were already causing ripples.

"May I ask how much you overheard?" Robert inquired.

"Most of the conversation," I admitted.

"I apologize for my brother's behavior," Robert voiced. "This is not the way I hoped you two would meet."

"There is no need to apologize," I assured him, raising my eyes to his face.

"Yet there is," Robert argued. "I have placed you in a position to become his enemy. The circumstances of our marriage opened the door for him to utter those vile insults. And those circumstances are of my creation."

"And of mine. I agreed to this marriage."

"Without a solid understanding of the family politics. I have used you, Lenora. The consequences of this you have just witnessed firsthand. My desperation to learn the circumstances of Annie's… well, my desperation has led me to make selfish choices."

"Your brother's behavior is not your fault." Robert offered a brief smile, averting his eyes from mine. "And your defense of my honor was… commendable." I offered a smile. "I hope you did not hurt your hand."

Robert eyed me sideways. "No need to worry, my dear. It is quite fine. I'm afraid my magnificent ability in a brawl is another fact I have kept hidden from you." He paused. "I do apologize, Lenora. This marriage must be far from what you hoped for as a young woman."

"There is no need for an apology. Your choices were not selfish. You have provided more than what is fair in this arrangement."

"Arrangement…" Robert answered, leaving the word

hang in the air for a moment before continuing. "Not quite the stuff of a young woman's dreams."

I chuckled, drawing a questioning glance from Robert, his brow furrowing at my reaction. "Given my circumstances," I explained, "I'm afraid I hadn't many dreams. Therefore, I can say without hesitation this marriage has provided me with more than I could ever have dreamt of!"

Robert's eyes met mine, and he studied them for a moment. "You are too kind, Lenora." He paused for a breath. "I regret disturbing you with Edwin's nonsense, though. It is nothing more than that, Lenora. Drunken nonsense."

"No bother. I was on my way to the library."

"Oh? I shall walk you," Robert suggested, offering his arm.

"Thank you," I said, accepting it.

"And what has you heading to the library? Considering making some changes? Removing it to add another parlor?"

"Absolutely not!" I exclaimed. "What a ghastly idea!"

"Ghastly? I should imagine the dusty library itself ghastlier than the idea of its removal."

"I happen to cherish your dusty library. What a treasure to have so many books, so many escapes at one's fingertips."

"A treasure? Am I to understand you are an avid appreciator of books?"

"I am," I admitted. "Books kept me company on a number of lonely nights at the orphanage. Though, the library there was woefully lacking compared to yours."

Robert smiled at me. "Compared to OURS," he corrected. "Though I must admit I am unaware of its contents. I have spent little time there. Is our selection sufficient?"

We reached the library doors. "More than sufficient," I assured him.

He smiled at me as we parted ways. "I am pleased you find it so. I shall leave you to your books, my dear."

I glanced down at the book on my lap, one that I found within our library after my arrival with a smile. The library far surpassed the one in my previous residence and had brought me many hours of enjoyment.

I opened the book to the marked page to continue my reading. As I settled into the first words of the chapter, a chill suddenly overtook me. I clutched the blanket closer to me, drawing it further up my lap. Perhaps the chilly air outside made my window seat too cold a place to read, I mulled. I glanced to the fireplace. Large flames still danced inside it, and I considered drawing closer to it for warmth.

Before I could make my decision, my fur blanket began to slide slowly off my lap, taking my book with it. I grabbed at it, pulling it back toward me. I snuggled into it, tucking it around me, and retrieved my book.

I had not read two words when the blanket began to creep toward the floor again, as though something weighed it down. I pulled it back, ensuring no parts of it remained on the floor. With a deep inhale, I returned to the pages of my book.

Within seconds, the blanket inched away from me for a third time. I grasped at it, now realizing the source was otherworldly. A powerful force tugged against my grip. "Show yourself," I ordered. Nothing appeared. Instead, the yanking grew stronger. I wrestled with it, clinging to the blanket as my book clattered to the floor. "Stop this nonsense at once! If you are not willing to show yourself, stop! You are acting like a child!"

The force on the blanket ceased and the lack of tugging in the opposite direction caused me to fly backward, striking my shoulders and head against the wall behind me. With a groan, I rubbed my head where it hit. The damage seemed minimal, though. I tucked the blanket around me again with a sigh and leaned over to retrieve my book from the floor.

Opening it to the marked page a second time, I attempted again to read the first sentence of the paragraph. Halfway through, an unseen force ripped the blanket from my lap, sending it flying through the air and discarding it on the opposite side of the room.

"Annie?" I questioned. "Is that you? Your trickery is not amusing!" I warned as I rose from the window seat and crossed the room. A red deer skin rug adorned the space in the middle of the room. As I trampled upon it to cross the space, the rug moved, pulled from underneath my feet. I landed hard on my backside as objects lifted from the various surfaces of the room and floated.

As I attempted to pull myself upright, a voice joined the fray. "Lenora! What's happening?" Robert shouted, alarm sounding in his voice. The floating objects, a variety of books, a large, red vase and a few knickknacks halted their airy dance instantly, crashing to the floor. By sheer luck, the vase landed on the chaise, preventing it from shattering against the hard stone floor. The porcelain trinket box I'd borrowed from another room in the castle did not fare as well.

"Oh, no!" I cried, reaching for a splintered piece of the small box.

"Careful," Robert warned, rushing to my side and removing the piece from my fingers. "Lenora, what happened? Were my eyes deceiving me?"

"No," I responded with a shake of my head. "Just a bit of mischief."

"Mischief? Lenora! Objects were floating about in the air. And how did you come to be on the floor?"

"My blanket," I explained, "was pulled across the room." I pointed toward it. "When I tried to retrieve it, the rug was pulled out from under me. Quite literally. I lost my balance and toppled over before the objects began their dance through the air."

"Are you quite all right? Are you experiencing pain anywhere?"

"I am fine. Though I am brokenhearted over this little box," I lamented as I stared at its broken pieces.

"I shall buy you another," Robert assured me. "Can you stand?"

"Yes," I nodded, accepting his hand to pull me to my feet.

I replaced the vase on the bookshelf and collapsed onto the chaise. "Was this…" Robert's voice trailed off as it often did before mentioning Annie's name.

I nodded again. "I expect so. A bit of mischief on her part."

"Mischief? She has come close to harming you. I cannot understand this behavior!"

"Something has perturbed her. Perhaps our absence."

Robert knit his brow. "Our absence?" He shook his head. "This is no way to welcome us home! She was not violent in life. I…"

"I am sure she was not," I reassured him. "But something irritated her. When the dead are agitated, they often lash out in this way."

"And you expect that our trip caused this?"

"I assume so. When we arrived home, Annie was waiting on the balcony."

Robert's eyebrows raised and his jaw opened as realization dawned on him. "Your gaze…"

I nodded. "Yes. But…" my voice trailed off as my forehead wrinkled in thought.

"What is it?"

"I am not certain," I replied, still lost in my reflection. "She did not appear upset. I had hoped we would finally have the chance to communicate. I imagined our absence may have been a constructive action."

"Yet, it appears not to have been," Robert replied, studying the mess on our floor.

"No, it does not appear so, does it?" I agreed. "A pity. But I shall keep trying."

Robert smiled at me. "I realize you will, though please be careful, Lenora. Her… hijinks… grow bolder. I loved Annie, but I do not want to see you harmed by her in her misguided distress."

"I shall be," I promised. Robert nodded to me. "Oh, were you searching for me? In all the commotion, I'd forgotten you arrived here. I assume you needed something?"

"I wanted to determine if the room had been prepared adequately for you. I worried Buchanan may not have built a fire and it may be too cold."

"Buchanan did not forget," I acknowledged, motioning toward the roaring fire. "Well, with that settled, I shall set to work tidying the room."

"No, I shall have Buchanan handle it. Perhaps you should rest, given the travel and… the latest events."

I gathered my book from the floor. "I shall read in my room."

"I hope you are undisturbed."

CHAPTER 9

Days passed before I encountered Annie again. Mr. Langford arrived with a ladies' maid in tow, having sorted the matter out in the course of two days. Ella Sinclair arrived at Blackmoore Castle with little more than I did. The girl, older than I, which seemed strange to me, had come from a reputable estate with good references in hand. Her previous employer had passed on. She did not mind the change of scenery and gushed about the beauty of the highlands and the estate despite the dreariness of the winter landscape.

I had never seen the grounds in the spring and summer, so I could not offer much regarding any changes, but her appreciation of the landscape matched mine, allowing us to converse easily.

Her arrival prompted a visit from Annie. On her first night while she assisted me in dressing for dinner, the door to my room creaked open. "Oh!" Ella exclaimed as she fussed with my hair. "My apologies, Your Grace, I must not have latched it properly."

Ella set the comb down on the dressing table. "Leave it," I instructed. "It is no bother."

"Of course, Your Grace," Ella responded, resuming her hair styling. In the mirror's reflection, I could detect the reason for the door's sudden and unexpected movement. I recognized the familiar dirty red dress and dark hair hanging around an obscured face.

Annie had visited to assess the new arrival. A new addition to the home could, of course, prove disturbing to her. I hoped she took Ella's arrival in stride and did not pester the poor girl.

I fixed my gaze on her as Ella put the finishing touches on my hair. My eyes offering a silent warning to behave. Ella noticed the direction of my eyeline and offered another apology. "Next time, Your Grace, I shall be sure to latch it."

I offered her a smile through the mirror. "It is not your fault, Sinclair. No amount of latching could have prevented it."

She stared at me, an odd expression on her face. Best she was prepared should my silent warning not be enough for Annie, I reflected. Her lips moved, but no sound came out as she struggled to form a response. She settled on, "I'm not sure I take your meaning, Your Grace."

I rose from my seat and faced her. "Have you heard any rumors regarding me? You have mentioned none, but I cannot discern if that is due to politeness bred into you or lack of knowledge."

"Rumors, Your Grace?"

"Yes. You make speak freely, Sinclair. If you have heard tales of my unique ability, please acknowledge this."

"I have heard no tales, Your Grace. Though, Lady Merton, my previous employer, was nearly a recluse for the latter part of her life prior to her passing."

"I see, then you should sit down before I explain."

"There is no need for that, Your Grace," Ella assured me.

In discussing my ability, I have often found bluntness to be the best approach. Dancing around the subject often led to confusion or misunderstanding. Therefore, I launched directly into my explanation. "The dead often walk among us. Most people do not witness them, but I do. And I can communicate with them," I responded, cutting to the chase. The admission took a harder toll than Ella was prepared for. She collapsed onto the chaise with my assistance. Her face turned deathly pale, her eyes wide and her jaw slack. I allowed her time to recover.

"Forgive me, Your Grace," she said after a few breaths, still clutching my arm, "I… I…"

"I understand," I assured her.

She swallowed hard and glanced at the open door. "The door…" she stuttered, staring at me, her eyes questioning.

I nodded in response. "Yes," I responded.

"A ghost?" she whispered, the words sticking in her throat.

"Yes," I confirmed, easing onto the chaise next to her and squeezing her shoulder.

She shook her head, her face paler than it had been already. Her eyes were wide and filled with fear. "There is nothing to fear, Ella," I assured her, choosing to use her first name to soften the conversation. "She was only here to observe. I warned you only in the event that you experience some anomalies. Being a new addition to the castle, she is curious."

"She?" Ella questioned, her eyes still wide with shock.

"The previous Duchess of Blackmoore," I explained. "Duke Blackmoore's first wife."

Ella nodded slowly. "Is she… dangerous?"

"No," I reassured her. "Beyond creating some mischief, she is not. And she would likely not target you with such behavior."

"And you can… see them? See her?"

"Yes, I can see them and communicate with them."

Ella sat silent for another moment. "Thank you for trusting me with this information, Your Grace," she said.

"While secrecy is not my objective, I do ask that you do not spread the information about," I requested.

"You may rely on my discretion, of course. And I apologize for my outburst."

I waved my hand, dismissing her apology. "There is no need for an apology. The information is difficult to comprehend and accept. Your reaction is better than most. And I trust and appreciate your discretion."

She squeezed my hand before standing. "How brave you must be, Your Grace. I am not sure I would possess the strength you display if I witnessed such things."

"I am no braver than any other, merely accustomed to the situation."

Ella offered me a tight-lipped smile and a nod. "Is there anything else before dinner, Your Grace?"

"No, thank you, Sinclair," I answered, returning to the formal method of address with her.

She curtsied before departing, pulling the door shut behind her. I pulled on my gloves, waiting to determine if Annie would return. She had disappeared during my conversation with Ella. I wondered if she would return or if her attention was focused on prowling after Ella. The novelty of her arrival would intrigue her.

The curiosity displayed on Annie's part during this encounter reminded me of my first encounter with her. Details flooded into my mind of my first experience with Annie.

One month after my arrival, on the eve of my birthday, I sat reading in my tower room late one evening. Nestled in the window seat, my book in my lap, I curled under a blanket. The quietness of the castle still amazed me. I found the stillness comforting. Engrossed in my book, I failed to notice the movement at the door.

I glanced outside into the night sky. The moonlight bathed the late autumn landscape in a luminous light. The stars in the sky were plentiful. From my perch in the sky, as I referred to it, it seemed as if I sat among them.

As I gazed out of the window, studying the twinkling lights, a reflection of red caught my eye. My brow furrowed, and I turned my gaze to the doorway. There stood the specter of Robert's first wife. She wore a red dress with black trim, the outfit she had died in. It was smudged with dirt and tattered.

Her black hair hung in tangles around her pale gray face. Her eyes sunk deep into her face; her lips almost blackened. She snarled at me, a hideous hissing sound escaping her lips. Anyone else witnessing this phantom would undoubtedly have shrunk away or perhaps shrieked at the sight, frightened by the menacing façade. I, on the other hand, failed to be alarmed. I had experienced sightings of the dead my entire life. Not all of them proved pleasant. Depending on the manner in which they had passed, the dead often did not appear or act as they had in life.

Annie proved to be no exception. The circumstances surrounding her death were tragic, shocking. Her mind, twisted enough to have thrown herself from a turret, still fought to recover from the circumstances.

Despite it having been years, I was likely the first person to witness her in her current form. She still carried with her all the emotional afflictions that drove her to her suicide. They displayed themselves in her physical manifestation, twisting her appearance into a gruesome presentation.

I stared at her, unafraid and unflinching. "Hello," I offered in a simple tone, trying not to sound aggressive or overzealous.

Her dark eyes widened and the sound emanating from her ceased. Silence filled the space between us. My gaze remained fixed on her. Abruptly, she turned, fleeing from the doorway.

I stared after her for a breath before my gaze fell to the floor. The reaction did not surprise me. Often the dead are shocked when their presence is acknowledged by the living. For the most part, they remain unnoticed, skulking about alone, unseen, unheard.

The shock Annie experienced would wane. At least now she realized that someone could communicate directly with her. I resolved to report my sighting to Robert over breakfast, though I would omit the details of Annie's appearance and leave those to his imagination. Robert's emotions only allowed him to view Annie as she had lived, not as she had died. I hoped to spare him any further pain by only reporting the progress.

* * *

I finished pulling on my gloves, disappointed by my lack of progress in the months I had been here. But the dead did not work on the timetables of the living. Annie needed time to adjust. Her death did not provide the escape she so desperately sought, and, in recent months, a number of changes rocked her current realm. I would continue to allow her to come to me, hoping to earn her trust enough for her to communicate on an increased basis.

Robert and I dined alone that evening. I took the opportunity to fill him in on the details of Annie's appearance earlier.

"I've had another sighting," I announced as we ate our main course.

"Oh? You appear unharmed. I hope this means progress was made, for your sake."

"No progress, really," I admitted. "She arrived to inspect Sinclair. I did tell the girl about my ability. I worried Annie may attempt a bit of mischief with her and did not wish her to be riled."

"Do you consider that wise? How did the girl take it?"

"Quite well," I commended her. "She was shocked but did not fall to pieces. Given the closeness with which we worked, I consider it best she understand my uniqueness. Also, I was not certain if she perhaps already knew about my ability."

"How would she learn of it?" Robert inquired.

"I know of no specific avenue by which she would learn of it, merely a guess."

"Did she know of it already?"

"No," I responded. "She was blissfully unaware. A luxury she is no longer afforded." A moment of silence spanned between us before I issued a query of my own. "How did you learn of my ability?"

Robert studied me for a moment before responding. "Lord Robertson informed me. He took on a girl from St. Mary's. Discretion was not the girl's strong suit. She confessed your secret to several other staff members, including Lady Robertson's ladies' maid. The tale spread from Lady Robertson to Lord Robertson and then to me."

I considered his response. "It seems a rather odd tale to spread within your circle," I mused aloud, not really expecting an answer. The information about an orphan's odd ability seemed of little interest to high society, no matter how unique it may be.

"Quite. He divulged the information to me when I was at rather a low point. We had held a séance to attempt to reach

Annie, which was disastrous. Lord Robertson offered the tale as a proposed alternate solution. I believe he meant to offer me hope. I am certain he did not expect me to pursue the avenue as zealously as I did."

"I see," I responded, parsing his answer in my mind.

Robert continued. "When I learned of you, I searched for information, questioned the girl who was your classmate and tracked you down at St. Mary's. You know the rest."

I offered a smile. "You spirited me here and offered me a new life, yes."

"I offered you anything I could because you offered me so much more. You offered me hope, Lenora. An avenue to reach out to my former wife, to determine why she..." He glanced to me, trying to force a smile on his face but it faltered, and he lowered his eyes to his plate.

"Let us not speak of it," I replied. "We shall concentrate on the hope you experienced instead."

Robert met my gaze, offering me a fuller smile. "Yes. Yes, we shall concentrate on the hope."

I nibbled at my carrots, a question nagging in my mind. I preferred not to ask it, realizing the pain Robert already endured by speaking of Annie's demise. Instead, I offered a pleasant expression as I glanced up from my plate.

Robert continued to stare at me for a moment. His eyes narrowed and he pursed his lips before speaking. "What is it, Lenora?"

I swallowed, avoiding eye contact. "What do you mean?" I responded.

"Something is on your mind," Robert presumed. "What is it?"

"It is nothing," I dodged, still avoiding his gaze.

"Lenora," Robert prodded. "I already know you well enough to realize something pervades your thoughts."

"My mind is clear," I assured him.

"You would fib even to your husband?" he teased.

The coquettish witticism roused a chuckle from me. "All right," I surrendered. "I confess a question is darting around my mind."

"What is it?"

"You mentioned an ill-fated séance. I was curious about it. Though if it is too painful a memory, we need not discuss it."

"Oh, yes," Robert responded. "It is not too unpleasant. We'd had… disturbances in the household since Annie's passing. A distant relative wrote to me and suggested it may be Annie reaching out and we may attempt contacting Annie through a séance. I had no experience in the matter, but the avenue provided a distraction in the form of research." I set my fork down, giving Robert my full attention, listening to the recounting. "I found a medium, and she recommended I gather several individuals to participate. I followed her instructions, inviting Lord and Lady Robertson, Edwin, one of Edwin's friends and his spouse.

"With the details set, everyone arrived on a stormy spring evening. I realize how stereotypical this must sound, like a gothic novel, but..." Robert's voice trailed off as though unsure he wanted to continue.

"Not at all," I responded, encouraging him to go on. "Please continue."

"Everyone gathered in the drawing room. Buchanan set up a large round table as instructed and the medium, Madam Goldstone was her name, explained that we should douse all but one candle, be seated, join hands and close our eyes. In retrospect, it was all very dramatic, I should have known better.

"After a few moments, the woman began moaning and told us Annie was near. She included various details about her as she described her entering the room and standing near the table. I inquired about her death, but no answers were forthcoming. I begged Annie to impart even the smallest amount of information through Madam Goldstone. Yet all the woman imparted were simple things such as how she loved me or missed me."

"She gave no other details?" I questioned.

"She gave one additional detail," Robert informed me. "As I pressed for more information, she conveyed a detail about Annie's death that struck me. Annie wore a red dress when she took her life. Madam Goldstone claimed she wore it because red was her favorite color. Immediately, I became suspicious as red was not Annie's favorite color. I assumed the information untrue and broke the circle by releasing Madam Goldstone's hand.

"She told me we lost the connection due to my inability to follow instructions. I informed her of her gaffe regarding Annie's favorite color. She claimed to only be repeating what Annie told her, but the information did not match. After an argument, the woman suggested we try again. Foolish of me, but I agreed. I was so desperate."

"Of course," I murmured, encouraging him to continue.

"What happened next..." Robert's voice trailed off again as he shook his head. "She claimed Annie returned. She babbled on about her suicide being the result of a terrible row we'd had recently. She continued that Annie had never recovered from the argument and the things said during it and threw herself from the turret in a fit of despondence over our failed marriage. It was at this moment that I broke the circle again and demanded the woman leave the house."

I raised my eyebrows at the statement and Robert continued speaking. "Annie and I had no such quarrel. Certainly none that would have caused such a reaction. The woman was a charlatan and had outed herself as such by trying to provide details that did not fit."

"Why would she take such a risk?" I pondered aloud.

"I came to learn later that the woman corresponded with anyone who may have details of the person in question prior to her séance. She used the details to establish herself as being legitimate."

"Yet she had certain details incorrect. How did she come to have incorrect information?"

"The details surrounding Annie's death were an embellishment created by Madam Goldstone. In an effort to appease me, since I had pushed for information, she created what she believed to be a likely scenario regarding a married couple. She assumed within the months leading to her death, there would be some trouble between us that I'd latch on to as the cause."

"Ah," I answered as realization dawned on me. "And there was no such argument."

"No, none."

"So, her less-than-clever lie allowed you to detect her ruse!"

Robert raised his eyebrows at me. "Yes."

"I can imagine how upsetting that must have been," I offered. "You hoped for answers and someone took advantage of that."

"It was devastating," Robert admitted. "The avenue I pursued offered me nothing. I considered it my last chance at finding information. After chasing the woman from the house and seeing most everyone off, I collapsed in a chair at the table. Lord Robertson was kind enough to stay with me. My mind was not well at that moment.

"I lamented that I would never learn the truth, and Lord Robertson offered me another way: you. He imparted the tale he'd heard from one of his staff. I made it my mission to find you."

My brow furrowed and Robert, noting my expression, inquired, "What is it, Lenora?"

"How did you know you could trust me?"

He smiled. "Because you were not using your gift for fame or fortune. I did research, inquired of anyone who knew you. It was clear you were no charlatan."

I returned his smile. "I hope I can provide more answers for you, true answers. I realize how her death troubles you."

"You have already provided me with more than I could have hoped for when I sought you out," Robert said with a smile as he resumed eating.

I returned to my meal as well, my mind turning to Annie and her less-than-cooperative behavior thus far. I silently wished for a better means of communication with her for Robert's sake. The man had suffered so much over her death already. I hoped to provide him some peace soon.

CHAPTER 10

Following dinner, I returned to my room, my mind heavy with thoughts. Ella awaited me, prepared to ready me for bed. I took stock of the girl as I entered the room, attempting to determine whether or not the news of my ability weighed on her mind. As she unfastened my dress, I noted her gaze falling constantly on the closed door.

"Nervous?" I inquired.

She grinned, a nervous chuckle escaping her lips. "A little," she admitted.

"There is no need to be," I reassured her. "Disturbances for most castle inhabitants are minor, if there are any at all."

"I still find it unsettling, Your Grace."

"Unsettling enough that you'd prefer to seek another position?" I queried.

"No!" Ella exclaimed. "I must admit to quite enjoying the change of scenery. And if I may be so bold to say, it appears we'll get on quite well, you and I." Ella stopped dead from her work, and I turned toward her. She looked me straight in the eye. "Please don't dismiss me, Your Grace."

"I have no intention of dismissing you, Sinclair. Though if it had been your wish to depart given the news, I would have provided you with a good reference, excusing your departure away as health-related given the dampness so as not to ruin your chances of placement. So, if you are not keen on staying given the situation, please do not let that discourage you. Though I hope you will stay. I agree, we will get on well."

Ella offered a smile and returned to unlacing my dress. "I prefer to stay, ghosts or not. And I promise to be brave. If you, Your Grace, can witness these things and remain as poised as you are, then I shall force myself to act as you do."

"I have the benefit of a lifetime of experience," I countered. "But in time, one becomes accustomed to these things. Though as I mentioned, beyond a minor disturbance, I do not imagine you will experience much. Most of the living are blissfully unaware of the dead's presence among them."

"It is odd to me," Ella answered as she helped me out of my dress and into my nightgown. "To have spent all my life never realizing they were among us. Rather gives me the chills though I am certain it will pass."

"It is the shock," I assured her. "Once the novelty wears from your mind, you will not give it much thought."

We finished the undressing tasks and Ella prepared my bed as I slathered lotion onto my hands and forearms. "Is there anything else, Your Grace?" Ella inquired before departing.

"No," I responded, turning to face her. "I hope you sleep well. If you are unable to sleep, please wake me."

"Thank you, Your Grace, though I hope it is unnecessary. Good night."

Ella opened the door to depart, finding Robert standing behind it. Startled, she jumped, then quickly corrected her reaction, adding a curtsy. "Your Grace," Ella murmured to him.

"Sinclair," he greeted her.

"Good evening, Your Grace," she responded as she stepped toward the doorway.

I rose from my dressing table as Ella closed the door behind us. "She seems to be handling your earlier admission well enough," Robert commented after the door closed fully.

"Yes," I answered. "I discussed with her the possibility she may prefer to depart from our employ, but she refused."

"Good news," Robert replied, his hands clasped behind his back. "I had hoped it would not become an issue. It is why I sought you out. To ensure you were satisfied with her services."

"I am quite," I assured Robert. "She is most efficient and personable. Mr. Langford should be commended on his selection."

"I shall pass the sentiment along," Robert said. "And I shall wish you good night. Sleep well, Lenora."

"Good night, Robert," I answered. Robert saw himself out, latching the door behind him.

I crossed the room and climbed into bed. As I nestled under the warm covers, the door to my room creaked open. A sigh escaped my lips, and I rose, shoving my feet into the slippers I'd just abandoned on the floor. I shuffled to the open door, ready to push it closed when a streak of red caught my eye.

Moving into the hallway, I caught sight of Annie hovering at the end. I locked eyes with her, expecting her to disappear in an instant. Instead, she held my gaze, before motioning for me to follow her.

Finally, I mused with some relief, Annie desired to do more than toy with me. The simple gesture spoke volumes, indicating a shift from suspicious specter to sincere soul. I nodded, acknowledging her signal, and stepped toward her.

Annie waited until I neared the end of the hall before

scurrying down the next corridor. Together, Annie and I wound through the halls. We approached the stairs leading to the fated turret, where her life had taken such a tragic turn.

I hesitated at the bottom of the winding stairway. My last experience with this room had turned unpleasant. I wavered about whether or not to follow Annie, who hovered above me on the stairs. Noting my hesitance, she beckoned me to follow her. "Can I trust you this time, Annie?" I questioned without receiving a response.

Instead, she repeated her gesture, coaxing me to follow. I shoved aside my reluctance, placing my foot on the first stair. I began the climb up. Satisfied that I was following, Annie resumed her ascent.

As I rounded the corner, Annie awaited me in the doorway. Something in her eyes resonated in the depths of my soul. A despondent, desolate hollowness was etched into those eyes, which I could tell now were brown. She receded further into the room as I arrived at the top of the stairs.

Annie stood by the room's single window, her back to me. "Annie?" I questioned softly as I took a few steps into the room.

Annie turned toward me. The forsaken expression replaced by something darker. Her expression alarmed me, and I retreated to the door. Before I could reach it, it slammed in front of me and I heard the distinct sound of a clicking lock. I tugged at the door, twisting the knob without any success. I pounded against the door, demanding it be opened.

I spun to face Annie again. "Open the door!" I shouted. Annie cocked her head, contorting her face into a twisted smirk. "Annie," I said, forcing my voice to remain calm, "I realize you are attempting to communicate with me. There is a better way to do this."

Annie narrowed her eyes. I continued. "I understand how confusing this must be for you. Most of the living do not notice you. They go about their lives, never recognizing your presence. But I am different, Annie. I have spent my entire life communicating with the dead. Please, Annie. Let us become allies."

Annie stared at me, her glassy eyes filling with a mix of emotions. For a moment, I expected her to weep and guessed progress may finally come. Then another noise broke the silence between us. "Lenora?" Robert called, jiggling the door. "Lenora, are you in there? Why is the door locked?"

The introduction of the new voice, Robert's voice, caused an abrupt change in Annie's demeanor. She lunged at me, grasping me by the shoulders with a shriek. I screamed as icy hands clutched at me. A powerful force pushed me from behind. I struggled against Annie and the unseen force pushing at me. "Help!" I shouted. "Annie, stop!" My hands clutched at hers, trying to pull them from my shoulders.

I barreled toward the window. The pane flung open and cold air rushed in from outside. I dug my feet into the floor in a desperate attempt to stop my progress. My efforts proved futile. I screamed as the window rushed toward me. The sound of Robert's voice calling to me met my ears. He sounded so far away.

My heart pounded and blood rushed into my ears as I slammed into the stone sill. I clutched at the stone casing surrounding the window as my body pitched forward. Annie had disappeared as I crashed against the window, leaving nothing standing between me and meeting a fate similar to hers.

My fingers scrambled to find purchase among the stones to prevent myself from being pitched out the window. The unseen hands that pushed at my back were unrelenting though. My strength was feeble compared to the force pressing against me.

Tears streamed down my cheeks as I hung further out the window, still desperately trying to clutch at the walls. The ground loomed below me in a dizzying display. The pressure against me soon proved too much, and I pitched headfirst out the window. As I tumbled, I managed to grasp the interior sill. I clutched at it, my legs flailing underneath me. As I dangled stories above the ground, I glanced up at the window. Annie loomed over me.

I called out to her for help. She glanced behind her as a loud splintering crack resounded through the air. Annie disappeared from my sight a moment later. At first, I assumed the sill had fractured and would fall away from the castle, sending me to my doom. But seconds later, strong arms grasped my forearms, pulling me upward.

Tears clouded my eyes, but as I was hauled through the window, I recognized Robert. He continued to pull, grasping hold of my waist as he hauled me into the room. I clung to him, a sob escaping me as I collapsed against him.

"Lenora, my God, are you all right?"

I nodded my head, unable to speak for a moment. "Yes," I managed to gasp out after a time. I inhaled a shaky breath, wiping at my face to clear the tears.

Robert hugged me to his chest, and I took solace in his embrace, allowing myself a moment to let my alarm diminish. Buchanan appeared in the doorway. "Your Grace, what has happened? Is Her Grace all right? I heard shouting."

I pushed away, trying to nod my response as I continued to catch my breath. Robert answered before I could. "No," he responded, still holding me close. "No, she is not all right. She has experienced quite a fright and was very nearly harmed beyond repair. I am taking her straight to bed. Have a hot toddy prepared to help calm her nerves."

"At once, Your Grace!" Buchanan turned on his heel and disappeared down the stairway.

I did not object to being spirited to bed or the beverage, feeling I needed both to calm my nerves. Robert gazed at me, pushing hair away from my face. "Are you ready?"

"Yes," I said with a nod, "I am able to walk."

"You will do no such thing," Robert scolded gently. "You are still shaking. I shall carry you." Reaching down, Robert swept me off my feet, cradling me in his arms to carry me to my quarters.

The gesture was not unappreciated. My legs remained wobbly from the experience and I longed to be in my bed. I decided not to protest, instead putting my arms around Robert's neck and allowing him to carry me down. "Please be careful of your leg," I warned.

"Oh, Lenora," Robert chided. "My leg is no issue, particularly compared with the circumstances you just endured."

Within moments, Robert spirited me through the halls and to my bed. He placed me gently down and pulled the covers over me. My arms ached from my struggle to hang onto the windowsill. I settled back into the pillows behind me to relax them. Buchanan arrived with my hot toddy and I sipped at it gratefully.

He dragged a chair to my bedside for Robert. "Is there anything else, Your Grace?" Buchanan inquired of Robert. "Should I fetch the doctor?"

"No, that isn't necessary," I voiced.

Robert held up his hand to stop me. "I shall decide what is necessary. We shall call for the doctor in the morning unless Her Grace takes a turn during the night. There is nothing else at this time."

"Would you like me to fetch Miss Sinclair to stay with Her Grace through the night?"

"No, that is not necessary, I shall stay with her," Robert

responded.

"Very good, Your Grace," Buchanan responded with a nod. "I shall leave you and check back first thing in the morning. If you require anything at all overnight, wake me at once, Your Grace."

"Thank you, Buchanan," we both said in unison.

I sipped at my warm beverage as he exited the room. I glanced to Robert, who fixed his gaze on me. "How are you?" he inquired.

I sighed before answering. "Given the circumstances, I am all right."

"This is becoming dangerous. You could have been killed tonight. As much as it pains me to say this, I must insist that you give up on your project."

"No!" I objected.

"Lenora," Robert lectured, "when I made the request of you, I did not realize the danger your life would be placed in. Had I not been there, you would have fallen to your death!"

My brow furrowed, and a shiver passed over me as I recalled the harrowing experience. Time would ease the shock I felt, but Robert remained correct. I easily could have lost my grip and tumbled to my death below, as his first wife had only three years prior.

While the thought disturbed me, I remained resolute in upholding my end of the bargain, if for no other reason than to satisfy my own curiosity. Robert, however, remained unsatisfied with the arrangement and continued. "I will not take the chance with your life. This ends tonight, Lenora."

"I will be more careful in the future," I promised. "But to give up seems unnecessary."

"If your reluctance stems from our arrangement, put it out of your mind. You owe me nothing."

"Neither do you," I countered. "However, my reluctance does not arise entirely from failing to uphold our arrangement. There is something odd here, and I am determined to get to the bottom of it."

"At what cost, Lenora?" Robert chided.

"I agreed to be more careful, so, with any luck, no cost. Still, as dangerous as the incident tonight was, something about it seems off." Again, my brow creased as I parsed through everything in my mind.

"What do you mean?" Robert questioned.

I shook my head before attempting to explain. "Annie wasn't the one pushing me toward the window. In fact, she remained in front of me until I reached it. After I pitched over the windowsill, I glanced up and Annie stood over me."

Robert's eyes glistened with tears that he blinked away before speaking. "I am so terribly sorry, Lenora," he whispered. I took his hand in mine, giving it a squeeze.

"I am not. I do not believe Annie intended to harm me."

"Did she help you when you were dangling from the tower window? Could she have?"

"Yes, she could have, but when you burst through the door, she disappeared. In essence, she didn't have the chance."

Robert remained silent for a moment. "I realize how difficult this is for you," I added.

Robert clasped a hand over mine. "I understand my Annie is no more. What is left is a shell, acting out in a desperate attempt to make sense of her fate." We remained silent a moment more before Robert continued. "You mentioned Annie did not push you. What are you suggesting then? That it is not Annie causing these disturbances?"

I shook my head again. "No. I am not certain. I do not detect any other presence but hers. However, I do not believe she intended to cause me harm. In fact, moments before we heard your voice on the other side of the door, I thought I had gotten through to her."

"If you detect no one else, then the danger must be a result of Annie's presence," Robert argued.

"No," I disagreed. "While the occurrences of this evening may have been of Annie's doing, I believe she did not intend to harm me as much as she was trying to communicate something to me."

Robert did not respond for a moment and I finished my warm drink, inching down under the covers.

"You should rest," he instructed.

"So, we are agreed that I shall continue, correct?" I queried before conceding to sleep.

Robert raised his eyebrows at me. "No, we are not agreed. I remain unconvinced that harm was not the primary intent of tonight's incident. However, you need rest. We may continue the discussion in the morning after you have been seen by the doctor."

"I do not need a doctor," I insisted.

"We shall not take a chance that you do and do not realize it. Now rest, dear."

I nestled my head on the pillow behind me. "You do not need to stay."

"I refuse to let you out of my sight," Robert responded. "So, I shall stay to ensure your safety through the night."

"Thank you," I murmured as I closed my eyes. My mind parsed through the events of the evening again, though I worked hard to push them from my mind. Yet I couldn't escape the notion that there was more to the story. That tonight's dangerous game was not a threat and contained no murderous intent, but that it was designed to impart some information.

As I struggled to fall asleep, details of Annie's death paraded through my mind. I had inquired about the circumstances in the days following our wedding. Buchanan provided answers to most of my queries.

It was a temperate day in mid-April when Annie had met her terrible fate. Robert had been out riding late in the morning before lunch. Edwin arrived to speak with him. Finding Robert out riding, Edwin stepped out for fresh air. As he walked, a scream broke the silence. He rushed in its direction, finding Annie's broken body on the ground below the turret.

She wore a red dress that day, which became bloodied and filthy in the fall. Edwin carried Annie to the house, and a doctor was summoned, but the injuries Annie sustained killed her instantly. Nothing could be done to save her. She had passed before Edwin happened upon her. Robert had fallen to pieces when he learned of her death, locking himself in his room for days at a time and refusing to speak to anyone. Her funeral was delayed as a result of Robert's inability to bring himself to bury her.

According to Buchanan, in the months prior to her death, Annie had become somewhat reclusive. She dismissed her ladies' maid and preferred not to travel at all. I had hoped to speak with the girl, but her whereabouts were unknown. The only other person involved that I had not spoken to was Edwin. Given his sentiments toward me, I did not imagine he would provide much information.

As my mind whirled around, images of my dangerous dance on the turret's windowsill flashed in my mind. Anxiety welled inside me as the reality of the situation smacked me in the face. For the first time in my life, my encounter with a ghost had turned dangerous. It had nearly turned me into one of them!

My eyes popped open as uneasiness overwhelmed me. In the dimly lit room, I made out Robert's form, dozing in the chair next to my bed. His presence brought me solace, settling my frayed nerves. I closed my eyes again and allowed myself to drift off to sleep.

CHAPTER 11

The fuss over me the following morning seemed endless. Servants flitted in and out, ensuring my every need was met as I remained abed, an order from Robert. I was not to move for the entire day and only could resume light activities the following day if the doctor approved it.

Dr. MacAndrews arrived by mid-morning to offer his opinion on my condition. The same doctor that pronounced the former Mrs. Fletcher deceased, I worried his presence may upset Robert or worse, Annie.

"Hello, Your Grace, how are we feeling today?" Dr. MacAndrews inquired while removing his stethoscope from his black doctor's bag. Robert looked on from the foot of the bed.

"Quite well, thank you," I responded.

"Duke Blackmoore informs me that you experienced quite a frightening incident last night."

"Yes, but I have recovered quite well."

Dr. MacAndrews pressed his stethoscope to my chest. "Take a deep breath for me, please," he instructed. I took several as he listened, moving the instrument around then requesting I sit up as he placed it on my back. He felt for my pulse, then gazed into my eyes and checked my throat. He checked my hands, both of which were scraped and bruised from my desperate clutching at the stone sill. "Have you any pain anywhere?"

"No," I replied. As I spoke, movement caught my eye. Annie appeared, stepping just inside the doorway. She stood staring in my direction.

"Lenora," Robert prodded, "are you quite sure?"

I shrugged, eliciting some pain from my arms and shoulders. "A bit of soreness in my arms."

"Where?" Dr. MacAndrews questioned. "Point to the location."

I ran my hands up and down each arm and onto my shoulder. "Hmm, yes," the doctor responded. "Yes, no doubt from clinging to the windowsill. And what of your mindset? Have you any terrible thoughts or strange notions?"

"No, none," I assured him. "Though the memory remains unpleasant, it does not disturb me greatly."

"Mmm-hmm," Dr. MacAndrews murmured. "Still quite an experience for a young woman."

"What do you recommend, doctor?" Robert inquired.

"I will tend to the wounds on her hands and I recommend two days of bed rest," he began.

"Two days?!" I cried, only to be hushed by Robert.

Dr. MacAndrews set about tending to the scrapes on my fingers and palms as he continued. "I shall leave a sedative to allow the duchess to rest comfortably. If any changes arise in either her physical or mental state, call for me at once. I shall return in two days to provide another check. If she has improved, we will reevaluate her activity level."

Annie continued to look on as Dr. MacAndrews finished cleaning and dressing my wounds. I glanced at her several times during the treatment. Buchanan arrived as Dr. MacAndrews packed his medical bag, leaving a bottle of a sedative and instructions with Robert.

Buchanan escorted the doctor out, leaving Robert and I along with our phantom. Annie still stood sentinel near the doorway. Robert eased into the chair at my bedside. "I shall have Buchanan send an extra spoon with your tea for your medicine." He noticed the direction of my gaze, glancing behind him before questioning me. "What is it?"

"Annie," I replied, my gaze unwavering.

"What?" Robert questioned, glancing again behind him. "Do not attempt to communicate with her, Lenora."

"She has been here since the doctor arrived to examine me."

"Ignore her. You must rest, Lenora."

I shook my head, focusing my gaze on Robert. "I am resting. And we have not yet finished our conversation from last night."

"You are meant to be sleeping, not arguing about pursuing a gambit that has proven far too dangerous."

"I cannot sleep for two days straight, Robert," I countered. "I agree to stay abed, but there is no reason I cannot rest while awake."

Robert heaved a sigh. "Lenora, when I brought you here, when we agreed to our arrangement, I never believed you would be placed in any danger. I did not understand that the dead do not behave as they did whilst alive. Under the circumstances, this project must cease."

It was my turn to sigh. "I do not agree. And Annie's presence here suggests that she did not intend to harm me last night."

"Perhaps it suggests she hopes to finish the job," Robert retorted. "Lenora, I will not continue to argue about this while you lay confined to your bed because you were nearly killed last night!"

"Fine," I acquiesced. "We shall reserve the argument for when I am up and about."

Robert offered me an unimpressed glance. "Has anyone ever told you what a stubborn woman you are, Lenora?"

"Yes, on several occasions. I paid them no mind," I replied, earning a chuckle from Robert.

Buchanan arrived with tea, providing an extra spoon for the medication prescribed by the doctor. "I do not need that," I objected. "I shall take it this evening."

"Lenora..." Robert began to object, but I hushed him with a wave of my hand.

"Do not worry. I shall not gallivant around the castle," I promised.

"No, you shan't. And I shall stay right here to make sure of it," Robert replied as Ella entered the room.

"Oh, Your Grace!" she exclaimed as she hastened to my bedside. "Mr. Buchanan told me you had suffered an accident. I wanted to come earlier but he preferred you not be disturbed."

"I am quite all right," I assured her. "And I shall continue to rest without requiring supervision. I do not wish to keep you from your work, Robert."

"Are you trying to get rid of me, dear?"

"No. However, I am an unnecessary distraction. I do not require oversight."

"Hmm," Robert murmured, pondering the situation.

"I shall stay with her, Your Grace," Ella promised. "I will be sure she receives the proper rest and care."

"There, you see?" I inquired. "I shall be well looked after."

"All right. I shall leave you under Sinclair's care. Do not climb from this bed," Robert ordered, offering me a kiss on the forehead.

As he departed, I noted Annie's presence, still standing quietly near the door. Her eyes stared at me, unwavering even as Robert passed her. Ella sank into the chair vacated by Robert. She grasped at my bandaged hand, her eyes falling to it.

"Oh, how awful this is, Your Grace," she lamented. "Did the doctor provide good news about your recovery?"

"Yes," I answered. "I've little recovery to do, Sinclair. I am perfectly fine, only a little disturbed by the alarming event."

"Of course, poor dear," Ella cooed at me. "Would you like a cool cloth for your head?"

"No, thank you, Sinclair."

She smiled in response before adding, "Perhaps you should sleep."

"If I feel tired, I shall sleep. Until then, let us pass the time by conversing. Tell me more about yourself."

"Myself?" Ella questioned.

"Yes. Then I can rest and learn more about you."

The request seemed to take Ella by surprise, though she obliged me, informing me about her life as a child in Glasgow. She imparted many colorful tales about her parents, siblings and her own upbringing, keeping me entertained until lunch was served to me.

The warm bowl of soup provided a satisfying midday meal and brought a sleepiness on me such that I wondered if the prescribed sedative had been sneaked into it. I found myself dozing off in the early afternoon as I read my book whilst Ella mended a dress.

When Robert checked on me before dinner, I had drifted off, only aware of his presence after Ella informed me. Whenever I awoke, despite the hour, I found Annie, the silent sentinel, posted near the door.

Robert visited me again after I'd eaten my dinner tray, this time finding me awake. "How are you feeling, dear?" he asked after kissing my forehead. Taking over for Ella, who departed to eat her own meal, he sunk into the chair.

"Quite well," I replied. "I even managed to sleep this afternoon."

"Yes, when I checked earlier you were asleep. Bravo, Lenora. I worried I'd have to tie you to the bed to keep you in it."

I shook my head at his droll attempt at humor. Robert searched around the room. "Has Annie departed?"

"No," I informed him. "She has not left since the doctor examined me."

"Where is she?" Robert said, still scouring the space.

"Just there," I said with a nod of my head, "near the door."

"It disturbs me that she has not left," Robert fretted, crossing his arms across his chest.

"There is no need to be disturbed, Robert. She has done me no harm in all her hours here. I do not imagine she intends to."

Robert pondered the statement, then shook his head. "Still, I am unwilling to leave you alone in the event that she may prey on you in a vulnerable moment." I smiled at Robert's statement, folding my hands across my lap as I settled into the pillows behind me. "Have you taken your medicine?"

"Not yet, though I promise to within the hour. Despite my afternoon nap, I feel rather exhausted. I slept fitfully last night given my experience."

"Then you should rest," Robert prodded, standing and filling the spoon with the liquid from the doctor's bottle.

I swallowed the bitter liquid. It sent a shudder through me and left a grimace on my face. "Oh!" I exclaimed. "I hope not to need that again. The taste is awful. It is worse than the food at St. Mary's!"

Robert settled into his chair. "Was it very difficult living there?" he inquired. "Oh, please, if it is too painful for you to speak of, ignore my query."

"It is not unpleasant, though I haven't many fond memories of the orphanage. And the food was quite terrible," I assured him.

Robert chuckled. "Mrs. MacAlistair should be delighted to know she has improved upon your previous experience with food."

"I do tell her as often as I can," I added. "Outside of that, the headmistress' cognizance of my cross often made life unbearable."

"How did she come to learn of it? Did you tell her?"

"No," I explained. "The nuns who left me there told her. She claimed she should have been commended for taking me in, given what they told her."

"You were at a convent prior to St. Mary's?" Robert questioned, his brow furrowing in confusion.

"Yes," I revealed. "I was there for one year, four months and ten days." I noted the confused expression spreading on Robert's face and continued my explanation. "My mother left me there just before I turned six."

"Have you any idea why your mother did this?"

"Because I was not a normal child. She grew increasingly disturbed about my ability and before my sixth birthday decided she could not tolerate anymore."

"How terrible. You poor child!"

I offered a meek smile, preferring to leave those memories closed off in my mind as I began to feel tiredness wash over me. I slouched further down in the bed, pulling the covers around me.

"Are you beginning to become tired?" Robert queried.

I nodded, stifling a yawn. "Then I shall leave you sleep after one more question," Robert said.

"What is it?" I said, this time failing to repress my yawn.

"When is your birthday, Lenora?"

"October 31," I informed him, surprised by the question.

"All Hallows' Eve?"

My eyes struggled to remain open as I answered. "Mmm, yes," I responded, sleep filling my voice, "another reason my mother considered me a wicked child." With that, I drifted off to a dreamless sleep.

CHAPTER 12

Over one month passed with no disturbances from Annie. Though she stayed in my room for the entirety of my bedrest, she beckoned to me no more. Even after Dr. MacAndrews freed me from my chambers, Annie only appeared to me on limited occasions and did nothing more than gaze at me from afar. If I approached her, despite Robert's objections over me "chasing after her," she disappeared. Simply vanished into thin air, leaving behind no trace.

On a few occasions, I ventured to the ill-fated tower, though never entered it. Despite my courageous façade, I remained spooked by the incident, and unwilling to explore my frightened feelings even within my own heart. Robert had the door removed, and the window boarded to prevent against any future incidents in which someone could be harmed. On my first visit there, after my near-fatal experience, I hovered a few steps down from the doorway.

My stomach somersaulted as I recalled the events that occurred on the previous occasion when I had entered that room. I shut my eyes as tears threatened. Finding myself unable to go any further, I descended the staircase and traversed the halls to my own tower. Odd how this tower could wrap me in comfort while the other could cause such angst.

It was the solace of my tower room that I sought on this early March afternoon. As February came to a close, my mind ceased being able to hold my past at bay. I dwelled upon it, as I always did at this time of the year.

It was the tenth of March when I'd arrived at the orphanage. A child of seven, I had lived at the Daughters of Charity convent from just before I had turned six. During my time at the convent, I'd helped clean and cook and took part in daily prayers. Despite being a small child, playing was forbidden. The nuns, aware of my odd ability, did their level best to keep me contained and solitary.

The older nuns were the only women I assisted. They kept me from any of the younger nuns, afraid I may poison them with my bizarre capability. "You'll lead people astray, Lenora," one of the older nuns warned on several occasions.

Though they never were cruel, the portion of my childhood spent there lacked any warmth or normalcy other children experienced. I longed for my mother, as I received no maternal care here. I yearned to run through my former back yard, the wind blowing through my hair, or swing on the wooden swing hanging from the large oak tree there. Instead, for most of the daylight hours, I was confined to my windowless room. Permitted no light in an attempt to prevent me from spotting any specters, I sat alone in a dark room for most daylight hours.

The treatment did little to stop my visions of those departed, who could visit whether or not enough light was available. I did not mind their visits. They were often the only normal interactions I had.

During the night, the nuns locked me in my room,

claiming it to be for my own protection. In reality, I discovered through overheard conversations that they feared the disturbances that may occur overnight should I rise from my bed and roam the halls.

After three months of this treatment, I managed to pilfer an old hairpin from one of the older nuns. I hid it in my pocket and, after the lights had been put out in the convent, I approached my locked door and attempted to pick the lock.

On that first night, the lock defeated me. It took me over a week to master opening my lock. The first time I did, I remained in my room, surprised by my own ability to triumph in my diabolical scheme to escape my confinement. As morning approached, the notion occurred to me that I should attempt to relock my door, so my hijinks went unnoticed.

I pushed the hairpin into the lock and fiddled with it until the knob no longer turned when I tried it. Satisfied with my work, I crept back into bed and slid under the covers after hiding my new tool under my mattress.

I spent the next thirteen months using my hairpin to escape nightly from my room. I traversed the halls, ventured outside into the courtyard garden, and even crept into the tiny chapel once or twice. During summer months, I enjoyed laying in the grass and stargazing. Especially exciting were the nights with a full moon. The moonlight basked the plants in the garden in its glowing white light, making them appear magical.

As my nocturnal excursions continued, I would sleep during the day while locked away in the dark. After dinner, I would count the hours until silence fell over the convent. I'd then slip from my bed, unlock my door and spend hours entertaining myself with games I made up, fantastical stories of knights and princesses and, of course, interacting with those lost souls who would visit me.

One day before 10 March, I sneaked from my room as usual as quietness fell over the convent. I crept down the hall away from the cells. As I rounded the corner into the hall leading to the courtyard, I picked up my pace. My bare feet slapped against the cold floor as I skipped along. Despite the chilliness still in the air, I preferred to stay barefooted until I reached the courtyard.

I made it halfway down the hall before my lighthearted scampering ground to a halt. I stood motionless, every muscle tense as I stared at the end of the hall. My eyes went wide, and my throat closed as I tried to swallow.

A figured stepped from the shadows at the end of the hall. Even in the dim light, I realized she was not a member of the dead. The white of her habit was visible even in the dark. As she moved into the moonlit hall, I recognized the face of the Mother Superior.

The stern expression she wore made her disapproval obvious. She approached, looming over me. I stared up at her, my hands clasped in front of me. "Mother," I greeted her.

She did not speak for a moment, her mouth set in a grim line. "What are you doing, Lenora?" she barked after a moment.

I considered my response. Should I lie or tell the truth? I decided honesty was the best policy. "I was going to the garden for some air."

"Going to the garden?!" she exclaimed. "You are meant to be in bed."

"I spend all day in my room," I countered. "I only wanted to get out for a bit."

"What you want and what you should have are separate things, Lenora," she lectured me. "You spend all day in your room to correct the illness from which you suffer. At night, you are not to do as you please. You are a child. You are to be in bed, sleeping like a normal child would be at this hour."

"I am not ill," I insisted.

Mother Superior grasped me by the arm, dragging me back toward the cells. "You ARE ill, child. Illness is not always physical. You suffer from a spiritual illness. The devil taunts you with these visions."

I struggled against her, but to no avail. Despite her age, she still possessed strength beyond that of a small girl. "They are real," I argued. "I am not ill!"

We arrived at my door and she opened it, shoving me inside without a word. The door slammed shut and the clank of the lock fastening sounded throughout the room. It echoed in my ears long after it settled into place.

I climbed into my bed, snuggling under my blanket as tears formed in my eyes. I still had the hair pin I used to unlock my door, but I dared not use it again tonight. I blinked back my tears and focused my energy on how I might avoid a punishment for my misbehavior.

The following morning, no one retrieved me as usual before breakfast. I huddled on my bed, my knees drawn to my chest as I heard the convent come to life. The hall became quiet again as the sisters gathered for morning devotions and breakfast. Perhaps this was my punishment, I reflected, as silence settled around me. I was to go without breakfast. While my stomach growled, the punishment was not so terrible. I could withstand it, I told myself.

The morning wore on with no one approaching my door. The sounds of the day carried on outside my room as I sat in the dark cell. As the lunch hour approached, the clanking of the lock releasing sounded throughout my room. The door cracked open, and I squinted against the light as it shined in from the hallway.

The outline of Mother Superior was framed by the back

light. I climbed from my bed as she hovered at the door. "Lunch," she said, leaving a tray on the floor inside the doorway. The door swung shut, and I heard the lock engage.

A small candle glowed from the tray, giving me enough light to retrieve the lunch setting and return to my bed to eat it. I set the candle on my night table and picked at the cold oatmeal in the bowl. The food, clearly left over from breakfast, had hardened into a lump. Even my intense hunger failed to make the meal appetizing.

I forced a small amount of the oatmeal down, gagging as it stuck in my throat. I pushed its hardened mass around the bowl as I pondered eating another bite. I scooped a small amount of the sludge from the bowl and brought it to my mouth. My lips formed a grimace as a whiff of it passed through my nostrils. I dropped the spoon into the bowl. It clattered against the dish, resounding through the room.

I sat crossed legged on my bed, my chin in my hands as I stared at the inedible food. My stomach ceased growling, the unappetizing food turning it enough to stop me from desiring to eat. With no window and no outlet from my room, I could not dispose of the food. I would surely earn myself another punishment for leaving it uneaten, but I could not stomach it.

The sound of the lock unlatching reverberated through the room. I leapt from my bed, my bare feet touching the cold floor. Mother Superior stood in the doorway, her features flinty in the flickering candlelight. She glanced at the barely touched food, then back to me. "Get dressed, Lenora," she said curtly.

I stood silent for a moment. "Now, Lenora!" she said, raising her voice. "And when you have finished pack your things."

My eyes widened and my breath caught. "Pack my things?" I questioned.

"Do not quibble with me," Mother Superior warned. "Do as you are told."

"But..." I began again.

"But nothing!" she snapped at me. "And finish your lunch." She spun on her heel, slamming and locking the door behind her.

The room darkened with only the light of the small candle flickering its feeble flame from my night table. My heart thudded in my chest as I pulled my tattered suitcase from under the bed. I changed into a dress, folding my nightgown and placing it in my suitcase. Why must I pack, I wondered? My heart skipped a beat. Perhaps my mother returned for me! The notion hurried my pace. This must be the reason Mother Superior requested me to pack.

I placed my limited belongings into the suitcase. I snapped it shut and set it on the floor near my bed. I used the dim light to ensure my dress was clean and unsullied. I sat on the edge of the bed, my hands folded in my lap. I wanted to be sure I was ready the moment my mother arrived. After one year, four months and ten days, I would finally be reunited with my mother.

Not wanting to wrinkle my dress, I sat unmoving. My muscles began to ache after an hour of waiting. Still, I sat unflinching on that lumpy bed until the lock released and the door swung open. I stood as the form of Mother Superior appeared rimmed in the hall's light. I searched behind her but found no one. Mother must be waiting in the foyer, I mused.

I gazed into Mother Superior's face, searching for answers as the candlelight flickered across her features. She glanced to my suitcase, then to me. "Are you packed?"

I nodded. "Yes," I answered, my voice breathless.

Mother Superior glanced to my bed. "You did not finish your meal?"

I followed her gaze, staring at the inedible lump of food in the bowl. My heart leapt into my throat and my mouth went dry. I hoped it would not be the reason I was kept from my mother for a second longer. I licked my lips, preparing to reply. My mouth opened and closed, but no sounds emerged.

Before I could respond, Mother Superior spoke again. "No matter," she said. "Come, Lenora."

A smile crept across my face and I grasped my suitcase's handle. I hurried across the room and followed Mother Superior into the hallway. The hall was empty of others. Mother Superior ambled down the corridor to the main entrance, her black habit flowing around her, making her appear to float. I nearly floated behind her, my excitement building with each step.

We reached the foyer. The late afternoon sun shined through the stained glass, painting the floor a rainbow of colors. My eyes darted around the space, searching for my mother. I found no one outside of Sister Mary Margaret. The young nun stood by the doors, a handkerchief clutched in her hand.

As we approached the door, Sister Mary Margaret sniffled, a tear escaping her eye. "Pull yourself together, Sister," Mother Superior warned. "Or I shall ask you to leave."

Sister Mary Margaret nodded, wiping the tear away and clenching her jaw. My brow knitted in confusion. As I approached her, she knelt on the stone floor in front of me. She offered me a genuine but wavering smile as tears threatened to spill from her eyes. She choked them back, pushing my hair behind my shoulders.

Of all the nuns, young Sister Mary Margaret had always been kind to me. On Christmas, she snuck me an orange and a small piece of chocolate. A family member had visited her and gifted them to her, and she had shared her bounty with me. On a separate occasion, she brought a small doll back, gifting it to me as a belated birthday present. Over my stay here, she had given me several other small items. Once or twice, she was caught and reprimanded for indulging me. It did not stop her.

"God loves you, Lenora," she whispered. "You are a special child. Remember that. No matter what they say."

I nodded. "I will," I promised.

"Be a good girl," she said, choking back a sob.

"I will," I reiterated. "Do not cry, Sister Mary. I shall be happy now. And I shall visit you when I am able!"

The statement seemed to upset her. She gulped back another sob and nodded in response. Sister Mary Margaret glanced to Mother Superior. "Come, Lenora," Mother Superior said, "it is time to go."

Before we parted, Sister Mary Margaret pulled me into a tight embrace, kissing my cheek. I returned her embrace before Mother Superior tugged at my arm. "Come along, Lenora," she instructed.

Sister Mary Margaret clutched my hand, giving it a squeeze. I returned the gesture before letting her hand drop. I offered one final smile as Mother Superior guided me through the door. We stepped into the cool March air. I expected to find my mother waiting on the sidewalk below. Instead, I found no one. A carriage awaited us on the road below. We descended the stone steps and climbed into the carriage.

Funny that Mother did not come for me. She must have sent for me instead, I surmised. I placed my suitcase on my lap as the carriage set off. As we wound through the streets, I wondered how long the journey home might be. My parents did not live in Glasgow, but rather in a small country town outside of it called Glenrock.

I searched the depths of my mind, trying to recall how long the journey took when my mother brought me to the convent. Just shy of six years old, I could not remember the duration of our trip. It did not matter, by nightfall I should be asleep in my own bed, I was certain. Contentment swelled in me. At long last, I would return to my home, to my mother and father, to my life. A smile passed over my lips as I gazed out the window, the buildings racing past me.

We continued for another fifteen minutes before the carriage slowed to a stop. My brow crinkled in confusion. Despite not recalling the exact duration of the journey between the convent and my home, I knew it was not this short. Outside the window, a ramshackle building rose multiple stories above the street.

Mother Superior disembarked from the carriage, suggesting I do the same. "Come, Lenora," she said.

I did not budge for a moment, still confused. Mother Superior's head popped back into the carriage. "I said come along, girl!" she exclaimed.

I climbed out of the carriage to the sidewalk, my suitcase in hand. My eyes lifted upward to study the battered building looming over me. What was this place, I wondered?

Mother Superior was already climbing the steps leading to the peeling black doors. I rushed to catch up to her. "Where are we?" I inquired.

"Hush, girl," she answered as she knocked at the door.

A child, slightly older than me, answered the door. "Yes?" she inquired.

"Sister Mary Xavier to see Headmistress Williamson. We spoke earlier this morning."

"Please, come in," the child instructed, standing aside as we entered the foyer. I gaped around, noting the dismal décor. A backless wooden bench sat outside a doorway. A wide staircase, paint peeling from the banister, led to another floor. A lone chandelier hung in the middle of the room, lighting the space dimly. No other items graced the area.

The child crossed the cheerless space, knocking at the door near the bench. After a moment, she entered the room, then returned to retrieve Mother Superior. "Wait here, Lenora," Mother Superior instructed, motioning to the bench. She disappeared through the doorway.

I set my suitcase next to the bench and climbed up to sit. My legs dangled in the air and I took care not to let them swing too much. A behavior unbecoming of a lady. I folded my hands in my lap as voices floated into the foyer from the room next to me.

It soon became clear to me why we were here. "Good evening, Headmistress Williamson," Mother Superior said.

"Ah, Sister Mary, welcome back. Please have a seat. You brought the child?" a woman's voice answered.

"I have," Mother Superior confirmed.

"Sister," the voice answered, "are you certain you cannot care for the child?"

"Yes," Mother Superior replied. "It is unfortunate, but the child is not normal."

"Yet you want to place her here."

"Your focus is different," Mother Superior said. "We struggle to educate the girl, to provide for her. And her... otherworldly capabilities scare some of the other sisters. I fear for their souls with her in our convent."

"At St. Mary's we attempt to offer a stable environment for these girls. If you fear for the souls of your own nuns, should not I be concerned for my girls?"

"I fear for the loss of faith. Your girls have not committed themselves to God."

"But they fear God. We train good God-fearing girls here, sister."

"I do not mean to impugn your reputation. Nor upset the balance of your school, but the girl is running wild with us."

"Sister, I find it difficult to believe you cannot manage a small child."

"We have no means to manage a small child. We have attempted to keep her isolated in the hopes it cured her. However, her behavior persists. And she has developed other poor habits."

"Poor habits?" the woman questioned.

"The girl needs a firmer hand," Mother Superior said, sidestepping the question neatly. "Guidance from a professional. She needs routine, structure."

"She will receive plenty of that here." There was a pause in the conversation, then the woman's voice continued. "And this strange behavior of hers, has she some mental disorder? We are not prepared to care for a child of this nature."

"No, the girl does not suffer from a mental disorder. She is disturbed, but not mentally. I prefer not to imagine the source of her troubles."

"Forgive me, sister, but I prefer to understand fully what trouble we may bring into this school."

Mother Superior sighed. "With the proper guidance, perhaps you will not invite any trouble."

"You place a heavy burden upon me, my teachers and my pupils."

"You are a school for orphans, are you not?" Mother Superior inquired.

There was a pause before the other woman responded. "Why, yes. Though I am not sure I understand the reason for your query."

"The reason, Headmistress, is that I did not need to request placement from you. I could merely have dropped the girl on your steps. As a woman of God, I chose to consult you. To make you aware of what to expect."

Another pause. "So, in other words, you have every intention of leaving the girl here regardless of our discussion."

"In short, Headmistress, yes. It is in the best interest of the girl. We cannot care for her." A rustling sound emanated from the room. "And now, Headmistress, I shall leave you to your work."

Mother Superior appeared in the doorway. She offered me a brief side-eyed glance before proceeding across the foyer. "Mother Superior?" I cried, a mix of emotions coursing through me. I leapt from the bench and ran after her, pulling on her habit.

She spun to face me. "Goodbye, Lenora," she said in a firm tone. "You must stay here now. It is in your best interest."

"But… but I thought you were taking me home!" I squawked, sobs filling my voice.

"Lenora, enough. I never told you that. Now unhand me."

Tears streamed down my face and thoughts raced about in my mind. Why was I being discarded? The convent, while not my home, was the only thing I had known after my mother left me. How would my mother find me if I was moved?

A voice boomed from across the room. "Miss Hastings!" the voice shouted.

I ignored her. "Please," I begged Mother Superior. "Take me back. I shall behave!"

Footsteps sounded behind me and the woman approached. She swatted my behind twice before smacking my hands away from Mother Superior. "I shall take it from here, sister," she assured Mother Superior.

Mother Superior nodded, her habit flaring out as she spun and crossed the foyer, disappearing through the door. I called after her, but the door slammed shut. I never saw her again. "That is quite enough!" the woman shouted at me. I fought against her, trying to break free of her grip.

It proved fruitless. She kept a firm hold on me, dragging

me across the room and into her office. She let go of my arms and slammed the door shut behind us. I jumped at the harsh sound.

The woman spun to face me, her green eyes cold. Her eyes narrowed, and she set her mouth in a firm line. She stood in silence, assessing me before she spoke. "Now, girl," she said, "I shall not tolerate this inappropriate behavior further. You may have evaded punishment at the convent, but you shall not at St. Mary's Orphanage for Girls! You will learn manners and proper behavior here! If you do not, you will be punished. Harshly, if necessary. Do you understand?"

I did not open my mouth. My mind struggled to comprehend everything that occurred. In an instant, I had been abandoned for a second time. Dumped unceremoniously in another place. This time in a home for orphans. A tear threatened to roll down my cheek.

She slapped me across the cheek. "I said, do you understand, girl?" the woman roared at me.

Stunned, I clutched my cheek as tears escaped my eyes. I nodded. "Speak up, Lenora! Answer when spoken to!" she shouted, swatting at me again.

"Ouch!" I shouted between sobs.

"Stop your infantile sobbing!" she shrieked at me. I could not control my sobs, still reeling from the events. "I said stop!" She grasped me by my shoulders, pulling my face near hers. "Listen to me, Lenora! You shall not behave in this manner here! You shall behave as a mature young lady! Now cease this crying at once and answer me!"

I choked back my sobs as she released me, nearly sending me sprawling onto the floor. I wiped at my face and sniffled. "I understand," I choked out.

"Say it again, this time, with your hands folded in front of you like a young lady."

I folded my hands in front of me. "I understand," I repeated.

"I understand, headmistress," she corrected.

With a sniffle, I repeated the words again. "I understand, headmistress."

She nodded her head at me, crossing the room to stand behind her desk. I turned to face her. "Now, I shall also not tolerate any nonsense like you displayed at the convent."

"I understand, headmistress," I repeated a third time.

Seemingly satisfied, she continued, informing me I would sleep in the attic.

CHAPTER 13

A chill passed over me as I recalled my first night in the orphanage. The anniversary of my second abandonment by my caregivers always brought a sense of sorrow over me. This year proved no exception. However, Robert planned a trip to Glasgow in a few days' time and invited me along. The dates would mean I would be in Glasgow on 10 March. The distraction would ease the melancholy.

A knock roused me from my musings. I pulled my gaze from the scenery to find Robert at the door.

"Hello, Lenora. I hope I'm not interrupting."

"Not at all," I said. "Please come in." I closed the open book on my lap and stood.

Robert entered the room, a small box in his hands. "This just arrived," he said, waving the box in the air.

I studied it, curious as to why Robert climbed to the tower with it. The small cream-colored box was wrapped with a sapphire blue ribbon. "What is it?" I questioned.

"Open it." He handed the box to me. I accepted it, my brow furrowing as I glanced at the object. I raised my eyes to Robert's, my gaze questioning. "'Tis a gift."

"A gift? Is there no end to your spoiling of me?" I questioned, sinking onto my window seat as I undid the bow.

"It is not spoiling for a husband to give his wife a birthday gift!" Robert retorted.

I stopped untying the ribbon. "It is not my birthday!" I exclaimed.

"No, it is not," Robert admitted. "It is a belated birthday gift. I was unaware your birthday had passed shortly after we wed. What a terrible husband I would be to miss my new wife's birthday just after our wedding! I hope I have redeemed myself with the gift."

"No redemption is necessary," I assured him. "And neither was the gift. Though I am delighted you thought of me."

"I hope you are keen on it," Robert replied, joining me on the window seat.

With the ribbon undone, I pulled the top from the box. Nestled in crushed paper inside the box laid a rectangular golden object. I lifted the small but heavy item out with care, studying it. Ornate decorations covered it. And a small bird was depicted on the top of the box where I also detected a hinge. "'Tis a singing box," Robert added. He reached over and pressed a small knob on the box's right side. The hinge on the top popped open, revealing a colorful bird. It chirped a tune as it flapped its wings.

I had never witnessed such a clever contraption. I marveled at it as its sweet song filled the air. "It is to replace the box that you lost when Annie… well, never mind," Robert said.

"The porcelain figurine?" I questioned, recalling my heartbreak when the object smashed to the floor.

"Yes," Robert replied with a nod. "This one is not as delicate and thereby, should not break! I hope you find it an adequate replacement."

"Adequate?" I questioned. "This is more than adequate. I have never seen such an object before. It is enchanting."

A smile crossed Robert's lips. "I am delighted you find it so."

"Thank you, Robert," I answered, offering him a kiss on the cheek. "I adore it! I shall keep it here in my tower room. Oh, unless I should like to listen to it before I fall asleep, in which case I shall take it to my bedroom." I chattered on, perhaps more than I should have.

"I am not certain I have witnessed you so excited before, Lenora," Robert mentioned.

"Oh," I murmured, wondering if I had babbled too much, "I am sorry. I did not mean to prattle on."

"Nonsense," Robert answered with a wave of his hand. "I am pleased you enjoy the gift. I was most anxious when I sent for it that you would not care for it."

"I do," I assured him.

"Good," he responded. He stood and kissed my forehead. "How are your preparations for our travel coming?"

"Excellent," I answered. "I am looking most forward to it."

"Hmm. I should think you would find it dreadfully boring. Have you plans?"

"Not at all," I assured him. "I am eager to visit Glasgow. I plan to visit with a friend from the orphanage."

"Eager to visit? Oh dear, perhaps you find Scottish country life dreadfully boring."

I chuckled at his comments. "No, dear," I responded. "I do not find country life at all boring. However, it was around this date when I arrived at the orphanage. I often find myself dwelling on the memory of that distressing day. But, with the travel, I shall have plenty to distract me. And I am eager to see how Tilly is getting on."

"Ah," Robert said with a smile. "I see. What a terrible

memory to commemorate. Well, I am glad to be of some service to you during this time."

"You are more than just some service," I answered, matching his expression.

His grin broadened. "I will see you at dinner. I am going riding."

"Please be careful," I warned him, recalling his injured leg.

"I shall, dear," he promised. His brow furrowed, and he added, "It occurs to me you have never asked to ride. If you enjoy it, ask Thomas, our stable hand, to prepare a horse for you whenever you like. The grounds are most beautiful to take in on horseback."

"I do not ride," I responded.

He paused a moment, as though uncertain how to respond. "Do not ride?" he repeated, his voice phrasing it as a question.

"No," I answered. "I never learned. Girls at St. Mary's had little use for the knowledge and no means to acquire it, anyway."

"Yes, I understand," Robert said. "Well..." He paused again, as though unsure. "I shall teach you. If you are keen to learn, that is."

"I should enjoy that," I responded. "I would like to take in more of the estate than I am able to walk."

He smiled at me again. "Excellent. We shall begin upon our return from Glasgow."

"I look forward to it."

He offered me another kiss on my forehead before departing. Alone, I turned my attentions to my new trinket. The brass box sparkled in the sun streaming through the windows. I smiled down at it, pressing the button to trigger the mechanism that released the bird. The little blue bird leapt from his hiding spot, his wings flapping and his beak opening and closing as he sang his merry tune.

I played it several more times before I worried I may break it on the first day I owned it. Instead, I returned my attentions to my book, though my mind wandered to preparations for my trip. As my mind listed items to be completed, my gaze fell upon the small singing box. Warmth filled my heart as I pressed the button, allowing the bird again to serenade me.

This March, I would not feel melancholy. Wistfulness would be banished by the small chirping bird. I had finally found my home.

My lips formed a broad smile. I reached for the box, caressing it. I closed my eyes, feeling its cool metal beneath my fingers. I rubbed the intricate details. My hand fell on the knob and I pressed the button again, freeing the bird to sing anew.

The song ended prematurely. My stomach jolted, and a lump formed in my throat. Panic rose in my chest as I assumed I had broken the trinket already. My eyes snapped open. I focused my attention on the small box, but something else drew my gaze.

Pale fingers rested on top of the box. I followed them up to a hand, wrist, arm and ultimately to stare at a pale face. Annie hovered over me; her fingers firmly pressed on the box. "Hello, Annie," I said. Her dark eyes bored into me as though she could study my soul. "You don't care for the bird's song?" She raised her hand, readying to swat the box away. "No!" I shouted, leaping from my seat and grabbing hold of the box. "Do not touch it. It is mine, a gift. I shall not see it broken." My eyes met hers. "Please," I added.

She lowered her hand, and I set the box on the table. "You haven't visited in some time, Annie," I continued. She stood unmoving; her mouth set in a grim expression. "I suppose we both needed a respite after the last encounter."

Her eyes narrowed, and she raised an eyebrow at me. "I

do not believe you intended to hurt me," I confessed. I paused. "Am I incorrect?"

Annie pointed to the singing box. I furrowed my brow, attempting to determine her meaning. "What is it, Annie?" I questioned.

Her arm did not move, continuing to point to the box. "The box?" I paused, assessing any reaction on her part. None showed. "It was a gift... from Robert."

Her arm lowered, and she nodded. I struggled to understand. "Does the gift disturb you? Is it the sound? Or perhaps the concept that Robert has given me a gift?"

Annie shook her head. The crinkle in my brow deepened. "I do not understand," I admitted. "You pointed at the box. What is it about the box?"

Annie swung her head in agitation. I paced the floor, my hand resting on my forehead. "It isn't the sound. It isn't the box itself. It isn't the fact that Robert gifted it to me. What is it?" I threw my hands out with frustration.

Her arm raised, and she again pointed at the box. I sighed and returned to pacing. "Not the box itself..." I murmured. "Not the gift..." I replayed the conversation in my mind, trying to focus on what triggered the nod from Annie. I halted my pacing, staring at her, throwing my arms in the air. "Annie, I do not understand what you are trying to communicate!"

Her arm, which never ceased pointing to the box, raised. I followed its trajectory. Her finger now pointed out the window. A horse rode from the stables, traveling away from the castle. I spun to face her again. "Robert!" I exclaimed.

Annie nodded her head slowly, lowering her arm. I smiled at her, a sense of achievement filling her. This marked our first successful communication! The smile was quickly replaced by a confused expression. "But what about Robert?" I questioned as the crinkle returned to my brow.

Annie continued to stare at me with her piercing gaze. I met her stare, squinting my eyes at her as though it may help me read her mind. "You are trying to communicate something about Robert. It is not your upset over the gift. What is it?" Annie stared, unflinching, in response. "Ugh," I groaned, shaking my head. I resumed pacing again as I attempted to solve the puzzle. "Do you wish to communicate something to Robert?" I asked, pausing in my ambling to gauge her response. She shook her head. "No," I said, resuming my pacing. "Are you unhappy with Robert?" I tried as my next query.

A slight nod. I smiled, proud of myself. "You are unhappy with Robert," I repeated. I paused a moment, thinking. "Is this… was he the cause…" A sharp shake of the head cut off my words. No, I pondered, no, Robert was not the cause of Annie's suicide. I chided myself for even beginning to suggest it. The Robert I was acquainted with could never drive a woman to suicide. "So, you are unhappy with Robert now, not before your death." Another nod. My mind whirled as I computed the information I possessed and tried to assimilate it into an answer.

"What has Robert done to upset you?" I queried aloud. Annie responded by pointing at me. I glanced down at my chest where she pointed as though perhaps a message would appear there. I raised my eyes to hers, my expression questioning. "Me?" I paused again. "Is it our marriage?"

Annie shook her head again. A snarling growl emanated from her. Her features darkened and her lips turned into a snarl. Frustration was growing inside her. "I am as frustrated as you," I admitted. I returned to pacing. "Oh! If you could only speak!"

She lowered her arm and her snarl ceased. Her features remained dark, but she made no move to leave. Her eyes bore into me. I breathed in a deep breath. "All right. I shall try again." I paused, gathering all the facts I had, walking across the breadth of the room. "Robert has upset you. And the upset involves me. It is not the gift, nor our marriage." I spun on my heel, ambling across the room in the opposite direction. I halted mid-step. My eyebrows raised and my jaw fell open. I twisted to face Annie. "You are upset that Robert restricted our communication! He removed the door to the tower and boarded the windows. He forbade me from pursuing our conversations!"

The darkness lifted on Annie's face and she nodded. I clapped my hands. "I have done it!" I exclaimed. I grinned at her, though she did not match my expression. "This is our first successful communication!" Annie's lackluster response to my delight dampened my spirits. I replaced my grin with a more serious expression. I continued, "You have no reason to be upset with Robert. He only means to protect me. In his mind, he judged you intended to harm me. The encounter nearly resulted in my death." A chill passed over me as I said the words and a lump formed in my throat. I swallowed hard, not allowing my mind to return to the fright I'd experienced. "Though I do not believe you intended to harm me, did you?"

Annie shook her head, her brown eyes fixed upon me. "I have told Robert this. But he does not understand, Annie. You must give him time." Annie's eyes flashed red for a moment, a dark expression crossing her face. "I shall make him understand," I promised.

Annie stared at me another moment. Then she flitted to the doorway. She hovered there a moment before motioning for me to follow. Robert's warning echoed in my mind for a moment before I chose to ignore it. I sped after her, catching her red dress disappearing around the turret's curving stairs.

I caught up to her at the bottom of the stairs. She led me through the hallways and straight back to the tower from which she'd thrown herself. I studied the steps ahead of me as Annie disappeared around the bend. My jaw quavered as I put one foot on the first stair. I steadied my jaw and my nerves and climbed after her. I reached the halfway point. The doorless portal yawned at me from above. Annie stood in the entryway; her eyes fixed on me.

I swallowed hard, a knot forming in the pit of my stomach. I took another step up, my legs wobbling, threatening to collapse. My teeth dug into my bottom lip as my eyes brimmed with tears.

My last experience here still frightened me. Perhaps more so now in retrospect than it had in the moment. While I maintained Annie did not intend to harm me, the recollection of dangling for those precious few moments from the tower window made my knees weak, my stomach somersault and my hands tremble.

I opened my mouth to speak as Annie signaled me to approach her. My parched throat found it difficult to push the words out. "I cannot," I finally managed before turning to flee down the steps. I stood at the bottom, my back against the stone wall as I gasped for breath to calm my frayed nerves.

A tear escaped my eye, running down my cheek. My fingers wiped it away as I fought to pull myself together. I'd never been afraid of the dead before. Though, to be fair, I still was not. Annie did not frighten me. Rather, fear of being harmed did.

Silly, I chided myself. Annie did not intend to harm me. The experience only provided a mechanism for communication between us. I must steel my nerves and continue my investigation. I filled my lungs with air, drawing myself upright and pressing my shoulders back. With a determined expression, I swung around the corner and climbed the staircase.

As I reached the halfway point, I paused. My gaze fell upon the open doorway. Annie no longer stood there. "Annie?" I called. I received no response.

I considered turning back. Annie must have gone, figuring I would not return. No, I insisted with a shake of my head. No, I would continue. I must. I climbed each of the remaining steps, firming my resolve and my mind with each footfall. I possessed the strength to reenter that room, I told myself.

I reached the top of the stairs, hesitating on the landing just outside the doorway. I peered inside, grasping the door-jamb to steady my legs, which threatened to betray me. An empty room stared back at me. My foot hovered over the threshold. After a breath, I placed it inside the room, followed by the other. I drew in another deep breath. I had done it. I had reentered the room and faced my fear.

"Annie?" I called again. "I am sorry. My nerves remain rattled after my last experience here. But I have overcome my fear."

I waited a moment but received no response. Annie did not appear. "Annie?" I tried a third time. I waited another moment. "Next time then."

I exited the room and rushed down the stairs. Despite the courage I displayed moments earlier, my trepidation over the room remained. I hurried to put distance between me and that fated space.

Over dinner, I broached the subject of Annie's visit with Robert. Annie's vexation with him may be mended with a simple conversation. At least I hoped so. "Annie visited me today," I announced as I stirred my soup.

"Oh?" Robert inquired, dropping his spoon from his mouth and staring at me.

"Yes," I continued. "As I listened to my singing box, she quieted it to draw my attention." Robert's jaw tensed, but I continued, determined to get my point across. "She is upset."

Robert's eyebrows raised, and he opened his mouth to speak, then closed it. I waited a moment, and he finally spoke. "SHE is upset?" he questioned.

"Yes," I responded. "She is upset… with you."

"With me?" Robert's voice raised a level, filling with indignation.

"She wishes you to realize she intended no harm to come to me during the last… incident. I suspected as much…"

Robert's disgusted sigh interrupted me. His hand fell to the table, rattling the dishes. "Lenora," he said, "we have been over this. The… incident, as you prefer to call it, nearly resulted in your death. I shall not have you carrying on with this."

"I am investigating, as is my task…"

"As WAS your task, Lenora. When I solicited your help on the matter, I did not realize the extent to which Annie would behave in such a contrary manner to the way in which she lived. It still baffles me that she engages in such destructive behavior!"

"She does not mean to be destructive! She is communicating. And while the incident frightened me, I must continue. She is desperate, hurting. I must help her!"

Robert closed his eyes for a moment, his jaw set. His displeasure was apparent. So be it. If we were to have a row, then we should have it, I thought. I would not abandon my mission to help this poor soul. Even if I chose to, Annie may not allow it. He opened his stormy gray eyes, stormier now because of his umbrage. "Lenora," he responded, his tone measured, "I have already explained that you owe me nothing. I no longer wish you to pursue this dangerous gambit! I recognized our arrangement hinged upon you providing information about Annie's death. However, I did not realize how dangerous of a task I requested. We are married. You are my wife. It is my duty to protect you, and I shall. From living or dead. I no longer expect information regarding the matter. Consider the arrangement concluded!"

"You no longer expect it, or you no longer desire it?" I queried. "It is an important distinction. And what of the other part of our arrangement? Am I to consider that concluded as well?"

Robert set his mouth in a thin line. "Let us not argue about the matter," he answered, collecting his spoon and returning to his soup.

"I do not wish to argue," I continued. "Merely to know the score."

"Damn it, Lenora!" he boomed, his spoon clattering to the table. "You know full well the score!" He paused, then continued, his voice lowered and containing no anger. "That was unfair. I apologize. Yet, you must realize I have come to care for you."

Robert's assessment was correct. I had suspected him to be keen on me, though I had no experience with such sentiments. My reaction was delayed, tainted by my life's experiences and confusion regarding our agreement. The delay caused Robert to continue speaking. "Though, I suppose I must again apologize. My offer included a lifestyle, not an emotional entanglement."

My pulse quickened as I realized my silence had been misconstrued as disapproval. "I do not object," I burst out. Over our brief marriage, I, too, had grown to care for my husband. I experienced an acceptance I had never known before, and his presence offered me comfort.

Robert glanced to me, before returning his eyes to his soup bowl. A slight smile crept across his lips as he retrieved his spoon. "I am pleased you do not. Then let us consider the matter settled. We shall remain married and you shall no longer be expected to pursue this inquiry. Are we agreed?"

"No, we are not," I responded. Robert lowered his spoon again, his eyebrows raised as he gazed at me. I met his glance. "I agree that we shall remain married, however, I do not agree to abandon my pursuit of information with Annie."

"This is unwise!" Robert argued.

"No," I disagreed. "Annie did not mean to harm me. When she visited me earlier, she made that much clear. It also remains clear that she needs help. Something disturbs her. I want to help her." I paused, then added, "And I realize, while you may not understand her behavior, find it dangerous and that you wish no harm come to me, you still desire to know what caused her to end her life. Besides, at this stage, I may become an unwilling participant in helping her. I prefer to control at least some of the situation."

Robert heaved a sigh. "Of course I wish to know the circumstances surrounding her decision," he admitted. He set his gaze on me. "But not at the cost of your life."

"I shall be careful," I promised.

"Lenora..."

"She needs help, Robert. MY help. And I have a healthy wariness of the tower room, which I am only just overcoming. But it aids me in acting prudently."

"You have not returned there since the... incident, have you?"

I broke eye contact, turning my gaze to my soup. "I followed Annie there today, though I did not enter. At first. My nerves remained too frayed. However, once alone, I entered the room for a moment only."

"Lenora, I wish you would not take such chances!" Robert chided me.

"The door has been removed, and the window boarded. And I was alone. The risk seemed minimal."

"I'd prefer the risk to be none."

"No risk is not an option," I countered. "Therefore, I shall work to minimize the risk to the best of my ability."

"And I shall work with you to ensure your safety."

I smiled at him. "Good, then I shall continue to seek answers with the utmost care!"

Robert nodded with a small sigh. "All right."

"NOW we are agreed," I said with a grin.

CHAPTER 14

Mists shrouded the grounds below the castle the following morning. I gazed out over the foggy landscape from my bedroom window. "Do you prefer the blue traveling suit or the peach?" Ella inquired. "Your Grace?" she questioned when I did not respond. I pulled my gaze from the scenery. "Your Grace, is everything all right?"

I offered her a brief smile. "Yes. The misty landscape captured my attention. Ah, the blue, please."

"The misty landscape?" Ella inquired, setting the blue traveling suit out for our trip the next day.

"Yes," I answered, motioning to her to join me at the window. She peered out before returning to her duties. "Romantic, isn't it? Beguiling and comforting yet also mysterious."

A chuckle emanated from Ella. "Romantic is not a word I would use to describe that fog, Your Grace."

I spun to face her. "No? How would you describe it, Sinclair?"

"Eerie, Your Grace," she responded.

I chortled at her comments. "Eerie?" I repeated. "Oh,

Sinclair, you let your imagination run too wild. Nothing sinister exists under those mists!"

She offered me a glance before holding up two necklaces for me to select from. "Sinister or not, that dampness chills you to the bones. It's unhealthy, this weather!"

"I thought you enjoyed the Highlands. The choker on the left, please."

"I enjoy the Highlands when there isn't a damp fog."

I rolled my eyes at her. "I enjoy the Highlands always."

"Will you be sad to leave even for the short period then?" Ella questioned as she placed a dress into my luggage.

"Very," I admitted. "Homesickness will set in on the first night."

"Why go?" Ella asked, then stopped short in the packing. "Oh, forgive me if that is too forward a question, Your Grace."

"It is not," I assured her. "I enjoy the traveling, though I also enjoy my home. And I plan to visit an old friend while in Glasgow."

"Oh?"

"Yes. Tilly, a friend of mine from St. Mary's."

"Was St. Mary's a private school?"

"No," I answered with a chuckle. "An orphanage."

"Oh!" Ella answered as she bustled about continuing preparations for my travel. "Did you volunteer there before your marriage, Your Grace?"

"No," I responded. "I was a student there before my marriage." Ella slowed in her motions for a moment before returning to her scurrying. It did not escape me. Her slight response spoke volumes to betray her surprise.

"I did not realize," Ella mumbled.

"No, you couldn't have. In any case, I hope to visit with Tilly while in Glasgow."

"I hope it is a successful visit, Your Grace!"

"As do I," I answered. "Have you any business to attend to while in Glasgow?"

"Business, Your Grace?"

"Yes," I replied. "Is there anything you would care to do while there?"

"I had not considered it," Ella answered, a frown crossing her face.

"Oh, please do consider it," I said. "I am certain you shall have free time to attend to anything that may interest you."

Ella remained silent a moment before saying, "If it is not too much, could I take some time to visit my mother?"

"Of course, Sinclair!" I responded. "I plan to visit with Tilly the day after we arrive. Would that time suit for your visit?"

"I am certain it would, Your Grace."

"Excellent. Please take the day then."

"I shall leave after you've dressed for the morning and return before dinner, Your Grace."

"Now it is my turn to wish you a successful visit," I answered with a smile. My gaze fell upon the singing box Robert gifted me the day before. A smile formed on my lips. "Have you seen this trinket box from Duke Blackmoore?"

"No, Your Grace. Is it new?"

"Yes!" I exclaimed. "A belated birthday gift. Come and see." Ella joined me and I pressed the knob, triggering the singing bird. He popped from his hiding spot, his little wings flapping and beak snapping open and closed. His tiny song filled the room.

The mechanism startled Ella, who recoiled before bringing her face closer to the object. Her jaw dropped open as she studied the box. "I have never witnessed anything like it, Your Grace!" she exclaimed.

"Neither have I until yesterday. Isn't it a fascinating piece?" I smiled at it as the bird finished his song.

"It is," Ella agreed. "You seem to be quite taken with it."

"I am," I confessed, setting it on my night table and admiring it. "I never believed something material could be so intriguing, yet I cannot take my eyes from this stunner."

"It is certainly a marvel," Ella concurred.

I smiled at the object a moment more. My brow crinkled for a moment and I glanced around the room. "Have you seen my book? The one I was reading last evening."

Ella ceased packing for a moment before she responded. "Yes. Downstairs in the sitting room."

"Ah, yes. You are correct," I answered, recalling it now. "After dinner, I read in the sitting room with Robert. I left it there. How careless of me. Thank you, Sinclair."

"Would you like me to retrieve it for you, Your Grace?"

"No, thank you, Sinclair. I shall retrieve it. Is there anything further on the packing?"

"No, Your Grace. I am finishing up the last pieces now and you shall be all ready!"

"Wonderful. Thank you, Sinclair. If everything is taken care of, I shall be reading in my tower room."

I left Sinclair finalizing the luggage and traversed the halls to the main foyer. As I descended the stairs, I caught sight of Annie at the sitting room doors. One door stood ajar, and she peered into the room. I reached the foyer floor and began to cross toward her. Before I reached her, she swung around, a pained expression on her face. I opened my mouth to inquire about it when she fled across the foyer, disappearing down the hall.

My gaze followed her, and I wondered about the incident. Should I follow her, I pondered? She moved too quickly for me to catch up, I concluded. I would retrieve my book as planned and hope she sought me out later. I pushed through the open door, searching the seats near the fireplace. There, on one of the side tables, sat my book.

I started across the room toward it when a figure stood from the chair Robert generally filled in the evenings. "Oh!" I exclaimed, startled by his presence. "I am sorry. I did not realize anyone was here."

He swallowed a mouthful of scotch. "Hello, Duchess," Edwin answered, acid in his voice.

"Mr. Fletcher," I responded, my posture stiffening. "I was retrieving my book. I shall only be a moment." I continued toward the book.

"Oh, please, do not let me stop you!" he exclaimed, his voice thick with sarcasm. "It is, after all, YOUR castle, Duchess."

I sighed, closing my eyes for a moment. I snapped them open and focused on Edwin. After a deep breath, I began, "Mr. Fletcher..."

"Oh, please, Duchess!" he said, waving his hand in the air to stop me. "Call me Edwin. We are, after all, family."

I grew weary of his derision, but I continued. "Edwin," I began again, "I believe we got off on the wrong foot. Perhaps we should try to begin anew and work toward a better result."

"Work toward a better result?" he questioned, as though rhetorically. He placed a pondering finger against his chin in a satiric display of reflection. "What a clever idea!" he said at long last. "Clearly it is your brains that prompted my brother to wed you." He stalked to the drink cart, pouring himself another scotch.

"There is no reason for us to quarrel," I responded. "I do not wish you any ill tidings."

"Oh, how magnanimous of you! No, you only mean to steal my inheritance."

"I have nothing to do with that affair," I informed him.

"Don't you, Duchess? As it stood, upon Robert's death, this property would transfer to me. With your recent nuptials, that is now questionable. So, I would estimate it has a great deal to do with you!"

"The property is a matter to be settled between you and Robert. It does not concern me. And I do not concern myself with it. Do not accuse me of causing a problem that is of your own making."

"Do not deceive me, Duchess. You cannot expect me to believe you do not whisper your plans into my brother's ear... and you do not use your..." He paused, gazing down at my body before continuing, "virtues to secure the result you desire."

My jaw dropped open at such a statement. I gathered my thoughts to respond, but a new voice joined the conversation, silencing me. "If you plan to speak to my wife in this manner, Edwin, I will bar you from this property."

Edwin offered me a wry glance, as though he'd caught me in something. "It seems your plan is working, Duchess. Soon, I shall not even be permitted to visit my family home."

"That will be of your own doing, Edwin, not hers," Robert responded. He glanced at me as he approached. "Were you using the room, dear?"

"No," I answered. "I only came to retrieve my book." I picked it up off the table.

Robert smiled at me. "Then would you mind leaving us to discuss some business?"

"Not at all," I replied. Robert kissed my forehead, and I strode away. Before pulling the doors closed, I said, "Good day, Mr. Fletcher."

His eyes narrowed at me as I pulled the doors shut. I did not linger at the door to overhear the conversation. Instead, I made my way to my tower room. As I settled into the window seat, my mind replayed the conversation with Edwin. I should likely never win him over, I concluded.

I focused on my book when another thought sprung into

my brain. What was Annie doing at the door when I descended the stairs? Was she curious? Did she miss Edwin? Perhaps he had been a bigger fan of Robert's first wife than me.

I set the book down, pondering the questions again. Perhaps if I could find Annie, I could ask her. I rose from my seat and traversed the halls to the other tower room. Remaining outside, I leaned in and called to her. I received no response. I waited a few moments, but she did not appear. I checked a few other areas, including my bedroom suite, however I could not find her. The mystery should have to wait until I returned from Glasgow, I determined as I headed back to my tower room.

* * *

Fog still clung to the moors the next morning as we climbed into the carriage for our journey to Glasgow. Romantic or not, Ella's assessment of the bone-chilling properties of the mist was accurate. I bundled tighter against it before suggesting Ella ride inside the carriage, fearing she may catch cold in the dampness outside. Robert agreed and situated her next to me inside the carriage for the ride.

I offered one of the books I had brought for the trip to Ella, which she gratefully accepted to pass the hours. We arrived in the late afternoon. After settling in and a brief rest, dinner was already upon us.

"Will you visit with your acquaintance?" Robert asked me as we dined.

"Yes. I hope to!"

"Hope to? Have you written her about our trip?"

"Yes," I replied. "Though I have not received a reply."

"Perhaps she has moved," Robert suggested.

"Perhaps," I answered, hoping she had. "Though she is

undoubtedly busy and perhaps it slipped her mind. At any rate, I shall attempt to call upon her tomorrow where she last resided."

"Will Sinclair accompany you?"

"No. Sinclair has plans to visit her mother."

Robert frowned. "Oh. I had hoped she would accompany you to visit, eh, Tilly, was it? Perhaps she can postpone the visit."

"Yes, Tilly," I confirmed. "I have no need of a chaperone. I have already given Sinclair permission to visit during the day. I will not renege on it."

Robert continued to frown. "Well…"

"I shall be fine," I assured him, patting his hand.

"You had better be," he answered with a smile. "My business should conclude shortly after lunch. I thought we may take a stroll in the park 'round the corner together. Are you keen on it?"

"Yes, it sounds very pleasant," I agreed.

"Excellent. Shall we meet at the entrance at, say, quarter to two? Will that give enough time for your visit?"

"Yes. Quarter to two will give me plenty of time."

"Wonderful. I shall look most forward to sharing the afternoon with you."

CHAPTER 15

When I retired for the evening, I laid awake in my bed. The last time I had been in Glasgow, I had laid awake as well. Worry for Tilly had consumed me then, as it did now. Worry over what, I did not understand. Perhaps anxiety crept over me at the prospect of Tilly's predicament. Becoming an unwed mother set both mother and child at a severe disadvantage. What would become of Tilly? Of the child? Would the child become another unwanted orphan being cared for by a callous caregiver? No, Tilly would not desert her child, I affirmed in my mind. Though what if circumstances warranted no other choice? My mind whirled and nothing I did could quiet it.

In an attempt to push the vexing thoughts from my mind, I considered my home. I recalled my tower room with its small library shelf. The comfortable chaise lounge, the cozy window seat, the small singing box I had left on my table there. All awaited my return. My mind turned to another awaiting me: Annie. I pondered over our last encounter. Why had she been hovering at the sitting room doors?

I fell asleep in the wee hours of the morning and was

awakened by Sinclair as she entered the room. "Apologies, Your Grace," she said as I stifled a yawn and stretched. "I did not mean to wake you."

"No apology is required," I assured her as she helped me with my dressing gown. "I confess I did not sleep well and slept later into the morning than I intended."

"Perhaps you should return to bed and rest," Ella suggested.

"No, I am quite well and prefer to pay my call as planned."

Ella nodded and helped me dress for the day. After breakfast, she set out on foot to visit her mother. I offered a carriage ride to her, though she assured me the walk on the bright spring day would be pleasant and not overwhelming.

Later in the morning, I embarked on my own journey to Tilly's brothel. As I navigated the streets, a knot grew in my stomach. I found my pace quickening with each step. Anxious to put my mind at ease, I dashed through the streets until I arrived in the less-than-desirable area of town. I approached Tilly's street and hastened to her building. The dilapidated stone façade seemed more somber to me somehow.

I hurried up the few crumbling stone stairs to the door and knocked. No one answered. I knocked again and waited, my foot tapping on the gray stone beneath me. Still nothing. Had the brothel closed, I wondered? I chuckled at the absurdity of that notion. Brothels did not often close.

I stepped back, glancing into the windows, searching for any signs of life. Lamps burned inside, confirming the presence of people within the building. I stepped back up to the landing and pounded on the door.

It appeared the third time was, in fact, the charm! The door opened a crack, and a face peered out. "What do you want?" she demanded.

I was taken aback but proceeded with my request. "I am here to visit with Tilly Anderson," I announced, struggling to see through the tiny crack in the door.

"She ain't here, go away," the girl responded. She shut the door. I pounded against it again. "I said go away," the girl repeated after opening the door a crack.

I pushed against the door, shoving it open further. "No," I insisted. "I demand to see Tilly." My trepidation about Tilly grew with each passing moment.

The girl seemed shocked at my determination. She fell back a few steps, and I pushed inside the building. She gaped around the room for a few moments as though uncertain how to proceed next.

Another woman appeared at the top of the stairs. She sniffled, wiping at her face. She glanced at me, then at the girl.

"What is this?" she asked.

"This… lady," the girl said, eyeing me, "pushed her way in here demanding to see Tilly."

The girl seemed to shudder at the statement. She swallowed hard, staring at me. "Yes," I confirmed. "I would like to see Tilly Anderson. Now, please. If you give my name, she will know it. We are friends."

"Friends?" the redhead at the stair's top squeaked.

"Yes," I repeated. "Friends." The two women shared another glance. "What is going on here?" I demanded.

"I think you'd better come at once, Miss… eh," the woman paused.

"Mrs. Fletcher," I finished for her. "Lead the way."

I skirted the rude girl and ascended the steps. As I approached the other woman, I noted her blotchy skin and red nose. She had been crying. My stomach turned over, though I assured myself a crying prostitute was likely not uncommon.

She led me up the remaining stairs and down the hall to a closed door. She glanced to me before opening it and proceeded inside. The distinct sound of sobbing filled the air as I rounded the bend into the room. Several women stood inside, a few crying, one wringing her hands.

My brow crinkled as I witnessed the scene. I scanned the room, searching for the reason behind their sorrow. The women who had summoned me to the room touched the shoulder of another and whispered something into her ear. The girl who stood in front of a bed, glanced over her shoulder at me then backed away. Only then could I comprehend their upset.

I gasped and tears filled my eyes as a sob shuddered through my body. On the bed lay Tilly's body, lifeless. Pale as the sheet she lay on, her open eyes stared upward, though saw nothing. Her colorless cheeks were slack, and her jaw hung open. One woman held Tilly's hand, sobbing over her, though it no longer mattered. She was gone.

"Tilly!" I cried as tears rolled down my cheeks. "No!" I rushed to the bed, placing my palm on her cold cheek. I collapsed onto the bed next to her body as another sob escaped me. After a moment, I closed her eyes and pushed a lock of hair from her face. "What happened?" I whispered.

No response came. I glanced around at the others, waiting for an answer. The woman who brought me to Tilly spoke. "She…" The woman paused, steadying herself as another wrapped an arm around her shoulder. After a sniffle, she proceeded again. "She had her baby this morning. But then she started bleeding. Lots of blood. And it didn't stop. Just kept coming." The woman choked on the words, sobbing with each sentence.

"Aye," a blonde woman added. "We tried to help her, even pooled some money to call for a doctor, but…" Her voice trailed off.

"She died before he got here," the rude girl who had followed us upstairs finished.

I glanced back to Tilly's exanimate form. Only now did I notice the faint traces of blood on the sheet that covered her body. Poor Tilly. Always so full of life, so exuberant, now cold and quiet. Another tear rolled down my cheek.

My thoughts were frazzled but one constant centered itself in my mind. I stood and faced the other women. "What of the child?" I questioned.

They gaped at each other, none certain how to answer. "Is it also…" My voice faded away, unable to finish the sentence.

"No," the blonde spoke up. "She delivered a healthy baby boy before…"

"Where is he? May I see him?"

The blonde nodded to the rude girl who disappeared into the hallway. She returned in moments carrying a small, swaddled figure. The tiny newborn mewled in her arms as he slept.

The girl handed him to me, and I stared down at his tiny face. He was wrapped in a stained white sheet. His coverings contrary to the child himself. Porcelain skin and pink cheeks like his mother's, I noted. And their mouths, identical. I wondered if he possessed her sparkling blue eyes. The only difference was the crown of dark hair on his head, the antithesis of Tilly's flaxen tresses.

He fussed, huffing and whimpering. "Shh," I offered. "There, there." I jostled him a bit to soothe him back to sleep. "Has the father been informed?" I asked, my eyes remaining on the child.

I glanced up sharply when I received no response. The redhead shook her head, sighing.

"There is no father," offered the blonde. My brow furrowed at her statement.

The redhead clarified it. "She don't mean that literal. But

we don't have no idea who he is. With our… profession… it's impossible to tell."

"Tilly seemed to know," I argued. "Did she not confide in any of you his identity? She seemed to believe he wanted the child."

A chuckle emanated from the rude girl. It turned into an uncontrollable laugh. Several of the women hushed her, but she continued to snicker. My brow furrowed further, and a frown crossed my lips. "That'd be Tilly, all right," she answered, calming herself after noting my expression. "She always insisted someone would be back for her." The girl rolled her eyes and met my gaze. "There weren't no father, no marriage proposal, no man wanting that baby. She dreamed it all up. Told herself that bedtime story to get through it, she did. There weren't no truth to it."

I glanced around the room and was met by a few nods. Rude as she may be, the girl was correct and most of the others acknowledged and confirmed her take on the unfortunate situation.

I looked down at the child in my arms. It was as I suspected. Tilly's dreams of marriage and family were only that: dreams. Poor child, I contemplated. What would become of him? Questions swirled in my mind as I struggled to process the events.

I gathered my thoughts before speaking again. I glanced up at the women. "What…" My voice trailed off. I stared into the room's corner. A blue-eyed, pink-cheeked, flaxen haired woman stared back. Tilly. My heart broke for her. It took all my strength not to weep again in that moment.

She approached me, glancing down at the child in my arms. She placed her hand on his head, her thumb stroking his tiny forehead. Tilly glanced up at me, tears filling her eyes. I offered her a sympathetic look.

"Please, Lenora," she said, sobs filling her voice. "Take him."

My expression changed to one of bewilderment. I glanced to the baby then back to Tilly. "Please, Lenora," she repeated. "Take him. Minnie is correct. He has no father. They cannot and will not care for him here. He will be left on the stairs of the nearest orphanage. He will grow up a street urchin. Please, I beg of you to take him."

My mind whirled. I could not take this child. I swallowed hard as I considered my next move. Tilly's assessment was correct. The child would be dumped at the nearest location. A terrible fate for a baby. I knew all too well the life he would lead. Yet, what could I do? Perhaps I could see to an appropriate adoption. Something better than an orphanage could arrange. Yes, perhaps...

My musings were broken by a touch on my arm. The redhead approached, gently pulling me back to reality. "Are you all right, Mrs. Fletcher?" she said softly.

Before I could answer the door burst open again. A rotund woman with a heavily painted face and a sour countenance stormed in. "All right, girls, enough is enough! Dry your eyes and put on a stiff upper lip," she announced. She swatted at one of the girls' bottoms. "We've got a mess to clean up before business starts in a few hours. Come on, come on! Much to do, we've..." Her voice trailed off as her gaze fell on me.

"And who are you?" she inquired.

"Mrs. Flet..." the redhead began, but I interrupted her.

"Lenora Fletcher. Duchess of Blackmoore."

I received several odd glances and a few gasps after announcing my position. "Duchess, is it?" the woman inquired. "If you are seeking your husband, he ain't here. We're closed. Or if you are looking to make trouble with one of my girls over the services she provided him, I will have to insist you leave. I don't permit nobody to harass my girls over the pleasures her husband has received."

"No," I explained with a shake of my head. "I am not seeking my husband nor to quarrel with anyone over any... services. I came to visit my friend, Tilly." I nodded to the body. "Though it appears I am too late."

"Oh," the woman said, her countenance softening a tad. She eyed me holding the child, then raised her eyebrows. "Will you be claiming the child then? As her closest next of kin?"

"I..."

"No! We don't know her from Eve," another woman objected. "We cannot just give Tilly's child to her!"

The plump woman raised her eyebrows further, setting her hands on her hips and staring at the girl. "This is a place of business!" she roared. "Not a nursery! We cannot raise a child here! Do you plan on tending to the infant with one hand while you hike your skirt with the other? If she don't take the child, it goes on the doorstep of the nearest orphanage."

I fluttered my eyelashes, focusing my attention on the child rather than the vulgar discussion.

The woman lowered her eyes, objecting no further. The madam turned her gaze to me. "Well?" she demanded. "If you are taking the child, let's get on with it. We have a business to run."

Tilly still stood in front of me. Her fingers stroking her baby's cheek. I glanced to her, then to the child. I met the madam's gaze. "Yes," I answered. "I am taking the child."

"Well, get on with it then. You can take the sheet if you ain't got another covering to wrap him in. And you girls get this mess cleaned up. No one wants a dead body staring at them while seeking the pleasures of a woman." The woman turned on her heel and removed herself from our company, slamming the door shut behind her.

"All right, girls, you heard Madame Blanche, the time for grieving is over," the blonde said, taking charge of the room.

The redhead busied herself at one of the dressers, searching the top drawer. After a moment, she pulled a light blue scarf from it. She approached me and offered it to me. "Here," she said. "This was Tilly's. She loved it, said the color was the most beautiful she'd ever seen. Take it to wrap the baby in."

I smiled at her, setting the child on the bed next to his deceased mother and using the scarf to secure the soiled sheet around him. Before I retrieved him, I dug in my purse and produced a few coins. "Please see that Tilly is buried properly," I requested of the redheaded woman. "I would do it myself, but I shall only be in town one more night."

She took the coins and nodded. I gathered the sleeping newborn into my arms. "Please make sure he is looked after well," the redhead pleaded, tears filling her eyes.

"I will. I shall write when he is settled to inform you of his whereabouts." I glanced across the room. Tilly now stood in the corner near the door. I approached her, but before I reached her, the rude girl stepped between us.

I braced myself for another bout of rude behavior. The girl reached to the child, caressing his cheek. A tear rolled down her cheek, and she quickly wiped it away. "Tilly stashed away a few nappies for him beforehand. Here." She handed me a small package, wrapped in a sheet.

"Thank you," I answered softly.

"Goodbye, little one," she replied, her gaze focused on the child.

I offered her a tender smile before I continued toward the door and Tilly. Tilly's eyes brimmed with tears, but she smiled at me. I nodded to acknowledge her emotions. She disappeared behind the door as the blonde swung it open for me.

I passed through and descended the stairs and crossed the foyer, stepping into the street. Only then did I take a moment to myself. I leaned against the doorjamb as I collected the thoughts whirling through my mind.

The tiny babe in my arms gave a soft grunt, wiggling and flailing his arms before settling back to sleep. I was no stranger to childcare, having tended several babies during my time at St. Mary's. However, my concern stemmed not from caring for the babe, but rather from explaining his presence. Still, the deed had been done. I had accepted the responsibility of placing the child. I would do my best to explain the situation to Robert and hope he could accept the temporary disruption to our lives. With any luck, I mused, Mr. Langford could place the child tonight.

I convinced myself all would turn out well as I descended the stairs leading to the brothel. I glanced up to the sunny sky, glad for a bright, warm spring day. I worried the child may catch a chill had the weather been damp.

As I began down the street, a clock tower chimed. Already half-past one, I realized. With a sigh, I hurried through the streets. Even at this frenzied pace, I would be late to meet Robert. The entire somber business at the brothel had taken longer than I'd expected. I used the time to practice what I might say to my husband. Explaining the sudden presence of a newborn may prove complex.

Our hotel came into sight and I hastened toward it. I rounded the corner, spotting Robert checking his pocket watch as he stood near the gates to the park. A sigh escaped my lips and my heart thudded in my chest as I crossed the street to the park.

As I approached him, he caught sight of me. His eyes widened and his brow furrowed in confusion. "I apologize," I puffed, winded from my hasty excursion through Glasgow's streets. "I was unexpectedly detained."

His eyebrows raised as he continued to stare at the babe in my arms. "Clearly."

"I can explain," I added.

"I hope so," Robert exclaimed, "as this is a most unexpected turn of events!"

The baby mewled, fussing as he wiggled in my arms. "May we walk as I explain?" I requested. "It may calm the child."

Robert motioned for me to proceed him into the park and I followed the path, taking a leisurely pace. Robert remained silent as we strode along. I waited a few moments before proceeding, unsure where to begin. "I am not certain where to begin," I confessed. "Though I shall try to make sense of this. Please know that I am most regretful of the inconvenience and beg your understanding in the matter." My words came in a breathless, clipped manner as I fretfully attempted to gain Robert's compassion. If I'd had use of my hands, I am certain I would have wrung them, though they remained clutching the child to my bosom.

Robert waved his hand at me. "Calm yourself, Lenora. I am not angry, only curious. Tell me what's happened."

Robert's understanding astounded me. I hoped his calm, measured manner persisted throughout my wild tale. I nodded, taking a breath before relaying the story. "It is Tilly," I said. "Oh, I am afraid I haven't been entirely honest with you. You see, Tilly… she left the orphanage to strike out on her own. It did not turn out at all as she expected. And… she fell into a rather bad way. I had hoped to liberate her from her circumstances by taking her on as my ladies' maid. But when I called on her to make the offer, I found her… unable to accept. She found herself in the family way. Only…" I struggled to make clear the more disgraceful details.

Robert nodded his head as I labored to explain. He raised his hand, ceasing my stuttering. "I understand. Presumably this sort of thing happens quite often in her profession."

I stared at Robert, aghast. "You..."

"Yes, I realized after our first conversation about her. You carefully danced around the details. It seemed obvious to me what you were attempting to hide. Of course, there was no need to dwell on such a vulgar topic, so I did not."

"You said nothing to betray your understanding to me," I mused aloud.

"It seemed important to you to protect the girl's reputation, so I said nothing." How kind, I reflected. "So, she has had her baby, I presume."

My mind snapped back to the matter at hand. "Yes," I said, glancing to the child.

"And she has asked you to care for it?" Robert queried.

"More or less," I replied.

Robert glanced to me and I ceased my walking. I faced him and explained further. "Tilly died this morning, shortly after birthing the child. I arrived too late. She was already passed. But... given my ability..." I paused, pushing back the tears that threatened to spill onto my cheeks.

Robert's expression softened, and he put his hand on my arm. I pulled myself together and pressed on. "She asked me to take the child. I could not deny her that request. Given Tilly's death, the boy was to be left on the nearest orphanage's doorstep. She begged me to provide him with better. I could not bring myself to refuse her. I grew up in an orphanage! I realized the life he would lead there. So, I took the child. I thought..." I paused again, glancing around the park as I searched for the strength to finish. "I thought we could find a placement for him. I realize the disturbance taking the child will cause, but it will only be temporary. I shall do the work myself to find the placement. And I shall care for any of his needs myself. I am accustomed to infants. I cared for several at St. Mary's. I promise it shall be no trouble to you. Though I understand if you object. If you do, please say it and I shall rectify my mistake at once." I babbled on, my voice growing frantic with upset. The child awoke in my arms during my frenzied speech and began to whimper. The whimper soon turned into a forlorn wail.

Robert took my shoulders in his hands. "Lenora, Lenora, stop, please." I ceased my chattering and stared at him, awaiting his decision. "You have worked yourself into a quite a state. And your upset has disturbed the poor child." I did my best to hush the baby, rocking him gently in my arms and shushing him. "Calm yourself, Lenora. I am not angry with you."

"You are most understanding, Robert," I answered, grateful for his kind and tolerant nature. "And I shall place him with the utmost haste."

He smiled at me, then at the child. His gaze lingered until I spoke up again. "I promise," I added.

His smile persisted, and I wondered what he found so amusing. "As far as I am concerned, the child has already found an excellent placement with a loving mother."

My brow furrowed in confusion. He could not mean... "Robert!" I exclaimed before my mind finished my thought.

"Am I mistaken?" Robert questioned. "Do you prefer not to keep the child?"

I remained silent for a moment. "I had not considered the matter," I admitted. "I acted in haste at the brothel with no plan."

"And have you considered it now?"

The crinkle in my brow deepened, the concept still incredible to me. "I am not certain what to say. I... Are you suggesting..."

"I am suggesting that we take the child in. Tilly wished

you to provide a good life for the boy. What better life than that of a Duke and Duchess' son? Unless you object to raising the boy, I cannot fathom a better solution."

I stood speechless. I had expected to receive, at best, a tongue-lashing about my lack of judiciousness and impulsivity. Instead, my husband welcomed the child into our home permanently. He provided a mechanism by which I could fulfill Tilly's final wish.

Tears sprang to my eyes. "I am speechless," I managed to breathe out. I struggled to compose myself.

"I hope these are tears of joy," Robert prodded.

"Yes," I replied, smiling at him. "Yes!" I wrapped one of my arms around his neck and kissed him on the cheek. "Thank you! Tilly would be most pleased." I bit my lower lip, staring down at the precious babe swaddled in her scarf.

"Oh!" Robert exclaimed, surprised by my reaction. "You are most welcome." He grinned at me. "He is a handsome little chap. I shall be proud to call him my son."

"Shall we finish our walk?" I asked after a breath.

"Yes. Unless you deem it to too chilly for the child. Or you are too weary to carry him."

"Too weary?!" I exclaimed. "I feel as though I am walking on air. You relieved a great burden from me, Robert!"

We continued down the path. "Is there a need to make arrangements for a burial?" Robert inquired.

"No. Given our departure tomorrow morning, I left a sum with one of the girls at the brothel and instructed her to provide a proper burial."

"Hmm," Robert murmured. "We could delay our departure and see to the services ourselves. If you prefer to attend for your friend."

I considered it. The paltry services the few shillings I'd contributed could afford would be a shabby send off, indeed. Plus, I wished to attend. I wished for Tilly's child to attend. "I should like to attend, yes. But not if it is too much trouble to modify our travel arrangements."

"Not at all!" Robert responded. "I shall see to it at once."

I nodded. "I shall visit the brothel to make arrangements for her body to be…"

"No, you shall not," Robert said, interrupting me. "I shall handle the matter. You shall attend to the important duty of seeing to our son's wellbeing."

Robert made a solid point. Someone must attend to the child. Though I could take him with me. "I…" I began.

"I do not wish to see you go into that dangerous part of town again, anyway. The matter is closed. Give me the address and I shall make all the arrangements."

I agreed, providing him with the information. We looped around, returning toward the hotel. Our conversation turned to discussing plans for our family's new addition. Mr. Langford would be tasked with drawing up the adoption papers, an assignment I was certain would shock him when he learned of it this afternoon. He would also assist in hiring the necessary caregivers for the child.

We reached the hotel, and I took the baby straight to our suite. Robert arranged for milk to be sent to feed the child, now fussing and likely hungry. I sat rocking the baby in my arms awaiting the arrival of his meal and Robert's return.

The door swung open, and Robert and Henry Langford entered. Robert glanced to me, holding the whimpering babe then around the room. "No milk as yet?"

"No," I confirmed.

"Where the devil have they gone for it? To the fields to milk the damn cow themselves?"

"I am certain it will arrive at any moment."

"I shall find out. The poor child is wailing with hunger!" Robert stepped into the hallway, only to return in seconds. "He is on his way now."

The man arrived with milk and a spoon as requested though Robert still groused at him about being late. I set straight to feeding the child as Henry admired him over my shoulder.

"Congratulations, Duke," he murmured, gazing at the child. "He is a handsome child."

"Quite," Robert agreed, his chest puffed. "He shall grow into a fine, strong man. He grasped my finger earlier whilst we walked in the park. His strength is impressive."

"And little mother seems to be like a duck to water with his care," Henry said, noting my ease with feeding the child.

"I have nursed many a babe at St. Mary's. They can prove finicky at the start, but with some perseverance, the task can be managed."

"We must arrange for the doctor to see him at once when we return home. And, of course, there is his christening to be seen to," Robert mentioned. "Henry has agreed to handle all the necessary paperwork. Oh, we shall need to name him! Have you any ideas, Lenora?" He checked his pocket watch. "If you have, give it to Henry for the paperwork. I should be off to make arrangements for Tilly's burial. Unless I am needed?"

I smiled at Robert. "No, dear, you may go. I shall finish feeding him and settle him for another nap."

Robert kissed my forehead and rubbed the baby's cheek before departing.

Henry poured himself a drink from the sitting area's bar. "Quite a surprising day," he noted as he sat across from me near the fireplace. "How tragic to have lost your friend, but how extraordinary to have gained a son."

"Indeed," I agreed. "Poor Tilly. I never suspected when I saw her only two months ago it would be our last meeting."

"She would be pleased you are caring for her child, I am sure," Henry said.

"Yes," I confirmed. "And I am pleased to do it. Though surprised. Robert suggested it. I had thought to place him for adoption. Robert's kindness flabbergasts me at times."

"You expect him to be disagreeable?" Henry inquired.

"No. Though I do not often expect him to be as agreeable as he always proves. It is quite something for a man to agree to raise another's child."

"Couples adopt often."

"Yes, couples who desire a child, who have planned for a child."

"Robert has always desired a family. You have provided him with one, whether or not you intended to."

"I hope it brings him happiness."

"It will," Henry assured me. "Have you given the child's name any thought? No rush, though I would like to begin the paperwork posthaste."

I gazed down at the child in my arms. "Yes," I said with a smile. "Yes, I have a name."

CHAPTER 16

I stared down at the sleeping baby next to me on the bed. His soft rhythmic breathing soothed me. After his feeding, he had gone to sleep shortly after a bit of rocking. With no bassinet, I laid him on the bed for a nap. Here he had slept for over an hour. I was content to read my book as he napped.

The outer door to our suite opened and shut. I assumed it signaled Robert's return. Not wishing to disturb the child, I remained on the bed. A light knock sounded at the door. "Come in!" I called just above a whisper.

The door opened a crack and Ella stuck her head inside. "I hope I am not disturbing you, Your Grace, but I wanted to inform you of my return."

"Oh, Sinclair! Welcome back! Come in. How was your visit with your mother?"

Sinclair slipped in the door, closing it behind her. "It went very well, Your Grace. Thank you for asking. Mother wished me to pass along her gratitude for allowing me the day off to visit. We …" Her voice trailed off mid-sentence. An odd expression crossed her face. Her mouth gaped open as she stared wide-eyed at the bed. "Is that a…" Her voice dropped off again as she motioned toward the baby.

"A baby, yes," I confirmed. "We have had some… developments on our end." I motioned for her to approach the bed.

Ella neared the bed. "Meet the newest Fletcher," I said.

"He is a beautiful child," she answered. "But…how?"

I patted the bed, encouraging her to sit. "It is rather a long, scandalous tale, but I shall explain."

"Oh, not if you do not wish to, Your Grace," Ella replied.

"I do not mind. I am only forewarning you, so you are not shocked by some of the more salacious details."

I explained to her about Tilly's circumstances, beginning with her departure from the orphanage to her untimely end. "I could not leave the child behind," I expounded. "I took him with the intention of finding a placement for him. It stunned me when Duke Blackmoore suggested we adopt him. Though I confess I am thrilled."

Ella smiled at me, grasping my hand in hers. "I cannot imagine better parents for the child. I am certain your classmate would be elated by the prospect."

I returned her smile, squeezing her hand. "Thank you."

"May I hold him?"

"Of course!" I exclaimed.

Ella scooped him up into her arms. The baby cooed, stretching his tiny arms before settling back into sleep. "What a precious child," she breathed. "What will you name him?"

I rubbed his cheek. "If you do not mind, I should like to discuss it with Duke Blackmoore first before I reveal the name. I have told Mr. Langford, only so that he may begin the paperwork for his adoption."

"Of course, Your Grace."

Ella patted the baby's bottom gently as she held him. I gazed over her shoulder, smiling down at the tiny form.

"Duke Blackmoore has gone to make arrangements for Tilly's funeral," I explained. "We shall have to delay our return to the castle until after she has been laid to rest."

"I am terribly sorry for your loss, Your Grace. I hope the funeral is not too trying for you. If you would prefer, I can care for the child while you attend."

"Thank you, Sinclair. Though if the weather holds out, I would like to take him. Perhaps you could attend as well. Then if the child becomes too fussy, you could assist with his care?"

"I should be most happy to, Your Grace," Ella agreed as she smiled down at the child. "He is a darling boy."

"I am quite smitten with him myself," I admitted with a chuckle.

"What an excellent mother you shall make, Your Grace," Ella said.

I smiled at the compliment. It would mark the first time I would tend an infant I was not expected to give away at a moment's notice. My previous experience at the orphanage prepared me well for the moment, though it wounded my heart on several occasions to hand a child I had cared for over to another.

As I gazed down at my child, I recalled the most recent of these incidents. Eighteen months before my departure from the orphanage, a newborn baby girl was left on our front steps. One of the teachers discovered the wailing child on her way into the building. The poor baby, stuffed in a basket without a stitch of clothing on, came with a simple note: *Please take care of her, I cannot.*

Newborn children require a great deal of care. The novelty of baby care wore off most girls after the first sleepless night. The baby, colicky from start, wailed most of the night. Tilly and I took turns walking the halls to soothe the child. In the wee hours of the morning, Tilly nodded off. I hadn't the heart to awaken her. Instead, I allowed her to sleep and cared for the child myself.

The baby nodded off as light broke over the horizon. I managed an hour's sleep before Tilly roused me to rise for the day, not wanting me to be disciplined for laziness.

After that night, the baby's care was left primarily to me with Tilly to assist. We spent six months taking care of the child who we named Bessie, short for Elizabeth. Without the ability to afford a wet nurse or formula, we used cow's milk and a spoon to nurse babies. On occasion we used dippy bread when milk was in short supply. But whenever I could manage it, I used animal milk, even if I had to forego my portion for the child.

One Sunday morning, Tilly and I set to feeding Bessie as we tidied the kitchen area. Tilly held the child in her arms, spoon feeding her milk as I wiped the counters. "One day we shall nurse our own children, Lenora," Tilly gushed.

I smiled at her. Tilly was a dreamer; I, a realist. We often possessed different opinions on what the future held for girls of our kind.

"Oh, do not give me that look," Tilly chided.

"What?"

"That knowing glance. I fully intend to have my own family one day, Lenora. Wait and see! I shall have six children and a loving husband!"

"My, my, such plans," I joked.

Tilly grimaced at me before bursting into a giggle. "You wait and see. I shall grab the world by the tail one day!"

"I hope you do, Tilly!"

Tilly did not respond. I finished wiping the last counter and washed the rag in the sink. I wrung it dry and turned to face her. Tilly stared into space, a silly grin on her face. Daydreaming about her future escapades had taken over her mind completely.

"Tilly!" I exclaimed, rushing over to her. "Stop daydreaming and pay attention! You've spilled the milk all over Bessie!"

Tilly snapped back to reality, glancing at the baby. "Oh!" she cried, spotting the stream of milk now dripping from Bessie's chin. I wiped the child clean and Tilly handed her over to me. "Perhaps you should finish. Golly, I hope I am better at feeding my own children."

"I am certain you will be," I assured her, relieving her of the baby and taking her place as she stood. I spooned more milk into the child's mouth.

Tilly stared at me from across the room. "Did you finish with the counters?"

I nodded. "Yes. Just the sink needs wiped."

I fed Bessie three more spoonfuls of milk before I set her against my shoulder to burp her. As I set to patting Bessie's back, I found Tilly still staring at me. "What is it?" I asked.

"You are so very good with her."

"She is not the first baby we have cared for here," I answered.

Tilly shook her head. "No. You are special, Lenora. You will make a wonderful mother one day." I did not answer, instead returning to feeding Bessie. Tilly set to her work, cleaning the sink. "You should not take such a negative view. You do not know what the future may hold!"

"Oh, to have your optimism, Matilda Anderson!" I exclaimed.

Tilly giggled and grinned at me. When we finished with our chores and Bessie's feeding, I changed then dressed her. I sat with her on the floor of our bedroom, reading to her. Tilly worked on a composition assignment, promising to relieve me soon so I may finish my work before classes tomorrow.

Footsteps sounded on the stairs, continuing down the

hall toward our bedroom. Headmistress Williamson appeared in the doorway. She glanced in at us, her face set into its usual frown. "Lenora," she snapped. "Clean up the child and prepare her to be seen by prospective parents. Bring her down as soon as you have finished. Do not delay."

"Yes, headmistress," I responded, a lump forming in my throat. Headmistress Williamson spun on a heel and disappeared from my sight.

"Perhaps they will reject her," Tilly offered.

I clung to Tilly's optimism with every fiber of my being, though a piece of my mind warned me to prepare for the inevitable. Babies were not often rejected by prospective parents. It was a marvel the child had gone this long without being claimed.

I closed the book and made sure Bessie was presentable. I fixed her dress, ensured her face was clean, and that she did not need her nappy changed. Satisfied, I carried her downstairs with Tilly following me.

A man and woman stood with Headmistress Williamson in the foyer. I slowed as I reached the bottom of the stairs.

"Ah, here is the child now," Headmistress Williams announced. She pulled the baby from my arms, offering her to the woman. "As you can see, the child is quite healthy. She sleeps through the night without trouble. She is a pleasant little darling, very alert yet never demanding or fussy."

I held back rolling my eyes. Headmistress Williamson rarely bothered herself with the child's care. She gave the same speech with every child, having no idea of any of their temperaments.

The woman accepted Bessie from her. "Oh, Charles," she breathed, turning to the man, "isn't she beautiful?"

"Mmm," the man murmured. "And she has no known diseases?" he asked Headmistress Williamson.

"None at all!" Headmistress Williamson assured him. "Healthy as can be!"

The woman rubbed her cheek. "Hello there, darling. Would you like to come home with us?" she asked Bessie.

"And the agreed upon sum for her adoption is set? No reduction in cost despite her age?"

"I am sure, Mr. Bedford, we can work out a sum agreeable to both of us."

My stomach turned. I held Bessie's blanket in my hands, her only possession. I clung to it, wringing it in frustration. Tilly would be proved incorrect. The couple planned to take the child.

"Do not dicker, dear," the woman whispered.

The man glanced to his wife holding Bessie. He nodded. "All right. We shall take the child, Headmistress." He passed her an envelope. "Please count it if you wish."

"I am sure there is no need for that!" Headmistress Williamson answered, shoving the envelope into her pocket. "Lenora, fetch anything that belongs with the child."

I stepped forward with the blanket, choking back my tears. "She sleeps with this," I choked out. "And she is fond of being rocked before bed."

The woman accepted the blanket. "Thank you," she offered. I stepped back and Tilly put her hand on my shoulder. "Oh, Charles, perhaps we should inquire after a nanny."

My heart lifted. They were in need of a nanny. I cared for the child for the first six months of her life. I knew her schedule, all her likes and dislikes, I knew the child inside and out. Perhaps we would not be separated. I could fit into the role of nanny!

"Yes," Charles agreed with Mrs. Bedford. "Yes, perhaps one of your girls would be suitable, Headmistress."

The woman nodded at me as Headmistress Williamson responded. "Oh, why yes! Yes, of course we can assist with that. St. Mary's turns out some of the best girls for service! I have the perfect girl in mind!" She stepped to the stairway, calling up. "Bertha! Bertha? Come down at once to my office!"

"Mr. and Mrs. Bedford, why don't we step this way into my office where we can discuss the matter further?"

"Oh," Mrs. Bedford said, hesitating. "What about her?" She nodded toward me. "She seems to know the child."

Headmistress Williamson glared at me for a moment before plastering a smile on her face and returning her gaze to Mrs. Bedford. "Please step this way and we can discuss it. I assure you Bertha will be a lovely addition to your home." She wrapped her arm around Mrs. Bedford's waist, leading her to the office. As they crossed the foyer, I heard her add, "Between us, Mrs. Bedford, I cannot recommend Lenora. Oh, she seems kind enough, but she is a troubled girl." They disappeared into the office as Bertha descended the stairs.

I swallowed hard as tears stung my eyes. I bit my lower lip and fled up the stairs to the bedroom. I flung myself across the bed as sobs wracked my body.

"She is a witch. Do not waste your tears," Tilly said, following me and closing the door behind her. She climbed onto the bed, wrapping her arms around my shoulders.

"I do not shed them over Headmistress Williamson," I said between sobs.

Tilly rubbed my back. "Do not cry, Lenora."

I continued to weep. "They have taken Bessie."

"They seem like a lovely couple."

"Yes, I recognize that," I responded. "And I hate myself for hating them but…"

"But you shall miss her," Tilly finished for me.

"Yes," I cried.

"One day, Lenora, we shall have all the happiness the world can offer. You must believe that."

I wiped at my face, sniffling. "There is no happiness in this world for me," I lamented.

"Lenora Hastings!" Tilly scolded. "Stop that talk this instant! I shall hear no more of it! We shall find happiness! Both of us. Even if you do not believe it, cling to the idea in moments like these. Together, we shall get through it!" She squeezed me tight. The warm hug eased my raw emotions. When I no longer sobbed, Tilly released me.

"You must finish your composition," I murmured.

Tilly responded by rising from the bed and grabbing her composition from the writing desk. She tore it in two and threw it in the trash bin.

"Tilly! What an impetuous thing to do!" I scolded.

Tilly grinned at me. "As long as it has stopped your mind from dwelling on your sorrows, I do not care."

"But now you shall need to rewrite it all!"

"It matters not. It was rubbish anyway. I can rewrite it if you promise to help me! But first, let us spend the afternoon playing a game." Tilly pulled a stack of cards from under one of the beds. "Rummy?"

I smiled as I recalled her devilish grin as she waved the cards at me. Sorrow grew in my heart over her loss, and I cursed myself for not coming to her aid sooner, for not insisting she leave the brothel earlier. I regretted not paying attention to my foreboding sense, vowing not to ignore such feelings in the future. Tilly, a true friend, was gone because of my disregard for my own instincts.

The baby yawned and stretched in Ella's arms. My mind snapped back to the present and to more pressing matters. His little mouth opened and closed before he began to whimper. "There, there, little one," Ella cooed.

"I should check the time. He may be hungry." I climbed from the bed and glanced at the clock in the sitting room. "It is later than I realized. I should feed him and dress for dinner. I imagine Robert will return at any moment."

I fetched the bottle of milk and spoon from the sitting room and relieved Ella of the baby. "That is quite an amazing trick," she murmured as I spoon fed the child.

"I've had a bit of practice at it," I informed her.

After the child was fed, I swaddled him in a blanket and settled him in a dresser drawer, a trick I learned at the orphanage. Ella busied herself laying out my clothes as I nestled him in to sleep. I dressed for dinner and awaited Robert's return in the sitting room. Ella and I sat near the fireplace reading.

Minutes turned to hours. After a time, I stared at the clock, wondering if the time may be correct. Robert's tasks seemed to take far longer than I had anticipated. I attempted to return to my reading but found my mind unable to focus. I stood from my chair and paced the room.

"Is everything all right, Your Grace?" Ella inquired.

"Yes," I assured her. "Only becoming fretful about Duke Blackmoore's return. The hour is growing late. I expected him earlier than this."

"Perhaps he has run into difficulty with the arrangements."

"Yes, perhaps," I agreed. I continued my incessant pacing as my mind whirled. Robert had planned to go to the brothel. Perhaps he had met with trouble there. The part of town where the brothel was situated was less than desirable. My mind concocted all sorts of scenarios.

I checked on the baby who still slept peacefully in my bedroom. I returned to the sitting room, plopping into the chair across from Ella. I found myself unable to stay there, though, and within moments, I resumed my pacing of the floor.

After another thirty minutes, the door to our suite

popped open. "Robert!" I exclaimed as he entered the room. "Thank goodness!"

Noting my flustered tone, Robert asked, "Is everything all right with the child?"

"Yes," I assured him. "However, the late hour concerned me. I feared something may have happened to you!"

Robert smiled at me and kissed my forehead. "No, I am quite all right, dear," he informed me. "Though I apologize for keeping you waiting for your supper."

"Did the arrangements give you trouble?"

"Not at all! I have arranged for her burial tomorrow afternoon. With no family, I saw no reason to delay it. She will be laid to rest at St. Agnes."

My brow furrowed. While I was pleased to know the arrangements had been completed with no trouble, I pondered why Robert had been delayed. Before I could inquire about it, a knock sounded at the door. Robert crossed to the door and opened it.

Three men entered, carrying a variety of things. "This," he said, pointing a finger in the air, his eyebrows raised and a grin on his face, "is what delayed me."

"What is all this?" I questioned.

"A few items for the baby," Robert answered. He grabbed a cylindrical item from one of the men's arms. He studied it, his lips pursuing as he stared at the object. "Formula! I am told this is the preferred alternative for a child in the absence of a wet nurse. We shall try it until a wet nurse and nanny can be engaged."

"And the rest?" I queried as the men set down the remaining items and departed. I stared at a small wooden horse. Brown in color with a black mane and tail, it sat on rockers. A little saddle sat on its back and leather reins flowed from its face to its back.

"Ah," Robert said, approaching the wooden animal and

setting it to rock. "A rocking horse! All the rage these days for children, I am told."

"A rocking horse?" I repeated, my voice questioning.

"Yes. A splendid surrogate for his nursery until he has his own horse, wouldn't you say? Though I do not imagine it will be long before I am buying the laddie his first pony!" Robert grinned from ear to ear. He picked up something else. I had never seen anything like it before. "And this is a zoetrope!" He spun a wheel underneath a cylindrical drum. "See, it makes the animal appear to be moving!" He continued on. "And this object is a magic lantern! You insert a slide here and it projects an image onto the wall! Most useful for his education!" My jaw hung open. I glanced wide-eyed to Robert. "Is something the matter, Lenora?"

"No," I answered, finally finding my voice. "I imagine he will find these items most entertaining as he grows."

"Yes, it is my sincere hope! I shall have them sent ahead of us with Mr. Langford tomorrow. Henry will return to the castle ahead of us to prepare the staff for the laddie's arrival. Buchanan will desire notice to prepare the nursery." Robert glanced around the room. Ella had wandered over to peruse the new items for the child. "Where is the little chap?"

"Asleep," I informed him, motioning to my bedroom.

"Do you mind if I take a peek at him before supper?" Robert questioned. "If you are too hungry, I shall wait."

"Not at all," I responded. Robert followed me into the bedroom and to the child's makeshift crib.

"A drawer?" he questioned. "Clever, Lenora. Did you give Henry a name?"

"Yes," I responded. "I hope you shall be pleased with it."

"I am certain I will be. What is it?" Robert asked, still cooing over the baby.

"Samuel," I stated.

Robert glanced to me. "Samuel?" A smile spread across his face. "My father's name."

"Yes," I answered, returning his expression. "I hoped it would please you."

"It does," he assured me. "Oh, we must also consider his christening. Shall we discuss it over our supper?" He offered his arm to escort me to dine.

"Yes," I agreed, accepting it. "Though I shall leave the details of godparents to you, Robert. I have no family or even acquaintances who may serve."

"Hmm," Robert answered as we navigated to the dining room. "I considered Lord and Lady Sinderby. A lovely couple."

"Whatever you suggest, dear," I agreed. "Though..."

"Yes?" Robert prompted.

"Would it be prudent to involve your brother?"

"Edwin?" Robert scoffed. "Lenora, with his behavior toward you, he is the last person I expected you to consider."

I shrugged. "I only considered him because I regarded it as an olive branch. Perhaps one from which to rebuild your relationship."

Robert frowned. "He is a drunkard and a troublemaker. Given his behavior of late, the olive branch should be offered from him to me, not the other way 'round!"

I nodded. "You are correct," I answered. "I shall not press the matter. Lord and Lady Sinderby are most suitable from my perspective. We shall ask them."

Robert glanced to me for a moment. "Quite right, yes," he answered. "I shall write to Lord Sinderby upon our return to Blackmoore."

CHAPTER 17

The following day brought bright spring sunshine to Glasgow. Mr. Langford set off early, his carriage laden with the items Robert purchased for Samuel. After lunch, we set off for St. Agnes church, where Robert arranged for Tilly to be laid to rest.

A mix of emotions, I focused myself on tending to Samuel as a distraction. The day warmed enough by afternoon to take the child, so I laid Tilly's blue scarf on his chest and swaddled him in a new blanket and took him. It proved to settle my nerves for the majority of the journey and even some of the service. Three of the girls from the brothel attended the simple service. I recognized the redhead who had given me Tilly's scarf, the vocal blonde and rude girl.

They stood apart from us during the service. I smiled at them whenever they glanced to me, though for most of the ceremony, they kept their heads bowed. After the service began, Sir Richard Prescott approached, standing at a distance.

I stared into the rectangular hole dug into the ground. The wooden box inside appeared so forlorn, so final. Its plain brown façade a direct contrast to the bright colors of spring. It served as another reminder of the finality of life. I fought to keep hold of my emotions during the funeral, though they got the better of me when we said our final goodbyes.

A sob escaped me, and tears rolled down my cheeks. Ella quickly swept Samuel into her arms to allow me a moment to grieve. Robert steadied me and I wept as sorrow swept through me.

After a moment, I regained my composure. I squeezed Robert's hand and wiped away my tears. Ella placed Samuel in my arms, and I focused all my energy on fussing with his swaddling.

As the funeral concluded, Sir Richard Prescott approached. He shook Robert's hand before turning to me. "My deepest condolences, Duchess Blackmoore."

"Thank you," I replied, surprised by Sir Richard's compassion in the matter.

"I was surprised to learn of your friendship," he continued. "Always a surprise from you, duchess." He raised his eyebrow at me, a wanton expression on his face. I had misjudged him. He offered no compassion. His curiosity drove him to seek out Tilly's funeral.

"If you wouldn't mind, Sir Richard," Robert chimed in. "My wife needs some time to grieve."

"Of course," Sir Richard answered. "Good day and again, my sympathies." Sir Richard strolled away, glancing back one last time with a lecherous wink. I stopped myself from shuddering.

Tilly's workmates approached me. "I shall wait for you at the carriage unless you require my assistance, Lenora," Robert excused himself.

I nodded to him in response.

"Might we take one last peek at the babe?" the redhead inquired.

"Of course," I answered, smiling away my grief and focusing on something pleasant.

"He's got a new blanket," rude girl responded. "Big and fancy."

"Yes," I answered. "Duke Blackmoore and I made the decision to adopt the child ourselves. He purchased a variety of items for the baby yesterday. I have kept the scarf you gave me with him though," I explained, pulling the blanket open to show them.

The redhead wiped a tear from her cheek. "Tilly'd be so happy he's being provided for." Another tear fell to her cheek. She reached to Samuel's cheek and rubbed it.

"What will you name him?" the blonde inquired.

"Samuel," I replied. "Duke Blackmoore's father's name."

"It's a good strong name," the redhead said with a sniffle. After a breath, she opened the ragged purse hanging from her wrist and withdrew a few coins. "Seeing as your husband took care of all the expenses, we no longer need this."

"Keep it," I blurted. I pushed her fingers closed and squeezed her hand.

"I couldn't..." she began.

I interrupted her. "You can and you will."

She smiled in response, dropping the coins back into her purse.

The rude girl suggested, "You will. To make up for our lost wages. We better be getting back. Madame Blanche is already sore at us for coming."

The redhead rubbed her thumb on Samuel's head and smiled at him. Rude girl tugged at her arm. "Hurry now, Alice!"

"Just a moment!" Alice insisted. She spun back to face me. "A bit of advice. Stay far away from that man." She pointed in the direction of Sir Richard. "He's a no good louse, that one. You'd do well to keep away from him."

I nodded at her. "Thank you," I said.

Rude girl tugged at her arm again. With a wistful glance to Samuel, she allowed herself to be led away. I sighed, snuggling Samuel closer to me and returned to the carriage where Robert and Ella awaited me. As I approached, I saw a third figure at the door. Tilly. She stood opposite Robert, her blonde hair flowing down her back. The color had returned to her cheeks and her blue eyes sparkled even from afar. She appeared as she had in life.

I smiled at her as I neared the carriage. She offered me a tearful smile in return. "You will raise him?" she queried.

I nodded. Robert noted my odd gaze, glancing between me and my focus point. "What is it?" he whispered.

"Tilly," I explained, without taking my eyes from her face. "She has come to inquire about her baby." Robert's expression betrayed a mixture of emotions including confusion, fear and discomfort. "She understands that we shall raise him. She is pleased."

Robert replaced his aghast expression with a soft smile. Tilly stepped close to me. She stared down at the baby, her hand finding his forehead. "My perfect boy," she whispered.

"We shall name him Samuel," I informed her.

"Samuel," she repeated. "Little Sam. It is perfect, Lenora."

"It pleases me that you approve, Tilly," I said, my heart soaring with contentment. "I shall always protect him."

"Please tell her we shall love him as though he is one of our own," Robert announced, his voice raised as though the dead were deaf as well as deceased.

A chuckle erupted from me at his tone. He offered me a strange look. I nodded to him. "She heard you. And she thanks you. If there is anything further you wish to convey, you can speak normally, they are not deaf."

"Oh," Robert murmured. "I did not realize she could hear me."

"She can," I assured him. "Though only I can see and hear her response."

"He seems a kind man, Lenora," Tilly responded, her eyes unwavering from her child. "I am so pleased that Samuel will have a loving father and you as a mother. If I cannot raise him myself, I am pleased you will."

"Robert speaks the truth," I assured her. "We shall love him as though he were our own." I paused for a breath before adding, "And possibly spoil him. Robert shall have the nursery filled with gadgets to amuse him before long. He already has made a good start!"

Tilly smiled up at me. She spent another moment gazing at Samuel before she bent to kiss his forehead. Samuel wriggled as her lips brushed his tiny head. Tears fell to her cheeks as she raised her head. She nodded to me as she stepped back.

She was ready to say goodbye, though could not find the words to do so. A simple nod was all both she and I could manage. I moved toward Robert to suggest my readiness to depart.

He smiled at me. "Ready?"

I nodded, and we all climbed into the carriage to return to the hotel. As I settled Samuel before afternoon tea, Ella fidgeted in her seat across from me. "Is everything all right, Sinclair?" I inquired.

"Yes, Your Grace," she responded.

"You seem… agitated. Did the funeral disturb you? Perhaps you should lie down."

"No, Your Grace," she answered. "It is only…"

"Yes?" I inquired.

"Well…"

My brow furrowed. "Speak up, Sinclair. There is no reason to hold your tongue."

"Your conversation with the child's mother," she blurted.

"What of it?" I asked, spooning more formula into Samuel's mouth.

"I do not wish you to consider me rude, however, I could not help but consider the situation so very odd. How extraordinary yet vexing for you, Your Grace."

"I have grown accustomed to it," I informed her.

"Do they speak with you as we speak?"

Robert, who was reading the paper in a nearby chair, set his paper down and joined the conversation. "Yes, I wondered the same."

"Some of them do, some do not," I explained. "Tilly conversed with me as she did in life." Robert's brow furrowed, as did Ella's as they considered my explanation. I shrugged and continued. "The reasons some can and cannot seem to vary. I assume the close relationship Tilly and I shared assisted in our communication, along with her concern for Samuel."

Robert spoke first. "Then Tilly behaved as she did in life, unlike Annie."

"Yes." I nodded. "Her concern for the child seemed to be a driving force in her communication. Her death still was likely a shock, though the matter of her child's wellbeing took precedence."

"I wish things were so simple with Annie," Robert said with a sigh.

"We are communicating more openly. I hope to reach this point. Her situation is quite different, though. As is the relationship between her and I. We were not acquainted in life. It shocked her to realize I could interact with her. She'll come 'round." I offered Robert a reassuring smile.

Ella, who had remained quiet until now, spoke up. She shook her head, saying, "Better you than me, Your Grace. I am not certain I could handle such matters. Even the discussion of them sets my nerves on edge."

I surmised the source of Ella's agitation from her comment. It disturbed her being so close to the dead. Most people do not realize the dead walk amongst us and, henceforth, never realize when one is close. It alarms the normal person when they are forced to face the concept that a spirit has stood in close proximity to them.

I did my best to set Ella's nerves at ease. "They are not generally harmful, Sinclair," I said. Ella nodded, giving me a nervous glance. My best attempt needed augmented. "There are no spirits here with us now. You may relax."

The last of my comments brought a slight smile and a deep sigh. I hoped that had done the trick. It is often easy to forget the trepidation that builds in others over a subject I had grown so accustomed to in my lifetime. I hoped, in time, those that shared my life would also find the situation normal.

CHAPTER 18

Blackmoore Castle stood tall on the hill. The carriage pitched at an angle as we began the climb toward it. A smile crossed my face, as it always did when I caught sight of my home. Samuel had endured the long ride home well, the jostling of the carriage lulling him to sleep for most of the journey.

The castle brimmed with activity as we arrived. Servants bustled from place to place, carrying out extra tasks to ready the castle for its newest occupant.

"I hope you do not mind, Your Grace," Buchanan said as he greeted us outside, "however, I dismissed the staff of their duty to greet you in order to finish the tasks needed to properly welcome the young master."

"Quite prudent of you, Buchanan," Robert responded.

We stepped inside, shedding our cloaks as Ella held Samuel. "Might I see the child?" Buchanan requested.

"Of course!" Robert exclaimed. I collected Samuel from Ella and sidled next to Buchanan, holding the child out for him to view.

"A most handsome laddie!" Buchanan said. He rubbed his

finger on Samuel's cheek and then against his hand. Samuel latched on to his finger. "Quite a strong little one, too!"

Robert beamed. "Yes, yes, he shall grow into a fine man."

"Indeed, Your Grace," Buchanan agreed. "The staff has been busy readying the nursery. If Her Grace would care to inspect it now, you may suggest some adjustments. I understand Mr. Langford is already engaging a wet nurse and nanny."

"Yes, I shall go there now. Until we have engaged a caregiver, I shall keep Samuel in my bedroom," I answered.

"I shall have the arrangements prepared at once," Buchanan answered. "Mrs. Thomson, will you show Her Grace the nursery?"

I followed our housekeeper up the stairs and through the halls to the nursery. Mrs. Thomson showed me the night nursery first, assuring me a bassinet would be placed in my bedroom until suitable childcare was brought on. I then perused the day nursery, appropriately set to face a southeasterly direction. It brought a smile to my face as I spotted the many toys Robert had purchased scattered in the large and well-lit room.

Overall, the day nursery had a pleasant presentation, and I congratulated Mrs. Thomson on her fine work. She inquired as to whether I should be reviewing the qualifications of those interested in the positions to care for the child, or if Robert preferred to review them. Uncertain, I informed her I would speak to Robert and provide an answer to her later.

With Samuel in my arms, I traversed the halls to speak with Robert on the matter. I arrived at Robert's office, where I expected to find him reviewing correspondence missed during our time in Glasgow. I discovered an empty office. "Where might your father be, Samuel?" I asked the child in my arms.

I navigated to the foyer in search of Buchanan. As I descended the stairs, I overheard Robert's voice coming from the sitting room. The doors were slightly ajar, so I entered, expecting to find him discussing something with Buchanan.

"Robert," I said as I pushed through the doors, "Mrs. Thomson wished to know if you preferred to review applications for Samuel's…" My voice stopped mid-sentence as I spotted another man in the room.

Edwin spun to face me. "Forgive me," I murmured to Robert, "I did not realize you were speaking with Mr. Fletcher."

Edwin's jaw dropped and his eyes widened. His eyebrows raised high. He guffawed, setting his brandy glass on a nearby table and burst into applause.

"Edwin, have you gone mad?" Robert questioned after his theatrical display.

"Not at all, dear brother!" He turned to me. "I offer you my congratulations, Duchess! I have far underestimated your unique abilities!"

"What nonsense are you prattling on about?" Robert demanded.

"Why, your wife's obvious talents, of course," Edwin responded. "The extraordinary qualities she possesses." For a moment, I assumed he had slithered through the more boorish gossipers and discovered my supernatural ability. "In an attempt to ensure her future here, she has conjured a baby from thin air!" He waved his arms around, imitating a magician. My face set into a frown at his comments. "And further, she has convinced you, big brother, to raise this child of enigmatic origin."

"Stop this behavior at once!" Robert bellowed.

"Oh," Edwin continued. "I underestimated the lengths you will go to, Duchess, to secure your place here!"

"I said enough!" Robert roared, grasping Edwin by the

collar. "I will not have you speaking this way about my wife or my child in this house."

Edwin wrestled himself from Robert's grip. "Your child?" Edwin questioned, his voice incredulous. "YOUR child? It isn't even HER child! Oh, Robert, she really has you wound around her finger, doesn't she? I always considered you too proud to raise another man's child."

"I will not discuss the matter further with you, Edwin. If you cannot control your tongue, we shall cease the discussion of our business immediately."

"I assume this development alters my prospects quite a bit?" Edwin questioned.

"I shall leave you to discuss business," I said.

"Oh no, no, please stay, duchess," Edwin responded. "Witness firsthand the product of your handiwork."

"Stop accusing Lenora of these things!" Robert shouted. "The product of her handiwork is the noble deed of providing a motherless child with a home. The world does not revolve around you and your needs, Edwin. It is a childish view to match your childish behavior."

"I assume this is why you summoned me?" Edwin queried. "To inform me of the demise in my future outlook."

I found the statement odd. Robert had requested Edwin's presence? Why? "No," Robert answered as I pondered Edwin's comments. "While it is true Samuel will be named as heir, that is not what I invited you to discuss."

So, I mused, Robert had invited him to the castle. For what purpose?

"Then what?" Edwin asked, his mind clearly pondering the same question.

Robert sighed, clasping his hands behind his back in his usual manner. "We are choosing godparents for Samuel's christening. Lenora, being kindhearted in nature, suggested you. Though I disagreed on the surface, in an attempt to model more of my wife's virtues, I reversed my decision and asked you here to discuss the matter with you."

Edwin did not respond. I read his expression to convey a mixture of confusion, regret and surprise. Robert continued, "Though I can see that this was a mistake. You have no tact nor courtesy. Your demeanor makes you both an improper and undesirable choice."

Edwin slammed his brandy glass on the table next to him. "Yes, I've always known that," he hollered before storming from the room.

The door slammed behind him as he departed. Samuel jumped in my arms at the noise and began to wail. Robert closed his eyes in frustration and disgust as I quieted the child. "I am sorry, Robert," I said.

Robert waved his hand, opening his eyes. "Do not apologize, Lenora. The man is an... well, never mind."

"I should not have suggested you ask him. It was not my place. The fault is mine."

"As the child's mother, it is your place. I had hoped the conversation would go differently, but, alas, even this olive branch he has spat out."

"Perhaps he will come 'round," I offered. "Though if you prefer, we may move forward with Lord and Lady Sinderby."

"Yes, I shall write to Lord Sinderby in a few days' time." Robert paused a moment. "Oh, you wished to speak with me? I had nearly forgotten with all the fuss."

"Yes," I replied. "Mrs. Thomson wished to know which of us would review those applying for the nursery positions. I should be happy to do it. Though, if you prefer to oversee the task, I have no objections."

"I leave the task in your capable hands. I prefer you to select the women you will entrust Samuel's care to."

I smiled and nodded. "I shall inform Mrs. Thomson to forward all correspondence on the matter to me."

"Are you pleased with the nursery? I have not had the chance to inspect it as yet."

"Very," I informed him. "The day nursery will receive excellent morning light."

"Yes, I can recall many a pleasant morning there with Nanny as a young laddie."

"And I am certain Samuel will enjoy many happy days there as well." The child began to fuss in my arms. Robert glanced to him, giving his cheek a stroke. "It is time for his feeding. I shall be in my bedroom with him." Robert smiled at me, kissing Samuel on the forehead, then me.

I took my child to my bedroom to feed him. When finished, I gathered him into my arms, intending to take him to my tower room for a nap while I read.

As I navigated the halls, I quieted Samuel with a lullaby. My focus on the child caused me to miss the figure lurking in the hallway just before the tower stairs.

The dark figure approached me and we nearly collided due to my carelessness. I noticed at the last moment, stumbling back a few steps as I exclaimed aloud my surprise. Strong hands steadied me from toppling over as I lurched backward.

"My sincere apologies, Duchess," Edwin said.

"Mr. Fletcher," I choked out. "I thought you had left the estate."

He paused, staring at me a moment, before answering. It was the first time I had gotten a good look at him. His eyes were stormy gray, a match to Robert's. His unruly dark, curly hair similar to Robert's as well, though his contained no streaks of gray. The family resemblance between the brothers ran strong. Though where Robert carried himself with a regal air and possessed a charming demeanor, Edwin's countenance suggested a troubled man. His features betrayed a man deeply disturbed by something. On the surface, I could not identify the source of these troubles, though.

"The fault is mine. I did not mean to startle you," he said. His voice, calm and measured, sounded unlike Edwin.

"It is no trouble, Mr. Fletcher," I answered. I glanced to Samuel to ensure his wellbeing after my startled outcry.

"Please, call me Edwin," he said. My brow furrowed, and I glanced to him for a brief moment. This new version of Edwin baffled me. "We are, after all, family. We have gotten off on the wrong foot, haven't we?" Edwin added when I did not respond to his comment. "For that, I apologize. It is also my doing."

I shook my head. "Think nothing of it," I stated, still uncertain of his motives.

Edwin paused for a moment. "I intended to leave the castle after our earlier conversation, but I returned before even collecting my horse. I…" His voice trailed off. I stared at him, waiting for him to continue. "I wished to speak with you. That is, if you are agreeable."

"To speak with me? Concerning what?" I questioned.

"I wished to thank you, Lenora. Oh, do you prefer I use your formal name?"

"Lenora is fine," I answered. "To thank me for what?"

"The gesture of including me as the child's godfather. I reacted badly, I realize, though it never occurred to me to have been considered for the role. I confess I was taken a bit off guard."

I heaved a deep breath, pondering my response. What was his aim, I wondered? This about face confounded me. Was he earnest in his remarks or was this some sort of game?

"There is no need to thank me," I replied. "I am only sorry the request proved to drive the wedge further than to close the growing distance between yourself and Robert, as it was intended."

"Yes, I understand, and you need not offer your apologies. The fault is altogether mine." I offered a slight, tight-lipped smile. "Though even I maintain I am a less-than-desirable choice for the role. I am certain you and Robert shall choose far better. And I shall be satisfied to be simply 'Uncle.' May I see the child?"

"Of course." I held the child out in my arms for Edwin to view. "Uncle Edwin, meet Samuel, your nephew."

Edwin smiled at Samuel. "Rather a handsome chap," he said. "I did not realize you planned to adopt a child. It all came as a shock to me, which is part of the reason for my poor reaction. I am not excusing it, though, I would prefer to explain. In the interest of establishing a better relationship between us."

"You are not required to explain to me, though I appreciate it. However, the child came as quite a surprise to us as well. We were not planning to adopt. An acquaintance of mine passed away, giving birth to Samuel. Robert suggested we adopt the child."

Edwin frowned. "His father did not protest?"

"No," I explained. "She was unwed, and the father not identified."

"Oh," Edwin exclaimed, surprise in his voice. "You are full of surprises, Lenora. An unwed and pregnant acquaintance? Wherever did you meet?"

I ignored the comment about my surprising nature. "His mother was a student at St. Mary's Orphanage when I was. So, you see, the addition of the child to our home was not intended to defraud you of anything. In fact, the decision had nothing to do with you. Only with our desire to help the orphan child."

"St. Mary's Orphanage? You were an orphan?" His face screwed up with confusion as he inquired after my humble beginnings.

"Yes," I confirmed. Edwin's eyebrows raised, and I added, "There is nothing salacious about the tale, I assure you."

"I did not mean to suggest there was. However, of late, my brother has been quite a recluse. I cannot understand how you could have met to begin with, but with the knowledge of your time at St. Mary's, I confess to be even further baffled!"

"Robert heard tale of my unique ability from a friend. One of my former classmates was in the man's employ and knew me well. After he discovered my talent, he had Mr. Langford collect me from the orphanage and ..."

Edwin held up a hand. "Unique talent?" he questioned.

"Yes," I stated. "I can communicate with the dead. I assumed you may possess this information already."

Edwin's eyes went wide and his jaw slack. "Communicate with the dead?"

"Yes. I can see and communicate with those who have passed from this life." I weighed in my mind the benefits and disadvantages of revealing more. It could not hurt, I reflected and continued. "Upon learning of this, Robert collected me from the orphanage and offered me marriage in exchange for helping discover the reason the first Mrs. Fletcher flung herself to her death."

Edwin's demeanor changed as I explained. His posture stiffened and his face hardened. Perhaps he did not believe me. Perhaps he judged me a charlatan, seeking an easy life. I added, "So, again, as you can see, our marriage was not an attempt to defraud you of anything. Only to set Robert's mind at ease regarding his former spouse."

Edwin continued to ponder the information in silence. "And have you discovered anything?" he inquired after several moments.

"Nothing as yet," I informed him.

"Have you... seen Annie?" he questioned.

"Yes," I admitted. "She is extremely disturbed, and our communications have been limited because of it."

"Doubtless! The woman was quite mad. That is what drove her to suicide. There is no mystery to solve, no reason to be discovered."

"That remains to be uncovered," I responded.

He raised his eyebrows at me. "Not in my opinion," he argued. "I am sorry to say, my brother has been quite foolish in his pursuit of this. The woman was mad, and that is the end of the matter. It is a waste of your and his time to delve any deeper."

"You were there that day," I said. "And I am sure in the months preceding it. Was there anything odd about the situation?"

Edwin shrugged. "No. It was all very tragic. I found her, you know? Happened upon her while walking. I attempted to save her, but she was gone. Horrible, horrible mess, that."

"And before that day? Was she at all despondent or erratic in her behavior?"

Edwin considered my question. "Perhaps," he responded. "Annie was... well, she was a daydreamer. A romantic. You know the sort. I believe those types are often prone to this form of behavior. They do not view the world clearly and, henceforth, are often disappointed by it. Really, there is nothing more to tell. I would abandon the pursuit if I were in your position. There is nothing to be learned."

I shrugged. "If I can help bring closure to the situation, I am pleased to do so."

"I must be on my way," Edwin said, backing away a few steps. "Though I think you shall find my assessment correct. If I were you, Lenora, I would not pursue this further. Leave the dead rest." With that, he spun on his heel and disappeared around the corner.

I stared after him for several moments before shaking my

head in disbelief at the conversation. His reversal in attitude befuddled me. Though his response to the revelation of my ability did not surprise me. I was accustomed to being shunned by people after revealing my nature.

I spun to continue on to my tower room. As I turned, I caught sight of Annie hovering at the end of the hall. Her presence surprised me, and I wondered how long she had been there. I had not noticed her when speaking with Edwin, though my mind was preoccupied with the conversation.

Our eyes locked for a moment before she disappeared up the tower stairs. I approached the stairway and ascended the steps. As I reached the top, my mouth dropped open. I gaped around the room. The chaise lay toppled on its side. The tables strewn around the room haphazardly. My books had been pulled from the shelves and scattered about. The draperies on the windows lay in a heap on the floor.

"Annie!" I exclaimed. I descended the stairs in search of help to restore the room. I fumed along the way. Her destructive behavior was becoming a nuisance. I had hoped we were past this, given the great strides we had made in communicating. Perhaps the trip to Glasgow induced another setback. Perhaps Samuel's presence disturbed her. I did not understand the reason, but I was determined to seek answers.

I found Buchanan below stairs and explained to him the situation. Ella relieved me of Samuel, promising to lay him for a nap in his bassinet and tend to him as I assisted with the restoration of my tower room.

While the staff and I cleaned, Robert entered. "What is all this? Buchanan informed me of some sort of commotion."

"Let us speak in private," I suggested. I preferred most of the staff members to remain unaware of the incident's true nature.

"What happened, Lenora?" Robert queried when we reached the bottom of the stairwell.

"I am not certain," I answered. I stared at the floor, remaining lost in my thoughts, and fell quiet after making my statement.

Robert raised my chin to face him. "Lenora, what is it? What are you keeping to yourself?"

"Nothing," I said. "But I can offer no explanation. After my conversation with Edwin concluded, I spotted Annie at the end of the hall. She flitted up the stairs and when I arrived at the room, I discovered it in disarray."

"Conversation with Edwin?" Robert repeated with a frown. "How dare he seek you out to harass you further?! I shall bar him from this house, so help me!"

I shook my head. "You misunderstand. He did not harass me. He apologized and sought to better our relationship."

Robert's frown remained, and he crossed his arms. "Hmm," he murmured. "I do not trust him. Do you believe him earnest?"

I considered the question. "I am uncertain of his intentions," I admitted. "Though his demeanor suggested his earnestness in the matter. He suggested we move forward with our plans to seek godparents, saying he was pleased to remain only an uncle to the child." Robert's eyes narrowed as he pondered the information. I continued, "I explained to him the nature by which we adopted Samuel so he could understand that we made no attempt to defraud him. And by extension, the origins of our marriage became a topic."

"And what did you tell him?" Robert inquired.

"The truth," I replied. "Though after learning of my ability, he made a fast exit. I am not surprised, most who learn of it prefer to flee from me as quickly as possible."

"So, you told him of your inquiry into Annie's death?"

"Yes, we discussed the matter some. I had not yet spoken with him about it and wished to do so."

"And did you inform him those original circumstances of our marriage no longer applied?"

"I did not."

Robert waved his hand at me. "No matter. I shall inform him, lest he attempt to use it against us in the future. To challenge the marriage."

"I understand and hope I have not caused any trouble by speaking with him. I determined telling the truth to be the best course of action."

"Quite right, Lenora," Robert assured me. "As always, your impulses prove correct."

"I hope it may lead to a reconciliation between you. I realize the situation between you is tense, but I do abhor a feud within a family."

"You are too admirable, Lenora. I am unworthy of your virtues."

I shook my head at him. "I suppose I am sensitive to it, having lost my family and spent most of my life without it."

Robert nodded, then moved on to the other subject at hand. "On to the other matter," Robert said. "You said Annie awaited you at the end of the hallway and proceeded up the stairs before you?"

"Yes," I said with a nod. "After my conversation with Edwin, I spotted her at the end of the hallway. She raced up the stairs ahead of me. When I reached the top of the stairs, I found the room in disarray."

Robert shook his head. "Why?"

"I haven't the slightest clue," I admitted. "Perhaps our trip. Something similar happened following our last trip to Glasgow. Our absence may perturb her."

Robert sighed. "I hope she has released whatever negative

energy our absence caused from her system. I do not wish you to be troubled by it further."

"As do I, though at least her anger seems restricted to creating minimal damage." I glanced up the stairs. "I should finish cleaning the room before checking on Samuel. Ella is tending to him, but I do not wish to leave him too long."

Robert grasped my hand, looping my arm through his. "The staff is more than capable of completing the task. Come, let us check on Samuel together. What did you tell the staff regarding the incident?"

"That a window blew open and a strong wind gust created the damage. Not a clever subterfuge, but it should do."

We traversed the halls discussing arrangements for Samuel's christening. I preceded Robert into my room through the open door. I halted one step into the room, causing Robert to bump into me. I swallowed hard, my eyes wide.

"What is it, Lenora?"

Ella read in a chair near Samuel's bassinet. Hovering over him stood Annie. She stared into the crib, her hands white-knuckled and clutching the crib's side. Samuel slept, oblivious to her presence.

"Annie," I whispered, my focus never leaving her.

"What?!" Robert exclaimed. "Where?" Robert's eyes shot around the room.

"At Samuel's bassinet."

The commotion drew Annie's attention. Her head whipped toward us, her eyes glowing red. Robert shoved me behind him. "Annie!" he shouted. "Do not touch that child!"

Ella leapt from her seat, her book clattering to the floor. Her eyes were wide, and her hands shook as she stared at me. "What shall I do, Your Grace?" she questioned, her voice high in pitch, her fear obvious.

I stepped around Robert. "Do not agitate her," I whispered. I raised my voice to a normal level, trying to steady it though it shook as I spoke. "Annie..." I took a step toward her.

"Lenora," Robert whispered, grasping my arms. I shook him off gently, keeping my focus on Annie.

"Annie," I repeated. "Something has disturbed you; I realize that. But it is not the child's doing."

Annie's red eyes faded, returning to brown. She glanced down at Samuel again, then back to me. A tear rolled down her cheek.

I stopped walking. "What is it, Lenora? What is happening?" Robert whispered.

I continued speaking to Annie. "You do not wish to harm him, do you?"

Annie returned her gaze to Samuel. She released one of her white-knuckled hands from the bassinet. Her gray-blue hand, its nails blackened and curling, reached toward Samuel. I shot forward with my arm extended, ready to slap her hand away if she harmed the child.

"Annie!" Robert roared behind me. Annie disappeared, fading into thin air.

"Oh!" I exclaimed, scooping the child into my arms and squeezing him close to my chest. I shut my eyes for a moment and took a deep breath. "She is gone," I reported.

Robert heaved a sigh of relief. "Was she here to harm the child?" Ella screeched, her voice still shrill with alarm.

"No, I do not believe so," I answered.

"You give her too much credit, Lenora," Robert chided. "She destroyed your tower room and then we find her here looming over our child." Robert sighed again. "Oh, Annie." He lowered his head, shaking it. "I loved you in life but what you have become in death I cannot understand."

Ella still shook from the experience. "It is all right,

Sinclair," I offered, grasping her hand in mine. "Calm yourself."

"I apologize, Your Grace. I remain unaccustomed to these situations."

"I understand. Sit down while you recover." Ella collapsed into the chair, keeping hold of my hand.

"I do not like this, Lenora. I am not comfortable with the latest developments."

"I shall remain guarded in my pursuit of any information. And I shall keep a close eye on Samuel, though I remain convinced she did not mean him any harm."

Robert shook his head. "Perhaps you should take Samuel and stay elsewhere for a time."

"That will only exacerbate the situation," I argued.

"I do not wish to see any harm come to either of you. That is my only concern," Robert countered.

"Perhaps His Grace is correct, Your Grace," Ella offered, holding tight to my hand.

"No," I retorted. "No, she does not strike me as dangerous."

"Lenora!" Robert shouted. "She has destroyed your tower room on multiple occasions and she nearly killed you! I shall not take a chance with your life or Samuel's!"

Ella gasped at the admission. I released her hand, wrapping my arm around her shoulder for comfort. "Robert," I responded. "It matters not if I leave. That will not solve the situation. Annie will continue to lurk in these halls, suffering as she does now. The only resolution for both her and the rest of us is for me to stay and continue my inquiries with her."

Robert paced the floor in front of me. He held his jaw taut. After a time, he shook his head but acquiesced. "I detest this, Lenora, but I shall accept it. Though perhaps it is prudent to remove Samuel from the castle until you have solved this."

"No!" I cried. "I shall not be separated from Samuel!" Robert raised his eyebrows at me, prepared to retort. Before he could, I continued. "You do not trust Annie, I realize that. But I hold firm to my conviction that she meant Samuel no harm!"

"Are you willing to bet the child's life on it?"

I sighed, abhorring the way the statement sounded. "I do not believe I am risking his life."

"What if you are incorrect?" Robert posed.

"If his life is under even the slightest threat, I shall remove him myself."

"You cannot guard him all day and night, Lenora. You must sleep."

"No, I cannot. However, we shall monitor him at all times. While I sleep, someone else may oversee him."

"None of us can perceive Anne's presence," Robert argued.

"No, but you are capable of perceiving harm to the child or the threat of harm, even if from an unseen force." Robert considered the statement. "Robert, we must end this. We must continue on the path for all our sakes."

"All right," Robert agreed. "All right. I despise the entire situation, but we shall keep on."

I nodded and glanced to Ella. "Sinclair? Have you the spirit to remain in this house as we work toward solving this?"

She sucked in a deep breath. After a moment, she nodded slowly. "Yes," she whispered, clutching my hand again. She nodded, sitting straighter. "Yes, Your Grace. I possess the fortitude to help you see this through. I will guard the child when you sleep."

"We shall take shifts," Robert suggested. "If you will take the first part of the night, I shall take the second."

We agreed upon a schedule and with that, disbanded. I remained in my room to nurse Samuel. His blue eyes flitted about his surroundings before settling on me as I fed him. I stared down at him, worry filling me for a moment. "Darling boy," I whispered to him, kissing his forehead. "I do hope I have not chosen poorly. If anything should happen to you... never mind." I could not finish the original statement. I convinced myself Annie's intentions toward Samuel were innocuous.

CHAPTER 19

As I cuddled Samuel in my arms, my mind turned to thoughts of my own mother. I tried to push them aside and focus my energy on Samuel but, like floodwaters, they rushed through my brain, overflowing any barriers I placed before them.

I stared at the now-sleeping baby. Already he had carved out his own space in my heart. In addition to the sentiments of responsibility and obligation, I felt a tenderness toward him. The simple word 'love' did not cover the enormity of what I experienced. I felt a strong attachment and the urge to protect and care for him. The concept of being separated from Samuel dismayed me. I could not imagine anything that would make me feel otherwise toward him.

I pondered over my emotions, wondering if they, perhaps, were intensified because of my grief over losing Tilly. Perhaps this would explain how a mother could leave her child. Had my mother not experienced these emotions? What did she experience, I wondered, when she held me in her arms as a newborn babe? Were her feelings different from mine? Or did they change as I aged? Would mine evolve in a similar manner?

Questions raced through my mind as I rocked Samuel to sleep. My thoughts settled on a conversation overheard between my mother and an acquaintance days before she left me at the convent. I had always considered it my undoing, though I suppose the problem began long before that conversation.

My mind wound through the memories of my sixth year on earth, the year that would change my life. In the spring before my sixth birthday, my father and mother spent an extensive amount of time shouting at each other. I did not understand the source of their argument. I only knew that their voices often passed through the walls of our home. I would listen to them after my bedtime, voices raised in an argument that would last for hours on some nights.

During the summer, my father departed for India. As a doctor, he traveled for the Crown to provide medical care to British citizens living abroad. On the day of his departure, he sat me on his lap and told me of an exotic land where he would spend two years. "Why must you leave?" I questioned. "Why are you not taking Mum and me?"

He stroked my hair. "It is very different there, Lenora. I shall go first and if it is suitable, I shall return for you and your mother," he promised.

After we concluded our talk, he set me down and proceeded to gather his belongings. My mother sobbed, begging him not to go. "Please," she cried, "please do not leave."

"Helen," he answered, grasping my mother's shoulders, "pull yourself together."

"Please," she whispered again, tears rolling down her cheeks.

My father released his grip on her, pulled on his jacket

and donned his hat. He grasped his traveling bag in his hand and exited into the outside air toward the waiting carriage. My mother raced after him.

"Please, John!" she screamed after him. "You cannot leave me here! You cannot leave me with this child!"

Without a word, my father climbed into the carriage. It pulled away as my mother stood weeping on our front walk. I followed her out. She bent over, grasping her thighs, gasping as sobs wracked her body. I put my hand on her back. "'Tis all right, Mum. Father will return for us. Until then, I am with you."

My mother groaned, glancing at me. She stalked into the house, leaving me alone in the front yard.

After my father's departure, my mother's behavior took a bizarre turn. She roamed the house, her eyes glazed over, clutching her Bible. She mumbled to herself before locking herself in her room. With each passing day, Mother grew more despondent and fretful.

As she served my breakfast one morning, she said, "Lenora, if anyone asks, you were born on 1 November. Do you understand?"

"But why, Mum?" I queried, before spooning porridge into my mouth.

My mother spun me to face her, dropping to her knees in front of me. "Listen and do what you are told, Lenora!"

"But I was born on 31 October!" I insisted.

"Stop this nonsense, Lenora. From this day forward, you were born on 1 November and not a moment sooner. Now, do you understand?"

I nodded, not understanding but not willing to disturb my mother further. I rarely experienced a warm moment with her, but I still loved her. And I tried to be an obedient child. I came to realize my birthday suggested some defect in my character. I did not understand what deficiency existed, but my mother considered it wicked for some reason. When I was grown, of course, I realized the lore surrounding the day, but as a child of five, I reacted by working to please my mother.

On several occasions, she would lock me in my room. From my window, I would spy her leaving the house. She would return several hours later and conduct bizarre undertakings. After one of her trips, she insisted on serving only white foods to me. This lasted for two weeks before she, again, left for the day after locking me in my room.

After the second trip, she told me she had "special plans" for us, that we were to play a special game. She instructed me to tell no one of the details or else we would not be able to play. After I promised to never tell a soul, she led me to our small library. The curtains were drawn, plunging the room into darkness despite the days' waning light. The area rug had been rolled back. Strange chalk markings decorated the floorboards. A ring of saltpeter was positioned in the center of the room. Candles rimmed the saltpeter ring.

The scene frightened me. I clutched my mother's hand, glancing to her for reassurance. She pulled her hand from mine. "Get inside the ring," she instructed. "Lie down and do not move from inside until I instruct you to. Do you understand?"

I nodded. I climbed inside the ring, careful not to disturb the salt or candles. I laid back, staring at the ceiling. My mother consulted several sheets of paper. She stretched her arms over me and repeated some incantation in a language unfamiliar to me. Her voice raised, she continued shouting.

She glanced down at me. I shook with fear, not understanding the meaning of the ceremony. She shouted again the strange words, her voice raising to a fever pitch. She stared down at me again, her eyes wide. The expression on her face frightened me more than the strange ritual. Raw panic shone in her eyes. Her face twitched and her mouth contorted into an odd shape.

"Mum?" I whispered.

The small sound caused her to descend further into her frenzy. She climbed on top of me, straddling me with her legs. She raised a candle toward the heavens, shrieking strange words before she began to shout, "DEVIL, LEAVE THIS CHILD!" over and over.

The hot wax began to drip on me as her frenetic rantings continued. I squealed in torment as the hot wax scalded me. Tears ran down my cheeks and I begged for my mother to stop.

I managed to wriggle free from under her. I crawled from the circle, gaining my feet as I reached the door. I clutched the doorjamb as my mother stared at me. "You are an evil child," she growled at me. "I shall stop you!" she screamed as I ran.

I sprinted to my room and crawled under my bedcovers. I clung to the sheets, weeping until I fell asleep.

The next morning, my mother ignored the incident. I found the library restored as though nothing had happened. I began to wonder if I had imagined or dreamed the entire incident. Life returned to a semblance of normal for several weeks.

As the leaves began to turn to fall colors, however, my mother locked me in my room and disappeared for hours. When she returned home, she fed me a meager supper of water and white bread. After, she lured me into the yard behind our home, telling me we would spend the night gazing at the stars.

A large oak tree stood several feet from our home. My mother led me there and stood me against it. "Do not move," Mother instructed.

"Will not the leaves block the stars?" I questioned.

"Hush, Lenora," Mother warned. She reached and grasped an object from the ground nearby. As she approached me, I noted she carried a thick rope. "Put your arms at your sides and do not move."

She disappeared around the tree. When she reappeared, she pulled the rope with her. She wrapped it around me, pinning me to the tree. "Ouch!" I complained. "Mum, this hurts!"

"Hush, Lenora!" she shouted. She secured the rope, testing its tautness. Satisfied, she glanced to the full moon rising overhead. She returned her gaze to me and, with a smirk, she spun on her heel and returned to the house.

"Mum!" I called after her. "Mum!" She continued walking as though she never heard my pleas. I wriggled in my bonds but found myself unable to move. In the distance, an owl hooted, lending an eerie tone to the quiet night.

As the night wore on, I wept. In a panic, I thrashed around, earning myself only brush burns as the taut rope tore at my flesh.

My mother returned for me at the break of dawn. My head lolled as I dozed from exhaustion. I snapped my head up and my eyes open as I sensed movement. My mother carried a large knife. She clutched it in her fist, staring at me for a moment. A tear spilled down my cheek.

"Mum?" I questioned, my voice hoarse.

She tightened her grip on the knife, then moved to my side. She sawed through the rope and I collapsed to the ground in a heap. Weary, I did not move. My eyes followed my mother as she stalked away from me. "Come in when you are able," she muttered, leaving me sprawled on the grass.

I fell asleep there, dragging myself into the house only after the lunch hour. I longed for my father to return. Perhaps that would correct Mother's odd behavior.

The only comfort I gained was from the arrival of my

maternal grandfather one week after Mother tied me to the oak tree. I hoped his presence would settle Mother. Another three weeks passed without incident before the ill-fated tea with the woman whose name escaped me.

I recalled the woman arriving for tea. I played nearby with a doll gifted to me by the woman upon her arrival. My grandfather hovered over me as I played, teaching me a new game.

My mother served tea, chatting with the woman. After a time, the conversation turned to me. "How much longer will John be away?" the woman inquired of my father.

"Oh, until next summer," Mother answered. "His last letter noted the beauty of India."

"Does he plan to move you there?"

"Oh, I certainly hope not!" Mother exclaimed.

"Quite right," the woman agreed. "The environment is far better here for raising a child. And Lenora will make a better match here than there when the time comes." My mother offered a brief smile, staring into her teacup. The woman continued. "I realize it seems far off, but her eligibility to marry will arrive before you know it!"

"Hmm," my mother responded.

"She seems a lovely enough child, Helen," the woman said, glancing to me. "Very pretty. She can make an excellent match."

My mother's eyes slid sideways to glance at me for the briefest moment. "Oh, yes," she murmured before trying to change the subject.

The women persisted in her inquiry. "Is not her birthday soon? Turning six?"

My mother waved her hand in the air as to dismiss the comment. "Yes, yes, a few days, give or take," she responded evasively.

"All Hallows' Eve, isn't it?" the woman pressed.

"No!" Mother responded; her voice raised.

The woman's brow crinkled. "My apologies, Helen," she said. "I thought..."

"No, no, no," my mother interrupted. "No, quite wrong. I went into labor on All Hallows' Eve. Oh, I did panic! But Lenora was not born until 1 November. All Saints Day!"

"Ah, I see. My apologies. Not that it makes any matter, though Eleanor told me the child was born on All Hallows' Eve. You should correct her. She is spreading some rather nasty rumors about the girl. And all based on her incorrect birthday."

My mother set her mouth in a grim line. "Yes, I am aware of the falsehoods Eleanor whispers behind my back. She is quite mixed up! It was a difficult birth, and I was in labor for quite a long time. But I assure you, Lenora's birth occurred on 1 November, mid-morning, in fact. After all, I was present!" My mother offered a nervous chuckle. "Oh, how I wish John was here to confirm this. I grow tired of defending myself!"

I stared at the women as they spoke, recalling the conversation with my mother. If asked, I should clearly tell the woman I was born on 1 November. Then Mother would be proud of me. Perhaps then she would cease her odd and frightening behavior. I waited for my opportunity. My grandfather's hand rested on my shoulder. I glanced up at him, a smile on my face. Grandfather would be proud, too. I would obey my mother, and this would please both of them.

"Even the child herself will tell you! She knows her birthday! Lenora, come," Mother called.

I stayed seated for a moment. My grandfather's hand still rested on my shoulder. He leaned forward and whispered in my ear. I crinkled my brow and glanced to him. He nodded in encouragement. I swallowed hard.

"Lenora!" Mother said again, impatience showing in her voice.

I rose and approached the table. "Tell the nice woman your birthday, dear," Mother instructed.

I stood straight, my hands clasped in front of me. I took a deep breath and said, "31 October."

My mother's eyes went wide. "Lenora! What have I told you about lying? Nice little girls do not lie. Now, tell the truth. When is your birthday?" My mother smiled nervously at the woman across from her.

I bit my lower lip. I glanced back to my grandfather, who nodded at me again. I turned to face my mother and her guest. "31 October," I repeated.

The comment vexed my mother. She drew her mouth into a thin line, her jaw set. "The child is confused. She overheard our conversation," my mother said as an excuse. "You realize how silly children can be."

"I am not lying," I insisted. "And I am not confused. Grandfather Murray said I should tell the truth. Never lie about who you are, Lenora, he said to me."

The woman's face expressed utter confusion. My mother's face reddened with fury. I did not understand her anger, though I detected it. "Go to your room!" she shouted.

Confused, I ran to the top of the stairs but did not proceed to my room. I slumped to the floor behind the banister, peering over into the foyer below. I overheard my grandfather speaking before he ascended the stairs to comfort me.

"You did nothing wrong, child," he told me.

Voices from below drew my attention before I could respond. "... should be going."

"Oh, please, stay. Do not allow the child to ruin our tea!" my mother said, chasing after the woman who appeared in the foyer below.

"Oh, Helen, I am sorry, but I must go."

"The girl is merely playing a game. You know children!"

The woman placed her hand on my mother's arm and shook her head. "Take care, Helen." She stepped toward the door, turning back before exiting. Her hand lingered on the doorknob. "I hadn't realized your father was still alive. I thought he passed years ago, before Lenora was born. I am so pleased to hear he is well and taking an interest in Lenora. Goodbye, Helen."

The women exited, pulling the door closed behind her. My mother leaned against the door, her forehead resting against the door jamb. Her shoulders slumped, and she pounded against the door with her fists.

After a moment, she whipped around, glaring up the steps. She spotted me peeking between the banister's spindles. Her face twisted and contorted as she thundered up the stairs. "You wicked brat!" she screamed at me.

My grandfather stepped in front of me, shielding me from her fury. "Do not blame the child, Helen!" he pleaded with her.

She stormed toward me, passing through him as though he was only air. I scurried backward on my rear. "Grandfather told me to tell the truth!" I cried.

"No more, Lenora! Stop this talk!" she screamed. I backed to the wall where I was pinned. She continued toward me. I attempted to dart to the side to escape down the hall. She grasped my ankles, dragging me back. Her hands pounded against me, striking multiple blows to my legs and back. "You are a devil child! Your lies have cost me more than I can calculate! First your father and now my friends! You little demon! No more!"

I squealed with sobs. "I am not lying. Grandfather is right there!" I shrieked. "Please, Mum! He's begging you to stop and listen to him."

My comments further incensed my mother. She grasped hold of me, carrying me like a sack of wheat. She tossed me into my room and slammed the door shut. I heard the lock engage before her footsteps retreated down the hall.

I collapsed on the floor, still sobbing. My grandfather stroked my hair as I laid there in tears. "Poor child," he whispered. "There, there, Lenora."

I grasped his hand in mine, squeezing it. He tugged on it and I rose from my position on the floor. He led me to my bed, and I climbed onto it, cuddling into my pillow for comfort. I fell asleep there, only waking hours later after the sun had set.

I glanced around, finding myself alone. I rubbed my sore eyes and climbed from my bed. Outside, the moon already rose overhead. I shuddered, reminded of my experience the month prior. I wandered to my door, turning the knob. I discovered the door remained locked.

With a sigh, I trudged to my small trinket box and retrieved a hairpin. After months of being locked in my room regularly, I had found a means of escape. On several previous occasions, I had witnessed my mother use her hairpin to open my father's liquor cabinet. I tried the technique on my door lock, finding it worked there too. My delight over my success caused me to clap my hands as I bobbed on my toes.

I used my trick to unlock my door. As I stepped into the hallway, I found the house dark. Mother must be in her bedroom, I concluded. I traversed the hallway, arriving at my mother's room. The door was ajar, but the room was dark. I pushed it open, stepping inside. "Mum?" I called softly.

I received no response. "Mum?" I questioned again. In the dim light, I made out a lump on the bed. I crept forward and stretched my arm out to touch her shoulder. "Mum?"

She jolted when my fingers grasped her. "Go away, Lenora," she groaned. Her voice was raspy, thick with phlegm from weeping.

I pressed on, despite her cold response. "Are you hungry, Mum? I can fetch some bread for you."

"No."

"I am sorry, Mum. I only wanted to tell the truth. I did not mean to upset you. I shan't do it again," I promised.

"Go AWAY, Lenora!" my mother said, raising her voice.

I swallowed hard, choking back my tears. I backed from the room. The moment I cleared the door, I spun and raced back to my room. I threw myself on my bed and wept. My mother remained angry with me. I was a terrible child who had disappointed my mother. I deserved to be punished.

After half of an hour, I quieted and lay staring out the window. My stomach growled with hunger, though I did not seek food. I fell asleep after a time despite my hunger, exhaustion overcoming me.

When I awoke, the sun had risen. I sat up and stretched. I had decided at the first opportunity to apologize and promise to be a better child. I considered seeking out my mother when a knock sounded at the door. My mother pushed through into the room. She appeared well, her hair kempt, her dress changed and her expression chipper.

"Good morning, Lenora," she said with a smile.

"Good morning, Mum," I answered, pleased to witness the change in her. She eased onto the edge of my bed, taking my hands in hers. I squeezed her hands. "I am sorry for being a wicked child..."

My mother shook her head, putting a finger against my lips. "Hush, child. We shall not speak of it. Instead, I have a surprise for you!"

"A surprise?" I questioned.

She nodded. "'Tis your birthday in a few days' time," she said.

"Yes," I responded. "But I shall tell no one! I shall insist it is not until 1 November."

"Lenora! Do not interrupt whilst I tell you about your surprise!" I bit my lip, lowering my eyes. "For your birthday, I have planned a special trip for us!"

My face rose, meeting her gaze. My lips formed a grin and my eyes widened with excitement. My mother smiled, pleased at my response. "Oh, how exciting it shall be!" she continued.

"When will we leave?" I queried.

"After breakfast!"

My grin widened. "Where are we going, Mum?"

"That, my dear Lenora, is a surprise! Though we must pack a few things for you! And we must hurry, Lenora. We cannot dally if we hope to leave on time."

I nodded, scurrying from my bed. My mother pulled a small, worn suitcase from the hall into my room. She plopped it on my bed and flung it open. I assisted her in packing a few dresses, a nightgown, and a pair of shoes. As she snapped it shut, I grinned at her.

"And now we shall have breakfast and be on our way!"

I giggled and clapped my hands. I rushed through my breakfast, eating all my porridge with no complaints. My legs swung under my chair with unbridled excitement. My mother offered a smile as she cleaned the pot at the sink. I grinned back at her, a giggle escaping my lips as my enthusiasm brimmed over.

In addition to my exhilaration over the adventure, it pleased me to see my mother happy. When I finished my breakfast, I carried my bowl to her to wash and helped her with the remaining breakfast chores.

After we finished, my mother said, "All done! Ready, darling?"

I nodded enthusiastically. She took my hand and led me

to the foyer. She draped my cape over my shoulders and gathered my suitcase in one hand. Her fingers closed around my hand and she led me outside.

"Where is your suitcase, Mum?" I inquired as we stepped out of the house.

"I sent my things ahead!" she informed me.

A horse-drawn carriage awaited us at the end of our walk. The sight made my mind whirl with possibilities. I trembled as we climbed into the carriage, unable to contain my elation.

We traveled for over an hour before the carriage teetered and ground to a halt. The coachman knocked at the door and opened it. "Stuck in a ditch, ma'am. Could you and the child climb out while I try to free it?"

My mother's eyes went wide. "No!" she breathed.

"It is not too chilly, and the sun is shining. It should be warm enough for the child."

"Please, try to hurry," my mother urged as we stepped down from the carriage.

The coachman spent half an hour freeing our stuck transportation. My mother paced the entire time, biting her fingernails. I attempted to soothe her, but she remained distraught over the delay.

Finally, the carriage pulled free of the ditch and we boarded and were off again. As Glasgow came into view, I glued myself to the window. The buildings and city's bustle excited me as a child. The city seemed mysterious and intriguing. I could not wait to explore it with my mother.

I glanced back at her; a smile stuck on my face. "May we visit a toy store?" I asked.

My mother offered a coy smile. "We shall see," she answered.

The carriage wound through the city's streets, arriving outside of a large, ornate building. As we disembarked, my mother spoke a few words to the coachman. He nodded and leaned against the carriage. My mother wrapped her hand around mine and we ascended the stairs to the building.

Mum pushed open one of the doors and pulled me into the large foyer. I gaped around at the space. I had never seen a space so large. The stones creating the floor seemed larger than me! Colorful stained-glass windows rimmed the length of the area, placed every few feet. The sun passed through the windows on one side, casting soft colors across the gray stones.

The scene delighted me. I raced to each window, studying each with great interest. They depicted various religious scenes. I skipped from one to the other, even examining the unlit windows carefully.

The colors splaying across the floor enchanted me. I imagined them coloring my light skin and tinting my clothes, turning me into a living piece of stained-glass. I held out my hands, inspecting the mosaic of pigments embellishing my skin color.

My multicolored hands brought a grin to my face, and I waved them around to catch different tints. I spun in a circle, feeling like a mythical creature come to life.

The appearance of a woman in a nun's habit interrupted my frolicking. "Mother Superior," my mother greeted her.

"Mrs. Hastings, I did not expect you."

"My apologies, but the situation is quite urgent. May we speak in private?"

The nun glanced between my mother and me. After a moment, she gave a curt nod. She approached me. "Appreciating the stained glass, child?"

I nodded. "Yes, very much."

"Let me show you where you can view more," she promised, reaching out to take my hand.

I glanced to my mother, unsure. She nodded at me. "Go

on, Lenora." I took the woman's hand and allowed myself to be led away. Before we rounded the corner to leave the entrance hall behind, I glanced back. My mother fidgeted with her gloves as she stared after me. She wore an odd expression on her face. I failed to understand its meaning at the time, though as I aged, I understood it all too well.

It marked the last occasion I would see my mother. Mother Superior left me in the care of two other nuns, one older and one younger named Sister Mary Margaret. She whispered something to the two nuns before stalking away.

Sister Mary took me to the courtyard. It amazed me to find a garden wrapped inside the building. I spent an hour exploring the greenery, staring up at the open sky ringed by the stone buildings and learning about the plants.

"This is wonderful!" I exclaimed. "May we show it to my mum?"

Sister Mary Margaret's eyes grew wide at the request and she smiled but did not answer. The older nun with us, Sister Thomas Aquinas, informed me my mother was not to be interrupted. I nodded, figuring I would show her later when we reunited.

Time wore on and after a while I began to grow restless, as a child of six usually does. "Is my mum still busy?" I questioned.

The two nuns exchanged a glance. Mother Superior's return interrupted any answer they may have provided. "The child is asking for her mother," Sister Thomas Aquinas informed her.

Mother Superior's stern face turned to me. "Come with me, child," she requested, holding her hand out to me.

I grasped her hand in mine and followed her, expecting to be reunited with my mother. Instead, she took me to an empty office. She sat me in a chair and rounded a large wooden desk, settling behind it.

"May I see my mum?" I asked.

She did not respond for a moment. I fidgeted in my seat. "Your mother had to go away," she stated at long last.

I frowned. "When will she return?"

Another long pause filled the air between us. "You will stay with us for the time being."

My forehead crinkled as I tried to process the events. "But..."

"Do not talk back, child. You shall remain here until such time as your mother returns."

"Did she say when she plans to collect me?"

"No," Mother Superior said. "Now, come along." She stood and rounded the desk. "I shall show you to your room."

That night I lay on the small cot in the tiny cell. No windows graced the space, only cold stone. I longed for my bedroom at home, for my dolls, my bed, my window overlooking the back yard. It would only be for a short time, I told myself as a tear rolled down my cheek. I would reunite with my mother soon.

CHAPTER 20

Samuel gurgled and fidgeted in my arms. My mind snapped back to the present time. I stared at the child. "I will never understand how you did it, Mum," I whispered.

"Your Grace," Ella said from the doorway. Ella's eyes darted around the room. "Is everything all right? Has… Has she returned?"

"No," I answered. "Annie has not returned."

Ella stepped into the room, approaching and leaning over my shoulder to coo over Samuel. "I heard you speaking and, for a moment, thought it was to… well, you know. I did not realize you were only speaking to this precious babe."

I smiled at Samuel. "I'm afraid my mind was wandering to my own childhood as I fed him."

"In the orphanage, Your Grace?"

I shook my head, rising to lay Samuel in his bassinet as he settled to sleep. "No," I confessed, returning to my seat. "Before the orphanage, I lived in a convent and before that," I said with a sigh, "I had parents."

"Did they pass on when you were still very young?" Ella asked, her innocence showing.

"No." I swallowed hard, composing myself before I continued. Emotions swirled in my head and my heart from the recollection of the painful memories. I hoped to avoid them spilling over for Ella to witness. "Just before my sixth birthday, my mother took me to a convent. She abandoned me there. I never saw or heard from her again."

Ella's jaw dropped and she knit her brows. "But why? And what of your father? Oh! Forgive me, Your Grace! It is not my place!"

I waved my hand at her. "Your request is not out of line. My father departed for India months before. My mother became increasingly disturbed. My ability troubled her. I suppose she could no longer tolerate it." I glanced wistfully at the ceiling, focusing on nothing in particular. I shrugged, firming my resolve and burying the volatile emotions. I shook my head, dismissing the memories. "I do not understand, though, how she did it. How she walked away from me. I cannot imagine deserting Samuel for any reason."

Ella shook her head. "You poor child," she murmured.

"For many years, I assumed the fault was mine. It was not until I was much older that I realized the failing existed on my mother's part."

"I should say so!" Ella retorted.

I glanced to her. "She did not understand," I offered. "I am not absolving her." I shrugged again. "But most people do not comprehend my ability. And my mind must create some reason why a mother might abandon her child."

I remained silent for several breaths as I collected my thoughts. When I glanced to Ella again, she offered a slight smile. "Anyway, let us not dwell on the matter. It is no longer my life."

Ella nodded. "We shall focus, instead, on the future. And it appears quite bright with this little fellow!"

* * *

The next week consisted of reviewing letters of interest for our nursery positions. Mrs. Thomson and I conducted several interviews before I selected a nanny and a wet nurse. Nanny Browne, a small, middle-aged portly woman with a resolute demeanor and a steady tone, exhibited attentiveness toward Samuel which pleased me. She would be assisted by Clara, who would serve as the child's wet-nurse.

I found myself unable to part with Samuel on the first evening. I requested that he remain in my quarters overnight. There had been no further instances of Annie visiting the child. However, I remained more comfortable keeping him close. While the sentiment may seem coarse, I chose to keep the child near to me.

Robert and Ella continued to assist me in monitoring Samuel. Annie did not return. Not for Samuel, nor for me. I remained uneasy. Annie's non-presence frightened me more than when she showed herself.

I wandered the halls in search of her. She hadn't disappeared. Where was she hiding? I checked in at the nursery several times per day. In addition to keeping a watchful eye, I enjoyed spending time with Samuel.

I often rocked him to sleep before his naps, singing him lullabies. One evening, as I dressed for dinner, Ella mentioned Nanny Browne's annoyance with my behavior.

She fussed with my hair longer than I hoped. "Leave it," I instructed. "I would like to check on Samuel before dinner." Her eyebrows raised as she glanced to me in the mirror. "What is it?" I questioned, noting her expression.

She shook her head. "Nothing, Your Grace."

My eyes narrowed at her. "There was meaning behind that glance," I insisted. "What is it? Do not be shy, Sinclair, say what is on your mind."

"I should not spread gossip, but I feel you should know, Your Grace."

"Know? Know what?"

Ella bit her lower lip, then met my gaze in the mirror's reflection. "Nanny Browne has mentioned her displeasure with the amount of time you are spending in the nursery." Ella continued to fuss with my hair as she chattered on. "I suppose I ought not to have told you, but she finds your behavior unusual and 'unbecoming of a lady.' Her words, Your Grace. I do not consider it right, her talking about you in that way."

I raised one of my eyebrows. "I see. You were right to inform me, Sinclair."

"She mentioned that your 'meddling' indicates some lacking on her part. As though you do not trust her to care for the child."

"That is not the case at all! I enjoy tending to Samuel. I realize it is not the trend, but I shall not have my life dictated to me!" I railed for a moment before considering Nanny Browne's viewpoint. I pursed my lips and shrugged. "Though I suppose I understand her frustration. I hired her to care for the child but prevent her from completing her job." I sighed. "I shall attempt to not 'meddle' in her affairs."

Ella met my gaze again. "She does not understand the situation. She lacks knowledge of the threat in the house."

"Annie has not shown any interest in the child or anyone, for that matter, in over a week," I told her. "Ah! You've fixed it!" I exclaimed as she managed to smooth the wayward piece of hair into my hairstyle.

"Yes!" Ella answered. "It is perfect now."

"Thank you!" I leapt from my seat, pacing the floor. "I

suppose I shan't check on Samuel until after dinner, lest I face Nanny Browne's wrath."

"Does it bother you greatly, Your Grace?" Ella questioned. "You seem perturbed."

"No, it's not that," I responded, continuing to pace. "It is Annie. Or rather, the lack of Annie."

Ella's brows raised. "If I were you, I would prefer not to have encountered her."

I reached the end of my route, spinning and returning across the room. "I do not prefer it. Something is odd."

"Odd?" Ella queried.

"Yes, odd," I responded. "Where is she? Where has she gone?"

"Perhaps she has… you know." Ella glanced to me, flitting her fingers in the air.

I rounded the bend, making another trip across the room. "No," I responded with a shake of my head. "No, she has not gone."

"Are you certain?"

"Fairly, yes," I answered. "No, she is lurking here somewhere. The question is when will she pop up again and what will she do when she does?"

Ella shook her head. "I am sorry, Your Grace. This must be frustrating and worrisome for you."

"It is, though there is not much to be done about it." I threw my arms out, allowing them to slap against my dress. "Well, I suppose I shall go to dinner."

"I shall see you after, Your Grace. Enjoy your meal."

"Thank you, Sinclair."

I exited the room, resisting the urge to go to the nursery before presenting myself for dinner.

Robert and I dined alone, discussing various topics. "The weather has been marvelous of late," Robert mentioned.

"Indeed," I agreed. "I have enjoyed watching the spring greenery begin to come to life from the tower's windows."

"I propose we take in the spring greenery at a closer view."

"Oh?"

"Yes, I thought tomorrow might be an excellent day to take you riding. It seems Annie's disturbances have died down and I expect an outing might be enjoyable for you."

I considered the proposition. We had discussed my learning to ride before we adopted Samuel. Samuel's arrival changed our plans, particularly after Annie's interest in him. Given that there had been no incidents with Annie and the child, I did not see the harm in it. "It sounds like an excellent proposition," I responded with a smile. "And it will help keep me out of Nanny Browne's hair." Robert's eyebrows raised, and he stared at me, waiting for me to continue. "Sinclair informed me Nanny Browne has taken issue with my interference in the nursery."

"Interference?" Robert questioned. "How dare she? It is your house and your child!"

"I may hover too much," I confessed. "Most women do not spend as much time in the nursery as I. She views my impingements as a slight on her abilities as a nanny."

"I am certain your judgement in the situation is appropriate."

"Still, I did not check on Samuel before dinner. And our riding expedition will keep me away for some time tomorrow. It will allow Nanny Browne room to breathe."

"I do hope you enjoy it," Robert mentioned. "The grounds are lovely in the spring."

"I am certain I will," I assured him.

The next day brought another sunny, warm spring day, perfect for my riding lesson. While I did visit the nursery in the morning, I allowed Nanny Browne free rein from mid-morning on, turning my attentions to my riding trip.

I met Robert at the stables in the late morning. The grooms already had our horses readied. Robert had chosen for me a steady mare, chestnut in color with a white streak down her nose. I learned her name was Lady as I greeted her, feeding her a carrot. Robert's horse, a large black steed named Charger, dwarfed Lady.

"I hope Lady lives up to her name," I quipped as I gained my mount on her back. Robert instructed me on holding the reins after I had adjusted myself into the side-saddle.

"She is a gentle horse. If anything, you may find her too slow!" Robert assured me.

Robert mounted his steed, instructing it to head away from the stable. Lady followed without much urging on my part. Robert offered instructions here and there. However, Lady's behavior proved above reproach. I found her easy to manage on my first outing.

We kept a slow, steady pace, meandering about the estate. I found the experience enjoyable. As we approached a field with a large oak, I spotted a table and several servants milling around. Robert planned a picnic as a surprise.

"I had hoped you tolerated the ride well enough to make it here," Robert said as he assisted me to dismount.

"I found it most enjoyable," I said as he escorted me to the table.

We enjoyed our picnic lunch under a cloudless sky. After lunch, we mounted the horses to return to the stable. As I settled into the saddle, a flash of color on the hillside caught my eye. I squinted into the distance, focusing on the color. My eyes widened as I realized it was Annie's red dress blowing in the breeze.

"Annie?" I whispered to myself.

The horse turned as I spoke, its eyes also catching sight of

Annie's blowing dress, of her disheveled form standing on the hillside. The sight caused the horse to panic. She reared; her eyes wide with fright.

I struggled to keep my seat, managing to hang on by grasping a fistful of her mane. The spooked horse turned in a circle before bolting in the opposite direction, racing away from the specter.

I shrieked in panic as I fought to stay on Lady's back. "Lenora!" Robert shouted behind me. I dared not glance back for fear of falling from the horse.

Thundering hooves pounded the ground as we fled from Annie. Lady raced down the hillside, heading into a wooded area and toward a stream that cut through the property. Branches tore at my face and arms. I lowered my head behind Lady's as she continued her mad dash.

Lady sprinted into a clearing near the stream, showing no signs of slowing. Without warning, she skidded to a stop, turning in circles. I attempted to soothe her as we spun in a dizzying loop. The horse panted hard, chomping on her bit, still spooked. She squealed and trumpeted, her distress obvious.

After three revolutions, Lady reared again. In this instance, I was unable to maintain my grip on her. I toppled off, landing hard on my backside and twisting my ankle. As I fell, movement caught my eye.

Lady dashed off as Robert and Charger rushed toward me. Robert leapt from his steed. He rushed to me, grasping my hand, worry etched in his face. "Lenora, my God, are you all right?"

"Yes," I answered without making eye contact. My focus remained straight ahead.

"Are you hurt? Did you jar anything?" Robert noted my gaze, adding, "What is it, Lenora?"

"A child," I answered. Near the stream's bank, a small,

dark-haired child played. The girl, around three-years-old, wore a light pink dress, her dark hair tied with a pink ribbon. She giggled as she splashed her hands in the stream's cold, clear water.

"Child?" Robert questioned, his eyes scanning the horizon. "Where?"

"By the stream," I answered. "Little girl?" I called to her.

The child snapped her head in my direction. Her small brown eyes were wide with fear. She stood and raced across the stream and disappeared into a thicket of trees on the other side. "No!" I called after her. "Wait!" I struggled to climb to my feet, wincing as pain flared through my ankle.

"Lenora!" Robert exclaimed. "What are you saying? I see no child."

With the child gone, I turned to Robert. "There was a child. About three, just there, near the stream. With brown hair and brown eyes. She ran when I called to her." Over Robert's shoulder, Annie stood on the ridge. My brows knit as I tried to piece the information together.

Robert huffed, focusing his attentions back on me. "Lenora, are you certain you are not hurt?"

"What? Oh," I responded, turning my mind back to the situation at hand. "Yes, I am unharmed. Lady ran off. I could not hold on to her, I am sorry. My ankle is sore, but with your help, I can stand and walk, I am sure. We can call for her as we walk."

"You shall do nothing of the sort," Robert enjoined. He wrapped one arm around my shoulder, cupping the other under my knees. He lifted me as he stood. "I shall carry you back to the castle."

Several of the servants, who had witnessed Lady's flight, raced toward us. "Your Grace! Is everything all right?" James, one of our footmen, inquired. He, along with Andrew, another footman, heaved deep breaths from their sprint.

"No," Robert answered. "Her Grace fell from her horse. Fetch the doctor at once, James. Andrew, collect Charger and search for Lady, she ran off in that direction." Robert nodded toward Lady's last known location. James rushed in the direction of the castle at full speed. Andrew took hold of Charger's reins, leading him in the direction Robert indicated.

"No," I objected. "A doctor is not necessary. And the castle is too far. I can walk, put me down."

"I will not hear of it, Lenora."

"Robert..." I countered, but found myself interrupted.

"Lenora, I said no! Have you no faith in my ability to care for you? I am not feeble!"

I sighed at him. "I have every faith in your abilities, Robert. But I also have faith in my own abilities to walk."

"You winced when stepping on your ankle. You will not walk on it until you have been seen by the doctor."

"You could have ridden on Charger and carried me with you."

"I shall not have you bounced about on another horse after your accident."

I acquiesced, finding myself unable to change the situation. Although, in truth, I appreciated being cared for. "Now, with that settled, tell me about the child."

My forehead wrinkled as my thoughts returned to the conundrum. "There is not much to tell. When I fell from Lady, I noticed her. She was crouched by the stream, playing. She had long brown hair and dark brown eyes."

"And you estimate her to be three?"

"Yes, give or take," I answered. "Who was she?"

Robert considered my question for a moment. He shrugged. "I am not certain, though I imagine there have been children who have died on the estate."

I shook my head. "But why did Annie want me to see her? Who was she?"

"Annie? What has she to do with this?" Robert asked.

"Yes. Annie is the reason Lady bolted. She appeared on the hill. When the horse saw her or sensed her, she ran."

Robert stopped walking. "Annie caused Lady to run?"

I nodded. "Yes," I answered. "She must have wanted me to see the child."

Robert continued toward the castle. "Lenora, she could not have known where Lady would have run to. Though it disturbs me that you have, again, sustained an injury from Annie's actions."

"She could," I contested. "During our wild fugue, Annie's presence may have escaped me. She could have guided Lady's direction without my knowing. She appeared on the hill above the stream's bank. She must have intended us to end up there. But why? Why did she want me to see the child?"

Robert shook his head. "I care not, only that you are unharmed."

"I am," I assured him.

"That remains to be seen," Robert countered.

I rolled my eyes. "I do NOT need to see the doctor!"

"I shall decide that. And do not roll your eyes at me, dear."

Robert trudged up the hill to the castle. As we approached, we were met by a bevy of servants led by Buchanan. "Your Grace," he greeted Robert, "I have sent a rider for the doctor straight away. I have a toddy being prepared for Her Grace and I have readied her bed."

"Oh, Your Grace!" Ella cried, racing after Buchanan. "Does it hurt dreadfully? How awful!"

"I am fine, Sinclair," I tried to interject, but the conversation between Buchanan and Robert continued over us. I had hoped to inquire about Samuel from Sinclair. With Annie's presence on the grounds, I doubted Samuel had been harmed, yet I desired to confirm that.

"I shall take her straight to her bedroom. Sinclair, prepare a cool compress for her to settle her nerves," Robert said.

Ella nodded, racing into the castle ahead of us. Buchanan preceded us, as well, overseeing the rescue operation and providing a clear path to my bedroom. Within moments, Robert settled me in my bed and a flurry of activity descended upon me. I was fussed over, my pillows fluffed, and a cushion placed under my ankle, a coverlet placed over me for warmth and a hot toddy shoved into my hands.

Robert paced the floor at the foot of my bed. Buchanan returned to the room to determine if any other arrangements were required. "Is there anything else, Your Grace?"

Robert flung his arms out in frustration. "Where the devil is the damned doctor?" he shouted.

"I sent the fastest rider, Your Grace. He should arrive any moment," Buchanan assured him. "I shall await his arrival in the foyer and send him to Her Grace's room at once."

"Robert," I chimed in as Buchanan strode from the room, "please! You'll wear a hole in the floor."

Robert sighed, shaking his head. Ella rushed into the room, a bowl of water and a cloth in her hand. "Here you are, Your Grace." She wet the cloth and laid it across my forehead. "Oh, you poor dear, is there anything else I can get you?"

"Please, will you check on Samuel? Have him brought here at once?" I requested.

"Lenora, you need not be attending to the child now. Leave him to Nanny Browne," Robert argued. Ella stopped mid-stride, unsure what to do.

"I am perfectly fine, Robert. Sinclair, please have Samuel brought. I want to ensure his safety," I said.

Ella nodded, disappearing from the room. Robert set his

mouth into a thin line, unhappy with me, but understanding my need to see the child. "Please, sit," I appealed to Robert.

With a sigh, he plopped onto the edge of the bed. I grabbed hold of his hand. "I am not certain how much more I can stand of this," he confessed.

I squeezed his hand in mine. "I only want to verify Samuel is unharmed. I am certain he is fine. Annie appeared at both our picnic spot and the stream. She could not have harmed him in any way."

Robert shook his head. "You were not so lucky," he lamented.

I groaned at him. "I am not harmed either!" I insisted.

Ella's arrival interrupted our conversation. Behind her trailed Nanny Browne, who carried Samuel in her arms. "Here he is, Your Grace. As perfect as can be!" Ella announced.

I reached my arms out to take the child, pulling him close to me. "Yes, there he is!" I exclaimed, smiling down at him. "Mummy simply wanted to visit with you!"

The doctor arrived minutes after, escorted by Buchanan and one other. "Duke Blackmoore," he said, greeting Robert. Robert stood to shake his hand. "We must stop meeting under these circumstances," he quipped.

"Indeed," Robert answered.

Dr. MacAndrews approached the bed, setting his doctor's bag on the foot. "Greetings, Duchess Blackmoore. Tending to little Samuel? While you are abed from a fall? Surely Nanny can manage!"

"Same thing I said," I heard Nanny Browne mutter under her breath.

"I find his presence soothing." Nanny Browne relieved me of the child to allow the doctor to examine me.

Dr. MacAndrews removed his stethoscope from his bag and listened to my heart and lungs. He examined my eyes and took my pulse. Then he moved on to examining my ankle. I winced as he moved it around. The ankle, now the size of a goose egg, was discolored from a bruise.

"And you cannot bear weight on it?"

"I have not tried, though when I attempted to stand, I did feel pain."

Robert stood at the foot of the bed, examining the process. "She could not bear weight," he interjected.

"Mm-hm," the doctor mumbled as he studied my ankle. "And can you feel this?" he inquired as he ran his fingers on my foot.

The motion elicited a giggle from me. "Yes," I answered, trying to contain my laughter. Robert shot me a stern glance, his forehead wrinkling at my reaction. "My apologies, doctor, I am ticklish."

The doctor chuckled. "And can you wiggle your toes?"

I nodded, demonstrating my ability by wriggling my toes back and forth. "Excellent!" Dr. MacAndrews stated. He folded his stethoscope and placed it in his bag.

"What is the prognosis, doctor?" Robert inquired.

"A minor sprain, nothing more. A few days of bedrest should do the trick. I shall leave opium for the pain."

"Thank you, doctor," I answered.

He nodded his head to me. "You are most welcome. And how is the young master? Settling into his home well? Not giving Nanny any trouble, is he?"

"Trouble? None at all! Oh, he is simply perfect!" I gushed.

Dr. MacAndrews nodded. "He will grow to be a strapping laddie! My initial examination of him proved outstanding! A healthy babe. My congratulations to you both."

"Thank you, doctor," Robert said, clapping him on the back.

"I shall return in a few days' time to check on Her Grace's

progress and the young master. Stay off that ankle," Dr. MacAndrews warned.

"I will ensure she does!" Robert promised as he walked him to the door. Buchanan waited outside to escort the doctor out.

Robert closed the door behind them. "See," I said. "All is well."

"All is not well, dear," Robert answered as he strode back to my bedside. "You have a sprained ankle." He sunk onto the bed's side, facing me.

"A minor sprain," I reminded him.

"And you must listen to the doctor's advice."

"I shall."

Robert kissed my forehead before continuing. "And you must abandon this investigation."

"Just a moment!" I objected.

"Lenora!" Robert admonished. "This is not up for discussion. This is the second time you have been seriously harmed in pursuit of this!"

"I have not been seriously harmed! I sustained a minor sprain of my ankle. It could have happened while riding, even without Annie involved. You, yourself, know the dangers of riding."

"It did not happen without Annie's presence. It happened because of Annie's presence. Lenora, please, I do not wish to quarrel over this."

"Then we shall not quarrel."

Robert's eyes narrowed at me. "But you have no intention on abiding by my request, have you?"

"I am unable to abide by your request. I have no control over the situation."

Robert sighed. "Please, promise you will be cautious."

"I promise." Robert issued another sigh. "Do not blame

yourself," I added, realizing the source of Robert's concern. "The fault is no one's, certainly not yours."

"I invited you for the ride," Robert stated.

"It is not your fault!" I maintained.

Ella's arrival suspended our conversation. "Your Grace, I retrieved several books for you to pass the time. If you are too tired, I can read to you."

"Thank you, Sinclair," I responded, relieving her of the books.

Robert stood, saying, "If you are certain you are settled, I shall attend to some business."

"Of course, dear," I answered.

"I shall stay with Her Grace," Ella offered.

"Thank you, Sinclair," Robert answered. He kissed my forehead and left us alone.

"Would you like me to read to you? Shall I fetch any medicines? Is there anything you need?" Ella questioned.

"Yes," I responded, pushing myself up a bit in the bed. "Could you seek out the family Bible? The one kept in the library on the pedestal?"

"Of course, Your Grace," Ella answered. "I shall fetch it at once."

She hurried from the room, pulling the door shut behind her.

"There," I said. "We are alone now. Perhaps now you might explain why you sent me to the stream to see the child."

The specter of Annie stared back at me. She had arrived with Dr. MacAndrews, following him into the room and taking her usual post by the door. It was the same spot she stood in when I had nearly fallen out of the tower. She had not left when the doctor did, nor when Robert departed. She stood, unwavering, staring at me.

"Nothing to say?" I questioned. I drew in a deep breath,

searching my depths for patience. "Why did you send me to the child?" Annie's eyes flashed red. I had hit upon something. "So, you DID send me there! Why?"

Annie turned, pacing the floor in front of me. I followed her as she strode back and forth across the floor. I narrowed my eyes, studying her form. Her shoulders slumped forward, her arms rigid and stiff. Her fists were balled. Something perturbed her. What?

"Annie," I tried again. "There is a reason you sent my horse on a mad dash toward that stream. You made sure I spotted that child. Who was she? What connection has she to this?"

Annie stopped in her tracks. She faced me, her eyes still glowing red, her fists still balled. At that moment, Ella burst through the door. Annie vaporized as she entered. "I've got it, Your Grace!" Ella called triumphantly. She waved the Bible in her hands. She perched on the edge of the bed next to me and pulled the book open. "Is there a particular passage you would like to read?"

"No," I replied. The turn of events with Annie frustrated me, though I did not expect answers to be forthcoming.

Ella offered a quizzical glance to me and ceased paging through the Bible. I motioned for her to hand me the Bible. I shut it and opened the cover. "I want to study the family tree."

Ella glanced over the book's top. "Will you add Samuel now?"

"No, not until the christening. Then he shall be added. I glanced at the tree, noting the addition of my name joined with Robert. The cross next to Annie's name did not escape me. No other names were shown in or after Robert's generation.

I followed the tree up, checking for female ancestors.

"What are you searching for, Your Grace?" Ella questioned.

"Female children who died at a young age."

"Whatever for?"

"When I fell from my horse earlier, I saw a child playing on the stream's bank. Annie must have shown her to me for a reason. Why? Who was she?"

"Annie?" Ella inquired, her face paling.

"Yes," I answered. "Annie spooked the horse and sent us on that wild race across the grounds. She also appeared at the stream."

Ella's eyes were wide as I disclosed the detail. "Your Grace! She is attempting to harm you! If she sent your horse into a frenzy, she intended to cause you harm!"

I considered her statement. This marked the second occasion on which Annie's actions caused me harm. Yet I remained steadfast in my conviction that she did not intend to injure me. "I disagree," I answered and returned to perusing the family tree.

"Your Grace!" Ella objected.

I set the Bible on my lap. "She is communicating. If she was attempting to harm me, she could have done it a dozen different ways by now."

"Communicating? Can she not speak?"

"She has not spoken yet," I responded. "She may lack the ability due to her traumatic end."

"But... you spoke with Samuel's mother. She spoke."

"Yes, she did," I confirmed. "But Tilly and I were good friends. And Tilly's death was far less violent. Tilly's circumstances were entirely different."

Ella shook her head. "It is all so complicated."

"It can be. Which is why we must keep at it. Who was this child and what has she to do with Annie? Why did Annie insist I see her?"

Ella leaned over the book to study the family tree. "Are there any children listed who match your vision?"

I shook my head. "No, I do not see anyone."

"Here," Ella said, "what about Fiona?"

"No. The dates listed make her eleven, far too old to have been the child I saw."

I snapped the Bible shut with a sigh. "No, there is no one listed here who died at that age."

Ella's shoulders sagged. "I am sorry, Your Grace."

"Do not be. This has helped."

"Helped? You have made no progress."

"That is where you are incorrect, Sinclair! The progress I have made is ruling out other female relatives. No female Fletcher child died at that age. So, it is not an ancestor of the Fletchers. Of course, it could be a servant's child. Though there is no reason for Annie to want to call my attention to her."

My mood turned pensive as I considered the information. Ella frowned as she processed my comments. Her forehead wrinkled as she, too, sought to contribute an idea. "Sinclair," I suggested. "Would you summon Buchanan? Perhaps he can shed some light on any children on the estate in Annie's time."

"At once, Your Grace," Ella declared, leaping from the bed. She hurried from the room in search of Buchanan.

"Annie? Annie, are you there?" I called to the empty room.

Annie did not appear. I waited for someone, alive or dead, to appear. I drummed my fingers on my opposite arm, the toes on my good leg tapping the air. Oh, to be able to walk, I lamented, frustrated by my inability to move.

Several minutes passed before my bedroom door swung open. Ella entered with Buchanan. "Miss Sinclair said you requested to speak with me, Your Grace?"

"Yes, Buchanan. I hoped to ask you about a delicate matter." Buchanan's eyes slid sideways toward Ella before glancing back to me. "You may speak in earnest in front of the both of us," I said. "Sinclair understands any information relayed here is to remain only between us."

Buchanan nodded in understanding. "Of course, Your Grace. What is the nature of your inquiry?"

"Are you aware of any female children, around the age of three, who passed away on the estate in recent years?"

Buchanan's thick brows furrowed, and he frowned, glancing at the floor. "Children?" his deep voice pondered aloud. After a moment, he shook his head and pursed his lips. "No. There haven't been any children on the estate in many years. The last children were His Grace and Mr. Fletcher!"

"No servants had any children? Please do not suppress any information for fear of appearances. The information shall go nowhere."

"Certainly not!" Buchanan assured me. "I have served in the household for many years, starting as a footman for His Grace's parents and working toward my current position. In that time there have been no scandals. A tight rein was kept on this household! There was no funny business tolerated under this roof!" Buchanan raised his eyebrows, wagging his finger in the air.

"I understand. And I am certain Duke Blackmoore appreciates your vigor in the matter. Thank you."

"Is there anything else I can be of assistance with, Your Grace?"

I considered the matter for a moment. I began to shake my head when an idea occurred to me. I glanced up at Buchanan. "Yes. Was the former Mrs. Fletcher ever with child?"

"No," Buchanan answered. "There were no children."

"And no pregnancies?"

Buchanan shook his head. "No, Your Grace."

My brow crinkled at the answer. Another dead-end. I nodded. "Thank you, Buchanan. I am sorry to have disturbed your day. And I appreciate your discretion in not mentioning this conversation beyond us."

"Of course, Your Grace." Buchanan bowed his head to me before departing.

Ella sunk onto the bed next to me. "Another dead end," I lamented.

"I am sorry, Your Grace."

"I suppose the next move is Annie's. Now, we wait."

CHAPTER 21

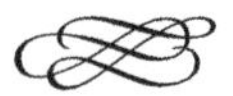

My ankle kept me abed for two days. Frustration grew in me as I sat unable to pursue any additional information. Though, I had no idea what information I would seek even if I was able. After three days, I could bear some weight on the ankle, though I remained cautious. I kept to my room, unwilling to traverse the long castle halls or climb the stairs to my tower room.

The books Ella brought kept me busy and, despite Nanny Browne's objections, I spent a large amount of time with Samuel. On the afternoon of the third day, I reclined on my bed with Samuel. His fingers wrapped around one of mine as I cooed at him. Tilly's blue scarf lay next to us. I kept it close to Samuel, insisting it adorn his crib regardless of Nanny's objections. I grabbed it and held it over my face before pulling it away in a game of peekaboo.

A knock sounded on the door and Ella entered when I called. "Your Grace," she said with a curtsy, "Mr. Fletcher is downstairs requesting to see you."

"Edwin?" I questioned with a frown.

Ella nodded. "Should I make your excuses, Your Grace?"

"No, I had better take his call. I do not wish to cause any further strife within the family."

"But your ankle! Can you manage a walk to the sitting room?"

I pushed myself up to sitting. "No," I admitted. "No, you are correct, I do not believe I should. Perhaps you had better offer my apologies."

"I shall pass it along to Mr. Buchanan."

I returned to fussing over Samuel. My mind dwelled on the repercussions of refusing to speak with Edwin. I hoped it caused no issues.

"I hope your uncle does not take this personally," I said to Samuel. "He can be quite melodramatic."

Samuel's blue eyes stared up at me as I spoke. I smiled down at him. A ruckus in the hall drew my attention from my child. Loud voices conversed for a moment before my door burst open.

"... most objectionable, sir!" Buchanan said, following Edwin through the door.

Edwin waved his hands at Buchanan. "I am her brother-in-law. I assure you there is nothing untoward. Besides, Miss Sinclair can chaperone." He grinned and winked at Ella who stood, her mouth hanging open in shock at the turn of events.

"Edwin!" said I. "What a surprise. Thank you, Buchanan, you may go."

Buchanan glanced between me and Edwin before turning on his heel with a huff and exiting.

"Lenora. When Buchanan said you were under the weather and abed, I took it upon myself to visit you here. I do hope it is not a problem. I have a gift for my nephew!" He waved a wrapped item in the air.

"How kind of you," I answered. "I am sorry I was unable

to take your call elsewhere. I am still unable to bear much weight on my ankle."

"Yes, terrible shame. And on your first outing with the horses. I hope it hasn't put you off riding entirely."

"Not at all," I assured him. "I do hope to try my hand again at it soon. I found it enjoyable." Edwin smiled at me. "You said you had a gift?" I prompted.

"Oh, yes!" Edwin exclaimed, passing the wrapped item to me.

"Again, how kind." I unwrapped it, finding a model ship in the package. "A ship!" I admired the item, turning it around in my hands.

"Yes!" Edwin exclaimed. "I had one like it when I was a boy. I enjoyed it in the nursery on many occasions!"

"How lovely. I am certain Samuel will enjoy it."

"I see the little chap is here rather than in the nursery," Edwin commented. "You are quite the hands-on mother." I nodded. "When Robert and I were children, we saw Mum for one hour per day, no more!"

"Yes, my methods are unorthodox, I realize, and quite distressing to Nanny Browne."

Edwin chuckled. He approached the bed, staring down at the child. "Such bright blue eyes!" he commented.

"Yes, I wonder if they will remain. I do hope so. They remind me so much of Tilly's."

"Tilly?" Edwin questioned.

"Yes, his mother," I responded. "Her name was Tilly." A crease formed in Edwin's forehead and his eyebrows pinched together. I continued, picking up Tilly's scarf, "She would have made a loving mother. This is her scarf. I brought it with me when I took Samuel. I try to keep it close to him. Silly, really, I suppose, but I feel he's comforted by it."

"That is her scarf?" he inquired.

I smiled down at it. "Yes," I answered, fondling it. "I understand she cherished it while alive."

Edwin stalked a few steps from the bed, his finger pressed to his lips. "Edwin?" I questioned.

He spun on his heel to face me. "Oh, yes." He waved his hand in the air. "Forgive my pensiveness. It is such a fascinating story. And you said… ah… Tessa, was it?"

"Tilly," I corrected.

"Ah, yes, Tilly. Tilly was a friend?"

"Yes. We spent several years together at St. Mary's."

"St. Mary's?"

"Yes," I confirmed. "The orphanage where we resided."

Edwin pursed his lips. "And she remained there after you came to Blackmoore?"

"No," I answered. "She left the orphanage several months before I did."

The crease in Edwin's forehead deepened. "I see," he answered, rubbing his chin.

His reaction puzzled me. His interest seemed odd, though perhaps he hoped his curiosity would be taken as polite. Edwin's gaze fell on Samuel. Several moments of silence passed between us before Edwin changed the subject.

"And how is your other project going, sister-in-law? Making any progress in your exploration of Annie's untimely demise?"

I waved the scarf over my face, peeking at Samuel as Edwin spoke. "Very little, I'm afraid," I responded, glancing to him.

"A pity. I realize how important the project is to you. Though as I mentioned when we last spoke, it is undoubtedly for the best."

"And as I mentioned when we last spoke, I disagree."

"So, Annie has not appeared further to you? No additional information?"

I stopped playing with Samuel to gaze at Edwin. I hoped my survey of him may provide some subtle hint regarding his inquiry. It did not. "No additional information," I responded, deliberately evading his question about Annie's appearances.

"Perhaps it is time to abandon the pursuit."

My eyes narrowed at Edwin. What was his motive? "That seems premature," I said. "I have only begun to make progress."

"Some things are best left alone, Lenora," Edwin responded, his gray eyes set upon me.

He seemed insistent that I cease in my search for answers. I did not wish to start an argument, yet I had no intention of backing down. As I pondered my response, the door swung open and Robert entered.

"Edwin," he said. "What in heaven's name..."

I interrupted his statement, recognizing the temper rising in his voice. "He brought a gift for Samuel. A ship!" I exclaimed, holding up the object. Robert's gaze flicked between us. "Is it not handsome? I am certain Samuel will be keen on it. Very thoughtful."

"Oh..." Robert paused, his forehead wrinkling. A slight smile crossed his lips, and he approached the bed, taking the ship from me. "Quite, yes." He studied it, turning it round in his hands.

"We had one similar..." Edwin began.

"When we were in the nursery, yes," Robert finished, his smile growing. "I remember it." He returned his gaze to the ship.

"I always admired it," Edwin replied. "It was one of my favorite toys. I thought it fitting to buy him one. I hope it shall provide him with the same entertainment it provided me."

"I am certain he will treasure it," I answered, catching

Robert's gaze. I gave him a slight nod and smiled broadly at Edwin.

"Yes," Robert agreed. "Very gracious of you."

"Well, I am the boy's uncle. It is my duty to add to his spoiling," Edwin said with a grin.

Robert gave a tight-lipped smile and a nod. The tension between them remained, though the gift seemed to ease some of it. "I shall place it in the nursery myself," Robert assured him. "In the same spot as where ours sat all those years ago."

Edwin nodded. A moment of silence fell over the room before Edwin spoke again. "Lenora appears quite an engaged mother. Very dissimilar to our mother."

Robert glanced to Samuel and me on the bed. "Yes," he agreed. "She has an obvious affection for the child."

"How admirable, given the unique way he came to you."

"Lenora is a very special woman, as I have mentioned."

"His mother…" Edwin began, testing the waters. "Was…"

"His mother," Robert interrupted, "is of no concern to anyone."

"Oh, I did not mean any disrespect. I merely am trying to understand the scenario to its fullest."

"The poor woman is dead," Robert answered. "Let us leave it at that."

"Of course," Edwin said, clasping his hands behind his back.

"Might I offer you some tea?" I chimed in.

"Oh, no, please," Edwin replied, waving his hand at me. "I have interrupted your recovery long enough. Though, Robert, there is a spot of business I hoped to discuss with you. Do you have some time?"

"Of course. We can speak in my study. I prefer not to hinder Lenora's rest with the bore of business."

"Certainly. Lenora," Edwin said, nodding his head to me,

"I wish you the best with your recovery. I hope to see you on your feet again, soon."

"Thank you, Edwin."

Robert tucked Samuel's ship under his arm, intent on delivering it to the nursery. He kissed me on the forehead before directing Edwin from the room to conduct their business.

I settled back on my bed, drawing Samuel into my arms. The crease in my forehead deepened as I considered the conversation that had just transpired. Ella, who had taken a seat on my chaise during my visit with Edwin, stood to depart.

"Did that seem odd to you?" I questioned before she reached the door.

She stopped, turning to face me. "The gift? A ship seems fitting for a boy," she answered with a shrug.

"No," I said with a shake of my head. "Not the ship. His interest in my progress with Annie."

Ella's brow crinkled. "Perhaps he was attempting to be polite."

"This is the second time he has asked about my progress. And the second time he insisted I abandon the gambit."

Ella held her arms out to her sides, adding another shrug. "I cannot imagine any other reason for his interest."

After a moment, I replied. "No, neither can I, though his interest seems more than casual."

"I am afraid I can offer no insight," Ella responded.

I glanced up to her. She shifted from one foot to the other, unsure as to what to provide as a response. I shook my head at her. "No, I do not expect so. I am quite at a loss, as well. Well, I shan't hold you back any further, Sinclair."

"It is no trouble, Your Grace. Shall I fetch Nanny to take Samuel for his afternoon feeding and nap?"

I stared down at the child in my arms. I did not wish to let him go, but the hour was growing late. "Yes," I said with a sigh. "I suppose I must give him up for his feeding and nap."

Ella smiled at me. "I find it charming how fervently you care for him."

I returned her smile. "Unorthodox, but then my life has never been normal. Why begin now?"

"There is nothing abnormal about you, Your Grace. I shall return with your dinner later." With that, Ella exited the room. In short order, Nanny Browne retrieved Samuel.

Left to my own devices, I retrieved my book from the night table. As I read, my interest drifted from the words on the page to the elusive Annie and eventually to Edwin's interest in the matter. Why did he insist on advising me against pursuing the truth?

I drifted to sleep asking myself that very question. When I awoke, the skies were already darkening. Swaths of red and purple cut through the sky outside my window. I yawned and stretched, wondering how late I had napped. I hoped it had not grown too late, though Ella should have had the good sense to wake me.

As my senses returned, the sound of sobbing reached my ears. I glanced over my shoulder to find Annie. Perched on the edge of my bed, she sat with her back to me. Her shoulders rounded as she doubled over, clutching at her belly and weeping.

"Annie?" I gasped, my voice just above a whisper and still filled with sleep. I pushed up to sitting, turning to face her. "Annie?" I asked again.

She continued her whimpering, rocking herself back and forth as tears continued to spill down her cheeks, and she choked through sobs.

"Annie, what is it?" I questioned. In an attempt to gain her attention, I reached to her, grasping her shoulder.

Her head whipped as though on a swivel toward me. Her

eyes glowed red. Tangles of black hair hung in disarray around her pale face. I removed my hand from her shoulder, pulling it quickly away.

Annie stared unblinking at me for another moment. "What is wrong?" I pushed.

Annie held her arms up as though cradling a baby. My eyes shot wide, and I leapt from the bed. "Is it Samuel? Has something happened?" I shouted, dashing to the door.

My hurried canter surprisingly produced no complaints from my ankle. I surmised the fear for my child trumped any pain I may have felt.

Before I reached the doorway, Annie blocked my path. She shook her head at me. "Stand aside!" I demanded.

Annie repeated her head shake. "Annie!" I exclaimed, my voice raising to a fever pitch. "If something has happened to Samuel, I must go to him!"

Annie shook her head a third time. "NO!" her voice boomed, reverberating through the room and knocking me onto my backside. Fury burned through me as I lay on the floor.

I struggled to stand and by the time I regained my posture, Annie resumed rocking the invisible baby with her arms. Fresh tears spilled onto her cheeks again. I ignored her, grasping the door's handle and pulling. The door was stuck fast.

Steadying myself, I pulled with all my might. The door did not budge. I whipped around to face Annie. "Open this door at once!" I ordered.

Annie ignored me, traversing across the room and sitting on the chaise. As she sunk onto the seat, she doubled over in sobs. She clutched at her dress and rubbed her belly.

The gesture made me pause. Perhaps her actions did not refer to Samuel.

"Annie, what troubles you? It is not Samuel, is it?"

Annie continued her actions, oblivious to my question. I approached her. As I tread closer to the chaise, only then did I notice a figure in the corner of the room. Lit only by the flames of the dying fire in the fireplace, the man hid in the shadows. A log shifted in the fireplace, causing a flame to leap higher, illuminating his face. I gasped as I recognized Edwin.

As if on cue, Annie spun to face him. Edwin shrunk further back into the shadows, shriveling away from her gaze. Annie opened her mouth and an ear-splitting shriek emerged. I clasped my hands over my ears and squeezed my eyes shut, hoping the raucous sound would soon cease. "Stop, STOP!" I cried.

My entire body shook, but I refused to open my eyes or loosen the grasp on my ears. My body shook again. This time I risked a glance, popping my eyes open to find Ella standing over me.

"Wake up, Your Grace!" she called.

My brow furrowed, and I glanced around the room. No one else greeted me.

"Your Grace?" Ella questioned. Worry etched her face.

I sat up, still searching the space. "I am all right, Sinclair," I assured her. "Though…" My voice trailed off as I struggled to the realization that what I had experienced was a dream.

"What is it, Your Grace?" Ella inquired.

"Annie…" I paused. "Has Mr. Fletcher left? Is Samuel well?"

The crease in Ella's brow deepened as I fired questions at her. "Mr. Fletcher? Yes, I believe so. Yes, Samuel is quite well. I checked with Nanny Browne before bringing your supper. Your Grace, are you quite well?"

"What?" I questioned, my mind distracted, still processing the events. "Yes, yes, I am quite well."

"Shall I fetch the doctor?" Ella queried.

"No, Sinclair," I assured her, regaining my composure. "I suffered only a disturbing dream."

"A dream, Your Grace? Was it very frightening?"

"Yes," I admitted. "It disturbed me and continues to."

"Perhaps I ought to fetch a toddy for your nerves," Ella suggested. "Or request a sleeping tonic so you are not troubled by it tonight?"

I shook my head at her. "That will not be necessary."

"You seem terribly distraught, Your Grace," Ella answered, wringing her hands.

"No," I disagreed. "Not distraught, disturbed."

"Disturbed sounds far worse, Your Grace. Should I inform His Grace?"

"No," I countered. "Something about the dream will not leave me. But what?" I asked myself.

Ella shrugged in response.

"Oh, I am sorry, Sinclair. Please, sit. Let us eat. Perhaps then my mind can come to some conclusion about why I received this message."

Ella relaxed into the chair near my bed, taking up her tray to eat. "Message?" she questioned.

"Yes. The dream concerned Annie. And Edwin, oddly. What could it mean?"

"Perhaps nothing," Ella suggested. "When I had a nightmare as a child, my mother assured me of that. 'Dreams are tricky things' she told me. They mean everything and nothing."

I considered the statement, disagreeing that this particular dream meant nothing. "I cannot shake the experience," I answered.

"What in particular disturbs you?" Ella asked.

I reflected on the dream as I swallowed the mouthful of stew. With a sigh, I admitted, "I am not certain. The dream was bizarre, as most are, but I cannot shake the concept that it contains a message. I awoke on the bed and heard a woman sobbing. I turned and found Annie sitting on the edge of my bed, weeping. I questioned her and she made a motion indicating a child." I repeated the motion Annie made. "I immediately leapt to the conclusion that something had happened to Samuel. I jumped from the bed and rushed to the door." I shook my head and rolled my eyes at my own stupidity. "I should have realized then it was a dream. My ankle gave me no pain."

"Was Samuel well?" Ella asked.

"I never made it to the nursery. Annie prevented me from reaching the door. She shouted at me and I fell to the floor. When I regained my footing, I found the door shut tight. I insisted she let me out, but she ignored me. She returned to her weeping and cradling the imaginary baby. Then she began pawing at her dress.

"I approached her to console her, then I noticed Edwin in the corner. He hid in the shadows. Annie noticed him and began to shriek. It was then that you woke me."

Ella pursed her lips in thought. "Perhaps your mind is burdened by your accident."

"No," I insisted. "There is some message. I am missing something. My mind is attempting to piece this together. But what connects Annie, Edwin, and an invisible child?"

Ella shrugged as she took another bite of dinner.

"This is the second instance involving Annie and a child. The first when she showed me the child playing near the stream. And this dream. Something disturbed her and when I questioned her, she indicated a child. But what ..." My voice trailed off as my mind worked to piece together the pieces.

"What is it, Your Grace?"

My eyes rose to meet Ella's. My mouth gaped open as realization dawned on me. "Annie... and a child.... Oh, I must speak with Dr. MacAndrews at once."

Ella leapt to her feet, setting her dinner tray aside. "Are you ill, Your Grace? I shall send for him immediately!"

"No, wait!" I shouted, stopping her. "I am not ill. I do not require the doctor for that. I must speak with him posthaste, however, it must be in the strictest of confidences. We shall make arrangements to travel to town tomorrow to call upon him."

"Call upon Dr. MacAndrews? But you are not ill? What are you saying, Your Grace?"

"I must speak with Dr. MacAndrews about Annie. Specifically, about her condition at the time of death."

"Her condition?"

"Yes," I said with a nod. "I believe she was pregnant."

CHAPTER 22

The following morning, I awaited the carriage's arrival from the drawing room. I still hobbled on my ankle, though I put on a brave front for Ella, insisting I was well enough to travel to town.

I tapped the toes of my good foot on the stone floor as I waited. The doors to the drawing room popped open. I pushed myself to standing, expecting Ella. Instead, Robert greeted me.

"Lenora," he began. "Buchanan tells me you've arranged for a carriage to go into town. For what reason, may I ask?"

"I wished to see the milliner. To arrange a new hat for the christening," I explained. It was not a complete lie. I planned to see the milliner along with the doctor. The latter was information Robert did not need.

"Is this a wise course of action? Your ankle may not yet be healed. Suppose it causes you trouble?"

"It is fine!" I insisted. I toddled about for a few steps to show him. I attempted to keep any winces to a minimum, hoping the pain I still experienced was not perceptible. "And if it plays up, I shall visit the doctor immediately. The pharmacy is very near the milliner. It would be an easy trip." I smiled broadly to add to my façade of confidence.

Robert studied me for a moment. I worried he may cancel my trip and dash any chance I had to discuss Annie in private with Dr. MacAndrews. "I could send for the milliner," Robert suggested.

"Not necessary," I countered. "And the fresh air will do me some good."

Ella entered the room. "Your Graces," she said with a curtsy. "The carriage is ready." She glanced between us, unsure.

I gazed expectantly at Robert. "All right," he agreed after a moment. "Sinclair, if Her Grace suffers in the least with her ankle, fetch the doctor at once."

"Of course, Your Grace," Ella confirmed with another curtsy.

I took care to walk steadily across the room and out to the carriage. I held back a whimper as I climbed into the carriage. As we were seated, Ella riding in the carriage with me, I breathed a sigh of relief. I had pulled it off.

"Your Grace?" Ella questioned. "I hope I did right not mentioning that you planned to see Dr. MacAndrews."

"Yes. You did," I assured her.

She crinkled her brow as the carriage lurched forward. "Why must we keep it secret from His Grace?" she inquired.

"I prefer to make the inquiry without disclosing it to Duke Blackmoore in case I am incorrect. I do not wish to upset him with the delicate discussion if there is no need."

Ella nodded. "I understand."

The carriage trundled down from the summit into town. While I planned to visit the milliner, my mind would not settle until I had spoken with Dr. MacAndrews. The carriage halted outside the pharmacy. We climbed from the conveyance and I entered the store.

"Good morning," the pharmacist called, "may I..." His voice trailed off as he glanced up from his work. "Duchess Blackmoore! To what do I owe the pleasure? Is there something medicinal you require?"

"Good morning, sir," I greeted him. "No, I hoped to speak with Dr. MacAndrews. Is he, by chance, still in?"

He gaped at me and swallowed hard before answering. "Yes," he squeaked out. He pointed to a door leading to the small back office.

"Thank you," I answered with a nod, making my way past him to the doorway.

"My pleasure!" he called as I disappeared through the door.

I entered the small room. Dr. MacAndrews bent over a table, packing his medical bag. "Good morning, Dr. MacAndrews," I announced as I entered the room.

Dr. MacAndrews swiveled to glance behind him. "Duchess Blackmoore!" He set down his materials. "Are you feeling ill? How is your ankle?"

"I feel quite well. My ankle is improving daily. I am careful not to overdo it."

"What may I do for you, Your Grace?" he asked.

I closed the door to the pharmacy. "I hoped to have a candid conversation with you about a sensitive issue."

Dr. MacAndrews raised his eyebrows. "Perhaps this conversation is best had at Blackmoore Castle with Duke Blackmoore," he suggested.

"The issue does not concern my health," I assured him. "I prefer Duke Blackmoore remain unaware of the conversation. He may find it upsetting. I do not wish to trouble him in the event I have made an incorrect assumption."

The doctor eyed me with some suspicion. "I must admit," Dr. MacAndrews said, his finger pressed to his lips. "I am intrigued."

"Then I shall proceed," I continued. "You are the doctor who declared the former Mrs. Fletcher deceased, correct?"

The doctor's eyebrows raised further. "Yes. I had the unfortunate distinction of having pronounced the poor woman dead."

I nodded. He confirmed the information I received from Buchanan. "And afterward, was a postmortem performed?"

The doctor's mouth dropped open for a moment. "Duchess Blackmoore, I must confess to be bewildered by your inquiry. What is it you hope to gain from it?"

I contemplated my response. "Are you aware of my unique ability? Perhaps Duke Blackmoore confided it to you?"

"He did not." The crinkle in his brow deepened.

"I will not mince my words. There is no easy way to say this. I can communicate with the dead. Because of my unique ability, my husband asked me to investigate the circumstances around Mrs. Fletcher's death."

Dr. MacAndrews's eyes widened. "I must admit to being thoroughly confused, Duchess Blackmoore. First, the circumstances of the former Mrs. Fletcher's death seem rather clear. And, forgive me, Your Grace, but… did you say you could speak with the dead?"

"No," I corrected, "I said I can communicate with the dead. Speaking is often not as easy. I see them, I realize they are there, I can sometimes speak with them but not always."

The doctor's mouth hung open as he processed my words. "You see the dead?"

"Yes," I confirmed.

"And what do they look like? Are they gruesome?"

"At times, yes. It depends on the circumstances of the death. Some of them appear quite macabre. However, some of them appear as they do in life."

Dr. MacAndrews paced the small room, his finger still

pressed to his lips. "Mmm-hmm," he murmured. "And how long have you suffered from these... apparitions?"

I stopped myself from rolling my eyes. "I do not suffer from any apparitions, doctor. Though I have seen the dead since my birth, or at least, my very early childhood."

"Forgive me, Duchess Blackmoore, but as a man of science, I..."

I interrupted him, holding up my hand and interjecting a comment. "As a man of science, you should understand there are things outside of our spectrum of knowledge."

"Yet..." Dr. MacAndrews paused. "It seems too fantastic to believe."

"All the same, I assure you, doctor, I can communicate with the dead." He fluttered his eyelids, his eyes still wide. "They are as plain as you are in front of me. In fact, your wife is standing not five feet from you at this moment. She passed four years ago from pneumonia. She recalls your holding her hand as she took her last breath. She appreciates the sentiment you expressed before she passed. She could hear you and she feels the same."

Dr. MacAndrews collapsed against the table containing his medical instruments. He remained silent for several breaths. I allowed him the moment. I had grown accustomed to the reaction.

"I... I am flabbergasted," Dr. MacAndrews finally choked out. "Many people are aware I remained with my wife until her last, though no one knows the circumstances that transpired." He searched the floor, his brow furrowing. "Is she... at peace?"

"Yes," I answered. "She is at peace."

Another moment passed in silence before Dr. MacAndrews spoke again. "And Duke Blackmoore is aware of your... gift?"

"Yes," I replied. "He learned of it through a rumor spread

by a former classmate of mine. He appealed to me to help discover the circumstances of the former Mrs. Fletcher's death. I obliged."

"Ah," Dr. MacAndrews said, wagging his finger in the air. "Duke Blackmoore has remained baffled by his wife's choice to end her life."

"Indeed," I answered. "And I wish to end his misery and put his mind to rest."

"I see. If you communicate with the dead, why inquire about an autopsy with me?"

"Communication with the dead can be difficult. Annie... Mrs. Fletcher has communicated with me on several occasions. However, understanding her messages has been troublesome. I am following up on a clue and hoping you can confirm some information."

"How did you gain the information from my wife?"

"Your wife provided it easily. She died in peace. She was not troubled. When she realized I could see and hear her, she spoke freely."

"And the former duchess does not?"

"No. It is clear her death was violent, and she is troubled by it. Communication is difficult at best. I am only just beginning to make any headway."

"And in what way can I assist?"

"By providing me with information. I presume you performed her postmortem, assuming one was completed?"

"Yes, I did. Along with an assistant from the police. A gruesome business, but done whenever an unexpected death occurs. I can assure you, the fall killed her."

"Thank you, though that was not the nature of my inquiry."

The crease in Dr. MacAndrews's forehead deepened. "Then what is?"

"Was Mrs. Fletcher with child when she passed?"

The doctor's eyebrows shot up and he paused for a moment before he spoke. He paced around the table, ceasing his ambling behind it. He spun to face me again. "What I am about to disclose, I have revealed to no one outside of the postmortem. Including Duke Blackmoore."

"I understand and will use the utmost discretion when discussing the subject with anyone, including Duke Blackmoore."

Dr. MacAndrews nodded. "The answer to your question is yes. Mrs. Fletcher was pregnant when she passed. I had not confirmed the pregnancy when she was alive. Though she was far enough along that she must have suspected."

"How far?" I questioned.

"About four months."

I nodded. Yes, at four months, a woman would know, I concluded. "Thank you, Dr. MacAndrews. The information helps. I have no additional questions at this time. I thank you for your time and your candid response. Good day, doctor." I turned to exit.

"Oh, Duchess Blackmoore," Dr. MacAndrews said, halting my departure. "Do let me know the results of your investigation. I am most fascinated by your ability. And by whatever answers you may find as to why the poor woman chose to end her life."

"I will," I assured him and took my leave. I exited onto the street into the cool morning air.

Ella greeted me. "Was Dr. MacAndrews able to help, Your Grace?" she inquired in a hushed tone.

"Yes," I responded. "Let us go to the milliner and discuss the conversation privately as we return to the castle."

Ella nodded, and we proceeded down the street at a slow pace, though my ankle withstood the jaunt. I concluded my business, and we climbed into the carriage to return to the castle. Once alone, I rehashed the story after reaffirming the tale would remain between us.

"So, you were correct, Your Grace!" Ella exclaimed.

"Yes," I answered, my gaze falling on the scenery as it passed outside the window.

"You do not seem pleased," Ella noted.

I pursed my lips. "It is true I gained the information I sought. But now I must piece together how it helps."

"But it explains why Mrs. Fletcher has shown you a child and motioned to you about a child."

"Yes, it resolves that mystery but adds several others."

"I am not sure I understand," Ella answered.

"The main question remains. Why did Annie fling herself from the tower? What caused her to choose to end her own life?"

Ella nodded. "And the confirmation of her pregnancy does little to answer that question."

"No, in fact, it confounds me further."

"How so, Your Grace?"

"If Annie was with child, why did she kill herself? Was she not overjoyed to provide Duke Blackmoore with a child? What would cause an expectant woman to become so despondent she would end her life and the life of her unborn child?"

Ella settled back into her seat, her gaze falling to the passing scenery as we climbed toward Blackmoore Castle. She possessed no answers, and neither did I. It reduced us both to silence as we parsed through the information at hand.

We arrived at the castle and I found myself greeted in the foyer by not only Buchanan but also Annie. She hovered at the top of the stairway, her gaze on me unwavering. I met her stare as I removed my gloves.

"Your Grace," Buchanan said as he collected my cloak,

"Duke Blackmoore requested your presence immediately upon your return."

"Oh!" I replied, handing him my gloves. "I shall go as soon as I have removed my hat."

"Very good, Your Grace. You will find His Grace in his study."

"Thank you."

I climbed the stairs with Ella in tow to remove my hat. Afterward, I navigated to my husband's study. My ankle, now swelling slightly, offered some protestation, though the pain was tolerable.

I took care not to limp into the study when I entered after a quiet knock.

"Ah, Lenora!" Robert greeted me, standing from his work and approaching me.

"Buchanan said you wished to see me at once."

"Yes. How was the outing? Did you secure a new hat?"

"I did," I reported. "And my ankle gave me almost no trouble. Though I believe I will rest it this afternoon. But not before I visit Samuel."

Robert smiled at me. "Before you depart, dear, I hoped to discuss a small matter with you."

"Of course," I responded.

Robert crossed behind his desk. "Edwin managed to become wrapped up in some sort of business arrangement with the vile Sir Richard. As a goodwill gesture, he took it upon himself to invite the horrid man to our home for a dinner party. It is against my better judgement, but he has put me in a rather tricky position."

"I understand, dear. I shall do my best to be a gracious hostess. When is the dinner party to occur?"

"As always, you prove gracious and valuable beyond measure, Lenora. In his infinite wisdom, Edwin extended the invitation for tomorrow evening. Though he mentioned there being no need to make arrangements for a balanced party. Apparently, Edwin is seeing to that. I shudder to think."

I suppressed a chuckle. "I shall be prepared and will discuss special arrangements with Mrs. MacAlistair."

"Good, thank you, dear. I have already had Buchanan warn her, though meal choice is best left to you and her." I nodded and turned to depart before Robert called me back. "Oh, Lenora?"

"Yes?"

"Sir Richard is... well, I am sure I do not need to remind you of his boorish tendencies. I apologize for subjecting you to a night with the man though..."

I waved my hand in the air. "I understand, Robert. Business is business. I shall entertain him for your sake and Edwin's, despite his churlish nature."

"Again, I am indebted to you. Though I shall do my best to ensure you are not found alone with him at any moment. Annie did not care for the man either. Why I continue to involve myself with him is beyond me. I suppose because Edwin entraps me into dealings with him."

"He is detestable, though, obviously he excels at business dealings."

Robert grinned at my response. "Indeed. You are quick-witted, Lenora. I enjoy that so."

I returned his expression. "I am glad you enjoy it."

"Give Samuel a kiss for me, won't you, dear?"

"I will," I promised before departing.

After visiting with Samuel and settling meal courses with a frazzled Mrs. MacAlistair, I lunched and returned to my room to rest my ankle. After my active morning, my ankle had grown to twice its normal size.

I planned to spend the afternoon reading and resting. My mind failed to focus on my book. Instead, it returned to my investigation into Annie's death. I flung the book onto the bed next to me as I pondered the latest developments. My suspicions were confirmed by Dr. MacAndrews this morning. Annie had been pregnant. She had likely been aware of her pregnancy, or at least suspected it, though she had sought no medical care. Why?

In the dream version of my message from Annie, Edwin had been present. Why Edwin? What had he to do with this piece of the puzzle? My mind stretched to fill in the gaps but found only blanks.

If Annie was about to provide Robert with his first child, what could have happened to drive her to such lengths? My mind searched and searched, yet found no answers. I brooded over my lack of progress. I settled one matter only to have more questions crop up.

I felt further from resolving the matter than I had when I arrived. "What am I missing?" I mused aloud. I recalled Annie lingering at the top of the stairs upon my return to the castle. Perhaps she had more information to share.

"Annie?" I called out. "Annie, are you there?" Silence met my query. I sighed. "Annie, you must provide me with more information!" Quietness hung in the room.

I crossed my arms in frustration. My foot tapped the air, and I pursed my lips. I must seek more information. Resolute, I swung my legs over the bed and slid to standing. I winced as my ankle objected to my activity.

I ignored it and proceeded to the hallway. I navigated to the fated tower room. I stood at the bottom of the curving stairway, vacillating about my decision to seek information. With a shake of my head, I dismissed any misgivings and decided to proceed. I swallowed hard as I placed one foot on the first step.

I forced myself up the stairs. My previous experience here still haunted me despite having been here several times since.

I stood outside the doorway and peered into the room. My breath caught in my throat as I spotted the boarded windows and the bare hinges.

I leaned into the room. "Annie?" I whispered.

Nothing moved or responded. I stepped inside, my hand still clutching the door jamb. "Annie?" I asked in a hushed tone. My eyes scanned the room, searching for any sign of the specter. I found none.

"Annie," I said, raising my voice to a normal level. "Annie, I realize what you have been attempting to communicate to me." I paused, awaiting a response. After a breath, I continued. "I know about the baby, Annie. I have deduced it! Are you proud of me? I have done it!"

No response greeted me. Silence hung heavy around me. "But now I need more! You were with child, what drove you to take your life? Please! Give me more information!"

My words echoed in the empty room. I waited with bated breath for any signal. None came. With a sigh, I retreated from the room. Dejectedly, I stepped onto the first step leading down the stairs. I took a wistful glance back toward the room. Movement caught my eye.

"Annie!" I exclaimed, racing back inside.

At this juncture, dear reader, I must pause. The memory of what occurred next remains painful and haunting. To this day, I have wondered if my decision to return to the tower was a mistake. Should I have continued back to my bedroom? Should I have left well enough alone?

In all honesty, I suppose the truth would always have come to light. I realize my discourse with the dead would mean I would likely have learned the truth, eventually. I suppose the point is moot. Though I still have difficulty with the memory, I shall press on so you are aware of the full story.

* * *

I returned to the tower room to find Annie. Her dark eyes were fixed upon me and her cheeks were tear-stained.

"There you are!" I said. "Oh, Annie. I am sorry this is painful for you. Though I have gained a piece of the puzzle. I realize what you have been attempting to impart to me. You were with child when you died."

Annie's specter shuddered as fresh tears streamed down her face. I continued, unaware of what troubled her beyond the death of her unborn child. "What disturbs you about the child so? I saw her playing by the stream. She is lovely. I…"

My words were cut off by Annie. Her figure charged at me and an icy hand clamped over my mouth. My eyes went wide with shock. I stumbled back a step, shrinking away from her. "I did not mean to cause you distress," I apologized.

Annie retreated across the room, her shoulders slumping as sobs wracked through her. After a moment, I tried again. "Annie," I said in a hushed tone, "what troubles you so?"

She did not answer. I urged her again. "Annie, please. I do not understand. I am stumbling in the dark. I have learned of your pregnancy, yet this seems to distress you more. Were you not overjoyed to learn you would give Robert a child? Were you unaware of the child? How does this play into your death? Please, I am struggling to understand, you must help me."

Annie turned back to me, her eyes blazing red. They bored into me and I shrank back from her piercing gaze. I wondered if I should, perhaps, leave. Annie's behavior continued to devolve as her upset grew. She balled her fists at her sides and growled.

It seemed an opportune moment to depart. I would learn nothing more, and my presence seemed only to antagonize Annie. I stepped backward toward the door. As I reached it, I turned, intent on descending the stairs.

However, I found myself unable to pass through the doorway. Despite there being no door on the hinges, it was as though one stood in my way. I pressed my hand into the empty space and found it unable to reach beyond the threshold. Mystified, I spun to face Annie.

Her face contorted into a mask of pain. I had never witnessed her this distraught. Even when she lured me to the tower and I pitched over the side, Annie remained calm. What disturbed her so? The thought flitted through my mind before worry replaced it. Why did she bar me from departing? What about the revelation of her pregnancy caused such strife?

"Annie..." I began to protest when Annie let out an earsplitting shriek. I clasped my hands over my ears and attempted to depart a second time. I could not.

When I turned to face Annie again, I found her huddled on the floor, her back toward me. I took one step toward her when I lost my footing. Invisible hands clutched at me. I struggled against them, but escape was impossible. The unseen force shoved me to the floor, my arm twisted behind my back. My chin scraped against the cold stone floor as weight bore down on top of me. Pain shot through my wrist and shoulder as my arm wrenched as I struggled to free myself. With my free hand, I sought to crawl away, my fingernails digging into the hard stone until they bled.

I was flipped onto my back. I lashed out at the air, attempting to stop whatever was happening to me. I screamed for help, but an icy, invisible hand clamped over my mouth, muffling any sound. A crushing weight held me in place and hot air swept past my neck. I experienced the sensation of lips being forced upon mine. I grimaced as hands grabbed me in unwanted places. The sound of ripping fabric reached my ears before pain shot through my body. I fought to free myself, but the task was impossible. Tears spilled down my cheeks as I bit my lower lip until it bled. Time stopped. Seconds seemed like hours and I fought to maintain my senses.

When the pain ceased and the weight lifted off me, I curled on the floor for several more moments, weeping. When I was able, I lifted myself from the floor, half-crawling, half-running to the doorway. I prayed my progress would not be impeded this time.

I found the way open, and I stumbled blindly down the stairs, tears clouding my vision. I choked on sobs as I scrambled through the hallways, desperately seeking the safety and comfort of my room.

I tumbled through the door, shutting it behind me, and stumbled to the chamber pot across the room. I retched several times before collapsing on the floor next to it. Curled in a ball, I remained there for several moments, tears still falling freely.

My mind struggled to comprehend the entirety of what happened and to push the horrible memory away. In only a few moments, my world had been turned upside-down. Physical and mental pain pummeled my very soul. As I grappled with the experience, I was unable to do more than lay still on the floor until my mind calmed.

Time passed without my realizing. I focused all my energy on calming my mind. I did not hear Ella enter the room. When she touched me, I recoiled. My body still trembled from my experience.

"Your Grace?" she inquired. "Your Grace, are you ill?"

I nodded, searching for my voice. "Yes," I choked out. I grasped her hand, and she lifted me from the floor.

"Oh, no!" Ella exclaimed. "Allow me to help you into bed." Ella steadied me on my feet, and I strove to cease the tremors in my body. "I shall fetch the doctor."

"No!" I exclaimed. "Please."

Ella raised her eyebrows but acquiesced. "As you wish, Your Grace. I shall have a toddy sent up along with a light meal."

"No, I could not stomach anything. But I would like to change."

Ella nodded, offering a sympathetic gaze to me. "Sit here," Ella instructed, easing me onto the edge of my bed. "I shall handle everything."

I swallowed hard, searching my mind for a response. My eyes stared ahead, focusing on a spot on the floor. After a moment, I forced myself to follow Ella as she flitted around the room.

"You should have rung for me at once, Your Grace," Ella offered.

"I… I was unable," I forced out.

Ella pulled my shoes off then stood, placing her hand against my forehead and cheek. "You do not feel feverish. From what symptoms do you suffer, Your Grace?"

I paused a moment, attempting to hold my emotions in check. "I…" I began. "I…" I tried again, my voice breaking.

"Your Grace!" Ella exclaimed, her eyes widening. She sunk onto the bed next to me and placed her hand on my shoulder. "I have never seen you like this. What is it?"

I met her gaze, tears forming in my eyes. One escaped, spilling down my cheek. "I cannot explain."

"Did you endure another experience with Annie?" Ella guessed.

I nodded. "Yes," I responded in a hushed tone. "It… disturbed me."

Ella offered a supportive smile before pulling me into a warm hug. "It is all right, Your Grace. You are safe now. I shall stay the night with you to ensure she does not disturb you again."

The genuine caring soothed me and for the first time since the incident, I began to relax. I pulled back and wiped my tear away. I nodded, managing a tiny smile in return.

"Now, let us get you into bed. And you should put something into your stomach. Perhaps some broth or bread. Even if you are nauseous, you must try to keep something down." I began to shake my head when Ella continued, "Do not fret, I shall not leave you. I shall ring for one of the maids."

Ella continued with my undressing. As she removed my dress and I slipped into my nightgown, I began to feel more normal. After a deep inhale, I said, "Thank you. The sentiment is very much appreciated." When she finished, I added, "Please give my apologies to Duke Blackmoore regarding dinner."

"Of course, Your Grace. Just allow me to ring for service." She retreated across the room and pulled the bell then returned to my bedside. "Feeling any better?"

"Yes," I said as I pulled the sheets a tad higher on my lap. "Yes, I am beginning to improve."

Ella took my hand in hers. "Can you tell me what happened? Perhaps it would help."

I bit my lower lip, wincing a bit as I hit the area I gnawed earlier. "Annie and I…" I paused. "I went to the tower."

"Your Grace!" Ella exclaimed. "Thank goodness you were not harmed!"

"No, I sustained no physical injury."

A knock sounded at the door and Ella rushed to answer it. Buchanan entered the room. "Mr. Buchanan," Ella greeted him. "Duchess Blackmoore is ill and unable to attend dinner this evening. She would prefer broth and plain bread to be sent up and her excuses made to Duke Blackmoore."

Buchanan's eyes widened under his thick eyebrows. "Shall I fetch the doctor?"

"No, Buchanan," I chimed in, "it is not necessary. Just the broth and bread, please."

"Yes, I shall see to it at once!" He turned his gaze to me. "Duchess Blackmoore, if there is anything else you require, please ring."

"I will, thank you, Buchanan. Could you see to it that Sinclair's meal finds its way to my room?"

"Of course, Your Grace," Buchanan answered before exiting the room.

Ella crossed back to my bed. She smiled at me as she sunk onto the bed. "Please, continue, Your Grace. What did Annie do that disturbed you so?"

I shook my head. "It is nothing Annie did to me. It is what she communicated to me that disturbed me."

"Which was?" Ella inquired.

I pursed my lips. "Something happened to her. Something terrible. I… I am uncertain if I can repeat it. My mind is still attempting to parse through it. Though I now believe I understand the reason she chose to end her own life."

Ella raised her eyebrows. "You have solved it?!" she exclaimed.

I pondered the statement. It appeared I had, though I had no idea of the culprit behind the vicious attack on Annie. Yet something stuck in my mind. "I am not sure," I answered.

"But, you said…" Ella began.

I nodded, interrupting her. "Yes, yes, though there are still unanswered questions." I glanced to her. "As such, please keep this conversation in your confidence."

"Of course, Your Grace," Ella agreed.

"Even from His Grace, at the moment. I am sorry to ask this of you, but I prefer to have all the facts at my disposal before I speak with Duke Blackmoore."

Ella nodded in agreement. "I understand, Your Grace." Silence fell over us before a knock sounded at the door. Ella raced to answer it. I spotted her curtsy, realizing it was not my broth but rather my husband.

"Good evening, Your Grace," Ella greeted him. Robert strode into the room. I hoped I possessed the wherewithal to face him after my encounter and the knowledge I gained from it.

"Good evening, Sinclair," he said with a nod. He turned his gaze to me. "Buchanan tells me you are ill? Shall I send for the doctor?"

"No, dear. That is not necessary. I fear I overdid things with my outing earlier. I do not wish to ruin the dinner party tomorrow, so I felt it best to put myself to bed and rest."

Robert's eyes narrowed at me as he considered my statement. I smiled up at him. "Are you certain I should not fetch the doctor?"

"I am certain," I assured him.

"I promise to take excellent care of Her Grace," Ella chimed in.

Robert glanced between us before turning his attention to me. "I merely overindulged myself. Despite my promise to rest after lunch, I found myself restless. I supposed a change of scenery might settle my nerves. I attempted to climb to my tower room." Robert clicked his tongue, shaking his head at me. "Yes, yes, I admit my folly. Which is why I have confined myself to bed for the evening. With enough rest, I shall be good as new by tomorrow for the dinner party."

"I am unconcerned about the dinner party, Lenora. My interest is your wellbeing."

"I shall be perfectly fine. Sinclair is taking expert care of me. I am beginning to feel better already."

Robert paused again, raising an eyebrow at me. "Well, if you are certain, then I shall allow you to rest. I will return after dinner to check on you." He kissed my forehead, and I squeezed his hand.

"I am sorry to leave you alone for dinner."

"Dismiss your concern, dear. I shall finish some overdue work on my accounts. I spent far too much time earlier reviewing the business Edwin proposed."

"Then I wish you a productive meal."

"Rest well, dear," Robert said before departing.

After the door closed, I whispered a thank you to Ella for her discretion. The next knock brought my meager meal along with Ella's. She sat at my bedside as we ate. My stomach threatened to revolt after the first few sips, but the plain bread seemed to calm it.

The meal fortified me as Ella suggested it would and I began feel more myself. After Ella plumped my pillows, I settled back, more relaxed than I had been.

"How are you feeling now, Your Grace?" Ella asked after she returned the trays to the maid.

"Much better," I admitted.

She offered a knowing smile. "I told you the food would help!"

I offered her a genuine smile. "Yes, you did, and you were correct." I grasped her hand, giving it a squeeze. "Thank you."

"Now, perhaps you should close your eyes and try to rest," Ella suggested.

I doubted my ability to rest given my experience, though I agreed to try. After a brief visit from Robert, I settled back for the evening. Ella eased back into the chair she retrieved. Within a few moments, I informed Ella she need not stay, though she disagreed. We came to terms with her staying under the bargain that she rest on my chaise.

With Ella settled under a blanket in my sitting room, I nestled under the covers. My trying experience took a heavy toll and, despite my restless mind, I drifted to sleep in moments.

I awoke hours later. I startled, drawing in a sharp breath as I spotted a figure near the foot of my bed.

"'Tis only me, Your Grace," Ella whispered as she straightened my bedcovers.

"Sinclair," I breathed, relief coursing through me. "You startled me."

"My apologies, Your Grace. I hoped not to wake you. I regret my clumsiness."

"No apology necessary. The fault is mine. I assumed you were Annie."

"Of course you did, poor dear. Shall I sit with you until you fall asleep?"

"No. Were you able to sleep?" I inquired.

"Yes," Ella answered. "I found the chaise most comfortable."

"Good," I answered through a yawn. "Sleep well, Sinclair."

She squeezed my hand and left me to sleep. I snuggled into my covers, hoping to return to my slumber. With my eyes shut, I breathed in and out in rhythm. After several breaths, my eyes popped open.

I scanned the darkness. Nothing appeared. I rolled to my back, staring at the bed's canopy. My mind whirled, thoughts raced in an endless parade. I longed for more rest before I faced the experience Annie shared with me and the repercussions.

I sighed and rolled to my side. I squeezed my eyes shut, willing myself to go to sleep. My efforts were not rewarded and within moments I surrendered to a sleepless night. I scooted to sitting as I allowed my mind to roam through the endless forest of questions.

Thoughts tumbled through my mind before it centered on one question: had I stumbled upon the reason for Annie's suicide? Had the attack on her drove her to such desperate lengths? Was there more?

The child Annie showed me, the child she carried in her womb when she died, was this child the product of the attack? Did this add to her anguish? Four months, I recalled. Dr. MacAndrews said she had been four months along when she died. She had lived with the aftermath of her attack for four months. Why had she then chosen to take extreme action? Was she unable to continue to live with the memory? Did she grow more despondent with each passing day? Did she learn of the child then? Was this knowledge what drove her over the edge?

Another question loomed in my mind. Who was the guilty party? Who committed such an abhorrent act?

I had chosen to say nothing to Robert yet. I could not. Not until I obtained more information. I could not inform Robert of the perverse assault on his beloved Annie and the resulting child, if my assumption proved correct on that front, without confirming the identity of the attacker. I could not burden him with that information without first possessing all the facts.

I vowed to seek out Annie at the first opportunity and pursue answers. I considered climbing from my bed and sneaking from the room to find her. I feared awakening Ella and did not wish to disturb her rest. Nor did I wish to endure the inevitable tongue-lashing I would receive from her if caught.

Instead, I bided my time, watching the sun crest the moors and dissipate the morning fog after hours of darkness.

Ella entered the room as the sky turned from red to orange. "Good morning, Your Grace," she greeted me.

"Good morning, Sinclair," I said, already climbing from bed. "Did you sleep well?"

"I did. You should have woken me. I have slept far later than I intended!"

I smiled at her. "I do not mind. I am pleased you were able to rest so well on your makeshift bed."

"Mr. Buchanan shall have my head if he learns of my late rising!"

"Then we shall make sure he does not learn of it!" I promised.

"And did you sleep, Your Grace?" Ella inquired as she helped me dress for the day.

With a sigh I admitted, "Not after we spoke last."

Ella paused. "Oh, I disturbed you. My apologies, Your Grace!"

"No, the fault is not yours. It is my own mind's fault."

Ella shook her head as she brushed my hair. "I am sorry you did not rest, Your Grace."

I dreaded breakfast this morning, uncertain I could maintain the charade with Robert. I managed to get through the meal and assure Robert of my well-being and ability to host the dinner party this evening.

After breakfast, I visited Samuel. I spent longer than I expected there. I found myself unable to tear myself from my son. Holding him in my arms soothed me. Though I lamented Annie's situation further. Some devil tainted the miracle of life for her.

I also did not yearn for my next task. I planned to seek Annie out. The confidence I possessed in the wee hours of the morning had dwindled. I no longer wished to pursue my inquiry. I avoided it as long as I could.

As the morning hours waned, I pushed myself to relinquish Samuel to Nanny Browne for his feeding. With a wistful glance, I forced myself to depart from the nursery and traversed the halls to the fated tower.

I stood at the bottom of the curving stairway, staring upward. My last visit here ricocheted through my mind. It cut at me like a knife, bringing fresh tears to my eyes. Twice I experienced peril in this room.

With a sigh, I forced my foot to climb the first stair. I must continue. I must find answers. I repeated the words aloud to myself as I climbed a second stair. My pulse raced and my heart thudded in my chest as the doorless entrance came into view.

As I reached the landing outside the room, I swallowed hard. My throat was parched and my mouth dry. I vacillated on my decision to enter. Perhaps I should inform Ella. No, I should not involve her. I did not wish any harm to come to her, physical or emotional. Still, perhaps someone should know I am here.

With a deep inhale, I set my shoulders and firmed my resolve. My dithering only delayed the inevitable. I must take this step. I must confront Annie. Whether I informed someone or not, I would still need to enter this room.

With solidified courage, I stepped through the doorway into the ill-fated tower room. My breath caught in my throat as I entered the room. I held my breath for a few moments as I gazed around. Memories of my last ordeal here flooded back to me in detail. I shuddered as I recalled the horrible sensation and fear I experienced.

"Annie?" I called out in a hushed and shaky voice. "Annie, are you here?"

Nothing stirred. "Annie," I called again, courage bolstering my voice. "We must speak."

Still nothing. So, I continued, hoping to draw her out. "I

understand now. I understand the emotions you experienced. I understand what drove you to take your own life."

The last comment garnered the reaction I sought. Annie materialized across the room. She paced back and forth, her fists balled.

"Annie," I soothed, "can you tell me who attacked you?"

She ignored me, continuing her agitated march from wall to wall. "Please, Annie," I entreated, "I must know. I do not wish to tell Robert without knowing all the facts. He will certainly wish to know who harmed you." Annie ceased her ambling at the mention of Robert's name, but the break was short lived. She resumed her pacing, clutching her fists tighter.

"If nothing else," I said, "perhaps we can prevent the man from doing to someone else what he did to you. Please, Annie."

She stopped and faced me. Her eyes burned red. My heart broke for her. The poor woman had been driven to her own death by the nightmare she endured. A nightmare which would have had a lasting effect on her life had she not chosen to end it. "I realize how you must feel. Because I felt what you did. Ashamed, alone. But you must realize what happened was not your fault, Annie. You must let go of any guilt you feel so you may rest."

I approached her and reached for her. She evaded my touch, turning her back to me. I proceeded despite the rebuke. Gently, I placed my hand on her shoulder. I felt her shrink away, but I held fast. "You mustn't hold yourself accountable for this, Annie. The fault lies purely with your attacker."

Her shoulders shook as she sobbed. "He fathered the child, didn't he?" I inquired. "Did you realize you carried it? Was it this that drove you to your decision?"

Annie spun to face me, shoving my hand aside. Her eyes

burned into me; a scowl set on her face. Fury replaced heartache, and a growl emanated from her.

"Annie," I attempted to reassure her, "your decision is understandable..."

"NO!" she bellowed, her voice reverberating off the stone walls surrounding us.

The admission, her first spoken word to me, stunned me. My eyebrows knit together in confusion. "Of course it is," I began when she rushed toward me. She drove me back toward the boarded window. Had the boards not been there, I would have pitched through again.

Pinned against the window, I struggled against her for a moment before pitching forward when she disappeared. I stumbled a step before righting myself. I glanced around the room. Annie was gone.

I smoothed my dress and stepped toward the doorless entry. I scanned the room one last time before retreating down the stairs. I had only succeeded in upsetting Annie. Perhaps she needed more time. More time to come to terms with the attack. More time to come to terms with my knowledge of it. I was not sure but either way, I would learn nothing else today, I surmised.

CHAPTER 23

As the sun descended in the sky, I dressed for the dinner party. My mind still attempted to sort through the situation with Annie. It found no answers, only questions. I made my best effort to turn my attention to the upcoming evening. I should need all my wits to deal with the uncouth Sir Richard.

"How is that?" Ella inquired after sliding the decorative comb into my hair.

"Perfect, thank you," I answered.

"And how are you feeling? Will you have the strength for the dinner party after your illness yesterday?"

"I have been asking myself the same question," I admitted. "I do hope so. It is important to Duke Blackmoore."

"Then I wish you the best of luck, Your Grace."

"Thank you," I said as I rose from the dressing table to pull on my gloves.

I exited the room, traversing the halls to the drawing room. Robert awaited me.

"How lovely you look, dear," he said, offering me a

brandy. I accepted, feeling I would need to draw on it for strength. "I do apologize for this intrusion."

"A dinner party is hardly an intrusion. I have been rather lax in entertaining as the mistress of the house."

"Nonsense. It is more than reasonable for you to have spent the first several months setting up your household before entertaining. Though I do not refer to the dinner party, but rather the company we shall keep while at it."

"Oh," I answered, realizing his meaning. "Yes. Sir Richard would not have been my first choice in dining guests. However, we shall make the best of it."

"I do appreciate that sentiment, Lenora," Robert responded as Buchanan appeared at the door with two couples in tow. I caught a barely perceptible grumble from Robert at the appearance of our guests.

I plastered on a smile and greeted them. Edwin and Sir Richard Prescott brought with them two women from Edinburgh, one named Susie and the other, Goldie. The two giggled together like schoolchildren and draped themselves over their escorts in a most obscene manner.

They polished off their drinks in short order, requesting a second prior to the dinner announcement. Only Edwin outpaced them in imbibing. By the dinner announcement, he had consumed enough alcohol to cause him to stumble as he stood from his chair. His companion found it most entertaining.

As we entered the dining room, I faced the reality of an impending conversation with Sir Richard Prescott, seated to my right. I smiled to him as we were seated.

"And how was your travel to our hamlet, Sir Richard?"

"Agreeable," he assured me.

He studied me in a way that disconcerted me. I pressed on in an attempt to alleviate my uneasiness. "I hope your stay has been agreeable as well. Though I am certain you are accustomed to more extravagant accommodations offered in larger cities."

"It is true, the town of Blackmoore is no London, yet it has its… charms. At least, Blackmoore Castle certainly does," he said with a wink.

I was glad I had not eaten anything yet, otherwise it may have flown from my stomach. I bit back the bile creeping up my throat and plastered on another smile.

"And how are you, Duchess?" he asked. "I heard you suffered an accident. Fell from your horse?"

Sir Richard was well-informed, I mused. "Yes, though I am quite well. I only twisted my ankle and have recovered from it already."

"How fortunate for you," Sir Richard responded. "I would so regret to see anything happen to you."

The remark unsettled me, though I could not say why. I suppressed a shiver as I experienced the sensation of an icy hand running down my spine.

"How kind," I forced out before turning to speak with Edwin. As we turned, I gathered from the glance I shared with Robert, the conversations on the other side of the table were no better.

"Good evening again, Edwin," I said.

"Good evening, dear sister-in-law," Edwin slurred. "And how lovely you look this evening."

"Thank you," I answered. "And how did you meet Susie?" I inquired.

Edwin chuckled. "Wouldn't you like to know," he said, tapping my nose with his finger.

I failed to find the response or gesture amusing, though I determined any follow up a poor idea. His avoidance of the question told me all I needed or desired, to know.

"She seems... very keen on you," I noted.

"Oh, she is... very, very keen," he rambled.

I was spared any further discussion when the first course arrived. The conversation turned toward the weather, the upcoming spring bloom and countryside farming. As the second course was served, we suffered the misfortune of the candles on the table blowing out. Mr. Buchanan tried three times to relight them, though each time they were snuffed out by some unidentifiable draft.

My stomach tightened as I wondered if the source may be otherworldly. We finished our meal with no further disturbances, and I felt the tension in my shoulders ease as I collected the ladies to return to the sitting room, allowing the men to discuss their business over cigars and brandy.

We settled onto the sofa and loveseat. I offered a nervous smile at them as I considered a topic of conversation. Goldie beat me to it. "So, Duchess, how d'you snag yourself a Duke?"

Shock showed plainly on my face, I am certain.

"Don't be shy," Susie encouraged. "We want to hear all the good bits."

Goldie nodded in agreement. "And the naughty ones," she added with a giggle.

"Perhaps we could discuss something else," I suggested. "Are either of you partial to flower shows?"

"Oh, come now, Duchess," Goldie replied. "Don't want to give up your secrets, hey?"

"I am afraid I have no secrets to give," I responded.

"Oh, hear that, Susie? She got no secrets to give. She don't want to share how she landed herself a Duke."

I resigned myself to the fact that I would have to tell them something to end the conversation. "We were an arranged marriage," I answered. "There is little more than that to tell. Now," I retorted, "perhaps a game of cards?"

I rose to retrieve the deck when the doors opened and Robert, Edwin and Sir Richard strode through. Relief coursed through me as Buchanan began to serve after-dinner drinks.

"That was quick," I whispered to Robert as Edwin and Sir Richard rejoined their dinner guests.

"I felt it best not to dawdle. It appears our female guests are rather vapid. I feared you may become bored," Robert answered with a smirk.

I suppressed a giggle before we rejoined the group. As I sat down, an icy gust of wind blew the doors to the foyer open. Buchanan rushed to close them. My jaw clenched. An eerie feeling settled over me. I glanced around, expecting to see Annie in the room, but found no uninvited guests.

I smiled at Robert, who continued his discussion on rural farming in the area. Within moments, the lamps lighting the room went dark. Susie yelped like a wounded animal, clutching Edwin's arm.

My suspicions rose that the incident was due to an unearthly presence. Buchanan rushed to relight the lamps in the glow of the fireplace. However, in this instance, the lamps refused to relight.

"I am certain we can carry on with only the fire's light," Robert assured him. Though I remained skeptical, certain something else prowled around the next corner to disturb our discourse.

The next incident occurred moments after we resumed our conversation. The vase of flowers on a side table crashed to the floor, shattering into pieces.

"One may suspect the castle is haunted," Sir Richard quipped. If only he realized how right he was, I reflected.

Buchanan dashed from the room to gather a maid to clear the mess. My gaze focused on the heavy draperies on the nearest window. I leapt from my seat as they began to rise into the air. Within an instant, they were ripped from their rods and discarded in a heap on the floor. An icy wind gusted through the room and the curtains rose and danced across it. Both Goldie and Susie issued sounds of alarm in response.

"Excuse me a moment," I said in a hurried voice and made my way to the door. I signaled Robert to follow me.

"Won't you excuse me for a moment?" he asked, setting his drink down before joining me in the foyer. "What is it?" he inquired in a hushed tone.

"Annie," I answered. "If they stay, she will continue her antics. We must disband the party."

Robert's brow furrowed. "Annie?"

"Yes," I answered. "She has been disturbed of late. I shall go to the tower and try to lure her there while you send our guests on their way. Please make my excuses."

"Yes, I will. Lenora," he said, catching my arm before I departed, "be safe."

I nodded in response and left him to deal with the closing of the dinner party. Robert's voice carried through the doors and across the foyer as I ascended the stairs. "It may be wise to conclude the evening. I shall make arrangements for the carriage to be brought 'round. Excuse me a moment."

With that settled, I disappeared into the upstairs hallways. With any luck, the foursome would soon depart. I wound through the halls, hurrying to the cursed tower room. I ascended the stairs without hesitation, shoving aside any dreadful memories.

I burst through the doorway and into the tower. "Annie!" I shouted, still catching my breath. "Annie! You have my attention. What is it you want?"

I spun in circles, searching the room for Annie. "Come now, Annie. You've frightened the guests enough. We are sending them home."

Annie appeared in the corner. Her hair hung limply

around her pale face. Her eyes glowed red, her lips curled into a snarl. I stared at her. "What is it, Annie? Something has disturbed you. What is it?

"I realize how disturbing the attack was for you. I understand now why you took your life, yet..."

Annie rushed toward me. She drove me back to the wall, her icy hand pressed over my mouth. She shook her head at me as we stood nose to nose. I stared at her with my eyes wide. My mind sought to find the meaning in her actions.

She removed her hand yet remained in close proximity to me. My brows knit and I asked, "What am I missing, Annie? What do I not understand?"

Annie released her grip on me. I paced the floor, attempting to piece the puzzle together. Annie's eyes followed me. "You were attacked. Someone forced himself on you." Annie nodded. I continued, "It resulted in a child." Another nod. "The attack coupled with the realization of your pregnancy left you despondent enough to take your own life."

Annie answered this statement with a shake of her head. Incorrect. But why? The crease in my forehead deepened. "The attack itself?" I questioned.

Another shake of the head. "Then what? What led to your suicide, Annie? If not the attack or the resulting pregnancy, what?"

Annie shook her head again. "What else can I be incorrect about?" I questioned aloud. "You threw yourself from this very tower for some reason!"

Annie shook her head. Frustration grew inside me and I struggled to hold my patience. "For no reason?" I suggested. I received no response. My eyes narrowed, and an idea occurred to me. I repeated a shortened version of my previous statement. "You threw yourself from this very tower."

Annie shook her head. She signaled something to me. My stomach dropped. I shook my head at her. "No," I murmured, lowering my eyes to the floor. "No, it cannot be."

CHAPTER 24

Annie's gaze bore into me. I raised my eyes to meet hers. "You did not end your own life. Someone... someone did that for you." Annie nodded. "Someone murdered you!"

Annie nodded again. My jaw dropped. "You were murdered," I whispered again. My mind whirled. "Who? The same man who attacked you? Who forced himself on you?"

Annie nodded. "Oh, Annie," I cried. A flurry of notions buzzed through my mind. I resumed pacing as I sorted through the details. This had been what Annie attempted to tell me the night I fell from the window. She had not meant me harm, instead she had been communicating to me that she had been pushed.

But who? I recalled our previous encounters and the dream in which Annie appeared to me. One detail stuck in my mind. Annie's torment in my dream was witnessed by someone: Edwin. In retrospect, many of our encounters occurred after Edwin had visited the castle. And Annie had exhibited curiosity whenever Edwin was present.

My stomach somersaulted at the concept. Edwin was a

scamp and a cad, but a dangerous man with a penchant for forcing himself on women? I could not accept it. Or did I prefer not to accept it?

Passing this news to Robert would be near impossible. I must be certain. I stopped my pacing and stared at Annie. "Edwin?" I questioned, my voice breaking.

Relief washed over me as Annie shook her head. Edwin was not the culprit. But then why did he appear in my dream, I wondered? Annie pointed to the floor. I shook my head, not understanding. She pointed again and signaled someone pushing her. The floor, I wondered? "Downstairs?" I responded.

She nodded. "Your attacker… was from below stairs? One of the servants?"

She shook her head. "Downstairs… but not a servant. Then who, Annie? Who else is downstairs? Obviously, it is not Robert. It is not a servant. It is not Edwin. The only other man in this house is…" I halted, realization dawning. "Sir Richard Prescott," I whispered.

Annie nodded, her lips curling into a sneer and a growl emanating from her.

Warmth spread through my body as my knees went weak. Of course. How could I have missed it? Sir Richard Prescott. The man who attempted to force himself upon me at the New Year's Eve ball. The man whose vulgarity knew no bounds. The man whom I had been warned about by multiple others. He attacked Annie, raped her, fathered a child with her against her will, then murdered her.

A clapping noise broke my train of thought. "Bravo, orphan duchess, bravo," Sir Richard Prescott said, stepping into the room. "I wondered if the rumors about you were true. And I wondered if Annie would impart the story to you."

I swallowed hard. He stood in the sole doorway, blocking

it. I could not escape. He continued. "I will admit, your marriage to Duke Blackmoore puzzled me. Though when Edwin told me about your special talent and your investigation, it became clear. After several inquiries, I learned you were no charlatan."

I stood alone in silence. Annie had disappeared when Sir Richard entered the room.

"You really should have listened to your brother-in-law and abandoned this, little orphan."

Sir Richard glanced around the room. With a deep inhale, he patted his chest. His hands clutched at his lapels and his chest puffed. "In this very room, Annie and I engaged in our… indiscretion."

"Indiscretion?" I replied incredulously. "You forced yourself upon her!" I shouted.

"We shall agree to disagree on the terms, orphan duchess. But when she confessed she was carrying my child and planned to tell her husband, well…" he paused, glancing at me with narrowed eyes. "I simply could not allow that to happen."

"So, you murdered her," I retorted.

"I really had no other recourse. Reputation is everything in social circles. A bastard child with another man's wife? That could have cost me far too much. Of course, from this height, it was simple to make it appear a suicide. I simply made myself scarce after she plummeted to her death and no one was any the wiser."

Silence filled the room for a moment. "Well, no one was any the wiser until you began poking around."

"And now the truth shall come to light anyway," I responded.

"That is where you are incorrect, orphan duchess. I murdered one woman to prevent the truth from surfacing." He raised his eyebrows at me. My pulse raced and my throat went dry. Tears formed and threatened to spill to my cheeks. I glanced around the room for any help. Sir Richard glanced to the boarded window. "This will not prove as easy as the first time. I suppose I shall have to make do."

He lunged toward me. I dropped to my knees and scrambled toward the door. He caught my injured ankle and pulled me backward toward him. My fingernails scraped across the stone floor as I tried to stop my backward progress. Pain shot through my leg and I cried out as I fought to free myself. His grasp tightened as I attempted to kick him with my free leg.

My leg found purchase and struck him in the chest. He fell backward, releasing my ankle. I scurried toward the door, climbing to my feet. I took one step toward the doorway when Sir Richard rammed into me, shoving me against the wall. Pinned, I was unable to move or fight. Tears spilled from my eyes as the rough stone walls scraped against my cheek. Sir Richard spun me to face him.

"I want to watch the life leave your eyes," he growled. His hands tightened around my neck. I grasped at them, desperately trying to pull them away. I was no match for his strength. As blood rushed into my ears, I struggled to breathe, my vision became fuzzy and my knees began to buckle.

CHAPTER 25

An icy chill passed through me and I assumed my life was leaving my body and death was replacing it. Over the rushing blood in my ears, I heard what sounded like a train being driven through a wall. Strong wind gusted around the room.

In an instant, Sir Richard's grip on me weakened. He stumbled backward several steps. I clutched at my throat, gasping for breath. Annie stood at the window. The boards were ripped off, one lay meters from Sir Richard. It must have struck him in the head, causing his retreat.

"GO!" Annie shouted.

In a panic, I flew from the room. I flung myself headlong down the stairs. Tears blurred my vision. I tumbled into the hallway. Regaining my balance, I fled down the hall. I glanced behind me as I heard footsteps on the stone stairs.

As I turned back, I collided into someone. I struggled as arms closed around me. "Lenora, Lenora, stop, it's me, it's Edwin."

"Edwin?" I choked out. "Edwin, you must help me."

A new voice entered the conversation. "Oh, good, you caught her," Sir Richard chimed in.

Horrified, I glanced back at Sir Richard, then to Edwin. What did he mean? Sir Richard continued. "Quickly, hand her over, I shall finish the job." Edwin hesitated, not moving. "Now, Edwin! We haven't much time."

"We shall be caught. It will not be like the last time!" Edwin warned. I struggled to free myself but was no match for Edwin's strength.

"Let me go!" I shouted.

"No, they will believe something preternatural occurred. We cannot allow her to leave. She knows, Edwin. She will tell, and it will mean the end for both of us. You played a part in Annie's death, too, remember."

Edwin paused again, and Sir Richard continued his attempt to convince Edwin to his cause. Edwin's grasp on me tightened, and I fought, fearing I was to be handed over to face my death. "And I wish to God Almighty I hadn't," Edwin spat out, shoving me behind him. "Run, Lenora, go!"

I tore down the hall as Sir Richard attempted to reverse Edwin's decision. "Edwin, you shall be ruined right along with me if this gets out. You will be disowned! Unwelcome anywhere, a social pariah."

"Leave, Richard. Go now and you may be spared. They can prove nothing, just get out."

I rounded the corner and their voices faded away. I sprinted down the hall, ignoring the screaming pain in my ankle. When I entered the hallway containing my room, I spotted Ella coming toward me. "Sinclair!" I screamed.

"Your Grace!" she exclaimed as I flung myself into her arms. "What is it?"

I sobbed as I clung to her, attempting to restore a feeling of safety. "Quickly," I gasped out. "You must fetch Duke Blackmoore."

"Of course, Your Grace," Ella assured me.

"Speak to no one, fetch His Grace and bring him at once to my room."

I sent Ella on her way, entering my room and bolting the door behind me. I paced the floor inside, my mind whirling at the turn of events. Moments seemed like hours and I worried that Ella may have been accosted or perhaps Robert. Had Sir Richard confronted one or both of them? I should have gone with Ella. I should not have sent her alone. Though I was weakened from the attack, I should have pushed myself. I fretted as I traversed the floorboards, my hand on my forehead.

Finally, the doorknob turned, and the door rattled in the jamb. I froze, staring at the doorway. A fist pounded against it. "Lenora?" Robert's voice answered.

"Yes!" I called, rushing to the door and unlocking it.

I hurled the door open and flung myself into his arms. "Lenora!" he exclaimed, holding me closer. "What is it?"

I pushed back from him. "Where is Sir Richard? Edwin?"

"Gone," he answered. "Buchanan put them in the carriage moments ago."

"Are you certain?"

"Yes," he answered, his brow furrowing. "Why?"

I closed my eyes as relief washed through me. So, he had departed as Edwin suggested. "Lenora, what is it?" Robert prodded.

I opened my eyes and stared into his stormy gray eyes. Tears threatened as I considered the information I had to share. I had solved the mystery, but I did not receive the answers I expected. The news would be as shocking to him as it was to me. But I must tell him. He must know the truth.

"I have learned the truth about Annie's death. It is... not what I anticipated. You may wish to sit down."

Robert's jaw dropped open as I told him of my discovery.

"You... she... you have learned what caused her to take her life?"

My breath caught for a moment as I formulated my next statement. "She did not take her own life, Robert," I answered.

"What?!" Robert exclaimed. "But she..."

I shook my head. "No, no, she did not throw herself from the tower, Robert. She was thrown from the tower to her death. She was murdered."

Ella collapsed onto the chaise at the admission.

"Murdered?!" he questioned. "By whom? Who would have murdered my sweet Annie?"

My lower lip trembled as his eyes searched mine. "Sir Richard Prescott."

Robert's voice raised an octave, incredulous at the statement. "What?! Why?!"

"I am sorry, Robert. The tale is rather sordid. It begins four months before her death." Robert stared at me, waiting for me to continue. "Sir Richard..." I paused, searching for the words to impart the difficult news. My voice broke as I imparted the next statement. "Forced himself on her. It resulted in a child. A child she learned of and planned to inform you of when Sir Richard confronted her. They argued, and he chose to end her life rather than allow the news come to light. He made it appear as though she took her own life." I did not mince words, regarding the best policy to be blunt honesty.

Robert collapsed onto the bed, his jaw agape and his eyes wide. He stared at the floor, unmoving, unspeaking. I placed my hand on his shoulder, willing him any strength remaining in me to help face the news. "I am sorry, Robert," I whispered.

We sat for several moments in silence. I studied Robert's face, trying to glean any hint of his reaction. His breathing turned ragged as his forehead crinkled. I worried he may have an episode of some sort.

Without warning, Robert rose. "Robert?" I questioned.

He strode to the door without answer. He flung it open with enough force that it banged off the wall, nearly snapping closed again. I chased him into the hall. "Robert," I questioned again, "where are you going?"

"To settle this," he growled.

"Settle it how?" I inquired, hurrying after him.

"Go to bed, Lenora. It is my affair now."

"It is not!" I countered. "You are in shock! I do not wish you to do something foolish!"

Ella, who had followed us into the hall, wrapped her arms around me. "Sinclair, put Her Grace to bed. She has suffered a shock."

"I shall not be put to bed like a petulant child, Robert!" I warned. "You are angry. Rightfully so! I am angry. But you mustn't react out of anger! The situation is already tragic. I have no desire to see it become more so!"

"I am a grown man, Lenora, I can take care of myself. Please, wait here."

"Robert!" I shouted as he spun on his heel and left me behind. "Oh!" I cried as Ella tightened her grip on me.

"Come, Your Grace. You should rest."

"Rest?!" I cried incredulously. "How can I rest?"

Ella patted my arm. "You must try. Come, at least lay on your chaise."

I allowed myself to be led to my suite, though I could not sit still. I paced the floor. "Perhaps you should undress, Your Grace," Ella suggested.

"No," I replied. "I dare not. In the event I am needed, I prefer to be ready."

Ella nodded, allowing me to return to my fretting and

pacing. After a few more moments, Ella said, "Perhaps if I read to you…"

"No. No, I am far too distracted, but thank you, Sinclair." Ella wrung her hands. "Do not distress, Sinclair. Your presence offers me as much comfort as I can bear at this time."

"How terribly anxious you must be, Your Grace. What terrible news about the former Mrs. Fletcher."

"Yes," I admitted. "Sir Richard's presence in the castle this evening must have been harrowing for Annie."

"And for you, Your Grace. You learned of her attack yesterday, did you not? It is what distressed you so, is it not?"

"It is," I responded. "Yes, I learned of the attack, but not the culprit. I only gained that knowledge this evening."

"You poor dear," Ella responded. After a moment she inquired of me, "Pardon me, Your Grace, but what are those marks on your neck? I have only just noticed them. Perhaps you should sit."

I glanced in the mirror. Purple-red bruises adorned my neck like an ugly necklace. "Bruises," I admitted.

Her brows wrinkled. "From?"

"Sir Richard. He trapped me in the tower after I learned the truth. He attempted to snuff out my life as he had Annie's." Ella's eyes went wide and she swallowed hard. "Annie saved my life. She flung one of the boards from the window across the room at him. It allowed me enough time to escape."

"My God!" Ella choked out. "The doctor should be fetched."

"No, no, Sinclair. I've no time for that now. Besides that, I am fine. Other than a sore throat, I sustained no damage."

"Why did you not tell His Grace?"

"His Grace has enough on his plate to deal with. I did not wish to add more."

Ella fell silent, and I collapsed to the chaise. After a

quarter of an hour, I could sit no longer. I leapt to my feet, resuming my pacing. Each passing moment brought more worry.

At long last, I heard the sound of hoofbeats in the distance. I prayed it was Robert and not news of Robert's demise. "Robert!" I exclaimed. I raced from my room and rushed down the main stairs to the foyer. Robert entered moments later.

"Oh, thanks heavens," I breathed, pressing my hand to my chest.

"I am fine, Lenora," Robert assured me.

"What happened?" I questioned.

Robert removed his riding gloves. "Annie's death shall soon be avenged."

"What do you mean?" I asked.

"I have challenged the swine to a duel. Tomorrow morning at sunrise."

"What?" I cried. "Robert, no!"

"It must be done," Robert answered.

"You could be harmed. Or worse!"

"As you were? He admitted his crimes to me. Including his attempt on your life! You withheld that information from me."

"It did not seem pertinent at the time. I did not wish to add to your misery," I answered.

"Lenora, I cannot allow that man's crimes to stand. I shall have the opportunity to avenge both you and Annie."

"And he shall have the opportunity to kill you!"

"I am an excellent shot, dear. You needn't worry."

"I shall worry! What kind of shot is he? Suppose he is quicker! Suppose he fires before you agree! Robert, please, I beg of you. Abandon this foolishness."

"It is not foolishness, Lenora. It is justice. And I shall have it. You cannot talk me out of it." Buchanan entered the foyer, collecting Robert's gloves and cloak. "Buchanan, see that the dueling pistols are prepared for tomorrow morning.

"I shall see to it at once, Your Grace," Buchanan answered before departing.

I threw my arms in the air in protest. "Lenora, there is nothing to be done. Go to bed. Tomorrow it shall be ended." He kissed me on the forehead, signaling the end to the conversation.

Ella allowed me a moment to fume before collecting me. "Please, Your Grace," she said in a hushed tone. "Let us prepare you for bed. You should try to rest."

I shook my head but allowed myself to be taken to my room. Ella assisted me in changing into my bedclothes, then promised to stay the night with me. I tossed and turned in my bed, unable to sleep or even rest. I climbed from the bed, pacing the floor. In the wee hours of the morning, I roused Ella to dress.

The hours crept by until finally the sky brightened. My stomach tied itself in a knot as the sound of hoofbeats reached my ears. Moments later, I overheard voices in the corridor. My door burst open and Edwin entered, trailed by a disconcerted Buchanan.

"Edwin!" I exclaimed.

"Lenora, I must speak with you at once."

"It is fine, Buchanan," I assured the butler.

"May we speak in private?" Edwin inquired, nodding to Ella, who remained in the room after Buchanan departed.

"You may speak freely in front of Sinclair," I assured him.

Edwin nodded, conceding his request. "You must have Robert call this duel off, Lenora."

"Must I?" I answered, my eyebrows raised high. "Do you not expect that I have tried?"

"Try again. Richard will not hesitate to kill him."

"No, I do not imagine he will. He has killed in cold-blood at least once already."

"Please, Lenora. I wish no more harm to come to my brother over this."

"Neither do I, though I have no control over him in the matter."

"But he will listen to you. Please, you must try again. It is on your behalf he fights!"

"He fights to avenge Annie's death," I countered.

"No. He did not offer the challenge until Richard admitted his attempt on your life."

I sighed, reflecting on his statement. "I shall try again," I promised.

Edwin stood unmoving. I issued a questioning glance. "There is one other thing…" he began when my door opened.

Robert entered. His eyebrows shot up, finding Edwin there. Anger shown plainly on his face. "What are you doing here?" he demanded.

"He has come to request that I stop you in this madness," I said.

"Get out. You are not welcome in this house!"

"Please, Robert," Edwin begged. "Please, I did not know it would go this far. As I explained, I owed him money. He asked for a few moments alone with her. I did not know it would lead to her death four months later."

Robert grasped him by the lapels and shoved him into the hallway. "I said get out. I do not wish to hear your excuses! You were complicit in her rape and death."

I heard Edwin's voice, though I could not make out the words. "Take him away," Robert said before returning to my room.

"Lenora, I am leaving now. I do not wish to argue. Only to notify you."

"Robert, please," I begged. "Do not argue, simply listen.

You do not need to avenge anything on my behalf. Please abandon this. For Samuel. Think of your son!"

"I am thinking of him, Lenora. I wish him to know that I would fight when faced with a difficult situation. I do not wish him to think me a coward."

"You are not a coward, Robert, please!"

"Lenora, I will not continue to argue. The matter is closed." Hoofbeats sounded again in the distance. Moments later Buchanan appeared to announce Sir Richard had arrived. I closed my eyes and shook my head.

Robert kissed my forehead and, without a word, departed from the room. I doubled over and Ella caught me, easing me back onto my chaise. "I cannot go," I said through sobs. "I cannot watch."

"Of course not, Your Grace. It shall all be over soon," Ella assured me.

I wiped away my tears and wrung my handkerchief in my hand. I vaulted from the chaise and circled the room. After several laps, I shook my head. "I cannot wait here." I hurried from the room.

"Your Grace!" Ella called after me. "Wait!"

She caught up to me as I descended the stairs. A footman crossed the foyer. "Where are they?" I questioned.

"The summit near the stables," he answered.

I nodded and raced from the castle. I ran as fast as my legs could carry me. Ella raced behind me. As we approached the stables, I gazed up to the summit. Two men stalked away from each other.

I hurried to climb the hill. I had nearly reached the top when two shots rang out. I halted in my climb. My heart stopped as though a bullet had pierced it. I scurried up the remainder of the hill, desperate to know the outcome.

CHAPTER 26

Gasping for breath, I glanced around the battleground. Robert lay sprawled on the ground, Edwin knelt over him. Sir Richard Prescott stood across the field, confusion on his face.

I rushed to Robert's side. "He's been shot," Edwin shouted. "Though not before he killed Prescott."

I pressed my handkerchief firmly against the wound near Robert's shoulder. Robert groaned. "Fetch the doctor at once," I shouted to Buchanan.

"I shall send our fastest rider," Buchanan assured me, racing to the stables.

Edwin clutched Robert's hand. "Please do not die, brother."

A shadow cast across Robert's face. I turned to glance behind me. Richard Prescott loomed over us. "Go away, you wicked man!" I shouted to him. "Leave this place!" He turned to glance at his dead body across the field. "Yes," I said. "You are dead. Now go! To the depths of Hell where you belong!"

I turned my attention to Edwin. "We must get him to his bed. You must carry him while I keep the pressure on the wound." My small handkerchief sopped with blood already. Edwin nodded. He began to lift Robert, but Robert groaned, causing Edwin to cease his attempt.

Robert's eyes flitted open. "Robert," I soothed. "Lie still. You are wounded but alive. You must let us care for you."

His eyes met mine. "Lenora," he whispered. "Fear not. You shall be well provided for."

"Do not try to speak," I warned, wishing him to conserve his energy and not wanting to hear his goodbye.

"Lenora, I . . ." he breathed before his eyes closed.

"Oh, no," Edwin groaned.

I swallowed hard as my blood-covered fingers sought a pulse in his neck. I prayed as I pressed my bloody fingers against his skin, searching for a pulse beat. I felt nothing. I closed my eyes, pressing harder. A slight thump reached my fingers. "He is alive," I announced. "Quickly, Edwin, we must get him to the castle."

Edwin breathed a sigh of relief and gathered Robert's limp form into his arms. I kept my fingers pressed firmly against the bullet wound as we traversed to the castle. With some effort, we made it, climbing the stairs and hurrying to Robert's room. Ella pulled back the bedcovers and Edwin placed Robert's slack form in his bed.

I kept careful watch on his shallow breathing as Ella retrieved a towel to hold over his wound. I prayed with every fiber in my being that Robert survived this. Ella offered to take over keeping pressure to the wound, though I could not bring myself to remove my hands.

Within the hour, Dr. MacAndrews arrived with an assistant. Buchanan showed him into the bedroom where he assessed the wound. "I shall need to remove the bullet. It is lodged in his chest," he said. "It is good he is unconscious. He shall not feel the pain."

"What are his chances?" I inquired.

"We shall know better when the bullet is removed. Mr. Fletcher, Miss Sinclair, please escort Duchess Blackmoore from the room."

"I wish to stay."

"It would be better if you did not," Dr. MacAndrews insisted.

"I am not squeamish. I can assist."

"I have my own assistant, well-trained in the medical field. I shall call for you as soon as I have completed the procedure."

I nodded, allowing Ella to direct me from the room. "We should take care of this, Your Grace." Ella nodded to me. I glanced down, first noticing my blood-stained hands, then realizing my dress was drenched in Robert's blood.

"I wish to stay close," I murmured.

"And you shall, as soon as we have changed your dress. You do not want His Grace to see this upon awakening."

I nodded and plodded along with Ella to my bedroom. My lower lip trembled as I scrubbed the blood from my hands. Ella redressed me in a clean dress, and we hurried back to Robert's bedroom.

"Anything?" I asked Edwin.

"No," he stated. "Nothing."

I paced the floor outside his room. "Let me bring you a chair, Lenora," Edwin offered.

"I am fine," I insisted. "I could not sit still if I tried."

Silence fell over us as we awaited news from the doctor. After a time, Edwin spoke. "I did not realize in either instance what Richard intended to do to Annie."

I stared at him. "I wanted you to know that, Lenora. After this is over, I will respect my brother's wishes. I will keep my distance. But I wanted you to know that I did not know his intentions."

I stared at him, trying to comprehend the reasoning

behind his admission. "I wanted you to know," he repeated after a moment. "You were one of the few people who offered me kindness, Lenora. I did not wish you to think ill of me. Though the part I played in this is inexcusable, I did not realize how serious it was until it was far too late."

I nodded at him, unable to respond. Dr. MacAndrews spared us any further conversation when he emerged from Robert's room.

"What news?" I questioned, rushing to him.

"I have removed the bullet," he answered. "And closed the wound. He remains unconscious. We must keep a careful eye that infection does not set in."

"When will he awaken?" I asked.

"I do not know," Dr. MacAndrews admitted.

"But he will awaken?" I prodded.

The doctor hesitated and my heart dropped. "There is no reason to expect he won't," he hedged. He then continued his instructions. "Keep cool compresses on his forehead and watch for any signs of fever. If he has any distress or becomes feverish, call for me at once. If he wakes, send for me."

"If?" I questioned.

"When," Dr. MacAndrews corrected with a slight smile of reassurance.

I nodded. "I shall sit with him."

I entered the room as Edwin saw the doctor and his assistant out. I dragged a chair to Robert's bedside and eased into it, grasping his hand in mine. I stared at his pale form, grey and quiet. His hand was cold against my flesh. I adjusted his covers to ensure warmth.

Minutes turned to hours, and the day waned to evening. Robert did not move, but his shallow, rhythmic breathing continued. As the skies darkened, Ella suggested I come away to rest.

"No," I argued. "I will not leave him until he is awake."

"I shall stay with him," Edwin offered. "I shall fetch you at once if he stirs."

I insisted on staying and Ella brought me a small meal and offered to stay through the night, but I sent her to bed.

As the night wore on, I dozed off, my head on Robert's bed. When I woke, the sun already shone through the windows. Robert still slumbered, his chest rising and falling gently. A hand squeezed my shoulder, and I reached up to grasp it. I glanced up, expecting to find Ella. Instead, Annie stood over me. She appeared different. Her dark hair was pulled neatly into an upswept style, framing her porcelain skin and rosy cheeks. Soft, dark brown eyes gazed down at me. Her red dress was bright, and no longer soiled.

She smiled at me. "Annie?" I asked. Realization dawned on me and tears sprung to my eyes. "You have come for him, haven't you? Please, no."

Annie smiled again and shook her head. My brow furrowed. She squeezed my shoulder again, then turned her gaze to Robert. She approached him and bent toward him. She kissed his forehead. "Be a good husband and father, Robert," she whispered. She gazed at him, a smile forming on her lips as her thumb rubbed his cheek.

Annie stood and strode away. I vaulted from my seat. "Annie, wait!" I called. She turned to face me. "You do not need to leave."

Her lips turned up at the corners. She spoke two words to me. "Thank you." She made a quarter turn, holding her hand out. A small child appeared, the dark-haired girl I had witnessed playing at the stream. She grasped Annie's hand, a grin on her tiny face. Together they walked toward the far wall, disappearing through it.

I stood in hushed silence, processing the experience. A noise sounded behind me. Robert groaned, and I spun to face him. "Robert?" I asked, racing to his side. I grasped his hand as his eyes fluttered open. "Robert?"

He blinked several times, then his eyes searched the room. "You are in your room. You were injured."

Ella knocked and entered after I called. "Your Grace, I thought I heard voices."

"Robert is awake," I announced. "Fetch the doctor!"

"Right away, Your Grace!" Ella ran from the room to send for Dr. MacAndrews.

"Lenora?" Robert questioned in a hoarse voice.

"I am here, Robert." I grasped his hand, squeezing it. His eyes found mine. "Lie still until the doctor has examined you."

"I saw Annie," he replied. I smiled and caressed his head. "She told me she was at peace."

"I saw her, too. Her appearance changed. She was no longer disturbed."

"She sent me back."

I paused a moment before asking, "Do you wish she had not?"

Robert smiled at me. "No. I asked Annie if I must die. I hoped her answer was no. I wanted to return to you, to my son." He paused, then added, "I love you, Lenora."

I smiled at him. "And I love you, Robert."

I clutched his hand tightly. I had my family. I found my home, my place in the world. In that moment, my heart was full. I could wish for no more. I hoped in that moment my life would settle, that I would experience no more unusual, uninvited drama.

This would not come to fruition. Though my other "adventures," dear reader, are stories for another time.

The End

Made in the USA
Middletown, DE
21 July 2021